Myth and Magic

Mae Clair

LYRICAL PRESS
Kensington Publishing Corp.
www.kensingtonbooks.com

Lyrical Press books are published by
Kensington Publishing Corp. 119 West 40th Street New York, NY 10018

All Kensington titles, imprints, and distributed lines are available at special quantity discounts for bulk purchases for sales promotion, premiums, fund-raising, and educational or institutional use.

Special book excerpts or customized printings can also be created to fit specific needs. For details, write or phone the office of the Kensington Special Sales Manager:
Kensington Publishing Corp.
119 West 40th Street
New York, NY 10018
Attn. Special Sales Department. Phone: 1-800-221-2647.

Kensington and the K logo Reg. U.S. Pat. & TM Off.
Lyrical Press and the L logo are trademarks of Kensington Publishing Corp.

First Electronic Edition: June 2015
eISBN-13: 978-1-61650-721-3
eISBN-10: 1-61650-721-7

First Print Edition: June 2015
ISBN-13: 978-1-61650-722-0
ISBN-10: 1-61650-722-5

Printed in the United States of America

AS CHILDREN THEY PLAYED GAMES OF MYTH AND MAGIC...

Veronica Kent fell in love with Caith Breckwood when they were children. As a teenager, she was certain he was the man she was destined to marry. But a traumatic event from Caith's past led him to fear a future together. He left Veronica, hoping to save her from a terrible fate. Twelve years later, Caith, now a P.I., is hired to investigate bizarre incidents at the secluded retreat Veronica manages. Returning to his hometown, Caith is forced to face his nightmares—and his feelings for the woman he's always loved.

THEN ONE DAY THE MONSTERS BECAME REAL.

After the callous way Caith broke her heart, Veronica isn't thrilled to see him again. But strange occurrences have taken a dangerous toll on business at Stone Willow Lodge. Forced to work together, Veronica discovers it isn't ghostly apparitions that frighten her, but her passion for a man she has never forgotten. Or forgiven. Can two people with a tarnished past unearth a magical future?

Visit us at www.kensingtonbooks.com

Books by Mae Clair

Weathering Rock
Twelfth Sun
Myth and Magic

Published by Kensington Publishing Corporation

For Gina Rutledge

For all the goofy things we've done, and the girl talk we've shared

From kids to adults and what the future will bring!

Acknowledgements

Thanks to Karen Fedderly who was there at the beginning, along with KK. Our Sunday circle was the starting point of this book, and I still remember it fondly.

A shout out also to my wonderful critique partners, Mary E. Merrell and Laura Lee Nutt for all the valuable feedback and for cheering me on through the writing process. Your input and help made the work fun.

Finally, to my wonderful editor, Corinne DeMaagd, who made working through edits and galleys a pleasure. I can't say enough about your impeccable eye for detail. Thank you for working so hard to make my story shine.

Chapter 1

"Stone Willow Hounded by Dead Dog"

Veronica Kent frowned at the newspaper headline. She'd hoped for a diversion from monthly budget projections, not another tabloid report to fan her irritation, but should have known better. Stone Willow Lodge and Breckwood Industries made it into Kelly Rice's *Coldcreek Herald* so frequently she'd been forced to become a regular reader in order to counter fallout. Managing the lodge for BI made it a necessity.

Standing, she pressed her hands to the small of her back and stretched. The clock on her desk read 9:14, an hour supported by the creaks and groans of the old house as the lodge settled around her. Her office was comfortable, a stroll down the hall from the main reception area, tucked around the corner from her suite. She should call it a night and curl up with a book on her couch. The budget reports weren't due until the end of the week and quitting time had been hours ago. If she had any sense at all, she would have met Merlin at the Jade Club.

Her gaze returned to the newspaper and its revolting headline. Curiosity got the better of her and she sank into her desk chair, focusing on the article.

"Stone Willow Hounded by Dead Dog"

Unexplained circumstances continue to escalate at Stone Willow Lodge where everything from random thefts to rumors of supernatural occurrences plague the struggling corporate retreat. Yesterday, the mutilated carcass of a dog was discovered in a guest suite. Avoiding specific details, Sheriff Duke Cameron would state only that the grisly remains, likely those of a stray, were found by a guest Tuesday evening. Not your typical turndown service.

Damn, the witch! Veronica bit her lip, silently fuming as she continued to read.

Site manager, Veronica Kent, was unavailable for comment, but Breckwood Industries chief operations officer, Aren Breckwood, insists the corporation has the situation under control. According to Mr. Breckwood: "Our primary concern is for the safety and continued enjoyment of our guests."

Stone Willow Lodge remains an established landmark in Coldcreek. The retreat incorporates part of the original Warren Barrister House, the site where Barrister brutally murdered his wife and children on a winter night in 1873. Coincidentally, an employee of the lodge claims to have seen Barrister's ghost, while several guests have reported the apparition of a sobbing woman roaming the hallways at night.

Fantasy or hoax? Either way, Breckwood Industries has managed to ensure their dying retreat is in the limelight once again.

Veronica flung the paper on her desk. Kelly Rice had been a thorn in her side since high school when they'd butted heads over everything from boys to clothes to grades. Kelly was determined to share Stone Willow's misfortunes with the rest of Coldcreek, writing up every mishap and problem as headline news.

Incidents had begun several weeks ago when one of the guests had spotted a "glowing apparition" by the lake. *A woman in a long white veil,* the guest, Kay Porter, had said. When she'd tried to speak to the mysterious woman, she'd retreated into the surrounding woods and vanished.

Other incidents followed: disembodied lights weaving through the trees, a room that stayed frigid despite attempts to heat it, locked doors yawning open, creaks and groans that had nothing to do with the settling of the lodge, even spoiled food and missing items.

Let me get my magic wand, Merlin Breckwood had joked. *I'll send the demons packing.*

Her sometimes-boyfriend rarely took anything seriously. Probably why their on-again off-again relationship never lasted more than a few weeks at a time. Like his three brothers, Merlin had been named for a character from myth, something that had played an important part in their childhood. If only myth still held the same magic.

The phone rang a shrill intrusion, and she snatched up the handset in an attempt to quell her irritation. "Hello?"

"Veronica, it's Melanie." The hesitation in the other woman's voice gave Veronica a sense of what was coming. "I thought you should know I ran into Merlin at the Jade Club."

"Who was he with? A blonde or a brunette?" Surprisingly, she didn't care. Twenty-nine and single. Her love life was going nowhere. "It's no big deal, Melanie. Merlin and I are in the friend stage again."

"Hmm…" Melanie didn't sound convinced. A good friend, she was the wife of Aren Breckwood, Merlin's older brother.

"I know exactly what Merlin's like," Veronica said. For all his outward sparkle, Merlin Breckwood was self-centered and thoughtless. A sad turn of events for a boy who'd been charismatic and fun-loving in childhood. "Merlin and I are…convenient. I don't think we were ever in love. He's free to see other people."

"What about you?"

Her throat closed up as she thought of Merlin's younger brother, Caithelden. "There isn't anyone for me. Pretty pathetic, huh?"

She'd been eleven when her parents had moved to Coldcreek and she'd met Caith. He'd been the boy with the funny name until Derrick Trask taught her how to pronounce it—*Caith-el-den*—pausing on each syllable until she got it right.

Her eyes shifted to a small framed photo on her desk, a cherished keepsake of better days. Eager young faces smiled back at her: Merlin, and his dark-haired brother Caith, Trask in a battered green ball cap, and her, all freckles and straight blond hair, as gangly-limbed as a newborn colt. It was the last photo of the four of them together.

"I don't want Merlin to hurt you," Melanie said.

"Don't worry. I told you we're just friends. One of these days I'm going to find someone as wonderful as your Aren and have a storybook romance."

"Well, you're probably right about Merlin. As much as I love the little brat, he's clueless about relationships. I say dump the cover boy and move on."

Veronica laughed. "I'll consider it. Right now I owe Aren budget reports."

"Mr. Taskmaster." There was a smile in Melanie's voice.

"He's adorable, and you know it."

"True, but it would be nice to see him blow a gasket now and then. Just to know he's human like the rest of us. I'll let you go. I know you're busy."

"Okay. Talk to you later." Veronica's thoughts returned to Caith as she hung up the phone. He'd been sandwiched between Merlin and Aren in personality, not as extroverted as Merlin, not as willing to bend as Aren. His stubbornness was the reason he'd left Coldcreek and his family twelve years ago after a horrible falling-out with his father.

Merlin was a pale imitation and a convenient replacement. Was it any wonder he flirted with other women? He had to know her heart had always belonged to his brother. She was a pathetic mess, in love with a memory.

Her eyes dropped to her desk calendar. The anniversary of Trask's death was fast approaching. Halloween. What might have been different if he'd lived? If they'd all grown up together, unscathed by tragedy? Caith might never have made the choices that drove them apart.

The phone rang a second time.

Thinking it was Melanie, Veronica snatched up the handset. "Hey, I thought you were going to let me get back to my budget reports?"

"Go to the lobby," a man's voice said.

"Excuse me?"

"Go to the lobby," the unfamiliar voice repeated. "I left something in the fireplace."

Click. The line went dead.

Suddenly uneasy, Veronica suppressed a chill. The familiar creaks and groans of the old lodge had stopped, replaced by unnatural stillness. She felt trapped, confined behind her desk, a target for a faceless assailant lurking outside. The hair prickled on the nape of her neck, sending a string of goose bumps racing down her arms. Crossing to the door, she held her breath then paused on the threshold, listening for telltale signs of intrusion. She'd always enjoyed the lodge's remote location, tucked in the woods of northwestern Pennsylvania, but at the moment wished it weren't so isolated. She couldn't hear anything over the frightened thumping of her heart.

Some creep's playing a game. He probably saw Kelly's article and thought it would be fun to scare me.

It was working.

Before the incident with the dog, Alma Kreider, Stone Willow's cook, had sworn she'd seen the ghost of Warren Barrister standing on the basement stairs. Veronica had heard eerie sobbing during a routine check of the vacant third floor two days earlier. Whether the occurrences were supernatural or contrived, they were mounting and unquestionably spooky.

Forcing herself to stay calm, she crept down the hallway, her tread light by nature. As a child, Merlin had compared her to a fairy queen, saying she looked the part with honey-kissed hair and green eyes. They'd been enraptured by myth and magic in those days, unaware there were real monsters in the world. Monsters like the men who'd murdered Trask and destroyed Caith's life.

Shaking the memories aside, she stepped into the lobby. All looked as it should be. The back of the check-in desk was visible, webbed in patches of velvety shadow. Towering glass windows hugged a cathedral ceiling, crisscrossed by thick wooden beams. Scattered rugs in earthy shades of russet, cinnamon, and pebble gray added warmth to the wide-plank pine floors. A fire crackled in the massive mountain stone hearth. Lew Walden, the lodge's caretaker, must have kindled it earlier. By habit, he'd return later to ensure it was out before retiring to his cottage at the southwest corner of the property.

I left something in the fireplace, the caller had said.

Veronica hugged close the collar of her bulky green sweater and padded across the waxed floor in stocking feet. She was still several feet away when her mind processed the sight.

A charred, cracked lump, broken by knobby protrusions of white, burned on top of the stacked logs. Something popped with the sound of cooking meat.

Choking on terror, she stumbled backward with a scream.

A severed human hand was swaddled within the dancing flames.

* * * *

"Drink this." Aren Breckwood shoved a cup of hot tea under her nose.

Veronica caught a whiff of vanilla and chamomile, but the soothing aroma did little to calm her nerves. She set the cup aside on an end table. "I'm not crazy."

"I never said you were."

Seated on a couch in the lobby, she tried to ignore the commotion swirling around her. Phone calls had brought Aren and the police. The few guests in residence at the lodge were gathered at the foot of the sweeping staircase, whispering among themselves as they watched the confusion. Lew Walden trailed the sheriff and two of his deputies as they inspected the fireplace and scoured the lobby. The fire had long since been doused, nothing but charred wood found in the hearth. A good hour had passed since she'd discovered the severed hand, but the grisly sight remained ingrained in her head.

"I know what I saw." She'd left the lobby only long enough to dash to her office and call the police. When she'd returned the hand was gone, the fire crackling undisturbed. "I'm not crazy."

"I don't doubt you, Veronica, it's just—" Aren halted when she looked quickly in his direction. "All right, all right." He raised both hands. "I know we've discussed it before. Something's obviously going on here."

"And you need to do something about it." She stood, hooking her shoulder-length hair behind her ear. "BI needs to take control or there isn't going to be a lodge left. Do you know how hard it is keeping the few guests I have? You and Galen have to do something. Soon."

Flicking a glance over her shoulder, she took note of the officers milling in the background. "The police already think I'm delusional. This is the fourth time I've called without proof. Most of the incidents have been things we can't prove or look foolish mentioning. If it weren't for the dead dog in the Hummingbird Suite, they'd have me committed."

Aren nodded. "Whoever's pulling these stunts has it down to a science." Frowning, he glanced around the room. "I left a message on Merlin's cell. I thought he'd be here."

"Didn't Melanie tell you? He's at the Jade Club."

"Again?" He scowled. "It must have slipped her mind. She wanted to come herself, but bringing the boys—"

"Would have been a mistake. Noah and Matt don't need to be exposed to this."

Smart, pretty, and poised, Melanie had twin nine-year-old sons with Aren. Sometimes Veronica positively envied her friend's life.

"You'll call and let her know you're all right?" Aren studied her sharply. "I mean…you are okay, aren't you?"

"Yes, I'm fine." She tensed, noting the approach of Sheriff Duke Cameron. There was little doubt she commanded the position of honor on his most-irritating-calls-from-whackos list. They'd grown up together but had never been close. Tall, with a slightly paunched middle and straw-colored hair, he was the same age as Merlin.

"Ms. Kent." Beaming an ingratiatingly false smile, Duke halted at her side. "We, uh…we seem to be coming up blank here, Veronica."

"Then you're not looking hard enough. I know what I saw, Duke."

"Veronica," Aren interrupted.

She sent him an annoyed glance, but he directed his next words to Duke, trying to soothe ruffled feathers. "It's not that we don't think you aren't trying, Sheriff, but these occurrences are getting out of hand."

Duke chuckled nervously, probably weighing his options. It was no secret Coldcreek's stability and wealth revolved around BI. It wouldn't do to make an enemy of its chief operations officer. "As I've told you before, Mr. Breckwood, there's just no proof. No signs of forced entry, no evidence left behind, not even traces of anything unusual in the fireplace. I can leave a man here for twenty-four hours as a precaution. We've done it before."

"That won't be necessary," Aren said.

Veronica wasn't so sure. The presence of an officer would provide an added measure of comfort to the guests, but the decision was up to Aren. Come morning, most would probably pack their bags and hightail it to the nearest exit anyway.

"What about the phone call?" she asked Duke. "Are you suggesting I dreamt that up, too?"

"We're not suggesting you dreamt up anything, Veronica. It's just..." Uneasily, he looked at Aren. "Based on our findings, there's little we can do."

"Understood." Aren offered his hand. "We appreciate your time, Sheriff."

Looking relieved to be off the hook, Duke shook Aren's hand and departed with a quick nod.

"The man is worthless," Veronica mumbled in disgust.

Aren chuckled. "You haven't liked him since he sent you that valentine in the eighth grade and said it was from Caith."

Leave it to Aren to remember something as silly as the valentine. Duke had sent it to her and signed Caith's name, thinking it a clever joke. To this day she wasn't certain who'd been more mortified, she or Caith.

She ignored the jibe, focusing on the problem. "We need to do something about damage control, Aren. After tonight, I wouldn't expect much help from county services." She hesitated, debating whether to broach an idea she'd entertained for the past week. With the police unwilling to help, there was only one alternative. "We need a private investigator."

Aren blinked. For a moment he appeared lost in thought, then a slow smile spread over his face. "That's brilliant, Veronica!" He gripped her shoulders and kissed her on the cheek. "This could all end up working out for the best. Excuse me. I've got phone calls to make."

Puzzled by his odd behavior, Veronica watched him dart away.

Chapter 2

Caithelden Lairen plucked the mail from the box at the end of his driveway and sorted through the letters. Two bills and a junk circular inviting him to take advantage of a twenty-percent markdown on costumes at the Halloween Emporium.

Not likely. He hated the wretched holiday, though anyone who didn't know him would find it hard to tell. His front porch was decorated with cornstalks and hay bales banked by bright orange pumpkins. A plump scarecrow with a floppy brimmed hat sat slumped in a wooden rocker. Despite his negative feelings, he did his best to make Halloween fun for his son, Derrick. Right now the kid was home from school with a cold, bored out of his mind, but not well enough to be out in the crisp autumn air. The tribulations of an eight-year-old.

The wind shifted and he caught the scent of hollowed-out pumpkins and dry leaves, odors that kindled memories of his childhood in Coldcreek. His gut tightened in reaction and he shoved the association aside, heading up the crescent-shaped walkway to his house. Typical New England with white siding and black shutters, the pristine Colonial was nestled in an upscale Massachusetts suburb. Since striking out on his own, he'd done well for himself. Not bad for a guy who'd ditched the family name and business and chose to be a private investigator instead.

He had his hand on the doorknob and was ready to enter when a gray sedan pulled into the driveway. The man in the passenger's seat lifted a hand and waved.

Aren?

He hadn't seen his older brother since Aren packed up his family and headed back to Coldcreek, leaving Breckwood Industries' Boston office in the hands of an underling. He'd grown weary of city life and wanted to go back to small town living. Or so he had said.

Dressed in a customary suit and tie, Aren stepped from the car. At thirty-eight, he wore his sandy hair longer than convention, the only edge to his appearance that didn't scream corporate America. The man who stepped from the driver's side was slightly shorter with neatly trimmed brown hair. Like Aren, he was dressed in a suit and tie.

Galen.

Caith couldn't recall the last time he'd seen his oldest brother. Eight years ago when Derrick was born? That had to be it.

Why would Galen show up now…and with Aren? Had something happened at home?

He tried to quell the reactionary knot in his gut. More than likely, the brothers had merely been at BI's Boston office for a meeting and decided to swing by. Interesting, given Aren must have coerced Galen into the visit.

"Hey," Caith said as the two approached. "What's the occasion?" He tried to keep the anxiety from his voice. "It isn't often I get the two of you together on my doorstep."

"Eight years was the last time." Galen held out his hand and Caith shook it.

Aren was more demonstrative, giving him a slap on the back with his handshake. When he'd lived in Boston, they'd connected frequently. Aren had been there for him when he'd struggled as a single parent with a newborn son. Later, his odd shifts as a cop on Boston's police force meant he'd frequently had to leave Derrick in the care of Aren and his wife, Melanie.

"Did something happen at home?" Caith was unable to get the thought out of his head.

"Nothing like that," Aren assured. "We were at the Boston office and wanted to run something by you. Can we talk inside?"

Caith nodded, his natural curiosity piqued. Galen rarely left Coldcreek. He shoved the door wide. "Come on in."

He led them to the living room, knowing Derrick was bound to make an appearance once he heard voices. He wasn't the greatest housekeeper but did his best to keep it clean and inviting for his son. He wondered what Galen thought of the potted plants in the foyer, the overstuffed rocker next to the fireplace, and brightly-colored rug on the hardwood floor—all things a bachelor usually wouldn't consider necessary.

Aren paused by the fireplace, his eyes skimming the framed photos Caith had placed on the mantle: Caith and Derrick on a fishing trip, grinning ear-to-ear; Derrick riding bicycles with Noah and Matt; Caith in uniform upon graduating Boston's Police Academy; their mother Morgana Breckwood; and finally a very old, aged photograph of Caith as a child with Merlin, Veronica Kent, and Derrick Trask.

Merlin was only a year older. They'd been inseparable in those days, but hadn't spoken a word in twelve years. What would he do if something had happened to Merlin? Or his father? He was estranged from both. Had been since he'd left for college at eighteen. "You want to tell me what's going on?"

"Dad, I'm bored." Derrick traipsed into the living room. Dressed in flannel pajamas, a brick-red robe, and unlaced sneakers, he looked like he should be in bed. His son was a mirror image of him with ink-black hair and winter blue eyes. But whereas Caith's hair was straight and neatly trimmed, Derrick's was a mass of unruly curls.

"Wow, Uncle Aren!" Derrick's eyes nearly popped from his head. With a cry of delight, he bounded across the room to hug his uncle and dance around him. "I can't believe you're here. Did Noah and Matt come with you?"

"Sorry, no. They're home in Coldcreek." When Derrick's face fell, Aren dropped a hand on his shoulder. "But maybe you'll get to see them soon."

"Cool. When?"

"That depends on your dad."

Derrick looked excitedly at Caith, then stilled when he spied Galen.

"Hello, Derrick." Galen smiled hesitantly. "You don't remember me, but I came to see your father when you were born. I'm your Uncle Galen."

"Are you from Coldcreek, too?"

"I am."

Derrick switched his attention to his father with an eager smile. "Dad, are we going somewhere?"

"You're going in the kitchen to finish lunch." Caith shot Aren a silent rebuff before refocusing on his son. "You need to eat the soup I made for you. It'll help with your cold."

"I feel okay." Derrick scuffed the carpet with a sneakered foot. "And soup's boring."

"So is staying in bed, but that's where you're going to end up if you don't finish your lunch." Dropping to an easy squat, Caith conversed with his son at eye level. "I have to talk to Uncle Aren and Uncle Galen. When you finish lunch, you can watch TV in the family room. Deal?"

Derrick nodded reluctantly. "Okay."

Caith ruffled his son's curly hair before nudging him toward the kitchen.

Behind him, Galen cleared his throat. "It's not easy, is it?"

Surprised, Caith turned. "What?"

"Being a single father. Raising a son." With a nod to the room and its comfortable, well-tailored furnishings, Galen sank into the nearest chair. "You've done well for yourself, even without the Breckwood name. I always wondered what made you pick Lairen."

Caith tamped down a slow burn of anger. He wouldn't get sucked into an age-old argument over his family name. "I got it out of a phone book. Stopped at Ralph's Subs on Fifteenth and Dock, had a few beers, and decided to change my name."

Aren stuffed his hands in his pockets. "Don't be cynical, Caith. We know why you changed your name." His gaze shifted to the mantle and the pictures of Derrick.

Aren had always understood.

So it won't happen again. So no one close to me gets killed by mistake. So Derry never has to go through what I did.

Caith shrugged, feigning indifference, and folded his arms over his chest. Perching on the arm of the couch, he braced one leg against the floor, the other swinging free, lightly tapping the hunter-green upholstery. "So, are you going to tell me what's going on? I can't remember the last time I had the family brigade in my living room. If Merlin were here, we'd be four brothers again."

"We never stopped being brothers." Aren paced to the bow window, then paused to study the sprawling front porch sheltered by chestnut trees. "Galen and I have a proposal for you, but you need to listen with an open mind. Do you remember the old Barrister House?"

Caught off guard by the change of topic, Caith frowned. "You mean that run-down place by Stone Willow Lake? We used to play there as kids. Wasn't there some kind of sect connected to it?"

Aren nodded. "Yeah, I think there are several Web sites devoted to its history, probably even some cult followers still around if you look hard enough. They don't bother us, so I don't pay attention."

"Us?"

"Breckwood Industries bought the place six years ago," Aren explained. "We renovated and turned it into an anti-stress retreat for top-level executives. We're low scale, nothing like the big corporate getaways. We run one and two week programs for small groups of employees—BI personnel and any other company that's inclined to have their workers attend. No cell phones, TVs, iPads, laptops, or newspapers. Sessions include relaxation, mental focusing, and a number of outdoor activities. There's no alcohol and no outside contact of any kind."

"Sounds rigid."

"We've done enough corporate studies to realize people in high pressure positions need an outlet or they reach a breaking point," Galen picked up. "The retreat's been remarkably successful. The BI employees who've completed the program have increased productivity in their respective departments. Their overall health has improved, their outlook on life, and their concept of work in general. Healthy, happy employees, particularly in upper management, translate to greater efficiency, which in turn generates increased revenue."

"Yeah, I recall something about BI being interested in revenue." Caith's tone was pointedly flippant.

Aren spoke quickly as if to forestall a rise of testiness from Galen. "The retreat is called Stone Willow Lodge, after the lake. We maintain a manager, caretaker, and a cook on site. Also a maintenance worker, guide, and some seasonal employees who drive from Coldcreek."

Caith arched a brow. "Guide?"

"He handles hiking, boating, and horseback riding. We also have a BI staff member who leads instructional sessions. For the most part, it's worked well. Until now." Aren paused, looking ill-at-ease. "Lately there have been occurrences we can't explain. Rumors are starting to circulate about the legend of Barrister House. Our guests have reported seeing strange lights in the woods, horses spooked for no reason, items missing from their rooms."

"Could be nothing more than a thief."

"It isn't only that." Aren stuffed his hands in his pockets and paced in front of the fireplace. "Things have gotten serious. It started with minor incidents, but has grown progressively worse. The mutilated carcass of a dog was left on a guest's bed. Alma Kreider, one of our employees, claims she saw someone in the basement. The next day we found some of our food stores damaged. Two of the guests got sick and blamed it on food poisoning. There have been other incidents, too. Blood splattered in the kitchen, a normally gentle horse threw a guest, a missing fishing boat."

"Did you call the police?"

Galen snorted. "Of course we did, but they can't be there twenty-four-seven. They're tired of us calling. The mess in the kitchen turned out to be red paint, and the horse was shoed improperly. My caretaker swears it was blood, and the guide insists he shoed the horse himself, something he's been doing since he was a kid on his father's farm. Last week, my manager claims she saw a severed hand in the fireplace. She called the police, but by the time they arrived, it was gone, and there was no evidence to indicate it was real. They wrote it off as night-time hysterics, but I know Veronica Kent, and I think you do, too. She isn't given to theatrics."

Caith tensed, suppressing a reactionary jolt. "Ron's your manager?"

"Since we opened." Galen tossed a suspicious glance in Aren's direction. "You mean all the years you palled around with Aren, he never told you Veronica worked for BI, or that she and Merlin dated? Even when Aren was in Boston, he knew everything that went on back home."

Veronica and Merlin dated?

Why not? Considering how he'd screwed up and hurt her. They'd all been close as kids. It was only natural her affection for Merlin would develop into something more.

Aren swiped a thumb beneath his nose. "That's irrelevant. And it's not why we're here." He looked at Caith. "Bottom line is we don't think Stone Willow is haunted, but something is going on. We need a private investigator."

Caith balked at the idea. "You're joking."

"You know Barrister House and you know the area. And despite what your driver's license says, you're still a Breckwood."

"Screw that." Incredulous, Caith paced behind the sofa. "You don't seriously expect me to believe Dad condones this?"

"He's in Canada," Galen supplied. "On vacation with Mom. They're not due back until the end of the month." He shifted uncomfortably and cleared his throat. "In time for the annual Halloween party."

Caith frowned. He hated the lavish costume party his parents had thrown every year since he was a kid. Even the memory brought a tang of bitterness to his throat. "Hire a PI in Pennsylvania. I'm not licensed to practice there."

"We don't want a PI in Pennsylvania," Aren said firmly. "We want you. Someone who has BI's interests at heart."

"What makes you think I give a rat's ass about BI?"

Aren scowled. "Maybe you don't care about BI, but I think you still care about the people who run it and the people in Coldcreek. Your family needs you, Caith."

What a load of garbage! Merlin needed him? His *father* needed him? "Where was my family when I needed them?"

Aren stepped forward until only the couch separated them. "Caithelden, I've never turned my back on you. From the time you left for college to your graduation from the police academy, and the mess you had juggling a newborn and a career, I've been there."

"I know that."

Aren had stood by him. At thirty, Caith was eight years younger, a gap that had seemed insurmountable in the days when football, girls, and cars had taken precedence, but they'd grown close as adults.

"I appreciate it, but you and Mom are the only ones." Caith sent Galen a pointed glance, but the older man remained silent, unmoved by the criticism.

"I need you in Coldcreek," Aren pressed. "I need you to do this for me, Caith."

"Don't manipulate me."

Galen shifted impatiently. "We'll double your usual rate, whatever it is. What's the matter, Caith? Are you still making the world a safe place to live or just shooting eight-by-ten glossies of cheating spouses?"

Caith glared at his brother. "Sixty-five percent of my business is corporate. I wouldn't be successful if it wasn't."

"So you're fighting white-collar criminals?"

"It was a white-collar criminal who killed Derrick Trask."

Galen dismissed the matter with a wave of his hand. "I didn't come here to dredge up the past."

"Bullshit." Caith paced to the fireplace, inserting distance between them to crush a spike of anger. "You expect me to go back to Coldcreek, a place I haven't set foot in since I was eighteen. A place where my best friend was murdered and I spent three days held for ransom in a root cellar. Knowing all that, knowing I'd have to take my kid there, you've got the gall to say you didn't come to dredge up the past?"

"Wait a minute." Aren raised both hands. "No one is saying this will be easy for you, but you can't keep the truth from Derry forever. He's got a right to know about his family. About what happened to you, and why he's named after your childhood best friend."

"The hell he does." Caith whirled on his brother. "He's eight years old. He doesn't need to know about the kind of monsters who kidnap and murder children. Not as it relates to me. I'm the single stable influence in his life and I intend to keep it that way."

"What about his family? His grandfather?"

"His grandfather never once tried to see Derry. He's never tried to see me."

"All right, forget it." Aren quickly changed the subject. "I don't want to dredge up old wounds either. The bottom line is BI is in trouble, and we wouldn't be here if we didn't value your skills as an investigator. With the exception of the last ten months, you and I have been together almost every day since you were twenty-two. I know the kind of work you're capable of, and..." His voice trailed off as he shrugged. "I'd be lying if I said there wasn't anything personal involved. Melanie and I have missed having you around, and I know Matt and Noah miss Derry."

"You're a sap, Aren. Galen's an ass and you're a sap."

"And you're as eloquent as ever." Aren grinned as if knowing he'd struck a nerve. "What's it going to be, Caith?"

"I have open cases."

"Anything that can't wait?"

Could he really go back to Coldcreek? Could he face the past? Veronica? Why the hell was he even considering it?

The thought of seeing her again...

"One I need to wrap up in the next few days."

"So finish it," Aren insisted. "By the weekend, you can be on a plane for Coldcreek. We'll put you up at Stone Willow Lodge. The family and Veronica will know why you're there, but to anyone else you'll be one more BI employee needing stress-relief therapy. Even if you're not licensed in Pennsylvania, you can still nose around and give us your professional opinion. I happen to know any private citizen with the gumption and knowledge can legally investigate a crime as long as they don't interfere with the police."

"It'll never work. Twelve years isn't that long. Someone will recognize me."

"Not if you stay at the lodge. It's only been in operation six years, and believe it or not, everyone employed there moved to Coldcreek after you left. We'll set you up with a fake identity, fake name. No one will make the connection."

Silently weighing the options, Caith roamed to the sofa again and propped on the edge. The money was enticing, but he'd never been about cash. The thought of seeing Ron again, of having a second chance to right his horrible wrong, had him waffling on the fence. He'd never stopped loving her. "What about Derry?"

"I already checked with Matt and Noah's school," Aren supplied. "Derry can attend with them while you're in Coldcreek. And he can stay at my place. Melanie and I would love to have him."

Caith jerked reflexively. "He wouldn't be with me?"

"Not at the lodge. Children don't fit with the concept of a corporate retreat."

A ripple of alarm shot through him. Leaving Derrick with someone else in Coldcreek...

"Listen up." Aren slid into a chair across from him and rapped a knuckle against his knee. "What happened to you and Trask as kids was a freak incident. You've got to stop being so overprotective. I'll look after Derry. You'll know where he'll be when you want to see him." He smiled, trying to lighten the mood. "It'll be good for him, and he'll enjoy the time with my boys."

Caith wavered. "I don't know."

Before becoming a private investigator, he'd been exposed to all manner of grisly crimes as a homicide detective. He'd seen the worst of humanity, forced to develop an exterior callousness. But there was one offense that still had the power to terrify him.

A hesitant shuffling drew his attention to the hallway. Derrick stood just inside the room, his expression hopeful. Realizing he'd overheard a portion of the conversation, Caith frowned. "Derrick, what are you doing here?"

The moment for retreat past, Derrick fiddled with the belt on his robe. As young as he was, he'd already picked up a number of Caith's childhood traits—ever-inquisitive, always exploring, dissecting some story or fact. It led him to frequently poke his nose where it didn't belong.

"Are we gonna stay with Uncle Aren?" Derrick blurted.

Caith's scowl deepened. "I thought I told you to finish lunch and then watch TV in the family room?"

"There's nothing on. It's all soap operas and stuff."

"Derry."

"I finished my soup." Derrick traipsed into the room and plopped on the couch beside Caith. Still fighting his cold, he sniffled. "How come we never go to Coldcreek, Dad? Even when Grandma visits, it's always here."

Caith stilled, not wanting to broach the subject. How could an eight-year-old understand the bitter rift that led him to cut ties with his father? Exhaling, he rubbed the boy's shoulder. "You'd have to leave school for a few weeks and your friends. What about Halloween? I thought you wanted to go trick-or-treating?"

"I can go in Coldcreek, and I heard Uncle Aren say I can go to school with Noah and Matt." Bowing his head, Derrick plucked at the seam on Caith's jeans.

"You were listening when you shouldn't have been."

"Uh-huh." Derrick exhibited just enough contriteness to pacify Caith. He'd obviously heard only the tail end of the conversation. Rolling his head against the sofa, he glanced up at his father. "Dad, can't we go to Coldcreek? I don't understand why you never wanna go home, and how come you won't talk to Grandpa or I can't see him?"

Caith sighed. Between Aren, Galen, and Derrick, he fought a losing battle. "All right, we'll go."

"Yes!" With a wide grin, Derrick clambered to his feet.

"Not so fast." Caith snagged his waist as he moved to dash away. "You're not going anywhere if you still have a cold this weekend." Cupping Derrick's cheek in his hand, Caith tilted his head, searching his eyes for signs of a fever. He pressed his palm to the boy's forehead. "Not too bad, partner."

"So we'll go for real?"

"We'll go for real." Caith grinned at his son's wide-eyed earnestness. "Now go watch some TV or find a book to read while I work out the details with your uncles."

"'Kay." Smiling happily, Derrick bounded out of the room.

Caith looked to his brothers. "Mission accomplished. It looks like I'm going home after all."

Chapter 3

Veronica took the afternoon off. With the all the strange occurrences taking place, the vacancy rate was climbing. She'd managed to keep the incident with the hand in the fireplace low-key, but rumors were spreading. It helped the police had come up empty, smoothing over her guests' jumpy nerves. Four remained at the lodge with five more expected by the weekend.

Leaving matters under the watchful eye of her caretaker, she agreed to meet Merlin for lunch at Coldcreek's Bristlecone Tavern. Set on the fringe of town, the converted stone farmhouse was normally too rustic for her GQ boyfriend who preferred sushi and bottled water over sourdough sandwiches and homemade pies. He probably wanted their relationship back on track, and was obviously willing to make concessions. They hadn't been exclusive for some time, but that wouldn't stop Merlin from wanting to cozy up if he was in the mood. She'd given up trying to figure out his motivations long ago.

As she pulled into the parking lot, Veronica spied his sporty black Mercedes near the entrance. Flipping down the window visor, she checked her reflection. Her skin still carried a lingering hint of tan from the late summer sun and the amount of time she had spent outdoors.

As a child she'd enjoyed hiking Pennsylvania's Blue Mountains, canoeing on lakes, and catching fish along the muddy banks of rivers and streams. It was why she'd bonded so well with Merlin, Caith, and Trask. They'd never really looked at her as a girl. At least Caith hadn't. Not until the night before he'd left for college, and their friendship had taken an unexpected turn after a shared kiss.

Snapping the visor in place, she slid from the car and headed across the lot, pushed by a brisk October breeze.

"You look great." Merlin smiled as she joined him at a table near the door. He bowed his head like a performer, offering a single red rose with exaggerated flourish. "I've been thinking about you all day."

"You're sweet, Merlin." She accepted the flower, twirling it beneath her nose to inhale the delicate scent. He often brought her flowers. Carnations, lilies, and red roses. Red because he thought it was her favorite. She knew his secretary was responsible for most of the flowers that came by courier, but never made a point to call him on it. The same way she never bothered to remind him yellow roses had been her favorite since childhood. Somewhere, years ago, she and Merlin had simply become convenient for each other.

"I already ordered you a soda." He slid a menu across the table toward her.

She set the flower aside. "I hope you weren't waiting long. I hit construction at the bottom of Fenbridge Road and had to detour."

"Yeah, I saw they're trying to widen that turn."

He seemed on edge, almost jittery. Physically not a hair was out of place, his wavy gold locks were brushed into gleaming strands behind his ears. He wore a white Ralph Lauren shirt with black pants and a sweeping coat of Italian leather. Shrugging out of the coat, he draped it on the chair beside him. Veronica knew he'd bought it during a March trip to New York, yet another month when their relationship had been in a nosedive. She'd long grown accustomed to his cavalier personality and flighty emotions, surface-ripples that never penetrated with depth. When had he become so superficial?

She flipped open the menu. "Merlin, is something wrong?"

"No. I was just thinking." He smiled secretively. "I bet Galen and Aren haven't told you about their latest scheme to stop problems at the lodge."

Veronica scanned the menu. She had a feeling where the conversation was heading. It had been her suggestion that prompted Aren to consider hiring a private investigator in the first place, though she had no idea if he'd followed through on the recommendation.

"Aren tells me what I need to know as Stone Willow's manager. He doesn't discuss everything BI-related with me."

"BI." He snorted softly, stretching his arm over the backrest of his chair. "My great grandfather started this business building carousels for amusement parks. My father expanded until it became a leading manufacturer of multi-faceted recreational rides. You'd think someone would wake up and realize Coldcreek is no place to headquarter a multi-million dollar company."

Veronica frowned. Privately, she supported Stuart Breckwood in his effort to keep BI where it was. "Your father never lost his small-town roots. Keeping BI headquartered here keeps Coldcreek afloat financially. Besides, there are BI offices in Boston and Baltimore for anyone who doesn't like hayrides in October or May Fairs in the spring. I thought you were considering taking Aren's position in Boston?"

"I'd rather have Baltimore." Merlin sipped at his imported spring water, and then bobbed a straw in the glass, upsetting a floating lemon wedge. "There's still opportunity for growth in Maryland with the right man calling the shots. Galen and Aren are bogged down. They're growing static and Dad's listening."

"Is that what's bothering you?"

Before he could answer, the waitress appeared with Veronica's soda and asked if they were ready to order. Finding little on the menu she didn't like, she settled on a hot turkey sandwich with provolone cheese and sourdough bread. Merlin ordered baked sole and wild rice, smiling at the pretty brunette who obviously found him attractive. Accustomed to his flirting, Veronica merely waited until the waitress left before continuing their conversation as though nothing had happened.

"What is it you want to tell me about Galen and Aren?"

Merlin shifted, forced to refocus on business. "I'm surprised they didn't already tell you since you're the manager. They think the way to solve the problems up there is to hire a private investigator and have him pose as a guest."

"An investigator?" Veronica tried to act surprised.

"You won't believe what those idiots did." Merlin smiled, but there was something off-kilter about his grin. "They hired Caith, Ron. My screwed up, black-sheep brother is coming home."

* * * *

Veronica sat on the bank of Stone Willow Lake, the lodge looming over her shoulder on a treed hillside. The setting sun gleamed on the surface, kindling an iridescent dance of magenta and gold. Across the expanse of the water, the opposite shore was visible, dressed in the russet and cinnamon shades of fall. According to legend, the lake burned with fire when fate was sealed. She'd seen that quirky event only once in her lifetime, on the evening before Caith Breckwood left for college.

Damn Aren for bringing him back! She'd made a reasonable suggestion to get BI out of trouble, never expecting he'd hunt down his PI brother. The last person she wanted to see was Caith. She'd been in love with him since high school, too afraid to tell him, fearful any hint of real affection might shatter their fragile friendship. He'd grown introverted after Trask's death, holding people at a distance. She'd stood by and watched him make a fool of himself over Kelly Rice only to have the prom queen dump him for the captain of the football team.

Idiot, she thought, and wasn't certain if she was referring to Caith, Kelly, or herself.

The first year following Trask's murder had been the worst. The trauma had left Caith emotionally unstable, frightened to venture anywhere alone, terrified those close to him might be plucked away and murdered. There had been counseling and doctors, lengthy stays in hospitals away from home. At first, the doctors had said it was best not to trigger memories, but eventually Caith returned to the town where he'd grown up, to the place where he'd been held captive and Trask was murdered.

Bidder Farm.

The house had stood abandoned for years until eventually the land was sold and a Quik-Mart sprouted in its place. She knew he'd never been comfortable going there, even after every trace of the dilapidated house and root cellar had been demolished. There were times, however, when he'd seemed almost recovered.

Like his last summer before college. She vividly remembered the two of them riding with Merlin in his red convertible, the top down, music blaring, the air rich with a mixture of honeysuckle, freshly cut grass, and chlorine from the community pool. But even among the laughter, there'd been sadness and distance in Caith's eyes.

"I don't understand why you can't be like your brothers and do what your father wants," she'd insisted.

Veronica closed her eyes, recalling Caith's agitation and pain. They'd spoken on this same bank, sitting, shoulder-to-shoulder, a seventeen-year-old girl trying to hide her feelings, and a long-haired eighteen-year-old boy trying to explain his.

"And become another BI cog?" Caith's eyes had flashed distaste. "My father wants me to become a business executive, Ron. To find ways to increase company revenue and expand the family business. I want to make the world a safe place to live. To contribute something beyond the next corporate advance. If that means being cut off from my family and the Breckwood fortune, I'll accept the consequences."

And he had. Instead of attending an Ivy League college as his father expected, he'd excelled at a less prominent eastern university. A straight-A student, his naturally inquisitive mind and innate problem solving ability had aided him well in his decision to pursue criminal justice. But it had also placed him at a permanent crossroads with his father, Stuart Breckwood.

That evening, sitting side-by-side on the bank of the small lake, it had hurt to think of life without him. She'd suffered through watching him date Colleen Parker and Toni Charleston, then make a fool of himself over Kelly Rice.

Behind them, the sun had sank into the horizon, the brooding shadow of Barrister House looming over their shoulders. Sun and moon merged on the water with the vermillion kiss of flame.

"Look at the lake," Caith whispered in awe.

Dazzling bands of ruby-red and flaming gold unraveled beneath the surface as though the sun melted into the water. Liquid silver defined the edges where moonlight webbed the shoreline in a sparkling tapestry of color and magic.

"It's beautiful," Veronica breathed, entranced. "Like it's on fire."

"Like the legend. Sealed fate." Caith lifted a hand, tucking a strand of hair behind her ear. "Ronnie..." His voice caught. "I...I'll miss you." Then as if sensing something he'd long overlooked, he'd leaned forward and kissed her, a shy, experimental touch of his lips. When she responded, he drew her into his arms, giving rein to something they would later regret.

Beneath the encroaching veil of twilight, they shared the electric passion of exploratory touches and moist, open-mouthed kisses. Kisses that sent her emotions careening out of control, her body responding in ways she hadn't imagined possible. Her skin burned with the need to be touched, her mind consumed with the desire to be loved only by him. Every fantasy she'd entertained about being in his arms had fallen dreadfully short of the reality.

Far too experienced for a boy of eighteen, he'd stroked, nuzzled, and caressed until her flesh burned with the same raging fire as the lake, and her body arched beneath his, silently begging release from the shocking torment. His lips brought ecstasy and his hands coaxed her over the edge.

All she'd cared about was him. The insatiable need for flesh-to-flesh contact and the raw, painful love in her heart.

The red-gold glow of the lake washed over them, and Veronica had willingly surrendered her heart with her virginity, certain there would never be another man.

The next day Caith had kissed her and left for college, promising to call. Three weeks later he sent a letter telling her the evening had been a mistake and he'd met someone else. Veronica never replied.

In the years that followed, she'd heard rumors from his family. How he'd supported himself through college on scholarship money and tips earned working nights as a waiter in a steak house. How he'd changed his name, eventually becoming a homicide detective with Boston's police force, then later a private investigator. He'd had a child with a woman he never married, taking up residence in an upscale neighborhood where homeowners worried more about the state of their lawn than who might be selling drugs to their children.

Veronica drew her knees to her chest, wrapping her arms around her legs. She propped her chin on her knees. It wasn't fair. Not of Aren, not of BI and, especially, not of Caith.

She could combat almost anything. The strange occurrences at the lodge, jittery guests glancing over their shoulders at every stray noise, even her staff spreading rumors about ghostly visitations and things that went bump in the night. But the one thing she couldn't fight, the one thing from which she'd never fully recovered, was her childhood love for Caithelden Breckwood and the damage he'd done when he'd broken her heart.

* * * *

Caith pulled the blankets beneath Derrick's chin, tucking them close. He sat on the edge of the bed, the mattress giving slightly under his weight. Beside him, the glow from a bedside light washed over the wall, illuminating a decorative paper border of freshwater fish, rods, and reels. A desk in the corner was littered with the toys his son liked best: fire trucks and police cars; yellow earthmovers with fat, oversized tires; and a drawstring pouch of colorful multi-sized marbles, a leftover of Caith's own childhood.

"Dad?" Derrick plucked at the blanket, sending an uncertain glance to his father. "Will I get to see Grandpa when we go to Coldcreek?"

Caith wet his lips. "He's not there right now, Derry. He's on vacation with Grandma. I don't think they'll be back before we leave."

Looking dejected, Derrick lowered his eyes and nodded.

As he'd often done in the past, Caith felt guilty over his son's quiet acceptance. "Hey." Leaning forward, he rested a hand on the silky crown of Derrick's hair. "You know Grandpa loves you. He sends you gifts and cards every birthday, every Easter and Christmas, and he calls you on the phone all the time."

"But I've never seen him," Derrick protested. "He won't visit with Grandma, and you never wanna go home."

"I'm going home now."

"But he won't be there."

Caith exhaled. A snippet of memory danced at the edge of his mind. A cold room, moldy and dark…the sharp reek of model car glue. His throat closed up.

"I know it's difficult to understand." He swallowed with effort, focusing on his son and the clear gaze of his eyes. The imaginary odor faded. "Grandpa and I have problems. Grownup things we need to work out."

"Is that how come our last name's different?"

"Is that *why* our last name's different," Caith corrected. His son groaned and rolled his eyes. Caith chuckled. "I think it's too late to be talking about this."

"Dad."

"It's past your bedtime, partner. Now give me a hug goodnight."

As he did every night, Derrick wrapped his arms around Caith's neck. Unwilling to let go, Caith kissed him on the temple, remembering a childhood when his father had done the same to him. When the days were filled with skipping rocks on the lake, shooting marbles after school, and climbing trees so high his mother had once grounded him for going beyond the measure of safety.

"Get some sleep." Caith rubbed Derrick's back. "Tomorrow, I'll take you to school and we'll talk to your teachers about going to Coldcreek."

"Okay." Derrick scrunched beneath the covers.

Caith tucked them close a final time, pausing to brush the floppy curls from his son's forehead. He switched off the light and stepped from the darkened room into the hallway.

With his back to the wall, he drew a slow breath, forcing quiet the childhood memories he'd resurrected. When he'd collected himself, he headed down the steps and into the kitchen where he found Aren. His brother was seated at the table, bent over his iPad, a cup of black coffee at his elbow.

"Where's Galen?"

Aren glanced up briefly before making a change to the screen. "He went back to the hotel."

"He didn't have to." Caith stepped past his brother and opened the refrigerator to retrieve a bottle of beer. Discarding the cap, he joined Aren at the table. "He could have stayed here."

"I think he's uncomfortable around you. It's been eight years since you've spoken."

"And that's my fault?"

Aren stared pointedly. "I'm not going to get into a debate with you, Caithelden. We've been down this road before."

"You're right." Caith took a swig of beer. "I'm an ungrateful bastard who bailed on his family, then committed the ultimate sin when I changed my name."

Exhaling loudly, Aren slumped in the chair. "We should probably talk about something else." Another tap on the iPad. "Galen and I have already started working out the details to get you in place at Stone Willow. Logan airport has an eight-fifteen flight on Saturday morning, or a later one at twelve-twenty. I booked you on the early flight but if you'd rather—"

"Cancel it."

"What?"

Caith set the beer on the table. Stifling a yawn, he rubbed his eyes. "I'll drive. I'd rather have my own vehicle."

"Caith, that's going to take you close to eight hours."

"Good. It'll give me time to clear my head." Reclaiming the beer, he rubbed his thumb over the label, more focused on the black and silver foil than his brother's frustrated stare. In the living room, the grandfather clock struck the hour, sending chimes like magic bells bouncing through the house. He smiled faintly. "When we were kids, Mom used to tell us every time a clock chimed, something magical happened."

"Mom used to tell us a lot of things. She named her kids for knights and a wizard."

"And a raven who collects souls of the dead," Caith added softly, thinking of his name and its dark association. "Why didn't you tell me about Ronnie and Merlin?"

Aren shook his head. "Does it matter?"

"We were friends once…Ron, Merlin, Trask, and me."

"You were. But that was before Trask died, before you left. I don't know what happened between you and Merlin, and I don't want to know. But I do need to know if you can work with Veronica. She's an integral part of Stone Willow. If you can't function with her there, we have a problem."

"Why would I have a problem with Ron?"

"Because of the way you left things." Aren leaned forward, folding his arms on the table. "I know what happened between you before you left for college."

Caith frowned. "There's a surprise."

Aren shrugged. "Veronica let it slip one night when she was visiting. She'd been having problems with Merlin and was talking to Melanie. I happened to be there." He shifted uncomfortably. "Look, there's no sense dancing around the issue. You slept with her, then bolted. You slept with a lot of girls back then. I just want to make sure Veronica won't be a problem."

"That was a long time ago." Caith didn't want to remember that night by the lake, his confusion afterward, or the mucked-up way he'd left things. "Let's get something straight, Aren. I'm going to Coldcreek to do a job and get paid. It's about money. Not about family, friends, or going home."

Aren scowled. "I'm disappointed in you, Caithelden. I didn't think it was ever about money. I thought it was about saving the world." Standing, he collected his iPad and coffee. "I think I'll finish this in my room. We can work out the details of the trip tomorrow. When you aren't being a jackass."

Not bothering to acknowledge the comment, Caith downed his beer. It wasn't his fault Derrick didn't know his grandfather or that Ron and Merlin had problems. They'd all made their choices long ago. Hadn't he done the same?

Like an idiot, he'd walked away from Veronica after their night at Stone Willow Lake. She'd twisted his heart, leaving him gasping and foolish, so head-over-heels in love it scared the hell out of him. People who got close to him ran the risk of ending up dead. It was why he'd ditched the Breckwood name. What happened to Trask would never happen to Derrick.

It was why he'd lied when he'd written that damn heartless letter to Veronica. There'd never been anyone else. His heart had belonged to her from the moment he'd given it that moon-drenched night at the lake, but he'd known it couldn't be. He wouldn't be responsible for getting her killed. It was better she found someone safe. Someone who didn't have a family with a multi-million dollar business, who wasn't a target for kidnappers, extortionists, and killers.

Trask had learned the cost of that friendship when the two of them sat hunched shoulder-to-shoulder in the damp basement of the old farmhouse. When he'd crouched in fear, certain he was going to die.

It should have been me. Stupid, fucking Trask, getting in the way like some kind of asshole hero.

Lurching from his chair, Caith snatched the empty bottle from the table and began to pace. He was going home…to Veronica and the guilt he'd left in Coldcreek. Like fog rolling across a hillside, the imagined taint of model glue returned. Was he out of his freaking mind?

But there was no turning back. He'd already promised Derrick, and the one thing Caithelden Lairen would never do was go back on a promise he'd made to his son.

Lies had consequences.

He wouldn't make the same mistakes as his father.

Chapter 4

Sunlight danced on the hood of the SUV, sending leaf-shaped patterns scampering across the windshield. Caith gripped the steering wheel with white-knuckle force, quelling a surge of panic. As the tree-lined streets of Coldcreek unfurled before him, a suffocating tightness grew in his chest, resurrecting the painful memories of a cold autumn day when he was thirteen.

Caith pedaled hard, racing down the hillside, head bent close to the handlebars as the wind whipped hair from his face. It was too cold to be biking. His lungs burned with frigid air, and his fingers were chapped where they gripped the handlebars. But none of that mattered in the race to reach the bottom of Spoon Hill first. Behind him, Trask pedaled for all he was worth but his shorter stature was no match for Caith's long-legged speed. Clamping down on the brake, Caith spun the back tire out behind him, doing a half donut when he reached the bottom of the hill.

"No fair!" Trask arrived a few seconds behind. "You had a head start."

Both boys laughed, flushed with excitement and the adrenalin of the race. Trask pedaled to his friend's side then stood balancing his bike, one foot braced against the asphalt. Traffic was non-existent, and the few homes scattered nearby were separated from the roadway by rolling fields and pastureland. It was the perfect place to race.

"Ron should have seen you," Trask said with a sly grin. "She likes you, you know."

Caith made a face. "That's stupid. She's just a friend." He stomped his foot on the left pedal and it spun in a frenzied circle as his heel slipped off.

Trask grinned as if sensing he'd struck a nerve. "She told Becky Kessler she'd like to be your girlfriend."

Before Caith could reply, a car rounded the bend behind them. With a glance over his shoulder, Caith moved his bike off the road along with

Trask. He had dismounted, squatting to check the pedal, when he heard the car slow. Gravel crunched beneath the tires as it rolled to a halt directly beside them. The hum of an electric window lowering into the door panel made Caith turn around. The car was sleek and shiny, a four-door black sedan.

"Hello, boys." A blond-haired man smiled from inside the passenger's side of the vehicle. He had a broad face, pockmarked on the right side. "Do either of you know where Candlestick Road is?"

Deciding they were out-of-towners, Caith stepped closer. There was another man on the driver's side, a shadowy figure he couldn't quite see, and another in the rear seat. "That way." He pointed to the right. "Past the cemetery at the end of Chapel Road." The moment he looked away from the man, he heard a metallic click. The hair prickled on the back of his neck, and the wind blew cold across his face. His gaze returned to the car, and his eyes widened when he saw the barrel of an automatic pistol pointed at his chest.

Trask made a strangled sound.

"Get in the car," the man with the pockmarked face ordered.

The back door popped open. A large dark-haired man reached forward and grabbed Trask by the wrist. Caith's eyes remained frozen on the barrel of the gun, his heart pounding wildly.

Sensing his fear, the man with the yellow hair sneered. "You're worth a lot of money to me Caithelden Breckwood. Now get in the car before we hurt your friend."

"Dad, it sort of looks like home."

Caith flinched, jarred by his son's innocent voice. Derrick sat in the back of the Ford Explorer, straining against the seat belt, engrossed in watching storybook homes and farmland roll past. Too tense to speak, Caith nodded. He inhaled raggedly as they passed the corner where Bidder farm once stood. The imagined taint of model glue tickled the back of his nostrils and, for one horrid moment, he thought he was going to puke.

Breaking out in a cold sweat, he dragged a hand over his face. Eventually the Quik-Mart dwindled from sight and he veered left, continuing into town.

It hadn't changed much. Some storefronts had been remodeled, and there were a few new businesses clustered near the center of town. The post office had received a face-lift but remained firmly entrenched on the corner of Sickle and Rosewood. The family-owned pharmacy where he, Trask, Ron, and Merlin had stopped after school each day to get sodas and licorice whips had been replaced by a coffee shop. A new McDonald's sprouted off the square and, farther from town, the community park had expanded to include a new ball field and swim club. Caith could just decipher the soaring roof peaks of the private, gated residence that had been his childhood home set back in the hills, overlooking the town.

Derrick bounced on the seat, grinning ear-to-ear. "When will we get to Uncle Aren's, Dad?"

Caith recovered his composure. His kid didn't seem to realize anything was wrong, and he wanted to keep it that way. "Soon." He shot Derrick a glance in the rearview mirror. "You know once I drop you off and go to the lodge, I won't see you every night?"

"I know." Derrick was looking out the window again, seemingly unaffected by the thought, his eyes glowing with eagerness. The trip had been long, and though Derrick had slept the first few hours, he'd eventually had to amuse himself. Too excited to read or watch a DVD, he'd asked endless questions about Coldcreek. Where did Uncle Aren live? Where did Matt and Noah go to school? When was trick-or-treat? Would he be able to go? The list went on and on. Caith had distracted him enough to play some travel games and they'd counted license plates from different states until it was time to stop for lunch. That had been nearly four hours ago, and Derrick was growing antsy again, eager to reach their destination.

"Will I get to see Grandma and Grandpa's house, too?"

Caith clenched his jaw. The roof peaks of the mansion rolled behind a crest of trees and were blocked from view. "They're not home, Derry."

"But we could still see where they live. Uncle Aren could take us."

"No."

"*Dad.*"

"I said no." Caith flicked another glance in the mirror. "Derrick, this is work for me, do you understand? I'm here because Uncle Galen and Uncle Aren hired me to do a job, just like the people who come to see me at home. I'm not going to have time for anything else."

"You just don't wanna see Grandpa," Derrick muttered, slumping in the seat.

Caith exhaled, silently counting to ten. There was no easy way to explain what had happened so many years ago to alienate him from his father. Without delving into Trask's murder, something he wouldn't subject Derrick to, there was no magical answer to explain why he wouldn't see Stuart Breckwood. Perhaps he should let Aren take the boy to the house. What harm would there be if Derrick went to see the place without him? His parents were in Canada. For that matter, he could go himself, without fear of encountering his father.

"Derrick, we'll talk about this later." The tone of his voice indicated the discussion was over.

Still sulky, Derrick went back to looking out the window, and for a while they drove in silence. Ten minutes later, they reached Aren's home, a renovated farmhouse six miles from the fringe of town. The property included an old barn, converted to a fort-playhouse for the boys, and a pond that promised excellent ice skating in the winter. Their collie-shepherd mix, Domino, and family cats, Biscuit and Charm, added to the warmth Caith always felt in Aren's home.

Melanie greeted him with a kiss, while the boys danced around hooting and hollering. The exuberant greeting was enough to make him momentarily forget his discomfort. Dinner followed almost immediately, pot roast with potatoes and corn, and Melanie's homemade deep-dish apple pie. Afterward, the boys disappeared, Noah and Matt eager to show Derrick their new home. While Melanie tinkered in the kitchen, making sure Domino stayed clear of Biscuit and Charm while they ate, Aren led Caith onto the back porch.

"I have most of the ground leased to a farmer," he explained, nodding off toward tall stalks of corn in the distance. "He rotates crops, but it's written into the lease he plants one field of corn every year for my use."

Caith raised an eyebrow. "I didn't know you wanted to be a farmer, Aren."

His brother chuckled. "Not even close. We just want to do something for the kids around here. I've hired people to help out. Remember those great hayrides we used to go on? They're few and far between these days. Farmers can't afford the expense or the time, and anyone who can isn't interested in making it happen." Aren shrugged. He scuffed a shoe against the plank floorboards. "Guess I want to change that. My wife and kids grew up in a city, Caith. Noah and Matt never saw farmland until we moved here. It's important they experience some of the things I did. I don't want them growing up with the corporate world as the only choice they have."

Caith studied his brother. "You're serious about this?"

Aren grinned. Dressed in jeans and a green pull-over sweatshirt rather than his usual suit and tie, he looked relaxed. "I know you don't like Halloween, but there used to be a time when you did. Before Trask."

Caith looked away.

"I'm planning a maze in the cornfield," Aren continued quickly as if to cover the sudden awkwardness. "I've got a crop of pumpkins we're going to harvest for the kids to face paint. We're going to have two weekends, starting on Friday night with the hayride and continuing through the next Sunday afternoon. The high school drama club has volunteered to act as staff, and they'll be in costume. Balin is heading things up for me."

Caith hadn't seen his nephew, Balin, in years, but knew Galen's son would be a teenager now.

"I've got vendors to provide hotdogs, pumpkin pie, caramel apples, and cider," Aren said. "If it goes over as good as I hope, I want to make it an annual event. I've got the ground. Why let it go to waste?"

Caith angled a glance at the surrounding fields. Once more a sense of déjà vu swept over him. Derrick had never been on a hayride or run giggling through rows of towering cornstalks. "What does Dad say about it?"

Aren shot him a suspicious look. "He's always loved the outdoors, and he's never outgrown his small town roots. He wanted to funnel BI money into it, but I told him I wanted to do this on my own. Dad's always supported anything that benefits the community, especially if it involves Coldcreek's children."

"Too bad he didn't feel the same about his own kids." Caith turned away before Aren could reply. Overhead, the sun slipped toward the horizon, melting into a brass-soaked ball. Caith stuffed his hands into his pockets. "It's not easy coming back. I've thought about it all day. About leaving Derry here."

Aren's face registered confusion. "Caith, we talked about this."

"I know we did, but I'm not ready to leave Derry that long. Not here, where Trask…" He exhaled deeply, reaching a decision. "I'll go to the lodge as a consultant, someone who's evaluating the program for you. It'll cause less suspicion when I start asking questions. I'll be able to come and go as I please, and see Derry whenever I want. You can tell people you know me from Boston. Our kids are friends, and Derrick's staying with you while I complete an assignment for BI. It's strictly credible you'd hire someone you can trust to evaluate the program. As it is, there are people who are going to recognize me. Let's face it, I look a lot like Dad. With any luck, I can avoid most of them."

"Galen isn't going to like it. We're changing something without his approval."

"Screw Galen. This is about my kid, my terms. I've got plenty of cases waiting back home if you want to scratch the whole deal."

"Why do you always have to be so bullheaded? Between you and Dad—" Aren broke off and shook his head. "All right. We'll do it your way. I'll advise Galen of the changes tomorrow, but I want you to go to the lodge tonight. There's a new group of guests arriving tomorrow evening. I'd rather you had the lay of the land before they get there." Frowning, he considered his brother. "The board isn't involved in this, but I'd like to update them twice a week as a courtesy. Stone Willow has BI connections, but it's a Breckwood family project, not a corporate venture. There are two working phones at the lodge, one in Veronica's office and one in Alma Kreider's room. You can use one of those to contact me. Cells work, but the reception is limited."

"Kreider's the cook?"

Aren nodded. "She lives at the lodge along with Veronica. Lew Walden, the caretaker, has a separate home on the property. Call when you can."

Nodding, Caith fell silent. After a moment, he cleared his throat. "Do, um…Trask's parents still live around here?"

Aren hesitated. "They left the year after their daughter graduated from high school. You would have been a college freshman then. They tried to tough it out, but it was too hard for them to stay."

Caith nodded. "Aren, Derrick's never been away from me for more than a night or two."

"I figured that. I remember in Boston when he'd spend the weekend with Noah and Matt. You were freaky about it then."

"This isn't Boston. It's worse. It's where Trask was killed."

Sighing, Aren clapped a hand on Caith's shoulder. "I know this is hard, Caith, but don't make your fears his. There's a reason you haven't told him what happened to you and Trask, and it's because you want him to grow up a normal little boy, something you didn't get the chance to do. Let him have fun while he's here."

He was being foolish. "You're right." The last thing he wanted was to ruin his kid's enjoyment. He'd spent the last eight years making up for the fact that Derrick didn't have a mother, doing everything he could to keep his life happy and fulfilled. While he might be a little on the protective side, he wasn't going to move into suffocation mode and chain his kid to an imaginary leash. Aren understood his fears and would take care of Derrick. "I should go while there's still light."

It was harder than he thought.

When he left, Caith gave Derrick a hug with instructions to listen to his aunt and uncle. Aren trailed him to his Explorer, assuring a final time he had nothing to worry about. As Caith opened the door, he spied Derrick's pouch of marbles in the back seat. A lump formed in his throat.

Retrieving the pouch, he passed it to Aren. "He takes them everywhere." Before his brother could respond, he climbed into the truck and started the engine. He never looked back as he headed for Stone Willow Lodge.

* * * *

Veronica sprinted down the steps, satisfied with her inspection of the guest suites. When the new arrivals checked in, they'd find everything in order. A relief, considering she'd be juggling Caith, too.

Aren had phoned to tell her his brother was on his way and to make certain she was comfortable with Caith's guise as a Breckwood consultant. It meant they'd be working closely. She'd never forgiven Caith his callous dismissal of her feelings, but assured Aren what happened between them had been nothing more than infatuation and puppy love. He didn't need to know how deeply their time together had scarred her.

"Veronica!"

She halted at the bottom of the staircase as Alma Kreider rounded the corner. A few months shy of sixty-five, her graying hair worn in a top knot, the cook was usually no-nonsense to the point of rude. Lately, she'd grown timid, casting worried glances over her shoulder and avoiding empty rooms after dark.

"I'm glad I found you. I've started a cobbler and need three jars of peaches from the basement." Alma fidgeted, twining her hands. "Lew said the breaker needs a new fuse, and the lights aren't working. I don't want to go down there."

Veronica should have known. With the sun setting and exaggerated shadows creeping from the walls, Alma was more likely to tangle with a rabid dog then venture into the basement.

It was nearing six in the evening. Beyond the towering windows in the lobby, darkness feathered the edges of the October sky.

"I'll go."

"By yourself?" Alma was appalled. "In the dark? After what I saw?"

"I'll take a flashlight. There's nothing down there but food stores and boxes."

Alma frowned. "Now, don't start sounding like Sheriff Cameron. I saw Warren Barrister's ghost, plain as day."

They'd had the same discussion numerous times. Veronica slipped a hand beneath Alma's arm and steered her toward the kitchen. "There are no ghosts at Stone Willow, Alma. If someone was in the basement, they're gone now."

"You don't believe me."

"I do. But whatever you saw wasn't a ghost." Veronica was careful not to upset her further, but didn't want to stoke rumors of the supernatural.

"What then?"

She bit her lip, unable to offer an answer.

As if taking that as a concession of defeat, Alma harrumphed her triumph and departed. Veronica headed behind the reception counter and rummaged through the cabinets until she found a flashlight. She tested the batteries, then walked to the basement wondering what else could go wrong. The breaker was another item in a long list of mechanical problems to plague the lodge. Coupled with those incidents that bordered on the supernatural, it was no wonder guests had started to imagine poltergeists behind every corner.

The hinges on the basement door creaked as she pushed it open, and she made a mental note to tell Lew to oil them when he took care of the breaker. She tried the light switch once, then flicked on her flashlight, angling the beam down the staircase. Darkness yawned below, layered in whorls of licorice black. Must and mildew tickled her nose, and a draft of cool air scraped over her cheek.

The cone of yellow light bobbed as she descended the steps. She paused at the bottom, sweeping the light to the far corners of the room, sending shadows scurrying from the beam. To the left, a floor-to-ceiling shelving unit loomed against the wall. Row after row of jarred vegetables and fruits cast back the reflected glow of her flashlight. Alma had canned most of the items, gathering the vegetables from a garden at the rear of the lodge, purchasing the majority of fruit from a local market.

To the right, a short set of block steps led up to an exterior exit. Rarely used, the metal storm doors were angled into the rear of the home, part of the original structure from the 1800s.

She felt an unnatural chill, but pushed it aside, realizing she was being silly. There was nothing in the dark that wasn't there in the light. Crossing to the shelving unit, she ran the beam of the flashlight over neat, orderly rows of canning jars, pausing to study the handwritten labels. Something moved behind her and a hand settled on her shoulder.

Veronica gave a startled squawk and lurched clear, her scream choked short by fright.

"Veronica, it's Caith." His voice struck her as the yellow beam washed over his face. Wincing, he raised a hand to block the direct path of light. She caught only vague impressions—coal black hair and eyes like crisp winter sky.

"Caith?" she echoed dumbly.

"Mind lowering the light?"

Veronica dropped the beam to the floor where it bounced off faded denim and brown work boots. She had a vague sense of his height, pinned between him and the shelving unit. He held a flashlight in his hand, smaller than hers, something that would easily fit into his pocket. Sidestepping, she swept her own light to both corners making sure there were no other surprises. "What are you doing in the basement?"

"I came in through the storm doors a while ago."

"They weren't locked?"

"Not when I got here."

She frowned, disturbed by the idea of Caith snooping around without her knowledge. "You could have saved me three years of gray hair by coming through the front door like everyone else."

"Sorry."

She doubted he was. He didn't seem contrite at all. Now that her eyes had adjusted, she could see him better. Wiry and lanky as a youth, he'd developed the muscle and definition that comes with maturity. Tall, broad of shoulder, and narrow through the hips, he carried a trim, athletic physique. His hair was shorter, black as the raven he'd been named for, and tapered against his neck in a becoming cut. Piercing blue eyes held her gaze, causing her heart to hammer faster. The good-looking boy she remembered had grown into a thoroughly handsome man.

He frowned. "What are you doing in the basement in the dark?"

"The light doesn't work."

"I figured that out."

Heat flushed her face. "So that private investigator's license is good for something after all?"

Caith chuckled softly. "Maybe we should start over."

Veronica opened her mouth to snap a reply. Before she could formulate a single pointed word, a shrill scream jarred her to the bone. She felt the blood drain from her face as the horrified shriek shuddered into silence, then started again, climbing in volume.

"Alma!" she cried.

Of one accord, she and Caith bolted for the stairs.

Chapter 5

Veronica clung to Caith's heels as he barreled into the lobby where Alma Kreider stood screaming. "Alma, what is it?" she cried, rushing to the woman's side.

White-faced, her eyes darting between Veronica and Caith, Alma pointed behind her. "The kitchen. There was a man outside. A horrible man. I saw him looking in the window." Covering her face with her hands, she began to cry. "It was ghastly. Like a scarecrow. A ghost." Her voice broke beneath hysterical sobs.

"Shh," Veronica comforted. Thankfully, all the guests were out on a hike with the guide, Ben Dunning, and hadn't heard the commotion. "It's all right now."

Caith snatched the flashlight from her and darted for the kitchen. Wrapping an arm around Alma's shoulders, Veronica led her to one of the low-backed sofas in the lobby. It took her close to ten minutes, but eventually she managed to calm the agitated woman. Alma's sobs had dwindled to sniffling by the time Caith returned.

"Well?" Veronica asked expectantly as he walked into the lobby.

The cold air had heightened the color in his cheeks, intensifying the wintry blue of his eyes. He shook his head.

"Nothing. I looked outside and the ground wasn't disturbed below the window." He scowled doubtfully at Alma. "The soil's soft enough to leave prints, but I couldn't find any."

"It's almost dark," Veronica said. "You could have missed them."

"Maybe." Unconvinced, Caith continued to look at Alma. "Are you sure it wasn't a trick of the light? A reflection of some sort?"

"I know what I saw, young man. You sound just like that Sheriff Cameron and all his cronies, not willing to believe a word of anything." Alma's eyes narrowed suspiciously. "Who are you anyway, and what are you doing here?"

Before Caith could answer, Veronica rushed to explain. "Alma, this is Conner Lairen. He's the consultant BI hired to evaluate the lodge and its anti-stress program. He'll be staying with us for a while."

"Consultant. Hmph." Alma's snort of contempt made her opinion clear. "Just what we need, a corporate busy-body sticking his nose where it doesn't belong. BI should get off their executive keisters and send us security instead of a paid snitch."

"I'll be sure to put that in my report." Caith motioned to the hallway. "Would you mind coming back to the kitchen and showing me exactly where you were standing when you saw, uh…whatever it is you think you saw?"

Alma's expression was hostile, but the belligerence helped dry her tears. Straightening her shoulders, she stood and traipsed from the lobby, her bearing defiant.

Veronica frowned. "I hope you make a better impression on the rest of the staff."

* * * *

Caith stepped into the kitchen, fully aware he'd made a mistake. No question about it. He'd thought he could waltz into the lodge, help Aren with his problem, and then vanish again with his pockets a little fuller. Stupid.

Especially since he'd never cared about money. Oh, he didn't mind an income that let him buy what he wanted, when he wanted, without having to worry about strapping his bank account. But cash had never been the driving ambition behind anything he did. And if he was honest with himself, money had absolutely nothing to do with his reasons for returning to Coldcreek. As much as he wanted to pretend otherwise, the pull of family was here. Family, and the woman he'd loved since he was eighteen.

He'd gotten over the initial shock of seeing her, but not the aftereffect. Even now, his palms sweated and his heart raced. He felt like a tongue-tied school kid with a crush. Raising Derrick didn't leave him time for relationships, and the sight of this woman, the one who'd haunted his dreams for the past twelve years, resurrected how much he wanted her.

"Where were you standing Alma?" Veronica asked.

Caith tried to concentrate on the question but was too preoccupied by how much she'd changed. She'd always been a tom-boy, lean and small-hipped. Still beautifully slender, her body had ripened with sexy curves. Small, pert breasts strained against the fabric of a teal sweater with a V-neckline, her long legs were luscious in soft gray slacks. Her hair was pulled back in a sleek pony tail, gold and gilded like the sun with just a hint of brown beneath. Clear, creamy skin warmed the minty green of her eyes.

"Mr. Lairen," Veronica snapped.

He jerked at her formality. Too late, he realized he'd been staring.

"Did you hear anything Alma said?" Clearly annoyed, Veronica stepped to the sink. "She was standing right here, a few feet from the window. I think it's obvious she wasn't imagining things."

Recovering, Caith glanced about the kitchen. It was large and roomy with cherry cabinets, mocha-colored counters, and a center island for food preparation. Copper pots and wicker baskets dangled from hooks overhead, adding a touch of warmth along with practicality.

Caith stepped to the window and ran his finger along the edge. The seal was tight and unbroken. With both women shooting daggers at him, he moved to Veronica's side. "There's your face," he said, with a nod for the pots. The reflection in the window didn't quite form features, but taken with the small baskets on either side, a quick glance could have produced a startled reaction.

"That's absurd," Alma hissed. "I'm not given to flights of fancy, young man."

"Maybe not, but everyone's been edgy. It's easy to misconstrue something when your nerves are rattled."

"I am not rattled!" Alma pressed her lips into a tight line. "At least, I wasn't until you showed up."

"Alma." Veronica tried to calm her.

"I'm going to my room for a little peace and quiet. Then I'm going to call Aren Breckwood and tell him what a fool he is for saddling us with a snitch who's as agreeable as arsenic."

Caith bit his lip to keep from grinning. He'd been called a lot of things in his day, but he'd never been compared to arsenic. Somehow he didn't think Veronica would find his amusement entertaining.

After Alma left the kitchen in a huff, he looked at Veronica. "I'd like to see the personnel file on her—I'm assuming you have one—and the rest of the staff while you're at it."

She stared in disbelief. "My staff? What for?"

"Because it's my job, and it's part of the investigation. Just because someone's on your payroll doesn't mean they can't have motive. Something's going on here. Until I find out what it is, everyone's a suspect."

Her eyes hardened. "Including me?"

He couldn't stop himself. The note of challenge in her tone was too tempting. Leaning forward until only inches separated them, he gripped her chin and lowered his voice to a husky whisper. "Butchering dogs isn't your style, Ronnie."

Her eyes widened as if she wondered what the hell he was playing at. She smelled incredible, earthy and spicy, like autumn flowers washed in rainwater. He had no business getting so close, but he could have easily drowned in those bewitching eyes. Her bottom lip trembled slightly as her mouth parted in shock. He hadn't meant to touch her. Hadn't wanted to reawaken the raw attraction between them. But it simmered below the surface, waiting to be unleashed. He'd never stopped loving her. Never stopped wanting her. Before he could think it through, Caith lowered his head to kiss her.

Veronica slapped his hand away, then slammed her palm against his chest, shoving backward. "My office is this way." Seething, she stalked from the kitchen.

Her anger crackled on the air even after she'd left. He deserved her hostility, was lucky she hadn't gone for his throat the moment she'd seen him. He'd made a mess of things twelve years ago and was making a greater mess now. He had no business flirting with feelings they'd buried. No matter his motives in breaking off their relationship, his actions had been inexcusable. Time didn't erase a wound like that.

As he followed her down the hallway, Caith berated himself for his thread-bare control. He'd always had feelings for her, but hadn't expected them to return with the force of a summer storm. As she sashayed ahead of him in those flattering slacks, he remembered his first glimpse of her when she was eleven and he was twelve.

"She's a girl," Trask explained, *"but she's okay. Becky Kessler said her parents bought that white house at the end of Ripplemill Road. The one where Bobby Claymore used to live."*

"Becky Kessler knows everybody's business." Caith huffed out a breath as he trekked up the hill beside his best friend, Merlin racing ahead of them. They'd spent the day slaying dragons and battling trolls along the edge of Stone Willow Lake. Grassy embankments, cool water, and leafy trees created a kingdom where Merlin was wizard and they were brave knights and warriors who triumphed over evil.

Caith sent his friend a black glare. *"Why'd you tell her we'd meet her anyway?"* Girls had no business in mock sword fights or challenging ogres. Even now, the slender branch he'd fashioned into a make-believe *sword dangled from his belt and bumped against his thigh as he walked. He liked the feel of it and wondered if a real sword swung that way. He'd have to ask his mother. She knew everything about folklore and myth.*

Trask chewed around a wad of bubble gum. "She isn't like Becky. She knows about legends and stuff. I saw her reading something on King Arthur. She told me she likes Robin Hood and some minstrel guy named Tal-Tali..."

"Taliesin," Caith finished for him. He'd grown up on myth, courtesy of his mother's family traditions. Over the years, he and Merlin had pulled Trask into their make-believe adventures.

"She thought your name was funny," Trask continued as the incline steepened and he dug in to keep pace. "She couldn't say it, so I broke it down for her. Caith-el-den."

"You told her my real name?"

"Don't be stupid. She already knew about you. Everyone knows about the Breckwoods. My dad says your father owns the town."

Caith shrugged, not wanting to talk about it. Sometimes he hated the reverence that came with the Breckwood name. "I don't care about that stuff. It's for Aren and Galen." They'd reached the top of the hill now, stopping beside Merlin who'd paused.

"Look there." Merlin pointed toward a copse of trees.

A thin knobby-kneed girl in a faded sweatshirt and dirt-stained jeans was doing cartwheels on the hillside. Her hair was long and straw-colored, streaming down her back in a tangled ponytail. A single yellow rose, snipped just below the bloom, was tucked into her hairband.

"That's Ron," Trask said with a goofy grin. He looked from Caith to Merlin. "Come on. You guys have to meet her."

She'd been distant at that first meeting. Distant and wary. After all, they were boys, and she was out of her element. But it hadn't taken long. She'd been better with the pretend sword than him and could outrun both Merlin and Trask.

He'd liked her from the start, then grown attracted to her about the time he turned sixteen. It was when he began to use sex as a crutch to ease the gut-twisting guilt he carried over Trask's death. There had been plenty of older girls, some from the local college, all willing to teach him. He hadn't cared about names or faces, and the need for escape made him a fast learner. For every moment he lost himself in the blissful mindlessness of sex, caring only for the release it brought, Caith treasured Veronica from afar.

She deserved to be loved and cherished. The older he got, the stronger those emotions grew. But she deserved someone better. Someone who wasn't tainted by death. Who wouldn't put her in danger simply by being at her side. He'd spent many nights waking in fear, his chest so tight he couldn't breathe, certain those who loved him would suffer.

The fear had never gone away. It had simply become bearable, distant.

Don't hurt him! Trask's voice echoed in his mind, resurrecting the sickening smell of model glue. *Please... you can't....*

Then bits of images he'd locked in a dark place he rarely allowed to surface: a damp room, the slant of greasy sunlight through a mud-splattered window, a man with a pock-marked face, the sharp, straight edge of a knife.

Don't hurt him! Trask had screamed.

Shaken, Caith dragged a hand over his face. He was grateful when he stepped into Veronica's office and could concentrate on something other than the past.

The room wasn't large, but homey, with bookcases, wooden file cabinets, and paisley curtains at the windows. A cherry desk topped with a computer screen, several folders, and scattered papers indicated the owner wasn't always tidy. Paper clips, pens, pencils, a discarded newspaper, and an empty coffee cup added to the clutter. He guessed Ron, as manager, was the only one permitted a computer at the lodge.

His back to the door, Caith slid into a chair across from the desk. "If you pull the personnel files, I'll take them to my room. You do have a room for me?"

Her gaze raked over him, decidedly cool. Most likely, she was still miffed about the near-kiss in the kitchen. Reaching into the top drawer of her desk, she snagged a key and tossed it at him. "The Blackbird Suite."

Caith caught the key in his left hand, his brows crinkling at her frosty tone. "Blackbird?"

"Stone Willow has three floors not counting the basement, which you've already seen." Veronica settled behind her desk. "The main level consists of my office and apartment, the lobby, kitchen, dining area, a room for gathering, and an enclosed porch to the rear. The second floor has six singular rooms, and the third, four suites—Blackbird, Hummingbird, Wood Thrush, and Nightingale."

"You gave me a suite instead of a room?" Caith tried to lighten the mood. "Someone must like me."

"Not me. It was Aren's idea. As he's the COO and you're his brother, I guess that entitles you to some privileges. Besides, most everything that's happened has been on the third floor or in the basement. We thought you should be where the action is."

"With the gobbly ghouls," a man inserted behind Caith in a sarcastic tone.

Caith spun quickly. The sight of the man poised in the doorway brought him to his feet. "Merlin."

He hadn't bargained on such a sharp reaction. Something dark danced up his spine. Time stretched like a taut rope as the two regarded each other in silence. Finally, Caith offered his hand. "It's been a long time."

Ignoring the overture, Merlin brushed past him. "Not long enough." Stepping around Veronica's chair, he placed his hands on her shoulders, leaning forward to press his lips against hers. The message was clear: *She's mine. Back off.*

"Merlin!" Veronica tried to swat him away, as if annoyed he'd use her as a trinket in a power play.

"You haven't changed much," Caith observed sourly.

Merlin chuckled.

"I was telling Caith about the lodge," Veronica interrupted with a sharp glance for Merlin. "He's going to be staying in the Blackbird Suite."

"How fitting." Merlin's gaze slid across the desk to Caith. "Blackbirds and ravens, eating the souls of the dead." The hint of a mocking smile stretched his lips. "Then again, you know all about dead things, don't you?"

"Merlin!" Veronica gasped at precisely the moment Caith launched himself at his brother. Catching Merlin by the collar, he slammed him up against the wall. "Shut up! You don't know what you're talking about."

Feigning innocence, Merlin held up his hands. "You're overreacting, Caithelden. It was a simple comment."

"Fuck you. It was about Trask." With a final shove, Caith released him.

"What if it was?" Merlin straightened his shirt. "You think you can waltz into Coldcreek and not have to face that? You think everyone's going to sidestep the issue so they don't ruffle your feathers? The hell with that. I lived through it, too."

"The hell with you." Caith headed for the door. "Veronica, when you've got the files together bring them to my suite. I'm going to unpack."

His fury carried him into the lobby and past the reception desk. He hit the front door with the flat of his hand, throwing it open. The force propelled it into the wall. Boiling, he took the steps two at a time. His Explorer was parked around the side of the lodge, tucked between trees where he'd hoped no one would see the vehicle until he was ready.

Mae Clair

But Merlin had.

Merlin had shown up and reawakened all the bitter blood between them. It shouldn't have happened. Brothers who'd been close in childhood torn apart by something ugly and vile.

He blames me.

Ignoring the enraged pounding of his heart, Caith wrenched open the back of the SUV and yanked his bags free. As he moved to close the vehicle, he raised his head and caught a startling glimpse of the house. Bracketed by the deepening night sky and tattered clouds, it looked somber and forbidding.

With a soft curse, Caith carted his bags into the lodge and to the suite he was certain Veronica had handpicked for him because of its name.

Chapter 6

Veronica couldn't decide who deserved her anger more. Caith had attempted to play on her emotions in the kitchen, while Merlin had shown up to stake his claim on her and toss ugly insinuations at his brother. As if they were still exclusive! She'd sent him on his way with a pointed rebuff, telling him she was busy and didn't have time for adolescent games. He'd left whistling a melody, hands in his pockets, having accomplished what he'd set out to do.

Typical Merlin.

Hiking up the final flight of stairs to the third floor, she adjusted the stack of manila folders tucked under her arm. Was she Caith's personal secretary now? How long before her irritating guest asked her to do after-hours work in his suite?

A slow burn rose from her neck to her cheeks. As much as she wanted to deny it, she'd felt the startling pull of attraction between them in the kitchen. Anger had made her wrench away, but even that bottle-rocket rage couldn't suppress what lay beneath—love she'd never truly abandoned, wounds she'd buried rather than healed.

If Alma doesn't lynch you for this Aren, I will.

Pausing before Caith's suite, she blew out a frustrated breath. She raised her hand to knock, but before she could complete the action, Caith opened the door. Had he been waiting for her? "How did you—"

"It's an old house, Veronica. The floorboards creak. I heard you coming down the hall."

She moved experimentally, rocking from foot to foot, coaxing a moan from the board beneath her feet. "I'll have Lew take a look." Brushing past him, she stepped inside.

He'd already scattered papers over the desk in the outer living area where a sofa, comfortable chairs, and a small dining table created a homey environment. Toward the rear, the door to the bedroom stood open, giving her a glimpse of a worn green duffle bag and small suitcase he'd dumped on the bed.

"Lew's your caretaker?" Caith asked, closing the door.

"And a friend." Veronica plopped the folders on the desk, grateful for the vista of lake and woodlands unfurling beyond the open draperies. The sight made her feel less confined, his presence not quite as overpowering as when they'd been in her office. "Before you ask, I trust Lew implicitly. I've known him for five years. And, yes, his file is in the stack with the others."

Caith overlooked her sarcasm. "How are your parents?"

"Enjoying retirement in Florida." She started for the door. "I have to go."

"Wait." Caith caught her arm, sending a jolt of unexpected warmth through her. "Ron, stay a minute. I need to talk to you."

He was too close, a sensation of nerve-tingling heat radiating from his hand. Needing to place distance between them, Veronica retreated to one of the stiff dinette chairs. "I have a lot to do, Caith. Four new guests arrive tomorrow."

"So business isn't all bad?"

"It's a trickle of what it should be. Fortunately, not everyone left after the last incident."

"The dog?"

"No, that was earlier. I'm sure Aren told you about the hand in the fireplace."

"He did, but I'd rather hear it from you."

"So you can tell me I'm crazy, too?"

He frowned. "I didn't say that."

Of course he wouldn't. It was his job to indulge her, ask questions that would make her rethink what she'd seen.

And what *had* she seen? How was her experience any different from Alma claiming she'd seen Warren Barrister's ghost? If she didn't believe the cook, writing the incident off as nervous fright, why should anyone believe her?

"Did you know Duke Cameron is sheriff?" she asked.

"I heard." He didn't seem impressed. "I understand no traces of evidence were found when his team checked the fireplace."

She bit her lip, realizing how foolish she must look. Flesh couldn't burn in flame without leaving some type of residue behind. And yet she'd been so certain…just as Alma had.

"Was there an odor?" Caith persisted.

Veronica blinked. "Odor?"

"Yeah." He pulled out a chair, spun it around, and straddled it backward. "Without being graphic, something like that couldn't burn without giving off a stench. You must have noticed it."

Veronica pulled her brows together. Why couldn't she remember a smell? Why hadn't the police asked her about it? No trace of charred flesh or human DNA in the hearth, and no odor that she could recall. Her story was pitiful.

"I don't remember an odor." She tried not to sound defensive. "But I certainly didn't imagine the phone call I got. A man called and told me to look in the fireplace right before I discovered that...*thing*."

"I don't doubt that." He shook his head. "Come on, Ron, don't look so angry. You remember how we used to talk."

"I remember how you used to talk, and I used to listen." The memory flashed bright and painful. She glanced at her hands, uncertain where the crush of emotion came from. "Then one day you stopped talking, and I knew you'd gotten swallowed up in all that guilt over Trask's death."

"Don't."

Veronica glanced up sharply. "It's coming up. Halloween, the anniversary. Caith, he wouldn't want you—"

"Was there a police report?" Lurching to his feet, Caith paced to the opposite side of the room. "On the incident with the hand? And the dog. What about the dog?"

Even after so many years apart, Veronica recognized his telltale signs of nervousness, short, choppy sentences and the way he roamed restlessly like a caged animal. Realizing he'd never made peace with Trask's brutal death, she sighed.

"There's an entire file of police reports." She indicated the folders on the desk with a nod. "Everything from the dog to the hand, and some others you probably haven't heard about. I also gave you a list of all the current guests and those expected to arrive tomorrow." Standing, she started for the door, then paused. "The Hummingbird Suite is empty if you want to check it, but I have someone booked for tomorrow. I try to keep the third floor vacant if I can since that's where the majority of problems occur. You and Dean Bowerman will be the only two guests on this floor. Unfortunately, he specifically requested the Hummingbird Suite, so there was little I could do."

Caith stopped pacing. "That's where the dog was found?"

Veronica hooked her hair behind her ear. "Yes. I think Mr. Bowerman has a side interest in the paranormal. I've had a few guests like him already."

Caith frowned. "A butchered dog isn't paranormal. Who found it?"

"George Stowe, an accountant with BI's Baltimore office. He was staying in the suite and went out for a walk. When he came back, the dog was on the bed. It appears to have been a stray."

"How long was Stowe gone?"

"Maybe an hour. It should be in the report. He packed up and left the next day. The majority of the guests went with him. I have to go now."

Caith crossed the room at a fast clip, reaching the door at the same time she did. He held it shut. "I wasn't through."

Anger sharpened her words. "I was."

"When did the incidents start?"

"A month ago, maybe more. Look it up, Mr. Investigator, it's your job." She pulled on the knob, but his hand remained firm, holding the door in place. He slumped against it, using his tall, muscled body to block her escape. Refusing to shrink away, she felt her pulse quicken.

"You're still stubborn, Ronnie." His voice was low and husky again, at its most dangerous. "When we were kids, you never wanted to be the damsel in distress." He raised his free hand, tracing a single finger over the smooth contour of her cheek, sending sparks of heat dancing like caged fire under her skin. "You wanted to be a knight on the front line, fighting for Arthur's kingdom."

"I was better than you," she croaked. The words barely came. Her heart thudded fast and hard against her breastbone. She despised him, loathed how quickly he could turn her resolve to mush. And yet she loved him. Still, always, forever. That was the horrid, wretched truth. If she didn't get free of him soon, he'd have her in bed again, only to saunter away in the morning to find someone else. The memory of past humiliation and pain made her back stiffen. "Get out of my way, Caithelden. I'm not playing games."

"Neither am I." He dragged her forward, then covered her mouth with his. The kiss was hot and desperate, crashing over her with the furious force of pounding surf. It took her breath away and left her senses spinning. Scorching heat unraveled in her belly and she nearly surrendered.

Caith groaned, hugging her closer.

The humiliation returned, sharp and glittering with a knife-edge like glass. It exploded in her stomach, shattering his carefully spun web of seduction. How dare he do this to her again? She shoved him against the door. "You bastard." Her hand cracked across his face.

He stared, unable to speak, his eyes heavily-lidded and glazed with an emotion she didn't want to see—need, desperate, crippling need. Sex had always been his drug of choice. This time when she reached for the door, he didn't stop her. Her face hot, she hurried from the room. She wasn't certain who she was angrier with, herself or him. He'd initiated and she'd followed.

After twelve years, the pattern remained the same.

* * * *

The next morning Caith examined the area outside the kitchen window, but even in daylight found nothing to indicate anyone had been there. He did a search of the Hummingbird Suite and the fireplace, finding nothing unusual. The remaining guests arrived, settled into their rooms, and to everyone's immense relief, three days passed without incident.

The staff, while on edge, tolerated him fairly well, answering questions when asked, grumbling only behind his back. In addition to Lew and Alma, Veronica introduced him to her guide, Ben Dunning, and a number of seasonal and part-time employees. He met the instructor who handled mental-focusing techniques for BI, a woman who drove from town each day, conducting her sessions with the same friendly intensity as a self-help guru. The guests were less intimidated and spoke freely. Bowerman even admitted to booking his stay solely in the hopes of encountering "resident ghosts."

On Thursday morning, Caith had breakfast with three of the guests, spent an hour talking to Ben, and then made his way to the boat house. When he arrived, Lew Walden was kneeling on the floor, running his hands over one of the wooden cradles for the johnboats. Stacked upside down, four on each side of the shelter, the eight boats looked like large empty nutshells.

"I guess they don't get much use in the fall," Caith said, walking inside. The place smelled of wet tarps, grass clippings, and linseed oil.

Lew glanced over his shoulder. "Not like the spring and summer when the bass are plentiful. Look here." Work-roughened hands motioned Caith forward, and he pointed to the timber cradle. "Wood-borers got to it, hollowed her out. She'll need replacing."

"Is there a boat ready if I want to go on the lake?"

Surprised, Lew stood. "Why'd you wanna do that? Ain't got enough to snoop around at the lodge?"

Caith hooked his thumbs through his belt loops. "Guess not." One of the skills he'd acquired as a private investigator was slipping into the speech patterns of anyone he questioned. With Lew, it was curt sentences, blunt and to the point. "When's the last a boat was out?"

"Don't track that stuff. Guests come, guests go."

"Lot are going now, aren't they, Lew?"

The caretaker narrowed his eyes. He wasn't exceptionally tall, just over medium height, but was stocky enough to be intimidating. Salt-and-pepper hair, worn on the long side, contrasted leathery skin and intense blue eyes. Caith guessed his age near sixty.

"Like I said, don't track that stuff."

The conversation went no further. Caith found a single boat docked around the side and took it onto the lake. The electric motor hummed quietly as water unfurled, blindingly blue in the bright October sun. The lodge dwindled behind, swallowed by a tree line still dressed in the gem-bright splendor of fluttering autumn leaves. Cool air scraped across his face as he steered around the bend. He beached on a familiar embankment where the wet grass smelled faintly of earth worms and tree-shaded moss.

"I'm a wizard. I was born during a meteor storm." Thirteen-year-old Merlin spun in a circle, his arms outstretched as he tilted his head to the sky. *"I can conjure magic from the lake. Make waves rise up on silver horses and crush ogres and trolls. I'm the mightiest wizard there ever was."*

Standing on the bank, Caith motioned to the lake with his wooden sword. It was hot, and the summer sun beat against the back of his neck like dragon fire. *"What about the sea monster?"*

"I'm a mermaid," Veronica said indignantly, kicking a spray of water into his face.

He laughed. She looked so silly paddling around in the water, her long blond hair soaked like seaweed. *"I say we stone the foul beast."* Grinning, he scooped a handful of muck from the water's edge. *"What say you, wise wizard?"*

"You don't stone mermaids, you idiot!" Veronica snapped. *"They're magical."*

With a mischievous grin, Merlin plopped to a seat on the grass. *"She protests, but do not let her objections sway you. She is a dangerous one, brave knight. Take care as you attack."*

Caith weighed the mud in his hand. "Trask." He pitched his voice to carry. "Our wizard advisor councils we take the offensive with this lake monster."

"I told you I'm not—"

"Who am I to argue with the mighty Merlin?" Trask broke from the trees on the far side of the bank, his expression gleeful. He scooped up a handful of mud as he raced down the grass. "The beast must die!"

"Don't you dare," Veronica shrieked.

Then all three boys were in the water with her, and spray and mud flew everywhere.

Caith grinned, but the memory was sad and whimsical. Trask was gone, Merlin despised him, and Veronica would vivisect him given the chance. She'd been cold since the incident in his suite, avoiding him whenever possible. He didn't know what possessed him to act the way he had. One moment he was blocking her path, fully in control, the next he'd behaved like a hormonal teenager. The sooner he resolved things at the lodge and returned to Boston, the better for both of them.

He hiked deeper between the trees. The soil was soft and muddy, carpeted with fallen leaves. A small animal had recently scavenged for food at the base of an elm, digging up clumps of earth. Random flecks of white riddled the ground and clung to patches of moss and protruding roots. Caith bent to examine the substance. Powdery in composition, it left a phosphorescent residue clinging to his fingers.

Curious, he went back to the boat and rummaged beneath the seat until he found an empty bait container. Carefully, he deposited a handful of the white-flecked soil in the receptacle, and then spent another half-hour scouring the surrounding grounds. Finding nothing out of the ordinary, he returned to the lodge. He located Veronica in her office, seated behind her desk, typing away on her computer.

"I'm busy," she said, glancing up when he stepped into the room.

"I won't stay long." He smiled smoothly, but her expression didn't soften. She wore black jeans with a gray tweed jacket and a cranberry T-shirt. Her hair was brushed back from her face, secured at the nape of her neck with a soft black ribbon. Indulging in a moment of sheer fantasy, Caith envisioned pulling the pert ribbon free and knotting his fingers in the rich cascade of honey-gold. With effort, he forced the images away. "Who saw the woman at the lake? The one with the white veil?"

Veronica looked puzzled. "Kay Porter, but that was over a week ago."

"Do you have a number for her?"

"She's with the Farzfold Corporation out of Wilmington." Veronica tapped a few keys, located the number on her computer, then scribbled it on a piece of paper. Passing it to Caith, she eyed him suspiciously. "Lew said you took out a boat."

"Does he report everything I do? I get the feeling he doesn't like me."

"There's a line for that, Caithelden." Her words were harsh, but her tone light. A sliver of amusement danced in her eyes.

Encouraged, Caith leaned forward. "So you've known him for five years?"

"Give or take. He used to live in Detroit, but moved here to be closer to his daughter who lives in Pittsburgh."

"Why not move to Pittsburgh?"

"I don't know. Maybe he doesn't like big cities." Her expression was a cross between suspicion and thoughtfulness. She tugged her bottom lip between her teeth.

Caith grew warm. "What about your guide, Ben Dunning? He seemed a little over-eager when I talked to him."

"You're not exactly the most welcome person here, Caith. The staff thinks you're evaluating their job performances and the success of the program as a whole. For all they know, you could advise Stone Willow be scrapped."

He couldn't pinpoint when he stopped listening, focused instead on the becoming tint of rose-gold on her cheeks. She was more bewitching than all the muse-daughters of Zeus and Mnemosyne combined. He laid his hand over hers where it rested on the desk.

She swallowed, a sure sign he'd unnerved her, but kept her hand where it was. "Ben's from a small town northwest of Coldcreek. He's worked here about two years. He and Lisa Cole, the BI instructor, have been dating off and on for the last few months."

"Like you and Merlin?" He regretted the stinging observation the moment the words left his mouth. Stupid mistake.

Veronica snatched her hand away. "You're out of line. My relationship with your brother is none of your business."

It was too late to back out. "Merlin, for crying out loud? You don't even look right together."

"How would you know? You spent one night with me. One night, Caith!" Her voice cracked with anger. "Then you flew off to college and dumped me for the first girl you could tumble into bed."

"Veronica."

"You didn't even have the guts to call. You sent me a letter. A letter, you son-of-a-bitch, too much of a coward to admit you were only in it for a good screw. I should have known better. You were always about sex and getting anyone you could into bed."

He hadn't wanted to do this. Not here, not now. Frazzled, he rubbed his temple.

Veronica stood, her anger bristling between them. "I met somebody," she spat, mimicking the words he'd used in the letter. "What we did was a mistake." Despite the venom, her eyes glittered with tears. "I hated you, Caith. Really hated you. You made love to me. Made me feel like I was the most precious thing in your life. And then you went off and had a child with another woman."

Her pain cut like a knife, but he wouldn't let her malign the single bright spot in his world. "Derrick came later."

"Was he a mistake, too?"

His face hardened into a stone mask. "Derrick's the best thing that's ever happened to me."

Veronica stood her ground. "Maybe I feel the same way about your brother."

The words were a blow to his gut. "You're lying. If you love Merlin so damn much, why is he never here? Why are you always fighting with him?"

Her eyes flashed emerald fire. "Who told you that?"

"Who didn't? He's not who you want, Ron. We both know that. I see it in your eyes every time I get near you."

"Your ego's bigger than your stupidity. Get out of my way, Caith."

She started past him but he caught her by the wrist and pinned her to the wall. He didn't know what he was doing, just that he needed to make her understand the conflicting snarl of emotion in his gut. He wanted her more than he'd ever wanted anyone, yet knew it would be a mistake. Another damn mistake. He'd had his chance twelve years ago and walked away when he should have stayed.

"That night—" The words struck in his throat. "What happened between us...I've never stopped wanting you."

"You expect me to believe that?" Her eyes were hard, brittle as glass. "You really take the prize, Caith, coming back after all this time with a story like that. You must think I'm an idiot."

Undaunted, he stroked her cheek. "Ronnie, you want me, too."

She slammed her palms against his chest, shoving backward. "Bullshit! I've already made one mistake with you, Caith. I'm not going to make another." Her voice was ice, frigid as arctic air.

He sucked down a breath, keeping his head lowered. "You're right."

Of course she was. He was scum. Dirt. Disgusting ilk of the lowest level. He'd done something unforgivable. He had no business thinking he could brush it off with a few choice words and the utterings of his heart. "I didn't mean to hurt you, Ronnie. I thought you should know I've missed you."

"And you should know I couldn't care less."

She shoved past him, stalking from the room, her anger like a storm cloud. It was a verbal slap in the face, not that he deserved any less. He yearned for the time when life was simpler, when feelings of love and lust had never come between them.

* * * *

Veronica stormed into the lobby, barely conscious of where she was headed. It didn't matter so long as she got away from Caith. Having him near brought a crush of memories and emotions tumbling back that left her shaken and weak, teetering on a precipice of uncertainty. She'd always loved him, even when he'd been wrapped up in Kelly Rice, so damn infatuated he couldn't see straight. She could still recall the slight she'd felt when he'd taken Kelly to their high school dance instead of her.

"You didn't go to the dance," Caith said as they walked one evening on the hilly roads surrounding Coldcreek. It was late spring in Caith and Merlin's senior year, the time when Merlin began to drift away, Caith was increasingly at odds with his father, and everything started to unravel. "I wanted you to know I was thinking about you, so I brought you something." He pulled his arm from behind his back, offering a single flower. A long-stemmed yellow rose. "This is for you."

She smiled, secretly pleased. "Thank you." Accepting the rose, she pushed on tip-toes, lightly brushing a kiss on his cheek. "You didn't have to. It was just a dance."

But it had been much more, and she'd wanted to attend with him. Even if it had been as friends, she'd wanted that memory of him by her side.

They started walking again. Veronica pressed the velvety petals against her lips, allowing the floral scent to engulf her. She hadn't wanted to see him with Kelly Rice. The prom queen was everything she wasn't, curvy and vivacious with curling black hair and smoky amber eyes. She slanted a casual glance at him. "Did you have a good time?"

"Nah." Caith grinned. "How could I, when you weren't there?" He slung an arm over her shoulders, tugging her close to his side as they walked. "We always have at least one dance together, Ron. We've done that ever since we were kids, and you dragged me, Merlin, and Trask to that god-awful harvest-thing in junior high."

She chuckled. "You were the only one who danced with me."

"Only because Trask and Merlin bet I wouldn't. I won four bucks that night, two from each of them."

"You danced with me for a bet?"

He kissed the top of her head. "Cut me a break. I was thirteen years old. Four bucks was four bucks. You think I would have danced with a girl for free?"

She pushed away from him. "That's whorish, Caith."

"Nah, men are gigolos, remember? Besides..." He flashed that grin again. The one she loved best, the one that reached his eyes. "You weren't the one paying me."

The magnificent smile faded as quickly as it came. He stared past her, abruptly ill-at-ease, looking over her shoulder. She didn't have to turn to know what lay behind her. Suddenly, the dance was no longer important. All that mattered was helping him ease the pain that plainly still twisted his heart. "Do you...do you want to visit the cemetery?"

"No!" Revolted, he wrenched away. Without waiting, he pivoted and sprinted down the hillside.

"Caith, wait!" She chased after him, her heart pounding. As long-legged as she was, she had a hard time matching his stride. "I'm sorry." She snagged his arm, dragging him to a halt. "It was a stupid suggestion. I just thought... You'll be leaving for college soon. It might be the last time you have a chance to—"

"Veronica, don't." He shook off her hand. "Some things are better left the way they are."

He'd never visited the cemetery. Not once after Trask died, not in all the years she'd known him. Morgana Breckwood had called her and Merlin together and told them the doctors thought it would help if Caith visited his friend's grave. That it would bring closure and healing. She'd wanted their help in convincing Caith it was best. Merlin had nodded and said he'd try, but he never did. Her own efforts failed, only succeeding in angering Caith whenever she mentioned it.

So the three of them continued to drift apart, year after year. Even as her feelings for Caith grew stronger, she felt him slipping away, locking his emotions in a place no one could touch. Rather than face the wrong in his life, he'd taken from her, used her, then let her go. Without a second thought.

He'd let her go.

Chapter 7

Caith returned to his suite, more on edge than he'd been since he'd arrived. Working with Veronica was damn near impossible. In Boston, she'd only haunted his dreams. Now she was under his skin like an itch he couldn't reach. The more he thought about her, the more he wanted to right his wrongs. A hidden, unreasonable voice insisted she could end up like Trask, but the fear of living without her was stronger still. Seeing her again awakened feelings he'd unsuccessfully tried to suppress most of his life.

He didn't deserve her. Of that he was positive. If there was any chance of them together, it had to be on her terms. He didn't believe she was serious about his brother, or Merlin about her. It was more like a friendship with benefits, of that he was certain. He'd treat her far better than Merlin ever could, the way he'd always wanted to cherish her. But she had to make the next move. He had to know she wanted him as much as he wanted her. That meant patience, understanding, and the willingness to listen and concede mistakes. It meant old-fashioned courtship.

He was woefully out of practice with dating. Derrick had seen to that. He tried to remember the last time he'd been intimate with a woman, and found it required a stretch of the imagination. A friend from the police force had set him up a few times. He'd done the dinner and dancing routine, occasionally winding up in bed at the woman's apartment. Thankfully, those incidents were rare. They always ended in awkwardness the morning after when regret replaced the heat of passion. The last true relationship he'd had was with Derrick's mother, a bond of convenience far more than love.

So, he'd do the dating thing…wine, dinner, whatever passed for entertainment in Coldcreek these days. Veronica was worth the effort. Eventually, he'd have to introduce her to Derrick.

He stopped abruptly, struck by an unpleasant thought. What if Veronica didn't like children? What if Derrick resented her?

Dropping into a chair, he fished Kay Porter's phone number from his pocket. He was being an ass. Veronica had always adored children, and he'd never seen his kid react badly to any of the women he'd introduced. Well, maybe the red-haired stockbroker, but he'd reacted badly, too.

With a tight grin, he punched Kay's number on his cell. Tonight he'd drive into town and spend time with Derrick. Placing daily phone calls had made him feel better, but four days without seeing his kid was too long.

Kay Porter answered on the third ring and Caith tried to concentrate on the matter for which he'd been hired. Earlier, before going to see Veronica, he'd left the bait container with the white-flecked soil on his desk. He bumped it now, locating a pad and pencil.

"Ms. Porter, my name is Conner Lairen. I'm a private consultant for Breckwood Industries, and I'd like to ask you a few questions about your stay at Stone Willow Lodge."

As Aren indicated, cell reception was limited. Coupled with Kay Porter's hesitation, Caith had his hands full trying to piece together the conversation.

Reluctant to talk at first, the woman eased under prodding. She'd taken a hike near dusk, skirting the lake. She'd been preparing to head back when a woman emerged from the trees on the opposite side of the bank.

"She just stood there staring at me." Kay's voice crackled through the spotty reception. "She had a weird white glow about her and was dressed in some kind of flowing gown. It looked vintage. You know… old-fashioned like something from another century. It might sound crazy, but with all that glowing white, I was sure she was a ghost."

"What did you do?" Caith asked.

"Nothing. I was too afraid to move, so I stayed where I was."

"Did she threaten you?"

"No. After a while she walked down the bank and disappeared into the trees. I went back to the lodge and told Miss Kent about it. Later, when I got back to Wilmington, I told my brother what happened. He did some research and discovered there was a religious sect associated with the house a long time ago. I think it had to do with the man who built it—Warren Barrister. My brother said Barrister's wife wasn't killed in the house. She drowned in the lake. He chased her there when she tried to escape. Do you think it could have been her?"

Caith made a note to check into the Barrister legend. Despite growing up in Coldcreek, he'd forgotten most of the details. "Legends have a way of getting out of hand. Myth, folklore. They get passed around so long, told and retold, the story gets distorted. If I asked three different people in Coldcreek about Warren Barrister and what he did that night, I guarantee I'd get three different versions."

"My brother is an expert in paranormal research." She was suddenly defensive. "What did you say your name was?"

He knew when it was time to back off so he thanked her for the information, apologized if he'd offended her, and ended the call amicably.

He glanced at his watch. Alma would be making dinner. The staff would avoid him, but he could probably coerce a few of the guests into telling him how their stay was progressing. Later tonight he'd give Aren the soil sample and tell his brother to use his BI influence to get it analyzed.

And then he would decide how best to go about softening up Veronica.

* * * *

Veronica passed the activity schedule to the nervous looking systems manager from BI's Boston office. "Ben Dunning is taking everyone horseback riding after breakfast tomorrow," she said with a bolstering smile. The physical awkwardness of some of the employees who enrolled for the retreat often surprised her. Wayne Hollis looked like a man most comfortable pushing papers behind a desk. A higher up in the corporate chain had probably encouraged him to complete the program.

"Yes, uh…thank you." He accepted the printed sheet of paper with a fidgety smile. "I think I'll go read now. Maybe find a quiet spot on the porch."

As he hurried from the lobby, Caith strolled down the steps. "You're lucky he didn't pass out. Horseback riding? Come on, Ron. The closest that guy wants to come to a four-legged animal is the computer mouse on his desk."

She ignored him, organizing a display of brochures on the reception counter. His manner was breezy, too confident. He'd certainly have no problems on a horse. She wondered what he would look like riding bareback, all that lean muscle moving in rhythm, thick hair flying in the wind. Abruptly warm, she bit her lip.

The front door opened before either of them could speak. "Delivery for Caithelden Lairen," Aren said, stepping inside.

Veronica turned in time to see a black-haired rocket streak across the floor. "Dad!"

Her breath caught in her throat when Caith snagged his son, still at full run, spun him around, and dangled him upside down. She'd only seen pictures of Derrick at Melanie's house, but he'd been much younger, and the amazing resemblance to his father hadn't been evident.

Caith grinned extravagantly. "Aren, why are you bringing me strange kids? I'm not sure who this is, it's been so long since I've seen him. Kind of a scrawny thing."

"Dad." Laughing, Derrick tried to claw right-side up. "Dad, put me down. There's a girl."

"A girl?" With a strong arm to his son's waist, Caith flipped him to his feet and set him on the floor. Aren joined them at the reception desk, a copy of the *Coldcreek Herald* tucked under his arm. "Derrick, this is Veronica Kent."

Derrick's eyes went wide at the name. "You're the one in the picture. The one my Dad keeps on the mantel. You, Dad, Uncle Merlin, and Trask." He puffed up a little straighter. "Dad says I'm named for Trask."

Surprised that Caith kept the picture, but more surprised that he'd told his son about Trask, Veronica offered a faltering smile. "It's good to meet you, Derrick. You look like your father."

"Everyone says that. And I like Derry better."

"Okay, you can call me Ron."

"Ron's a guy's name."

"When we were kids, she was like a guy." Caith sent her a lopsided smile. "She climbed trees, had mud battles, and even beat me in a sword fight."

Derrick's eyes grew round as he looked at Veronica. It was clear she'd soared three notches in his esteem. "Cool!"

Caith ruffled his hair. "Miss me?"

Derrick grinned at him, making Veronica's heart melt. He was such a good-looking kid, all curly black hair and wide blue eyes, and he obviously adored Caith. "You won't believe what Matt, Noah, and I did today."

Caith looked at his brother. "Where are Matt and Noah?"

"Melanie has them. Back-to-back dentist appointments."

"Uncle Merlin took us on this really cool hay ride after school."

Caith's brows drew into a hostile crease. "Merlin?"

Veronica sensed alarms going off. If there was one person who got under Caith's skin nearly as much as his father, it was his brother. The transformation on his face alerted her he was close to losing his temper. Derrick didn't need to witness a scene between his father and uncle.

Snatching up his hand, she smiled encouragingly. "Derry, do you want to see the rest of the lodge? I think Alma has some chocolate cake in the kitchen."

He nodded eagerly.

Ushering him around the reception counter, she led him down the hall. Even then, she heard Caith's voice rise in anger behind her.

* * * *

"You let Merlin take my kid?" Caith felt like he'd been gut-punched.

Heaving a sigh, Aren set his copy of the *Coldcreek Herald* on the reception counter. "Why do we have to do this? It's not as bad as it sounds." Still dressed for the office, his charcoal suit and pin-striped tie made a sharp contrast to Caith's navy Dockers and stone-washed denim shirt. "Melanie was with them. I told you about the hay ride we're planning for Friday. They were with the farmer who's arranging it for us. He's a friend of Merlin's."

"Since when does Merlin have friends who don't wear imported suits and drive Porsches?"

Aren shot him an ugly frown. "You can be downright nasty when you want."

"I left my kid in your care."

"So I let him go on a hay ride. What's the problem? He was with his cousins and his aunt."

"And an uncle he's never met before."

"Is that what's bothering you?" Aren shook his head. "You've gone off the deep end. Derrick never met Galen either, but I didn't see you acting like a jerk when he showed up at your house." Smiling tightly, he held up his hand. "Uh, wait a minute. Maybe you did. It's hard for me to tell anymore, since you've been a general ass for the last twelve years."

"Fuck you."

"Ditch the nastiness, Caithelden. The only reason you don't want Merlin near Derrick is because you have a problem with him."

Caith ground his teeth, turning away. "You don't know what you're talking about."

"Let me take a wild stab at it." Aren snagged his arm, holding him in place. "Your problem with Merlin is about Trask. And your problem with Trask is he got killed saving your life."

"Shut up!" Caith flung off his grip. Before he could think it through, he drew his fist back and popped Aren in the jaw.

"Hell, Caith!" Staggering, his brother shrugged off the blow. In the next instant, he had Caith by the collar and slammed him into the wall.

"What the fuck is wrong with you? You think conking me is going to change what happened to Trask? I brought Derrick here because it doesn't matter anymore. Read page two of the *Herald* and you'll see what I mean."

Giving Caith a violent shove, he started for the door.

"Wait." Caith dragged a hand over the back of his neck. "I, uh…I didn't handle that very well."

Aren paused halfway across the lobby. "If that's your way of saying you're a fucking ass, we'll call it even."

The hint of a smile ghosted over Caith's lips. "You know, Aren, I don't think I've ever seen you lose your temper, and I know I've never heard you swear." Looking away, he thumbed open the *Herald.* "How about if I let you take a whack at me later and we call it even?"

Frowning, Aren rubbed the corner of his mouth. He loosened his tie and joined Caith at the counter.

"So is this more bad news or the usual *Herald* drivel to make me feel at home?" Caith asked, thumbing open the paper.

"Someone's been talking to your old girlfriend, Kelly Rice." Calmer now, Aren rifled a hand through his sandy hair, tidying his appearance. "And don't think I'm going to forget I owe you a cheap shot."

"Not anytime soon, huh? Ron tells me there's a line for that." Caith flipped to page two. He gave a low whistle as his eyes hit the headline. "'BI's Private Lies' by Kelly Rice."

Veronica returned to the lobby with Derrick in time to hear his comment. "Another stinging article?" she asked, joining them at the desk.

"More like an obituary," Aren countered. "I get the feeling she wants to bury BI."

"Her family owns the paper," Veronica pointed out. "She can say what she wants."

Derrick tugged at Caith's sleeve. "Dad, what's an obit…bit… "

"Obituary," Caith said for him. "It's something I have to discuss with Uncle Aren and Veronica. How about giving us a few minutes, partner?"

"Then what?"

Derrick was the picture of hope and eagerness. Feeling a protective tug on his heart, Caith dropped a hand on his shoulder. Four days in Coldcreek and he hadn't spent a single moment with his kid. His brothers had been with Derrick more than he had.

"We'll drive into town and stop wherever you want. Deal?"

Derrick grinned ear-to-ear. "Deal." He wandered away to explore the rest of the lobby and Caith returned his attention to the paper. He read the article aloud.

"Breckwood Industries has been hiding more than corporate failures at Stone Willow Lodge. The anti-stress retreat recently welcomed a new guest in the guise of Conner Lairen, a corporate evaluator assessing the program for continued longevity. Despite BI's attempts to deceive employees and guests, Lairen's true identity is Caithelden Breckwood, a private investigator and the youngest son of Stuart Breckwood, owner and president of Breckwood Industries. Lairen was hired by his family to probe the recent rash of unexplained occurrences at the lodge.

"Born and raised in Coldcreek, Lairen left the area twelve years ago after a well-publicized falling out with his father. Since then, he has served on the Boston police force as a homicide detective, retiring after seven years to begin a private investigation firm. He dropped the Breckwood name shortly after leaving Coldcreek, apparently finding a life of anonymity preferable to the undeserved and excessive awe surrounding his family.

"Left to wonder why BI has resorted to underhanded snooping, one can only assume there is something to hide at Stone Willow. Perhaps Caithelden Lairen, nee Breckwood, should stop to consider why he left Coldcreek in the first place, and he might recall a kidnapping-murder that scarred this community far deeper than anything that goes bump in the night.

"Reputed to be in town with his eight-year-old son, Lairen is making a name for himself and BI in ways he never intended."

"Damn her!" Caith sent the paper soaring over the counter. "She's got no business putting Derry in the news. She can drag my name and BI through the headlines all she wants, but she leaves Derrick out of it!"

Looking puzzled, Veronica retrieved the paper. "How did she know you were here? As a private investigator, I mean? No one at the lodge knows who you are except for your family and me. And even if the staff or one of the guests suspected you were an investigator, they wouldn't know you're a Breckwood."

"Someone told her," Aren said darkly. "Someone made sure she knows. She's never been kind to BI in her column, but she's downright vindictive when it comes to Stone Willow." He studied Caith thoughtfully. "Throwing you into the mix seems to have kicked her grudge-holding into high gear."

Caith scowled. "There's nothing personal if that's what you're driving at. I haven't spoken to her since high school."

"Maybe that's the problem," Veronica ventured. "You might have forgotten Kelly, but she's never gotten beyond Coldcreek where you can't turn a corner without being reminded BI and the Breckwoods support the town. You're salt in an open wound."

"*She* dumped me, Ron, and it's been twelve years. There was never anything exceptional between us."

"Except Breckwood money. She missed out on a joint bank account."

Surprised, Caith laughed. "When did you get so cynical?"

"Not long after someone sent me a letter."

Unprepared for the verbal slap, Caith eyed her sharply. Before he could say anything, Derrick wandered to his side. Having exhausted all of five minutes exploring the lobby, he was clearly bored. "Dad, are you done yet? You said we'd go where I want."

"Yeah, Derry, we're done." Caith folded the paper Veronica had set on the counter. With a smile for his son, he shoved aside the recent unpleasantness. "So, what do you want to do, partner? Ice cream, video games, or just stay here and check out the lake?"

"I want to go with Uncle Aren, and I want you to come, too."

"Back to the house?"

Aren exhaled loudly. "Not exactly. Galen's stuck at the office handling a crisis with Boston Corporate. He wants me to stop and pick up some paperwork for him."

Suspicious, Caith frowned. "Pick up paperwork where?"

"At Dad's."

"Forget it."

"But you promised!" Derrick tugged on his hand. "Grandma and Grandpa aren't even home."

"Derrick," Caith warned.

"You should go," Veronica coaxed at his side. "Show Derry all those great places we used to hide as kids. I'll go with you."

Derrick grinned at her over the counter, his eyes bright with excitement. His kid had just found a co-conspirator.

"Looks like you're out-voted, Caithelden." Aren glanced at his watch. "So let's get moving. I want to be home before Melanie gets back with the boys."

Caith glanced from Derrick's expectant face to Veronica's challenging stare, then to Aren. None of them were playing fair. Irritated, he glared at his brother. "If I do this, you just forfeited your cheap shot."

"Deal. Now get your butt in the car. I can only handle one moody eight-year-old at a time."

* * * *

Before they left the lodge, Caith retrieved the soil sample he'd taken at the lake and gave it to Aren to have analyzed. Derrick wanted to stay at Stone Willow that night, and since there really wasn't a need for pretense any longer, and Aren was willing to bend the rules, Caith agreed. He took his own vehicle, getting Derrick settled into the back while Veronica rode with Aren. The drive wasn't long, and within twenty minutes they pulled into the circular driveway at his parent's gated residence.

Caith had forgotten how brooding the house appeared with its distinctive gothic lines. His father had it designed around his mother's love of folklore, incorporating massive chimneys, steeply arched windows, and multiple roof peaks. A marble fountain, littered with dry leaves, dominated the center of the driveway. Caith remembered playing there as a child, the water spouting up in magical streams, glittering with the glow of multi-colored lights. His father had often joked he would have been happy with a simple cape cod, but would settle on nothing less than a storybook castle for Caith's mother, his queen.

When they stepped from the car, Derrick abandoned him, racing to the house after Aren. Caith moved far more slowly, walking around the side, re-familiarizing himself with the grounds. Treed and landscaped, the earth unfurled in flat parcels and gentle slopes, connected by cobblestone paths and raised gardens. Statues of stone, marble, and iron made a host of fantastical sentries beneath trees and trellised walkways. No garden gnomes for his mother. Brooding gargoyles, fierce dragons, and majestic unicorns guarded the Breckwood estate.

Caith eyed the entrance to the nearest garden, still blooming with late fall flowers. A black bird, forged from iron, perched on a gothic-looking gate, its wings unfurled to the sky.

"Mom, what does my name mean?"

With a soft smile, Caith's mother brushed the thick hair from his forehead.

"You're the raven, Caithelden. Strong and swift, like the bird from the Myth of Orlen. It was born after a mighty battle when Prince Kenrick fought his brother Prince Orlen for the throne of their father."

"And Prince Kenrick died." Caith knew the legend. He'd heard it countless times.

"Yes. But Orlen wept, sobbing bitter tears that he'd slain his own flesh. No one could console him, not even his men. So a wizard was summoned, and from Orlen's tears he conjured a raven to carry Kenrick to the next

life. And that is why the raven haunts battlefields, collecting souls who pass from one world to the next."

"Derry went inside with Aren."

Caith jerked when Veronica appeared at his shoulder. Frazzled at being caught unaware, he nodded curtly.

She looked past him to the gate with its dark sentry. "Bird watching or reminiscing?"

His immediate retort, a defensive reaction, died on his tongue. Her expression was open, almost playful, those remarkable green eyes betraying a thread of the mischievousness he remembered from childhood. Although it was dark, he saw her face clearly, outlined in the soft glow of solar lighting. Her hair glimmered with the kiss of awakening starlight.

"Remembering." What good was the past? With her face upturned to his, her lips petal-soft and inviting, all he wanted to do was drown in the present. To claim her mouth with his and sink in the slow emersion of a mind-numbing kiss.

Disturbed, he jammed his hands into his pockets. "I should go inside and get this over with."

Veronica touched his arm. "We used to have fun here. Do you remember?"

The light pressure of her fingers seared his sleeve with fire. He kept his hands in his pockets, fighting the desire to drag her against him. "I remember."

"Your father made us that great play fort in the trees. He came out and pretended to be a troll so we could attack him with our swords. He spent all afternoon with us…letting you and Trask jump all over him and pull him down into the grass. Merlin turned him into stone, but I did something to set him free. I remember he threw me over his shoulder and said in a loud troll-like voice that I was too scrawny to eat."

Caith chuckled. "You were scrawny. Like a toothpick in jeans." He looked her over from head to toe, his gaze lingering on her slender curves. "But I wouldn't think of calling you that now." Snatching her hand, he pulled her toward the front of the house. "Come on, Ron. Time to go into the dragon's lair."

* * * *

Caith found Derrick and Aren in the back by following the trail of his kid's coat, sweatshirt, and shoes. He picked up each item as he went, locating his brother and son in a two-story formal drawing room with an elaborate buttressed ceiling.

Derrick was flushed, one side of his shirt hanging sloppily over his pants. He looked like he'd run a race and still had massive amounts of energy to spare. Typical. Caith didn't know where the kid packed his endless supply of enthusiasm.

"Uncle Aren showed me your old room, Dad. He said it's still the same."

Caith set the clothes aside on an ornate high-backed chair, and cast his brother a suspicious glance. "What do you mean?"

"Go see for yourself." Aren shrugged nonchalantly. "Everything's the way you left it."

"I wanna see downstairs." As if realizing his father wasn't the best choice of tour guide, Derrick appealed to his uncle. "You said there's a pool table and a big fireplace. Come on, Uncle Aren, I wanna see."

"I'll show you, Derry," Veronica offered.

She'd been to the house often enough over the years, Caith guessed she knew it like her own apartment.

"Okay!" Grinning, Derrick bolted into the hall. The sound of his stocking feet thumping across polished hardwood echoed through the room. After a few seconds, the sound evened out into a long, gliding slide. "Dad, you should see this, it's so cool. Like ice."

Caith pinched the bridge of his nose. "He's gonna knock something over."

"Let him enjoy himself." Veronica nudged Caith toward the front of the house and the multi-tiered staircase leading to the upper level. "Do something with yourself, Caithelden. Aren has paperwork to collect. I'll look after Derry."

He frowned, uncertain. "All right. Just, uh…don't say anything about Trask. I never told him what happened when I was a kid. Let's keep it that way, okay?"

After she left and Aren departed, Caith wandered upstairs. The house was much as he remembered, sprawling and lavish with high vaulted ceilings, gleaming woodwork, and gothic-inspired windows. The furnishings included a blend of Victorian antiques, Celtic artwork, and medieval-inspired decor—ornate wall tapestries, claw-footed chairs, massive candlesticks, and minted replicas of broadswords, sabers, and shields.

When he opened the door to his bedroom, it was like stepping into the past. Aren hadn't lied. It was exactly as he remembered. The household staff had kept the room clean and tidy, but otherwise hadn't disturbed a thing. The same artwork and posters hung on the walls, now terribly dated for the passing of time. The same books stood on the shelves, everything he had loved to read from T. H. White's *The Once and Future King* to Conan Doyle's master detective *Sherlock Holmes*. Both had helped him pass numerous Halloweens, closeted in his room as he tried to block the noise of his parents' lavish parties below.

Shoving the memory aside, Caith opened a few drawers, rummaging through the clothes he'd left behind, the trinkets he'd collected over the years. When he found a Swiss army knife he and Trask had used to slice their thumbs, mingle their blood, and declare themselves brothers, pressure mushroomed in his chest. Breathing deeply, he nudged the knife aside and unearthed other mementos.

A pack of matches from an out-of-town bar where he'd had his first underage drink, a cigarette lighter from the one and only time he'd tried to smoke. He'd swiped it from his dad's desk. Later, Trask had stolen two cigarettes from his father's pack of Kools, and they'd snuck into the trees for their first taste of nicotine. Both had pretended to enjoy the smoke, neither wanting to be the first to wuss out, even though they'd coughed and gagged through most of it.

Idiots.

There was a glow-in-the-dark yo-yo, a magnifying glass in a leather case they'd once used as a talisman against an imaginary army of trolls, and a faded green ball cap, frayed and worn at the edges.

Trask had rarely been without it except that fateful day when the black car had rolled to a stop behind them. Pulling the cap free, Caith slumped to a seat on the bed. It was only a hat, and Trask was gone. He set it aside and reached for the top drawer on the nightstand. Unlike those on the dresser, it refused to budge. He fiddled with it, applying force, and tugged harder. The increased pressure made it pop too quickly. The whole thing came free in his hand, disgorging a half dozen tubes of model glue, their sides split and oozing.

The odor struck Caith in the gut like a sledgehammer.

A cold room, moldy and damp. The dismal slant of fading sunlight through a mud-splattered window, washing the room in a sickly gray haze. Trask's shoulder was pressed against Caith's, both of them trembling with terror and cold.

A dark-haired man sat at a table, ignoring them as he calmly pieced together the plastic sides of a model truck. The stench of glue, sharp and astringent, filled the room until Caith couldn't breathe. Until that lone scent encompassed every horror and fear he associated with his kidnapping.

Lurching from the bed, he bolted for the bathroom and doubled-up over the sink. Memory ripped through him with a viciousness he hadn't felt in years. Grinding his teeth, he swallowed back bile until the sickness and memories passed. When he could breathe easier, he returned to the bedroom where he carefully examined the drawer. It had been rigged with razor blades, triggered to split the tubes when forced opened. Whoever had orchestrated the feat had been careful to use fresh glue for maximum affect.

Only one person knew what that odor did to him, someone he'd told years ago. Merlin had welcomed him home in a manner he wouldn't forget.

* * * *

Veronica didn't remember being as exhausting as a child. Derrick was everywhere, racing from room to room, wanting to know this or that story, more curious than his father had ever been. Knowing Caith as she did, she wouldn't have thought that possible, but the difference was rooted in their personalities. Caith had been quietly analytical as a child while Derrick was charged like a live wire.

She told him about sea serpents, ogres, and trolls. About playing by the lake and in the woods. About sitting up at night and sharing stories under the stars. Every word sent a stab of painful whimsy through her heart, but Derrick was all eagerness and grins, forcing her to shelve her melancholy. When she heard a car out front, she guessed Melanie had arrived with the boys instead of going straight home.

"Let's go upstairs. I think your Aunt Melanie is here with Noah and Matt."

Derrick raced ahead of her, outdistancing her on the staircase. She heard his feet thump across the floor, then stop suddenly. A split-second of silence followed before his voice tumbled down the stairs, raised in excitement. "Grandma! Grandpa!"

Veronica's heart lurched to her throat. Imagining every horrible scene in the book, she darted up the staircase, around the corner, and came to a skidding halt in the Great Room. Caith was nowhere in sight.

"Veronica." Morgana Breckwood stopped fussing over her grandson long enough to spare a glance, her face rosy with delight. She wore a pencil skirt with low-heeled boots and a drape-front cardigan, her short blond hair styled in a becoming bob. As always, the picture of casual elegance. "What are you doing here? How did Derry—" She broke off laughing as her husband swept Derrick up into his arms.

"So this is the voice on the phone?" Stuart Breckwood asked with a wide grin for Derry. An older image of Caith, Stuart was slightly taller and broader through the shoulders, but his eyes were the same winter blue. Gray peppered the black hair at his temples, lending a distinguished look befitting the owner of a prominent company.

"Grandpa." Derrick measured the name with the man, grinning like he'd fallen into Christmas morning. "I can't believe you're here. Dad said you were in Canada."

At the mention of Caith, something flitted through Stuart's eyes too fast for Veronica to read.

"We decided to come home early." Morgana leaned forward, kissing her grandson on the cheek. "We never expected to find you here."

"I'm staying with Uncle Aren and going to school with Matt and Noah," Derrick said proudly.

Morgana looked to Veronica for clarification.

Her face grew warm. Nervously, she hooked a strand of hair behind her ear. "It's...it's a long story."

"It doesn't matter." Stuart grinned, as delighted as Veronica had ever seen him. "I don't care what the reason is as long as I have the chance to see my grandson." Cupping the back of Derrick's head, he kissed the boy on the forehead. "Eight years old. Look at you! The spitting image of your father."

"I suppose you think I've kept him from you all these years."

Caith's tightly controlled voice drew four gazes in his direction. Veronica let a small gasp slip as he walked into the room. Something was wrong. Something beyond this unexpected, nerve-wracking reunion. Had something happened while he was upstairs? His skin was gray, his features tight and strained. He carried a green ball cap which he slipped into his rear pocket by the bill.

Stuart set Derrick on the floor but made no move to speak. Sensing the sudden tension in the room, Morgana swept from the group and embraced her son. "Caith, why didn't you tell us you were coming? It's so good to see you."

Caith gave her a fleeting smile. He wrapped his arms around her and kissed her temple. "Missed you, Mom."

Encouraged by his affection, Derrick darted to his side. "Dad, can we stay? Can we stay here?"

"We're going back to the lodge." He laid a hand on Derrick's shoulder. "Go find your coat and shoes."

Veronica saw the angry defiance the moment it hit Derrick's eyes. "I don't want to. I wanna stay here." He folded his arms over his chest, sulky and angry.

Disaster. Veronica knew Caith had reached the end of a dangerously short rope. His temper had been on edge from the moment he'd learned about Derrick's interaction with Merlin. Every event since had been kindling for the fire. Clenching his jaw, he crouched in front of Derrick and gripped the boy by both arms.

"I'm not in the mood for games, Derrick. If you think making a scene in front of your grandparents and Veronica is going to change how I'll react, you're wrong. Now go find your coat and shoes. I'm not going to tell you again."

Veronica winced at the control in his voice, knowing a storm brewed underneath. Derrick's bottom lip trembled. A bright sheen of tears appeared in his eyes, but to his credit, he blinked them back. Caith released him and he went wordlessly, if slowly, in search of his shoes.

Stuart glowered. "He could have stayed. You don't have to."

"You mean you don't want me to."

"I didn't say that."

"Then you'd better roll out a fucking red carpet, because I don't see any welcome signs."

"Caithelden!" Morgana's voice cracked between father and son, stopping Stuart cold when he would have snarled a reply. Her eyes burned as she spun to confront her son. "I've missed you dearly, but that doesn't give you the right to be rude. Clean up your language this instant and show some respect, or I'll toss you out on your tail-end."

Caith clenched his hands. "Don't worry. I'm leaving."

"Looks like I'm missing a party." Aren came back into the room with Derrick. His emerging grin faltered at the ugly expressions that greeted him. He chuckled in a clear effort to lighten the mood. "Hey, I'm one of the good guys."

Stuart glowered. "We'll see about that tomorrow. Two o'clock." He glanced from Aren to Caith. "I want you both at BI. Merlin and Galen, too. And you, Veronica."

"I don't work for you," Caith snapped.

Stuart smiled thinly, as if enjoying the upper hand. "Oh, but you do. At least for now. I understand BI hired you, and like it or not, I'm still President of Breckwood Industries." He stepped closer, as if measuring the man the eighteen-year-old had become. "I expect you there, Caith. For once in your life, do the right thing."

Chapter 8

Veronica rode to the lodge with Caith and Derry. They stopped briefly at Aren's to retrieve some of Derry's clothes, along with his bag of marbles, then headed for Stone Willow. It was a tense drive with Derry occasionally muttering how unfair it was that he couldn't stay with his grandparents. Caith ignored him, but by the third repetition of the protest, his composure snapped.

"Maybe we'll go back to Boston and that'll settle everything," he said.

Derry immediately fell into moody silence. Veronica felt like a tightrope walker doing a balancing act between the two. "Why do you think your parents came home early?" she asked Caith.

"Three guesses. In my book, they all start with the letter M."

It took a moment to realize what he was insinuating. "You think Merlin called them?"

"How else did my father know I was working for BI? Aren and Galen weren't going to tell him."

"It could have been any member of the board."

A snort of derisive laughter told her what he thought of the idea. "There isn't anyone on BI's board with the nerve to call my parents on vacation. My father doesn't mix business and pleasure."

"So you immediately want to blame Merlin?" Looking at his profile, Veronica felt her irritation ratchet higher. She'd played peacekeeper all evening and had reached her limit. "You're being unreasonable. Why don't you just admit you want to slander Merlin?"

Caith sent her an annoyed glance. "That's crazy."

"Your attitude is crazy. Merlin's successful, he's well-liked, and your father backs him in everything he does. That's what really bothers you, isn't it? If Merlin wanted to spend a year filming the mating habits of rhinos in Africa, Stuart would finance the expedition."

"The mating habits of rhinos?" Surprising her, Caith chuckled. "You need to get out more, Ron. Stone Willow must be getting to you."

"Don't change the subject."

Caith cast his son a look in the rear-view mirror as if fishing for a co-conspirator. Apparently, he'd decided to ditch his moodiness. "Derry, did you know Veronica used to pretend she was a mermaid in the lake at Stone Willow? You should have seen her. She was really bad at it."

Not ready to abandon pouting, Derry managed grudging interest. "How come?"

"She couldn't swim. She just kind of paddled around."

"I did not," Veronica protested hotly.

"Until I showed her how to swim."

"You are such a liar. Trask was the one who showed me."

"Oh. So, I guess you couldn't swim?"

Caught, Veronica exhaled in frustration.

Behind her, Derry giggled and sat forward as far as the seatbelt would allow. "Dad taught me to swim when I was a little kid. I can hold my breath underwater a really long time." Warming to the conversation, he glanced at his father. "Can we go swimming in the lake, Dad?"

"It's too cold for that." Reaching into his back pocket, Caith pulled something free and tossed it to Derry. "Here, partner, this is for you."

Veronica turned in the seat as Derry examined a ball cap. It was dark in the car, but enough light filtered through the windows for her to realize what he held. "Where on earth did you get that?"

"I found it in my room. Guess it's been there all this time. I remember Trask's mother wanted me to have it after the funeral."

Derry's eyes grew round with reflected moonlight. "Was it Trask's, Dad?"

"Yeah, Derry, it was his."

"Wow, that's cool." He ran his hands over the bill, sat back in the seat, and tugged it over his head. It was a little big, but that didn't stop him from grinning ear-to-ear.

Later at the lodge, Veronica waited until she was certain Caith had Derry tucked into bed, then tapped lightly at his door. He answered within seconds, looking haggard from the strain of the evening.

"Can I talk with you?" she asked.

"Derrick's out." He motioned her inside, then nodded toward the bedroom. "He's a sound sleeper, but I don't want to leave him alone. I'd feel more comfortable talking here instead of downstairs."

She moved past him into the living area. Ever since their harsh exchange of words in the car, she'd felt guilty for her crack about Stuart. Before he'd left for college, Caith had once confided how hurt he'd been his father didn't support him. She was certain Stuart favored Merlin's every idea now because he feared losing another son. Caith might not realize it, but he'd taken the wind out of Stuart's sails when he'd packed up and struck out on his own.

Twisting her hands together, she turned to face him. "I want to apologize, Caith. I said some things tonight…about your father. Things I shouldn't have said."

"They were deserved." He grinned tiredly. "Maybe I do always look for a motive when it comes to Merlin. It was bad enough before, but it's harder now."

"Why?"

"I thought that would be obvious."

He moved closer, and with that slight advance, Veronica's heart pounded. It wasn't so much what he said, but the way he looked at her. There was heat in his eyes, raw and unchained like the flame of an ancient forge. His fingers brushed the back of her hand, and her mouth went dry. Scintillating sensation shot through her.

"The two of you were together." His voice was soft and tender, laced with a sincerity that made her heart pitter-patter. He was everything she'd ever wanted and everything she'd ever hated. He'd left her, and the pain of that parting could still bring tears in the middle of the night.

His fingers tracked up her arm, curling around her elbow. She'd always been tall, but felt dwarfed by his height as he applied pressure to her arm, willing her to step forward. His hair was impossibly thick, his eyes intently blue. The scent of spicy aftershave clung to his skin, mingled with the fresher scent of bath soap. He must have hugged Derry after giving him a bath and tucking him into bed for the night. The thought of that image, of father and son, made her heart constrict in ways his sensuality couldn't touch.

The day had brought other changes, too—the faintest hint of stubble along his jaw, a smudge of ghost-gray shadow beneath his eyes. He looked exhausted, rumpled, and as sexy as hell. It took every effort to resist when he tried to pull her forward.

"You had your chance, Caith. All those years ago. Why can't you accept Merlin and I *are* together?"

"You're not. I know you're not." He tilted his head and the light struck his eyes, turning arctic blue to moon-silvered smoke. Cupping her cheek, he traced his thumb slowly to the peak of her upper lip. "You love him the way you've loved him since we were kids. There's no fire with him, Ronnie. He's comfortable and familiar."

She wanted to deny it, but his gaze was mesmerizing, the murmur of his voice hypnotic. His thumb dipped lower, rested on her lips, then feathered across the bottom one. Unconsciously, her mouth parted. He tipped her chin up to his, drawing closer. "I want to kiss you."

The pronouncement sent a shiver through her.

Feather-light, his touch played across her lips. Lowering his head, he dropped his voice to a silky whisper. "I want to go on kissing you." His mouth hovered over hers. "Until you don't know night from day, and all you want to do is kiss me back."

"Caith, no."

He turned his attention to her cheek, caressing her skin with the warm whisper-sigh of his breath. She felt the wild race of his heart through his shirt. His tongue tickled the shell of her ear and sent a shockwave rocketing up her spine. Gently, he traced her lips with his thumb, urging them apart.

"Let me kiss you." His voice was low, a seductive rasp, but no longer steady.

She'd affected him. The knowledge thrilled her, made her lift her lips closer to his. A single kiss didn't mean she'd end up in bed with him. A kiss didn't mean she'd sold her soul.

"Dad?"

Derry's sleepy inquiry wrenched her back to the present, dousing her with a bucket of cold water. Caith released her. Flustered, he stepped backward and scraped a hand through his hair.

"Derry, what's wrong?"

Veronica flushed. It was far worse being caught with Caith by his son than one of his brothers. She tried to smile at Derry, but heat crept across her cheeks. He stood in the doorway to the bedroom, incredibly sleepy-looking in rumpled pajamas, his black curls tousled over his forehead.

"I don't feel good," he protested.

"Okay, partner, we'll get you something," Caith said reassuringly.

Veronica felt abruptly cheap and dirty. She'd come to apologize, not be seduced. Heaven only knew what Derrick thought of her now. Then again, maybe Caith routinely entertained women in the bedroom. He certainly hadn't lost his knack for reducing her to a simpering fool.

Furious, she headed for the door.

"Ron, wait." Caith hesitated halfway between her and Derrick.

"Goodnight, Caithelden."

"Dad."

"It's okay, Derry, I'm coming."

As she stormed out the door, the last sight Veronica had was of Caith crouching in front of his son, gently cupping his face as if searching for signs of fever.

* * * *

Veronica's mind wandered even as she tried to focus on the book she was reading. She'd changed into a short nightie the color of antique lace, then curled into bed, intending to lose herself in the gutsy exploits of the heroine from her latest mystery novel. Unfortunately, her encounter with Caith kept interfering.

She hated how close she'd come to losing herself in their almost-kiss. How she'd wanted his heat to engulf her and sweep her into a tide of sensual pleasure. What right did he have evoking feelings like that when he would pack up and leave in a few weeks? He'd return to Boston and forget, as he'd done before, that she even existed.

Too keyed up to read, she snagged a silk robe from the foot of the bed and headed from the apartment. The shimmery fabric whispered against her bare legs as she walked up the steps to the third floor. There hadn't been any unusual incidents lately, but that didn't mean she couldn't poke around. Pausing at the head of the stairs, she looked down the darkened hallway. It wouldn't do to be found wandering at night by one of the guests, but she only had to worry about Bowerman and Caith on this level.

Something flitted through the darkness at the end of the hall, followed by a sliver of sound. The volume was low at first, a bare murmur that rose sharply in pitch before plummeting like a cresting wave. A woman's eerie sobs echoed through the corridor, magnified by the hush of night-time stillness. The hair prickled on Veronica's neck. She knew the sound, had heard it before. Two weeks ago it had chased guests from their rooms, been ridiculed in the *Coldcreek Herald* by Kelly Rice, and written off as a cheap Halloween trick by Sheriff Duke Cameron.

A spectral figure appeared at the end of the hall. Cloaked head-to-foot in ghostly white, a woman moved noiselessly across the worn floorboards. Only days ago, Caith had pointed out how the aged boards creaked, yet the woman walked without awakening a squeak of sound. Generous waves of white hair concealed her face, her body insubstantial, nearly translucent. Releasing a chill wail, she pressed a lace handkerchief to her mouth, turned the corner, and vanished from sight.

"Wait!" Veronica bolted down the hall, her heart hammering out a frantic beat. Had she just seen a ghost or was someone playing another trick? Rounding the corner, she came to a dead end at the closed door of the Hummingbird Suite. The ghostly apparition had vanished without a trace. Raising her hand to knock, she hesitated, debating the wisdom of waking Dean Bowerman.

"Veronica."

Startled, she whirled to find Caith and Derry behind her. Bundled into a thick robe, Derry was wide-eyed, looking more curious than frightened. Caith was shoeless, his shirt hastily thrown on, fully unbuttoned and hanging over his belt. She caught the gleam of something metallic in his hand.

"Did you hear the sobbing?" she whispered.

"Hear it? It woke us out of a sound sleep." He eyed her suspiciously. "What are you doing up here?"

"I…" What did she tell him? That he'd so enflamed her thoughts she couldn't concentrate on anything but him and had gone wandering as a diversion? "I saw something. A woman at the end of the hallway. I followed her here."

The door opened behind her revealing a bleary-eyed Dean Bowerm. "What's going on out here?" A thin man with an elongated face, he was dressed for bed in tan pajamas and a belted blue robe.

Caith brushed past him into the suite.

"Excuse me, what do you think you're doing?" Bowerman demanded.

"Mr. Bowerman." Veronica spoke quickly as Caith moved away to do a sweep of the adjoining rooms. "Did you…did you hear anything, or see anything unusual just a short while ago?"

Appearing flustered, he pressed his lips together. "I was sleeping, Ms. Kent. Sleeping. I thought that's what the lodge was supposed to be about. Relaxation. I hardly think it soothing to have someone barge into my suite in the middle of the night." He stopped abruptly, his face undergoing a startling transformation. "Oh, no. Something happened, didn't it? Something paranormal. The one night I decide to get some rest and I miss an occurrence." Plainly agitated by the thought, he shook his head. "What did I miss?"

He spun around as Caith came back into view. For the first time, Veronica got a good look at the item in his left hand—a heavy duty flashlight like a cop might carry. Given it wasn't lit, had he intended it as a weapon?

"You really didn't hear anything?" Caith asked.

"I told you I was asleep." Bowerman exhaled noisily. He retreated into the room and dropped into the nearest chair with a despondent shake of his head. "I can't believe I missed an occurrence. It's the whole reason I signed up for the retreat in the first place."

Caith slanted Veronica a doubtful look. "There was a woman sobbing. It woke me and my son."

"I sleep with earplugs," Bowerman explained. "Old habit from my college days when I had an off-campus apartment by a railroad crossing."

"What brought you to the door?" Caith persisted.

Bowerman shrugged. "I heard talking."

"With earplugs?"

Clearly irritated, Bowerman scowled. "Of course not. I'd already removed them when I woke up." He eyed Caith disapprovingly. "Everyone knows about you, Mr. Breckwood, about why you're here. Guests might be cut off from the outside world, but we've overheard the staff talking about the column in the *Coldcreek Herald.*"

"My name is Lairen."

"Personally, I think you're wasting your time," Bowerman continued as though he hadn't heard. "Not everything that happens has a rational explanation. There are numerous documented accounts of paranormal happenings throughout the world, many scientifically proven. If I were BI, I'd hire a paranormal researcher, not an investigator."

"Such as yourself?"

Bowerman chuckled. "I'm a marketing manager. I just happen to enjoy reading about the unexplained." Standing, he tightened his robe. "And since I seem to have missed the opportunity, I'd like to get some sleep now."

Caith hesitated in the doorway. "One last question. You said you opened the door because you heard talking. What woke you in the first place?"

"Thirst. I wanted a glass of water." Patience gone, Bowerman sneered. "It might come as a shock to you, Mr. Breckwood, but most people don't like being questioned like a criminal." He turned his attention on Veronica. "If I were you, Ms. Kent, I wouldn't pass out any how-did-you-enjoy-your-stay evaluations." The door clicked in place with a resounding snap.

"You have a gift with people, Caith," she observed dryly.

He scowled. "No one's that defensive over a few simple questions. He's hiding something."

"Is that your professional opinion?"

"It's my only opinion." Catching her arm, he steered her away from the door. "Derry, come on. We're going back to the suite."

"Without me," Veronica protested as he walked her down the hall. But she didn't make an effort to pull away. It felt good to have his hand wrapped securely about her arm, her body held firmly to his side.

"I want you to stay with Derry," Caith said as they neared the Blackbird Suite. "He had a stomachache earlier, and I don't want to leave him alone." He pushed the door open and waited for Derry, who followed reluctantly. The boy was obviously more interested in what might be happening in the hallway.

"Dad, was it a ghost? Do you think it'll come back?"

Veronica was surprised to hear hopeful excitement in his voice as she stepped into the suite.

"No, it wasn't a ghost, and no, it isn't coming back."

"How do you know?"

"Because it's late and any sensible ghoul or school-aged kid should be in bed. Now, get going, partner. I'll be back in a moment to tuck you in."

"*Awwright.*" Derry dragged out the word as if he'd been given the worst punishment in the world. Delaying as long as possible, he disappeared into the adjoining bedroom, closing the door behind him.

* * * *

Caith's gaze swiveled to Veronica. From the moment he'd seen her in the hallway, her bare legs flashing beneath the satiny folds of her robe, he'd been dangerously distracted. "The next time you go ghost-hunting, you might want to wear something more practical."

"What does that mean?"

He pressed nearer, not caring when her eyes widened in surprise. Hooking his finger into her belt, he tugged. The creamy fabric unraveled easily, leaving her long legs bare, the tops of her thighs brushed by the lacy silk of her skimpy nightie. Heat surged through him, staggering and lava hot. He swallowed hard, fighting the desire to put his hands on her. With her hair loose against her shoulders, her full lips innocently parted, she was every inch a siren. He'd never wanted a woman so badly in his life, but he'd made a vow.

Her terms.

With a groan, he leaned forward, pressing his brow to hers. One touch, just one. He skimmed his fingers across her hip and felt her tremble. "Do you know how badly I want you?"

Her voice quavered. "I know you've always been about sex."

The words drove a fist into his gut. The desire drained out of him, replaced by something cold and empty. "Will you stay with my kid while I check the lodge?"

As if unable to trust her voice, Veronica nodded.

He shut his mind down, forcing himself not to think about her as he retreated to the bedroom to get Derrick settled. Afterward, he buttoned his shirt, tucked the ends into his jeans and pulled on a pair of shoes. Veronica was waiting in the living room when he returned.

"I'll try not to be long." His voice was tight, bordering on hostile, but he couldn't control the anger. Did she care anything for him at all?

"Caith."

He halted at the door, frowning over his shoulder.

"Be careful." She said it almost as if she cared.

* * * *

The door clicked shut, allowing Veronica to release her mental walls. With a sigh, she collapsed on the couch. Why did every moment with Caith end in confusion?

Every time he drew near, her resolve wavered. The bitterness she'd once harbored grew less with each hour they spent together. She'd wanted him to touch her, to take her back to the place only he could unleash. To make her feel the way she had when he'd coaxed passion from an inexperienced girl for the first time. She wanted his arms around her, strong and demanding, until his roughness and her silk melted into something that was a blending of both.

It was too much, and she was too tired. By the time he returned two hours later, she'd fallen asleep on the sofa. The closing clack of the door woke her with a start, jolting her from a restless sleep. The room was mostly dark, illuminated only by a low-wattage lamp in the corner and a faint glimmer of moonlight bleeding through the curtains.

Veronica switched on a light, wincing as the brightness stung her eyes. "What time is it?" she asked, spotting Caith.

He dropped into a chair across from her. Like her, he was clearly tired, but his eyes were vibrant blue, intensely aware. Analytical by nature, he was likely in overdrive, determined to find a logical explanation for the night's otherworldly events.

"After two. Sorry to keep you so late." He scuffed a hand through his hair. "How's Derry?"

"He's been sleeping since you left." Veronica swung her legs from the sofa, arranging the folds of her robe for modesty.

Caith noted the action with a tightening of his mouth. "Who has keys to the lodge, Veronica?"

Startled, she sat straighter. "Why?"

"Because the storm cellar doors were unlocked. Again. Whoever's pulling these stunts is probably coming in through the basement. Kind of coincidental Lew hasn't fixed the breaker, don't you think?"

For a moment Veronica couldn't speak. Her throat closed up as the insinuation washed over her. "You don't actually think Lew has anything to do with—"

"I told you before everyone's a suspect. Now, who has keys to the lodge?"

Anger spiked through her, putting her on the defensive. "Myself, Lew, Alma, your mother, brothers, and father." Standing, she tugged the robe close about her throat. "It's late. I'm going back to my apartment."

"Wait." He stopped her at the door.

The heat of his hand where it gripped her arm felt like the most seductive sensation on earth. As irritated as she was, she couldn't deny her attraction for him. Even angry, she was drawn by the flare of magnetism between them, every glance, every touch, sizzling with suppressed desire. She felt herself falling into his eyes, an untamed place that had trapped countless women before her, but vowed she wouldn't make the same mistake twice. "Let go of my arm."

"The night you found the hand in the fireplace," he said, ignoring her. "Who was the last person in the lobby before you got there?"

Her back stiffened as she realized where he was headed. "Lew. He checked the fire before retiring." Inborn stubbornness kicked in. "You're wasting your time, Caith. Sheriff Cameron's already talked to Lew and cleared him. Now let go of my arm."

He tightened his grip as if testing the balance of power.

It was strength against will, male pride against female indignation. If she pressed the issue, he'd release her. He'd never hurt her, never force her. Twelve years couldn't change the gentleness of spirit she'd fallen in love with as a child. Suddenly, the confrontation was no longer about the lodge or the insinuations against Lew. It was about past and present, the lies and secrets they'd buried for twelve years.

"Do you believe what you said earlier?" There was an edge to his voice, cold and brittle as winter. "Do you think my feelings have always been about sex?"

Startled by his abrupt change of topic, Veronica blinked. She remembered the girls' locker room in high school, and how Kelly Rice and Toni Charleston had swapped stories about how good Caith was in bed. What he liked to do and how much they enjoyed it.

"Everyone knew that about you, Caith. Even your parents. Your father looked the other way, and your mother pretended not to hear the gossip. They accepted it as your way of coping. I was stupid enough to believe you meant it when you made love to me that night on the bank. Stupid and naive."

His grip loosened.

"Did you love Derry's mother, or was she about sex, too?"

Fury flashed in his eyes. It died quickly, replaced by rigid acceptance. As if stung, he released her.

"We met in college." Caith moved away from the door. "We had a good relationship, but we weren't in love. Not the way two people are supposed to be. So, yeah, I guess it was about sex, but she didn't mind." He shot Veronica an accusing glance. "We were careful, but somehow she got pregnant. She didn't want a husband or kids. I wanted my son." He stepped nearer, raw conviction in his eyes. No matter how else he'd failed, she understood he wouldn't allow himself to fail as a father.

"We agreed Derry would be my responsibility. Eight months after he was born, she died in a car accident."

Veronica didn't know what to say. *I'm sorry* didn't seem appropriate. Her anger drained along with the hostile thoughts she'd harbored. Before she could respond, he tugged open the door.

"It's late as hell, and I'm tired. I'll see you in the morning."

The dismissal stung. Tired of playing by his rules, she pushed past him. "I don't think so. I have a date with Merlin."

* * * *

Veronica tried to concentrate on her French toast and coffee but lacked the appetite. Merlin said something about the hayride Aren had planned for tomorrow, but the words faded into background noise along with the din of the restaurant. Last night, after telling Caith she was meeting his brother in the morning, she'd had to scramble to arrange the date. Thankfully, Merlin had been agreeable when she called and suggested an early breakfast.

The restaurant off Main Street was crowded and noisy, filled with people stopping for a cup of coffee or a quick meal before beginning the workday. Outside the sky was overcast, threatening rain, fueled by a mass of soot-black clouds. A strong wind scattered leaves over the street, sending them swirling between cars and dancing against the restaurant's circle-top windows. The front door opened admitting three BI employees and a blast of cold air. It gusted between the tables, but Veronica barely felt it.

Her gaze strayed across the street where the office for the *Coldcreek Herald* was sandwiched between a bakery and a dry cleaning establishment. Recalling Caith's vow to confront Kelly Rice, she expected him to arrive any moment, his mood as black as the gathering storm. Her focus strayed to her watch. By now he would have dropped Derry at school and worked up a healthy anger in anticipation of tangling with his high school flame.

"Ron?" Merlin watched her expectantly. "Have you heard anything I've said?"

She flushed guiltily. "I'm sorry." Retrieving her coffee, she sipped the tepid liquid. "Daydreaming, I guess."

She was miserable. Miserable because she couldn't keep her mind off Caith. Miserable because she used Merlin to make his brother jealous, and miserable because she didn't feel the slightest spark of attraction with Merlin. Caith had been right. Merlin was safe and familiar, a good friend, but not the man she wanted for a lover.

Unaware of her thoughts, Merlin poked his egg-white omelet with a fork. "Aren says my father called a meeting for two o'clock to discuss the lodge. I hear you'll be there."

She nodded. "So will Caith." She wasn't certain why she made the observation. Maybe because Caith was in her thoughts. Sensing a blunder, she glanced at Merlin, but he only grinned.

"My father and Caith. I wouldn't miss that for the world."

The wicked delight in his voice made Veronica frown. She had a nasty image of him as Pan, dancing on a hickory stump. "The meeting isn't about confrontation, Merlin. It's about correcting the problems at Stone Willow."

He snorted. "Don't be naive. My dad wants to teach Galen and Aren a lesson, and he wants an audience when he does it. My guess is he's going to fire Caith."

"Fire Caith?" Veronica's voice cut out. She hadn't considered the possibility, but hearing it now, she realized Merlin was right. She wouldn't put it past Stuart to do something so rash.

But would he risk alienating his youngest son further with Derry in town? The conflict left her queasy. "I can't believe Stuart would do something so impulsive." Her hand tightened around her coffee cup as she imagined the horrible scene at BI later that afternoon.

Merlin shrugged. "Caith didn't want to work for BI before. This could be my dad's attempt at payback. A sort of 'we weren't good enough for you then, we don't need you now' attitude."

She remembered what Caith had said the previous night on the drive to the lodge. "Did you call your father while he was on vacation and tell him Caith was here?"

"What does it matter?" His tone was confirmation enough.

"You *did* call him." Before she could object further, she caught a flash of movement from the corner of her eye. Caith's Explorer swung into an angled parking stall before the *Coldcreek Herald*.

Stepping from the vehicle, he spared a glance across the street. Despite the weather, he wore a long black coat unbuttoned to the elements. It flapped around his legs, billowed by the wind. When he turned and stepped inside the newspaper office, Veronica gathered her purse. "Merlin, I have to go."

He swallowed the last of his grapefruit juice. "You hardly ate anything."

"I know. I'm sorry." She inched out of the vinyl bench seat. "I just—"

"This is about Caith, isn't it?"

Dumbstruck, she halted. He watched her silently, his expression unreadable. His gaze flicked toward the window. "I saw his car, Ron. It was hard not to with you looking across the street every five minutes." He slumped against the seat. She expected him to be annoyed or dejected, but he seemed resigned.

"I knew this would happen. You've been in love with him your whole life."

"That's. Not. True." Her mouth clamped shut on each word. The noise in the restaurant was suddenly louder. Her ears heated with embarrassment, and she slid quickly back into her seat.

"It's partially my fault," Merlin offered. "I'm not attentive. I get distracted easily."

"With blondes and brunettes." She couldn't believe they discussed it so calmly. At the mention of Caith, her heart had quickened, blood thundering loudly in her ears. Now seeing Merlin's easy smile, she relaxed, sensing they had reached an understanding. The pretense was gone, along with anger and guilt. Kinship returned, renewing the bond they'd shared as children.

"Guess we were never meant to be lovers." Merlin reached across the table and took her hand. "We've always been better friends. I'll be the first to admit you've put up with me longer than I deserve." His lips curled in a sly grin. "So you're dumping me for my black sheep, pain-in-the-ass brother?"

"Merlin, I never said I was in love with Caith." Was she so blatantly obvious even he saw through her? The realization rolled over her like a storm. Unconsciously, she tightened her fingers over his. She couldn't deny it. Not to Merlin.

"He doesn't have to know we've decided to be friends." The wicked delight was back in his voice. "Let's have fun with this, Ron. There's nothing I'd like more than pissing off my little brother."

Appalled, she withdrew. "I don't play those games, Merlin." Even as she said the words, she cringed. Hadn't she invited Merlin to breakfast hoping to make Caith jealous?

"So you're just going to let him call the shots?"

"No one's calling anything." In an effort to collect herself, she stood. "I really have to go."

"All right, but remember what I said. I've been angry at Caith for the last twelve years. Longer if I think about it."

"I've never understood why. You were so close."

"Maybe, maybe not." He shrugged. "Things happen. People change. That's for me and Caith to work out. In the meantime"—he grinned, the smile devilish and wide—"I'd be happy to play your lover a little longer."

On impulse she leaned forward and kissed him on the cheek. "You're a good friend, Merlin. I'll see you later today at BI."

As she hurried from the restaurant, it occurred to Veronica she hadn't declined his offer a final time.

* * * *

"You have no right telling me what I can and can't print."

They were the first words Veronica heard as she pushed open the swinging, glass-fronted door and stepped into the cluttered office of the *Coldcreek Herald*. Voices rose in the background, angry and defiant, male and female, tangling one upon another in an effort to be heard.

The front office was divided into three cubicles and a small reception counter. Papers tottered in stacks on two of the desks, sloughing toward overspill. The walls were dark and dated, dressed with inexpensive brown paneling. One sheet had cracked down the center and someone had hung a painting of two men in a fishing boat, hoping to hide most of the flaw. The room was empty, but it was easy to follow the trail of voices to the rear.

"Damn it!" Caith slammed his fist on a heavy metal desk as Veronica stepped into the back room. "You leave my kid out of your trash tabloid and gossip column. If I see him mentioned again, I'll slap this two-bit rag with a lawsuit so fast you won't have time to cry editorial freedom."

"You think you can threaten me?" Kelly Rice stood on the other side of the desk, looking imperious in a short blue skirt, silk shirt, and tailored jacket. Curvy and vivacious, the former prom queen had retained her lofty beauty. Her hair was long and flowing, as black as Caith's, her eyes the color of antique brass. Even angry, there was something seductive about her.

"Your name isn't Breckwood anymore, Caith." Stalking around the desk, Kelly confronted him. "Even if it were, BI doesn't own this town. The newspaper belongs to my family and I'll print what I damn well please. If you don't like what you read, stop snooping around the lodge and go back to Boston. As long as you're here, you're fair game. So is your past, and so is your kid."

Caith lurched forward, then halted abruptly as he struggled for control. A vein ticked in his temple. When he spoke, restrained fury bristled on every word. "Listen to me, you vindictive bitch. I might not be able to stop you from printing your editorial garbage, but if anything, *anything* happens to Derry as a result, I'll haul your ass into court and bleed this sleazy tabloid for every dime its worth. I might not be a Breckwood, but I've got the means to make your life miserable."

"You *are* threatening me." Her lips curved in an unsavory smile. "Perfect for my next column. And to think I was going to have to dredge up all that dirt about your past. This is so much better."

"Caith." Veronica stepped forward before the situation grew uglier. "This isn't solving anything. Let's go."

"I should have known you'd show up." Kelly raked Veronica with a demeaning glare. "You belong in this hick town, right along with all the poor saps relying on the mighty Breckwoods for their paycheck every Friday."

Enough was enough. Veronica had tolerated the swill Kelly printed in her paper because she had no choice, but she wouldn't be insulted face to face. Stepping forward, she pushed between the woman and Caith. "I'm not sure why you have this insane vendetta against the Breckwoods, but it's obvious you've lost all objectivity. The *Coldcreek Herald* is one tiny paper, Kelly, and it doesn't amount to anything stacked against a respected news journal. I think a few of the larger papers might be interested in how you're using the first amendment to wage a personal battle against BI."

"What does that mean?"

"It means I have a friend at the *Central Tribune*. Jeff would find it interesting to see how you're abusing your editorial license. I can almost guarantee he'd do an article, plastering your name in the paper for a change."

Kelly's face grew white. "You're bluffing." With effort she recovered her poise. "I've known you too long, Veronica. You don't have it in you. Even now you're tagging along on Caith's heels, hoping for a crumb. Just for the record, he's not that good in bed."

"Probably because of his partner. I had no complaints."

Kelly's eyes widened in shock, providing Veronica a momentary thrill of one-upmanship. Before she could think it through, she turned, wrapped her arms around Caith's neck, and kissed him hard.

He flinched, unprepared for her forwardness. A second later, she lost command of the kiss to his firm control. Wrapping one arm around her waist, he tugged her tightly to his thigh. The pressure of his leg wedged between hers sent her senses into a tailspin. He kissed her like a man with every intention of stealing her soul.

"Get a room," Kelly snapped in disgust.

Shaken, Veronica tore free. Hot color flooded her cheeks. Mortified, she spun and hurried from the office. Outside wind and rain gusted into her face, biting and cold. Blindly, she raced across the street, humiliated she'd acted so brazenly. Her fingers trembled as she fumbled in her purse for her car keys.

"Veronica!" Caith's voice bounced behind her, half lost in the drone of traffic and the blustery bite of rain. She shivered, hating the sudden sting of tears in her eyes. The rain made her hands slippery, and the key ring tumbled from her grip, plopping onto the wet asphalt.

Before she could move, Caith reached around her to retrieve the keys. He opened the door and shoved her into the dry interior of the car. Within seconds, he climbed into the passenger seat.

"What the hell happened back there?" His eyes were turbulent and biting. "Was that some kind of sick game you two play about who gets who in bed?"

The hostile sting of his words brought an unexpected surge of rage. "You are such an arrogant S-O-B. I just saved BI, you, and your son from becoming tomorrow's headline. She would have printed every smutty half-truth she could find after the threats you made."

"You don't know anyone at the *Central Tribune*, do you?"

"What if I don't? It's a better bluff then you pulled." Falling back into the seat, Veronica tugged her coat closer. "I'm cold and I'm wet. I want to go home. Get out of my car, Caith."

"Not until you tell me what that kiss was about."

Veronica sighed. She scraped a hand through her hair. It was wet and clung to the side of her face, chilling her to the bone. She wanted him to go away, to leave her alone so she didn't have to remember the heat of his lips on hers, the hard, muscled lines of his body making her yearn for closer contact.

His coat was wet and smelled of rain. *He* smelled of rain, every wonderful inch of him exuding the same raw power as the storm. Beads of moisture clung to his face and hair, and for one irrational moment, she wanted nothing more than to brush them aside.

"Veronica."

She faltered as the images scampered beyond her reach. Snatching her keys from his hand, she found the one for the ignition and jabbed it home.

"I'm not leaving until you tell me what that kiss was about."

Her patience was gone. "It wasn't about anything. It was just my turn to use you."

As soon as she said the words, she knew she'd hurt him. Rather than making him angry or defensive, she'd struck where he was vulnerable. Determined to keep her distance, she slanted a look in his direction. His expression never changed, but the damage was there, buried in his eyes.

"Good job." Caith popped the door and stepped into the rain.

Chapter 9

Veronica returned early to the lodge, stripped off her wet clothes, and rummaged up a dry sweater and pair of jeans. Wanting to forget the morning and everything that transpired, she locked herself in her office, concentrating on paperwork. It was nearly noon when she began to regret her behavior and fret over Caith's absence. His Explorer had been parked out front for hours, but there was no sign of him. Distracted, she wandered into the lobby, then continued to the back porch where a mental focusing session was taking place.

Enclosed by walls of glass, the porch was inviting even when rainy and overcast. Her guests generally preferred it during the day, avoiding it after sunset when the night sky shuttered it with darkness. She lingered a few moments, listening to the instructor while watching the class. Dean Bowerman was absent, searching for ghosts no doubt, but the remaining guests were intent on the session. With any luck, they'd carry the benefits back to their jobs, producing the results the program was structured to achieve. Caith was nowhere to be seen.

Deciding it was just as well she hadn't run into him, Veronica headed back to the lobby. She encountered Lew coming from the basement as she rounded the corner. He plunked a tool box on the reception counter, pausing to mop a handkerchief over his brow.

"Breaker keeps blowin', but I think I got it fixed now," he offered as way of greeting.

"Good." Veronica hated the doubts Caith had put in her head about Lew. He'd always been a reliable worker and didn't deserve her wariness. "Maybe Alma will be brave enough to go downstairs now."

Lew chuckled, arranging pliers and electric gauges in his tool box. His casual reaction helped ease her tension. Outside, the rain lessened, lightly pattering against the windows.

"Lew." She hesitated, uncertain how to proceed. "Have you seen Conner Lairen this morning?"

"Huh?" With a grunt, he looked over his shoulder. "You mean Caith Breckwood?"

She frowned. "Caith Lairen," she corrected, deciding not to deny the obvious. "Have you seen him?"

"Hard to miss. He's been skulkin' around the basement all mornin'. Can't rightly tolerate snoops under foot."

"He's doing his job." Veronica wasn't certain if she was defending him or BI. "There was another problem last night. A woman sobbing on the third floor. Like before."

When Lew didn't answer, but continued to arrange items in his tool box, Veronica leaned forward. "Don't these occurrences bother you? Especially with everything that's happened lately?"

"That's just it." He faced her squarely. "I'm done tryin' to reason it. Let it happen. It's BI's problem."

Most of her staff had been edgy since Caith's arrival, but Lew in particular had grown surly. She wasn't certain if his resentment came from having an "intruder" at the lodge, or from BI's attempts to conceal Caith's profession and identity. Deciding to let the matter drop, she returned to her office where she passed the time compiling figures for her weekend report to Aren. When two o'clock neared, she gathered her purse and headed out front. Caith's Explorer remained parked in its usual spot, but there was still no sign of him.

Anxious over the looming meeting, she climbed into her car. Did she really care if Stuart fired Caith? Her entire world had been turned upside down since his arrival. She'd been a fool to tell Aren they could work together.

Caith had made it all too clear he wanted more than a working relationship, and she simply wasn't willing to reciprocate.

* * * *

Caith tugged at his tie. He didn't know why he'd bothered with it. The black jeans and button shirt were his usual style, the tie was something he reserved for clients.

He swore softly as the irony struck him. BI was a client which meant he had to act the role of a professional investigator without the bitterness of an estranged son. When accepting the case, he thought he'd be reporting to Galen and Aren. His father's return had changed that.

He'll probably fire my ass.

It was just as well. Then he could go back to Boston and the uneventful life he'd led before Aren and Galen arrived on his doorstep. He could forget about family and Veronica, and what she did to him.

Pushing the thoughts aside, he steered his Explorer through town, heading to the north end where Breckwood Industries was headquartered. There were plenty of other businesses on the same street, but BI's sprawling multi-tiered office building dominated the area. The manufacturing plant was several miles outside of town, set among open fields. Here, smoked glass and steel complemented manicured shrubs, leafy trees, and lighted cement walkways.

Caith pulled into the parking lot and killed the engine. A sea of chrome engulfed him, row after row of countless automobiles. He'd forgotten how large the complex was, how many people BI employed, most driving from neighboring towns where employment was minimal. He spotted Veronica's Volvo and Aren's Lexus parked in reserved spots near the front.

Stepping from the Explorer, he shrugged into his long black coat. Coupled with the tailored white shirt and black tie, he presented a passable image for a business meeting. His jeans might be faded, but they were clean and fit well. Stuart would probably sneer over his lack of a suit, but Caith didn't give a shit. Not really.

Steeling himself for the confrontation, he headed for the main entrance. As he stepped beneath the shadow of the overhang, bits of memory returned. He'd come often as a child, taking the elevator to the top floor, racing down the hall to his father's office, eager to share some bit of news about school or play. As he'd gotten older, they'd talked more about the future and Caith's place in the business.

And all the while Caith had kept silent, afraid to tell his father the truth—that he didn't want to be part of BI. That he wanted to make the world a safe place to live, so that what happened to Trask wouldn't happen to anyone else. If he'd been honest from the start, maybe things would have worked out differently. Maybe there wouldn't be a black gulf of bitterness between him and the man who'd raised him.

The memories washed away as he stepped into the reception area. It was large and open, updated with mocha-colored ceramic tile and a marble reception counter veined with burgundy threads. Potted plants and half-moon seating in shades of burgundy and cream complemented soaring glass windows and an atrium ceiling. Bypassing the receptionist, Caith headed down a short hallway to a set of elevators. A black roster mounted on the wall listed each office in gold leaf. With a glance to confirm Stuart was still on the top floor, he pressed the up-arrow.

His father's executive assistant eyed him critically, but there was no mistaking his resemblance to Stuart or his unusual name. After a brief pause, she led him to a conference room where Merlin, Aren, Galen, and Veronica already waited.

"So. You decided to come after all." Slouching with his shoulder against the wall, Merlin straightened when Caith entered the room. "I was sure you'd pull a disappearing act rather than face Dad."

Ignoring him, Caith shrugged out of his coat and draped it over the back of the nearest chair. Galen, Aren, and Veronica were already seated at a rectangular conference table. Aren fidgeted nervously, drumming his fingers against the top while Veronica pretended interest in the floor and Galen merely scowled. The tension in the room surged with undercurrents, ready to erupt at the slightest provocation.

Caith pulled out a chair and sat down. When the silence continued, swelling noticeably, he looked between the three. "Is it my tie?"

Aren relaxed with a mild chuckle. "I'm glad someone still has a sense of humor." He slid a manila folder across the table. "Here are the results of that soil sample you wanted."

"You're quick." Caith studied it briefly. "Pretty much as I figured. Maybe I'll get a chance to discuss it before Dad cans my ass."

Merlin strolled to the table. "What makes you think you're getting fired?"

"Don't be coy, Merlin. You've been counting down the hours."

"Minutes." With a thin smile, Merlin leaned forward and flicked a finger beneath Caith's tie. "At least you came dressed for your funeral."

"Back off." The command came from Galen. Startled by the hostility in his voice, Caith swiveled toward him in surprise.

Merlin let out a choked snort and slumped into the nearest chair. "What's this? Sir Galen of the Square Table ready to right all wrongs?"

"I'm not kidding." Galen's expression was dark. "Whatever's been eating at you two for the last twelve years gets shelved until this conference is over. It's awkward enough without having you sniping at each other."

"Damn." Merlin released a patronizing sigh. "And I was so looking forward to the fun."

"Merlin," Veronica warned.

"Don't worry, hon." He caught her hand, bringing it to his lips for a showy kiss. "Nothing that happens will spoil our plans for the evening."

His gaze slid across the table to Caith. "Business has no place at a romantic dinner for two."

Veronica snatched her hand free.

Caith barely had time to register the insinuation before the door swept open and his father strode into the room.

A man who knew how to command attention, Stuart Breckwood let his gaze settle on each of them before coming to rest on Caith. "I want this out of the way as quickly as possible." Curtly, he settled into a chair at the head of the table. "I go away for a few weeks and Stone Willow sprouts headlines in the gossip column. Anyone know why Ms. Rice has made it her personal goal in life to slander BI?"

Intent blue eyes swept the group, but no reply was forthcoming. "I see. Anyone want to *guess* why this woman is becoming a colossal pain in my ass?"

"It's just a two-bit tabloid," Merlin ventured with a disinterested shrug. "Let her spew her poison. What harm can it do?"

"What harm?" Stuart glowered at Merlin. "Coldcreek is about small town ideas and small town ways. If the people here believe what Ms. Rice prints about Stone Willow, they'll believe anything she prints about BI." He tossed a copy of the *Herald* on the table. "This garbage is already filtering through our corporate offices and into neighboring firms. Thank God, she hasn't taken it online yet."

"Skilled executives don't worry about seeing blue and white lights dancing in the trees," Galen said sharply.

"No. But they do about butchered dogs on their beds, and meals that give them food poisoning. Stone Willow has never been exceptionally profitable. We know that. The question is, should it continue?"

Looking alarmed, Veronica sat forward. "You're not thinking of closing the lodge?"

"We should be addressing this with the board," Aren commented on her heels.

Caith's father dismissed the notion with a backward wave of his hand. "The board comes later. This is about Breckwood interests and Breckwood money. Most of what's invested in the lodge belongs to us as a family, not a firm. Should we close it?" His glance shifted to Veronica, and he paused. "It's always been a pet project, so I'd like to keep it running. I can't do that without concrete answers. I'm not going to have BI's name attached to something that's becoming a joke and-or liability. Caith?"

Expecting to be dismissed rather than included, it took Caith a moment to respond. He cleared his throat. "I can't give you anything concrete, but

I can tell you someone is staging an elaborate hoax. I know how they're doing it. I just can't tell you who."

Merlin crossed his arms. "A hoax? There's a newsflash."

Galen shot him a warning look before turning and addressing his question to Caith. "How's it being done?"

"I don't want to say until I have all the answers. Assuming I'm still on the case." Caith looked directly at his father, putting him on the line. Now was the time to drop the axe if it was going to fall. When Stuart gave a marginal nod, he continued. "The person or persons doing this are gaining access through the basement. After last night—"

"What happened last night?" Aren interrupted.

"Sobbing," Veronica explained. "The same as before. A woman on the third floor."

"Who conveniently disappeared outside the Hummingbird Suite. I remember when we were kids there were rumors about the house being filled with secret passages." It irked Caith he couldn't spend more time in the Hummingbird Suite. Once Bowerman left he'd be able to do an exhaustive search. Or maybe he'd have to convince Veronica to move their resident ghost hunter to another room.

"That's right." Aren snapped his fingers. "According to legend, Warren Barrister had passages built into almost every room because he was so paranoid. Wasn't he involved in some kind of secret society or cult? Tolmar…Tolar, something like that?"

"But the Barrister house was remodeled," Veronica protested. "Only portions of the original structure are intact."

"And part of that includes the basement." Caith leaned forward. "I did some scouting this morning and found a passage that leads from the mechanical room to the Hummingbird Suite. A convenient way to drop off a dead dog if you don't want anyone to see you. And a quick way to disappear if you're a woman pretending to be a ghost. Or someone projecting a holographic image."

"Holographic?" Galen frowned. "Are you saying—"

"I'm not sure what I'm saying. I'm looking at facts. Kay Porter reported what she thought was a ghost at the lake. A few days ago I found traces of phosphorescent body paint in the same area. The lab results confirm it." He tapped the folder Aren had given him. "I've read the reports from Duke Cameron's forensic team on the hand Veronica saw in the fireplace, and there's no trace of evidence. Even if an appendage were removed, there would have to be something left behind. A residual trace of skin or charring. If it were something other than a hand, like a fabricated composite, there'd be indications of chemical or material residue."

"I didn't imagine it," Veronica said tightly. "I saw it clear as day."

"All tricks easily accomplished by someone familiar with effects technology."

Galen frowned. "You mean like movie-making FX?"

Things were going deeper than he wanted at the moment. "That's one application. Government agencies have been using effects technology to induce everything from mild hypnosis to supervised mind control for years. I'm not saying that's the case here, just that it's a possibility. I checked around town earlier and couldn't find any place that sells body paint, but it's not hard to obtain. You can buy it online, and with Halloween around the corner, even costume shops carry it."

Aren frowned. "I got a shipment from a place in Cleveland a few months ago through an online order. Mom gave me the name. Melanie and I wanted it for the hayride. We're planning on having greeters in costume."

"Any missing?"

Aren shrugged. "I don't check it regularly. It's stored in the barn."

"That still doesn't explain why any of this is going on." Galen shook his head. "Assuming someone is using an elaborate means of pulling these stunts, why are they doing it? What do they gain?"

Silence fell over the group. Caith felt his father's gaze shift to him. "Caith?"

"I don't have an answer."

"Then get one. And get Kelly Rice off my back while you're at it." Finished, Stuart stood. He was halfway to the door when he hesitated and glanced over his shoulder. "By the way, I'm to convey a message from your mother. You're all expected for Sunday dinner. One o'clock. That includes you, too, Veronica." Before anyone could protest differently, he left.

Releasing a pent-up breath, Aren slumped in his chair and grinned. "You see that?" he said to Caith. "You got a stay of execution."

He snorted. "Only because he wants to see Derrick. The longer I'm in town, the more time he gets to spend with his grandson."

"There's always a motive with you, isn't there?" Galen prepared to leave. "Don't screw this up."

Typical.

"I don't tell you how to run BI, Galen. Don't tell me how to do my job."

"Like you'd listen anyway," Merlin countered.

Caith flipped up his middle finger.

"You two are worse than my twins." Aren shook his head. "Do everyone a favor and get it together before Sunday. If you act like this in front of Mom, she'll choke you both. Come on, Veronica." Standing, he took her arm, plainly prepared to follow Galen from the room. "I'll buy you a cup of coffee."

* * * *

Caith tugged his tie free as they left. Might as well get his beef with Merlin out in the open. "Veronica's not interested in me if that's what this is about."

Merlin stretched, propping his feet on the chair beside him. He folded his hands in his lap. "Obvious. Why look twice when she has me?"

As they'd grown older, it had been hard to tell when Merlin was playing a conceited ass or *being* a conceited ass. Caith chose to overlook the comment.

"Why did you leave glue in my bedroom?"

"Huh?" Merlin raised a brow. "You want to translate that, Investigator Lairen?"

With effort, Caith controlled his temper. Beyond the closed door, he heard murmuring and guessed Aren, Galen, and Veronica conversed on the other side. "At the house, in my old bedroom. Someone put tubes of model glue in the nightstand, then rigged the drawer so they'd split apart when I opened it."

Merlin shrugged indifferently. "What? No plastic trucks?"

"Don't play games with me." Shoving his chair back, Caith leaned over the table, splaying his hands on top. "You know damn well you're the only person I ever told about"—he ground his teeth, tripping over the words—"what that smell does to me."

"That's the price of confidence." Merlin leaned forward until his face was only inches from Caith's. "And how would I know you were going to the house, Mr. Detective? The last place I'd expect a chummy family guy like you to go?"

Caith swore. He paced to the opposite side of the room where he braced one hand against the wall. Through the window, he could see the parking lot below. Overhead, the sky had begun to clear, charcoal gray receding before quiet blue. Emerging sunlight danced off the windshields of countless cars aligned in neat, orderly rows. "No one else knows about the glue, Merlin."

His brother gave a long-suffering sigh. "I hate to break it to you, Caithelden, but I don't give a shit. You don't rank high enough for me to waste my time planting glue. Maybe you should start thinking about who wanted to get you to the house in the first place. About who knew you'd be there."

"No one knew I'd be there."

"Maybe." Dropping his feet to the floor, Merlin stood. "Then again, maybe you pissed off a really nasty ghost with a grudge."

Caith looked over his shoulder. "Aren't you a little old to be putting stock in stories about Warren Barrister?"

Merlin smiled thinly. "Who said anything about Barrister? I was talking about Trask."

Caith let the remark wash over him as Merlin left the room. He didn't understand his brother's anger now any more than he had twelve years ago. The more biting his comments grew, the more confused Caith became. There'd been times during the last summer before he'd gone away that they'd been free and easy with one another, but more often than not Merlin had been distant. After Trask's death, they'd drifted apart. When Caith left for college, nothing but silence followed. Somehow, someway, it all came back to Trask.

Caith carried the thought with him as he left BI and headed for the town library. He found what he was looking for in the local interest section, a book combining the history and myth of the Barrister House. He scanned it briefly, then drove to the elementary school to pick up Derrick and his nephews. He smiled broadly at the sight of his son wearing Trask's old ball cap as Derrick climbed into the back seat along with Noah and Matt. Earlier, Caith had adjusted the band on the hat for a better fit, and Derrick deemed it one of his favorite possessions. With the three boys chattering non-stop about school, the impending hayride, and Coldcreek's trick-or-treat scheduled for the following week, Caith headed for Aren's farm.

"Dad, can we take Ron to the hayride with us?" Derrick asked.

Surprised, Caith flicked a glance in the rearview mirror. "You want Ron to go?"

"Sure. I like Ron." The three boys shared a secret glance, and Derrick grinned. "You like Ron, too, don't you Dad?"

Muffled giggling came from the rear. Apparently, Derrick had been conspiring with his cousins, sharing the tale of catching his father and Veronica nearly kissing. "Yeah, partner, I like Ron, too."

More giggling, and this time Caith smiled. It didn't hurt to have Derrick on his side playing matchmaker, no matter how clumsy the attempts.

Veronica might decline a date with him, but he doubted she would with his son. That might make him unethical, but he needed all the help he could get. By the time he pulled in the driveway at Aren's farm, the boys were once again discussing the hayride and trick-or-treat.

Preparations had advanced considerably since his last visit. The fields surrounding the house had become graveyards and shadowy lairs for zombies and ghouls. Strategic lighting, coupled with an endless array of props and false fronts, transformed the picturesque farm into a Halloween extravaganza. Volunteering to handle most of the special effects, the high school drama club came equipped with fog-making machines and an assortment of ghoulish makeup and costumes. Galen's seventeen-year-old son, Balin, a tall, blond-haired boy, flashed a grin at Caith's arrival.

"Uncle Caith!" Although he'd lost touch with Galen over the years, Caith had continued to send his nephew cards and gifts on birthdays and holidays. For his part, Balin had visited a few times when in Boston with school friends. "Are you dressing up tomorrow night, too?"

"I'm just here to help," Caith said. The thought of dressing up in costume made him cringe.

Spying him from across the field, Aren waved him down, then immediately put him to work. Shortly afterward, rain set in, limiting their accomplishments. Derrick, Matt, and Noah raced through the house, ready to explode, tracking mud across the floors, dancing rings around the adults. Galen showed up briefly, muttered his support, then left before anyone could coerce him into helping. A half hour later, Caith's mother and father arrived.

Derrick went from excited to ballistic, leading his grandfather out back, making sure he knew every scrap of knowledge Derrick had acquired about the event. Caith stood on the rear porch, listening to the rain patter overhead, quietly watching his son and father interact. Easy and effortless in each other's company, it was evident they'd already formed a tight bond.

Regret tugged at him. He'd once shared the same kind of relationship with his father, but it was too late to go back now. Tragedy, time, and bitterness had destroyed that closeness. After a while he pulled Aren aside, and together they went to the barn to check the supply of phosphorescent paint. It didn't surprise him to find a small amount missing.

Aren gave a low whistle. "So someone's using my stuff to cause problems for BI?"

Caith squatted beside the paint Aren had stored under a tarp. The barn smelled musty, still thick with the pungent odors of horse, hay, and oiled leather. Aren kept no farm animals, but the smell was as much a part of the structure as the packed earth beneath their feet. "When's the last time you checked this?"

"When the shipment came. I signed for it and stored it back here. I didn't think I was stashing gold or anything I needed to padlock."

"I want the name and phone number of the company you bought this from." Caith stood. "The amount that's missing is too small to sustain anything long term. Whoever took it probably used it to get started, then would've had to order more."

Aren frowned. "Caith, the drama club got a huge supply two weeks ago. I gave them my contact at Otherworldly Props, then funded the order. They're using it at the hayrides."

Caith glanced aside at the sound of footsteps in time to see his father enter the barn.

"Aren." The older man shook rain from his coat and hair. "Melanie's looking for you. The kids are having problems with the fog machine."

"I'm coming." Aren turned back to Caith. "How about prints? Can you lift anything?"

"It's doubtful. The kids have been playing in here, and you've had people in and out for weeks planning the hayride. It'd be like trying to isolate a print on a public door knob."

"Do what you can." Flashing a parting grin, Aren jogged from the barn.

Caith turned back to the paint, tugged the tarp down, and secured it at the bottom. A long pause preceded the tread of footsteps behind him.

His father cleared his throat. "Derry's a good kid. I appreciate you letting me see him."

"You could have seen him anytime. All you had to do was come to Boston." Stubbornly, Caith chipped at the gap between them, doing his best to broaden the chasm. God forbid they should ever bridge it. Standing, he stuffed his hands in his pockets and turned. "I want you to have a good relationship with Derrick, but that doesn't mean anything has to change between us."

Stuart's eyes glinted with frost. "You wouldn't want that, would you?" Beyond the open door, rain drummed the earth, echoing in the near empty shell of the barn. "You'd rather carry around all that anger than sort through the hostility."

Caith chuckled bitterly. "Since when did you decide to play peacemaker?"

"Since you let me see my grandson. I don't want to trip over all that bullshit you're carrying around every time I want to see Derry. I want a healthy relationship with him."

"What about a relationship with your son?" Caith couldn't keep the acid from his voice. Why the hell did it have to feel like he'd been punched in the gut? Before his father could answer, he shoved past him and stalked from the barn. If he had any doubt why he still had a job, his father made it clear.

Because of Derrick.

He exhaled. He supposed he should be grateful, but gratitude came with the high price of swallowing his pride. A flicker of temptation made him consider dropping the case, but the thought was short-lived. He'd be failing Aren and Veronica, and despite how he felt about his father, Derrick idolized the man. He wouldn't use the kid as a bargaining chip.

Which meant he was screwed.

Deciding to call it a night, he rounded up Derrick, intending to head back to the lodge. His son, however, had other ideas. With all of the hayride prep going on, he begged to stay overnight. Reluctant at first, Caith talked it over with Aren, then eventually agreed.

It was after ten by the time he returned to the lodge, and most of Stone Willow's guests had retired for the night. In an effort to get his mind off the ugly encounter with his dad, Caith retreated to the enclosed porch. Outside, darkness enveloped the woods, broken only by patches of shell-white moonlight. Switching on a small lamp, he settled into a chair with the book he'd picked up on Warren Barrister.

Veronica had yet to return, missing since six o'clock when she'd left for dinner with Merlin. Ever since his brother had mentioned their plans at BI, Caith had inwardly seethed over the date. The thought of the woman he desired in the arms of his brother was more frustrating than his encounter with his father.

Annoyed, he tried to distract himself with the book.

Written in the early 1930s by a local historian, it detailed the legend of Barrister House in cumbersome language. Caith found a single reference halfway through the first chapter that made him pause:

There is some debate whether Warren Barrister was a Tolar, but most historians of merit discount it as unsubstantiated myth.

The next paragraph branched into Barrister's arrival in America at the age of twenty-seven from Great Britain. A tedious account of how he'd established himself in the community followed. Wading through the thick prose, Caith found his mind wandering.

He glanced at his watch. Ten-twenty-five. Irritated, he flipped a page.

Breakfast *and* dinner. Veronica might as well have spent the entire day with Merlin. How much could two people have to talk about anyway? Swearing softly, he rubbed his eyes. Merlin probably had his hands all over her, touching, kissing, doing everything Caith wanted to do.

"Damn." He tossed the book onto the coffee table. He had hoped when she'd kissed him at the *Coldcreek Herald* office, she'd felt the same rekindled longing he did, but apparently that wasn't the case. How could it be when she was with Merlin, probably melting into his brother's arms? She had just wanted to use him. Paybacks were a bitch.

"Caith?"

Light from the bright overheads washed over him, making his pupils contract. He turned in his chair to find Veronica had wandered onto the porch. With a hand to shield his eyes, he shook his head. "Turn off the lights. They're too bright."

She complied, plunging the room into soothing shadows but for the muted table lamp. "What are you doing out here?"

"Reading." He stood, frowning down on her as she approached. He scrutinized her face, searching for some evidence of how she'd passed the hours with Merlin. Still angry from butting heads with his father, growing angrier at her innocent arrival, he couldn't keep the sting from his voice. "Dinner is really getting late these days, huh?"

Her mouth thinned. "What does that mean?"

"Exactly what it sounds like. I thought you had a lodge to run."

"Which doesn't include twenty-four hour service. You're not my keeper, Caithelden." She started to turn away, but he snagged her arm.

Veronica tensed, her eyes flashing anger. "Get your hands off me."

"Is that what you said to Merlin, or did you let him do what he wanted?" He knew as soon as he said the words he'd made a dreadful mistake.

"You arrogant bastard!" She yanked free, the anguish on her face so gut-wrenching, it left him speechless. Tears sprang to her eyes, spilling over her lashes. "God, I hate you. I really do."

She ran for the door.

"Veronica!" Caith surged after her, stumbling when his leg collided painfully with a chair in the semi-dark. He never slowed, catching her just inside the doorway. "Let me explain."

He pinned her to the wall, pressing forward until her scent overwhelmed him. She smelled of vanilla and spice, a combination so contrastingly warm and exotic, it made his head reel. His anger drained as though it had never been. Moonlight spilled through the surrounding windows, turning her hair to silver wheat, her skin to porcelain cream.

"Get your hands off me." Tears glistened on her face, bright as starlight in the darkness.

He hated himself for that pain, knowing he was the cause.

"I'm sorry." The words spilled out of him. He couldn't stop them anymore than he could his lips from tasting her cheek, her tears. "I didn't mean to hurt you. I just..." His mouth found hers, seared her lips with heat. He cupped her face in his hands. "Ronnie, I've been going crazy thinking about you with him all night."

She wedged an arm between them. "You don't care about me." Her eyes were bright, still glittering with tears. "You only want a taste of what you had from me years ago."

"That's not true." He bowed his head against her forehead. "Let me show you. Let me make love to you." He kissed her again, slowly this time, sliding his tongue between her lips as if he had a lifetime to kiss her. He willed her to melt, poured his soul into the kiss, igniting a tide of blistering heat to engulf them both.

She relaxed, cautiously inviting. That small victory made him groan low in his throat. He nipped her lips, enjoying her startled intake of breath. "I could kiss you forever." His voice was low, a murmur against her skin. He raised a hand and brushed her hair aside. "Tell me what you want, Ronnie."

* * * *

Veronica couldn't speak. When she stepped onto the porch and spied him sitting alone, her heart had leaped to her throat. She'd been so fearful Stuart would fire him, that he'd leave and she'd never see him again. She should forget him, but it was impossible when he kissed her.

Once and again. Her lips grew swollen and moist beneath the attention. She had wanted this. She'd let Merlin coerce her into a dinner date engineered to make Caith jealous, but she hadn't expected it to work so quickly or effectively. She wasn't ready to go to bed with him. "You only want sex."

His crutch, the way it had always been.

His breathing grew rasp. "Is that so wrong?" His mouth found hers, hungry and demanding, so thoroughly possessive she lost herself in his passion. Just as quickly he retreated, smiling slightly as he looked down on her. He traced a finger across her lips, followed with an agonizingly insubstantial brush of his tongue. "Let me make love to you."

He was good. Too good. Veronica felt her resolve slipping. She shivered as he found the top button on her blouse and eased it free. Every nerve in her body screamed for her to run, but he kissed her again, over and over, and she couldn't deny she wanted him, needed him. That she had always wanted him.

Another button followed.

"Caith." She placed both hands on his chest. "Not here. The guests…"

"Are all in bed. You don't think I'm going to let you go now, do you?" His voice was husky, so thick with desire it left her trembling. If she had any doubt of his need, it vanished when he pressed against her. Before she knew what she was doing, she surrendered and allowed him to lead her to the sofa.

"Do you have something?" she asked breathlessly. "Protection?"

He nipped at her lips. "It's not like I carry something around with me."

She would have imagined him a condom-in-the-pocket kind of guy. "I'm on the pill, but—"

"If you're asking whether or not I'm clean, I am. There haven't been a lot of women since Derry."

She wasn't sure she believed the second part, but he wouldn't lie about the first. Wrapping her arms around his neck, she dismissed the last of her inhibitions. "As long as I'm the only one you think about tonight."

She wanted him every bit as much as he wanted her and allowed that passion to drive her. When he groaned, heaving against her, she snared his mouth beneath her own, more demanding than he had been. Breathless, she rocked against him. "Caith." His name came on a tortured gasp, desire commanding that every inch of him fill her.

He shuddered beneath the onslaught, fisting his hands in her hair, dragging her forward. Eagerly, she tugged at the buttons of his shirt. Two popped and pinged across the floor. He seemed shocked by her aggression, but quickly took control of the kiss, trapping her against the couch.

Their clothing ended on the floor, and she abandoned herself to the exquisite sensations induced by his touch. He stroked and nuzzled her body, carrying her ever closer to a peak that resonated with the memory of that long-ago night on the bank of Stone Willow. She'd loved him then and loved him now. Release raced through her; together they tumbled over the edge. The explosion of pleasure left her gasping and vulnerable. Slowly, sanity filtered back and they lay twined together on the couch.

Caith bowed his face into her hair. "I don't want to let you go."

But he would. Like before.

His bangs were damp with sweat. It made her realize how out of control they'd been. No love, no passion. Just need and mutual attraction. She was as much to blame as he. His lips brushed her throat. "I could make love to you all night."

Not *I love you* but *I could make love to you*. Tears pricked her eyes for the second time that night. She'd made a horrible mistake, allowing him to seduce her, believing he cared. Believing that somewhere beneath all that sensual coercion, he might feel tenderness.

What did she expect? When push came to shove, she was as guilty as he, practically ripping his clothes from his body.

"Ron." He kissed her, brushing his lips tenderly against hers. The gentleness in the action left her confused.

Trembling, she disentangled herself. "I have to go." Had she really made love on the porch? What was she thinking?

Thankful for the darkness, she scooped up her clothing. She pulled her loose skirt over her hips and slipped into the blouse unbuttoned. Had she really behaved with so little inhibition, tumbling into his arms? Shame made her cheeks burn. He'd taken what he'd wanted and scored his victory.

"Ron, what are you doing?"

She tripped over her shoes, collected the ruins of her panties and bra.

"Veronica." Caith stood and zipped his pants. "Stop rushing."

He was standing too close, his eyes reflecting pinpricks of light in the darkness. His shirt hung unbuttoned, the ends of his belt dangling loose from his jeans. With his black hair tangled, his bare chest banded by moonlight and shadow, he exuded all that was male and dangerous.

Veronica's heart quickened. "I have to go."

She started to turn away, but he caught her arm and drew her back. Hooking a finger beneath her chin, he tilted her head up. "What's wrong?"

"Nothing." The last time they'd done this, she'd been head over heels in love, giddy with the magic of what had passed between them. Now there was only emptiness and thorns, a gut-wrenching certainty she'd made a mistake. "Please, Caith. I just... I have to go."

She wrenched free, no longer able to keep the tears inside.

"Ronnie." His voice echoed in her ears, but she ran headlong from the porch, clutching her shoes to her chest. By the time she reached her apartment, she was sobbing in earnest. Slamming the door behind her, she pressed against the frame, too miserable to move.

The memory of his touch rolled over her with heightened awareness, nearly as staggering as the stroke of his hands. With a little imagination, she could feel the warmth of his mouth over hers, the press of his body. She'd never wanted that to stop, never wanted him to stop touching her or loving her.

"Ronnie." Caith's voice sounded on the other side of the door in combination with a sharp rap. "Ronnie, open the door."

Sniffling, she pulled herself together and straightened with a small measure of dignity. "Goodnight, Caith."

She turned the lock, clicking it loudly into place. He knocked a second time, protesting, but she walked into the bedroom, blocking his objections from her mind. She wasn't a child. She'd made a mistake and would live with the consequences.

But she'd be damned if she'd let it happen again.

Chapter 10

The following day Veronica steeled herself for the inevitable confrontation. It didn't take long for Caith to hunt her down. Shortly after eight-thirty in the morning, he barged into her office, his expression black, his mood foul.

"You mean you're not going to lock the door on me?" he snapped, coming to an angry halt in front of her desk.

Schooling her face for composure, Veronica looked up from the papers she was sorting. "I'm busy, Caith. Can't this wait?" She was surprised by how callous she sounded.

"No, it can't wait." He leaned forward, his hands on top of the desk, forcing her to face him. "I want to know what happened last night. I want to know why you took off the way you did. One minute you couldn't keep your hands off me, and the next—"

"Don't." Despite her vow to handle things as an adult, Veronica fought the urge to snap at him. She moved the papers aside, stacking them methodically in hopes of stalling for time. Knowing Caith wouldn't be put off, she drew a breath and plowed ahead. "We needed to get past having sex. Now that it's over, we can concentrate on what's happening at the lodge without distraction."

"That's it?" Caith stalked around the desk. He grabbed the arm of her swivel chair, and spun her around to face him. "That's all it was to you? Sex?"

"What did you think it was?"

His expression was thunderous. "So you're going to forget it happened? Forget about me?"

"Isn't that what you did twelve years ago?"

He rocked backward as if slapped. His face went white, then hard. "I get it. This is payback."

"Don't be stupid." Veronica shoved from the chair. "I'm making an observation. And I'm letting you know I have no intention of continuing an intimate relationship with you. The lodge is more important."

"It wasn't last night. If this is about Merlin—"

"It has nothing to do with Merlin." She'd prepared for this moment all night, rehearsing what she'd say when confronted, but every attempt at driving him away only made him more persistent. "I don't know why it even matters to you. In another week or two, you'll be back in Boston."

"Is that what this is about?" The anger left his eyes, replaced by something intent and dangerous. Taking her hand, he raised it to his lips. For the first time, she noticed a stubble of shadow framing his upper lip and jaw. He hadn't shaved and looked like he'd barely dragged a comb through his hair. He was dressed in yesterday's clothes, a sure sign he'd had no other thought than finding her when he'd awakened. She guessed his sleep had been as restless as hers.

"Let go." She tried to pull away, but he tightened his grip, lightly brushing a kiss across her knuckles.

"Do we have to talk about Boston? Can't we talk about how we feel now?"

"And how is that?" Exasperated, she yanked her hand free.

He was worming under her skin again, making her question her decision to keep him at a distance. Another woman would probably take the two-week fling, enjoy the great sex, but she couldn't. He'd leave and this time she wouldn't be able to pick up the pieces.

"If last night wasn't about sex, what was it about?" she asked.

She'd cornered him. There it was. That flash of panic in his eyes. Any whisper of commitment and he was ready to hightail it to the nearest exit. A buried part of her had secretly hoped to hear him pledge his heart.

"I…I just…" He faltered.

She returned to her desk, all crisp efficiency, able to dismiss him now that he'd confirmed her suspicions. He was shallow and self-centered, interested only in sex and a no-strings-attached fling. He hadn't changed.

"I have work to do, Caith. As you bluntly reminded me last night, BI pays me to run a lodge."

He hesitated, his expression caught between regret and anger. With a curt nod, he left the room, tugging the door shut behind him. Veronica picked up the nearest paper, blindly latching onto the first thing that sprang from the page—words, numbers—she didn't care. It was better to lose herself in the mundane day-to-day functions of Stone Willow and forget about what had happened.

Forget Caith.

Imagining they had a future together was simply too painful.

* * * *

Caith bowed his head against the closed door. His chest was tight, his breathing ragged. She'd blindsided him just when he'd thought he was turning her around.

If last night wasn't about sex, what was it about?

She'd thrown out a challenge and he'd failed miserably. She hadn't been searching for anything permanent, just an assurance she meant more to him than a body in the bedroom. He couldn't even manage frickin' lip service. Rolling his hand into a fist, he rested it against the door. How pathetic was that?

The moment she'd tossed out the words, he'd felt the familiar sense of panic kick in. Someone would hurt her. Someone would take her away. As foolish as it was, he couldn't get past the fear. By staying silent, he'd reinforced her belief he was shallow and self-serving, interested only in sex.

Exhaling loudly, he turned and slumped against the door.

Time for damage control.

* * * *

Veronica yawned and rubbed her eyes. The numbers on the computer screen grew fuzzy, edging out of focus every time she blinked. She was already an hour overdue for lunch, but Alma usually set something aside when she worked late. The persistent rumble in her belly convinced her that addressing the accounts payable could wait. She tucked the paperwork inside a folder, preparing to call it quits when Alma appeared in the doorway.

"Look what came for you." The cook grinned ear-to-ear, a long, narrow box cradled in her arms. Veronica recognized the soft mauve cardboard and silver lettering that belonged to the town florist.

"These must be from Merlin." Alma shoved the box in her lap. "Well, don't just sit there. Hurry up and read the card."

Veronica smiled. "I think you enjoy flowers more than I do, Alma." She slipped the card free of a velvet ribbon. Lilies, carnations, and red roses were a matter of routine whenever Merlin acted foolishly, forgetting a date or her birthday. After their dinner last night, they'd agreed to be friends, nothing more. Were the flowers Merlin's way of saying good-bye?

Puzzled, she opened the card. Instead of the computer-generated note she expected from the florist, a strong, left-handed slant scrawled over the page:

One for each year I screwed up and another for last night. I'm sorry I've been a jerk.
Caith

Veronica's lips parted in shock.

"Well?" Alma persisted.

She tugged at the ribbon, pulling it free. "They're from Caith." Tossing the lid aside, she brushed back the fragile tissue paper. Tears stung her eyes. "He remembered."

Yellow roses. Thirteen yellow roses. *One for each year I screwed up and another for last night.* She wiped her eyes. "I can't believe he remembered after all this time."

Alma shook her head. "I don't understand you. Merlin sends you flowers at least once a month and all you say is 'they're nice.' This"—she waved her hand in the air, groping for the right word—"*person* sends you roses and you sniffle like a waterworks."

"You wouldn't understand. They're *yellow* roses." Veronica dabbed at her eyes with a knuckle.

Alma leaned forward, silently counting. "Thirteen. What kind of fool sends an unlucky number of flowers?"

"I think it's the perfect number." Veronica gathered the bouquet into her arms, savoring the rustle of paper, the heady floral scent. "Excuse me. I want to put these in water."

She was worthless the rest of the day. The vase stood on the corner of her desk. When she retired for the night, she planned to carry it to her apartment. It wasn't fair he could strip her defenses so easily. He'd done something foolishly romantic and the gesture had awakened memories of the tender, kind-hearted boy she'd fallen in love with. Somewhere beneath Caith's walls and masculine bravado, that part of him remained.

It was almost six when Derry found her in the office, chin propped in her hand, staring dreamily at the roses. He peeked around the corner, Trask's ball cap holding the unruly curls from his face. Caith had picked him up after school, bringing him to the lodge for dinner, but she'd avoided the dining room. To be more precise, she'd avoided Caith.

"Ron, aren't you going to Uncle Aren's hayride?" Derrick leaned in the doorway, one arm tucked behind his back.

She'd forgotten it was Aren's opening night. Caith and the arrival of the roses had occupied her mind most of the afternoon. "I don't know, Derry."

Outside, darkness was starting to fall, Halloween-black and starlit. The rain had departed overnight, but the temperature had taken a downward turn. She'd already helped Melanie with preparations over the preceding two weeks. If she went tonight, it would be as a spectator. Would Melanie and Aren even miss her if she wanted to stay snug at home?

"I think I'll stay here, Derry."

"But you could come with me and Dad. *Pleeeease?*" He tromped across the room, extending the hand he'd kept hidden. "Dad says thirteen is an unlucky number, so this is for whatever he messes up tonight."

Struck speechless, she stared at the yellow rose, uncertain if she should be angry or amused.

"Okay, partner, I'll take it from here." Caith stepped into the office, dropping an affectionate hand on Derry's head. "How about waiting for me out front?"

"Okay." Unaware anything was wrong, Derry handed his father the rose and bounded from the room. Pounding feet echoed down the hallway, fading around the corner.

Caith extended the flower. "Offer's still good."

"Does that mean you're planning on messing something up?"

She was surprised he was going to the hayride considering he'd always associated Halloween with Trask's death. But Derry clearly wanted to go, and she had the feeling Caith would do almost anything for his son.

Stepping to her side, he swiveled her chair around, an easy motion unlike the force he'd used earlier that morning. He was subdued, almost reflective. "I've got a bad habit of screwing things up. It's a pattern with me." He crouched beside the chair in a one-legged kneel and slowly trailed the yellow bloom down her arm. "But I don't want to make any more mistakes with you, Veronica."

When she didn't say anything, he nodded toward the vase on the corner of her desk. "Did you like the roses? Yellow was always your favorite."

"It was a sweet gesture." Looking down on him, she found herself holding her breath. He was clean-shaven, his thick hair neatly combed. When he wasn't being angry or seductive, his eyes were gentle. Unable to stop herself, she lifted a hand to his cheek, drawing back at the last minute. "Let me get my coat and I'll go with you and Derry."

He grinned, flashing a heart-stopping smile. Catching her hand, Caith pulled her to her feet. "It's a date."

* * * *

By the time they reached Aren's farm, the festivities were in full swing. Caith smelled roasted peanuts and caramel apples, odors that brought back memories of childhood. The air was crisp, overseen by a cloudless black sky and a full moon the color of an overripe orange. Food vendors offering barbeque, french fries, apple cider, and slices of homemade pumpkin pie competed for space with colorful activity tents.

Children played at apple dunking, pumpkin painting, and passing gooey unidentified objects in the dark. Every now and then, a girl squealed in frightened delight, or a young boy made a showy fuss of holding something that looked like oozing pig brains. Costumed ghouls appeared and disappeared, beckoning guests to follow to the hayride. A short distance away, the entrance to the corn maze was guarded by three witches huddled over a bubbling cauldron. Rumbling moans and high-pitched shrieks exploded from speakers mounted on poles scattered around the field.

Despite the costumes and effects, the horror element was minimal, geared to be fun and nonthreatening for children. Tiny, bare light bulbs dangled from wires strung between poles, lighting the fields like midday. Dressed in a tattered black robe, his face painted with garish white makeup, Aren roamed the crowd, passing out free sacks of candy corn.

"Here, for my favorite brother—zombie teeth. Don't say I never gave you anything."

Caith caught the small sack Aren tossed him and handed it to Derrick. "Now I know what you look like when the suit comes off."

"Funny."

"Dad." Derrick tugged on Caith's sleeve. "Let's go to the hayride. Look, there's a corn maze, too. I gotta find Noah and Matt."

"They're with your grandfather in the story tent," Aren offered.

Derrick grinned. "You look cool, Uncle Aren." Still holding onto his father's sleeve, he looked up at Caith. "Will you dress up when you take me trick-or-treating, Dad?"

"We'll see."

Veronica chuckled. He shot her a warning glance, but Aren was already ahead of her, leaning forward to talk to Derrick.

"Tell you what, Derry. If your dad can't find a costume, I'll get him one. He used to love trick-or-treating when he was a kid." Straightening, he grinned broadly at Caith. "He used to dress up along with Trask, Veronica, and Merlin. It was like playing trolls and ogres and getting rewarded for it."

"I know all about trolls and ogres," Derrick said proudly. "Ron told me about it. But Dad doesn't like Halloween anymore."

"I thought you wanted to find your cousins." Caith redirected the conversation with minimal effort.

Derrick nodded eagerly. "Then can we go on the hayride?"

Taking Veronica's hand, Caith slipped it into the crook of his arm. "Sure, partner. Let's go."

They located the story tent as the latest session was breaking up. Noah and Matt had just finished passing around chunks of egg-coated Jello, rumored to be vulture eyes in the dark. Wound up from the storytelling, the boys immediately cornered Derry and shared how cool and disgusting it was to hold the slimy globs in their hands. After a few moments of general confusion, the kids all talking at once, Derrick turned to his grandfather. "Are you going with us on the hayride, Grandpa?"

"No, I've got to find your grandmother. She's helping Aunt Melanie with the pumpkin painting." Caith's father tugged the bill of Derrick's ball cap, giving it a firm jerk over his eyes. "You have a good time, kiddo, and stick with your dad." He gave a short ruffle to Matt and Noah's hair, said good-bye to Veronica, and then glanced awkwardly at Caith. "See you Sunday."

When Caith didn't respond, Veronica elbowed him in the ribs. Scowling, he grunted something resembling an acknowledgment. As his father left, Caith steered the small group toward the hayride. Derrick, Matt, and Noah raced a short distance ahead, grinning at the costumed performers who wove through the crowd.

"They're having a great time." Veronica kept her hand firmly hooked in the crook of Caith's arm as they walked. "They remind me of you, Merlin, and Trask when you were kids. Maybe a little younger."

"They need some scrawny girl to balance things out." Caith grinned at her, amused by the gleam in her eyes. "You were pretty good at keeping the three of us in line. Trask used to say—" He stopped abruptly, stung by the thought of his dead friend.

Veronica tightened her grip on his arm. "I miss him, too, Caith."

"It's not the same."

"I know."

Her eyes were soft when she looked at him, and for a moment, he imagined something beyond concern. Something that hinted she felt the same about him as he did her. It was all too quick, much too fleeting.

"You knew him a long time before you knew me," she said.

Caith exhaled. "I can't remember not knowing him. He was always there from the time our kindergarten teacher put us together at the same activity table. Sometimes, he was more like a brother than Merlin. I think about what he'd be like now...if he'd lived."

"Caith Breckwood!" He jerked as the name exploded behind him. Surprised, he turned to the sound of pounding footfalls. A tall, solidly built blond-haired man bore down on him at full tilt.

"Hey, I thought that was you." The newcomer caught Caith's hand in a firm grip. "I see Kelly splashed your name all over the *Herald*. So you're a cop now?"

"Was." It took Caith a moment to realize he was talking to Nick Fontaine, Kelly Rice's ex-husband, and the man she'd dumped him for in high school. "I'm a private investigator. Thanks to Kelly, that's not a secret anymore."

"Yeah, she does like to twist the knife. I got it firsthand in our divorce." Nick grinned and gave Veronica a quick nod. "I saw Ron here first—how ya doin'?—and figured it had to be you with her. Veronica Kent and Caith Breckwood. Kind of like old times."

Caith glanced aside, scanning for Derrick, making sure his son and two nephews were only a step away. "It's Lairen. Caith Lairen."

Nick snorted. "Maybe in Boston. You come to Coldcreek, you're a Breckwood. Your family owns the whole fucking town."

Caith was uncertain what to make of Nick's broad grin. Normally when people talked about Breckwood money and influence, it wasn't in a flattering light. He flicked a glance through the crowd, conscious of Derrick and his cousins digging into their bags of candy corn, of the milling press of people. The throng made him uncomfortable.

You come to Coldcreek, you're a Breckwood. Your family owns the whole fucking town.

He might as well have hung a neon sign on his chest. His unusual name, his resemblance to his father, Kelly's article... If there was anyone who didn't know who he was, they had their head under a rock. He looked around for Derrick.

Derrick Lairen. Derrick Breckwood. It didn't make a difference. His son's uncanny resemblance to him marked Derrick as a target for anyone devious enough to use a small boy for extortion.

The astringent scent of model glue overrode the aroma of caramel apples and spicy barbeque.

"Sorry, Nick. I gotta get going. I'm taking my son to the hayride." Moving beside Derrick, he dropped a hand on the boy's shoulder, a warning to anyone lurking in the crowd to stay away. *He'll never suffer what I did.*

Nick didn't seem to realize anything was wrong. "Sure. You take care of yourself. Hey, before I forget…one of those ghouls in costume asked me to give you this." He pressed a scrap of paper into Caith's hand and grinned. "Wait till I tell the other guys I saw you."

Caith wasn't sure who the "other guys" were, but didn't care. He wanted to get free of the crowd and get Derrick into the wagon where there were less people and less chance of his son being stolen away. He was overreacting, the long dormant sense of panic kicking into high-gear, but couldn't choke it down. The reek of model glue was overpowering.

"Caith, is something wrong?" Veronica's eyes were wide with worry.

He stuffed the paper into his pocket. "Do you smell anything?"

Puzzled, she paused. "Barbeque. And french fries."

"And glue." Noah grinned as though it were a game. "I smell glue like the kind you use to build plastic airplanes."

Frazzled, Caith scraped a hand through his hair. "I thought I was imagining it. Veronica, stay with the boys."

He sprinted a short distance beyond the light-illuminated fringe to an area of bordering shadow. It was difficult to see but he focused on the scent, closing his mind to the memories the odor conjured. After five minutes of hunting through the grass, his hand encountered something sticky and wet. Caith nearly gagged when he passed his fingers beneath his nose.

Glue.

There was no tube, just a huge loose mound as though someone had dumped a quart of it in the grass. He wiped his hands on his jeans, but the wind shifted and the odor struck him full in the face. Lurching backward, he choked down a wave of nausea.

"Caith." Veronica caught his arm as he stumbled onto the lighted midway. "What's wrong?"

Bending double, hands on knees, he waited for the clean air to absorb the odor.

"Dad, you okay?" Derrick looked worried, his blue eyes abnormally large beneath his ball cap.

Caith shot him a reassuring grin, able to breathe again. "Yeah, partner, I'm okay. How about we go on the hayride now?"

A little subdued, Derrick nodded. As they started walking, the boys in front, Veronica slipped her hand into his. "There's something you're not telling me."

How the hell did he explain a glob of glue in the grass? He'd sound like an idiot. He wanted to go back, scan the area for tracks, trampled earth, footprints. But it was dark, and countless people had trooped across the fields in the last few days, especially tonight. Someone must have dumped the glue when he was talking to Nick. If Merlin was the only person who knew the scent triggered reactionary panic in him, and if Merlin wasn't involved, how did he account for tonight and the incident at his parents' home?

"Caith, you're worrying me."

Veronica watched him, her brows drawn together in an anxious frown. He found himself grateful for her concern. Last night, she'd closed a door in his face; now she walked with her hand twined in his.

"Guess I'm not used to being a Breckwood again."

It was partially true. Walking through the crowd, he saw people looking at him, glancing over their shoulders. Once he heard someone whisper, "That's the one Kelly wrote about in her column."

Kelly Rice, prom queen. She'd dumped him in high school and was making his life difficult now. Caith slung his arm over Veronica's shoulder and tugged her close. "I don't do well with attention." He brushed his lips against her temple, lowering his voice to an intimate murmur. "Unless it's in private."

Her back went rigid. "We're friends, Caith. Enjoying each other's company. Let's keep it at that."

They'd reached the line for the hayride. The boys returned to their previous state of exuberance, cutting short anything further he might have said. Caith dug out his wallet, bought five tickets and three glow sticks for the boys, and then remembered the scrap of paper Nick Fontaine had given him. What had he said? *Some ghoul in costume asked me to give this to you.* A member of the drama club? Or someone who'd arrived in costume, hoping to blend in?

He pulled the paper from his pocket and creased it open. Typed words became visible as he tilted it toward the light.

If you want to know who's responsible for what's happening at Stone Willow, meet me behind the Jade Club. Monday night, 10:00.

There was no signature, no name of any kind, but he hadn't expected one.

"Dad, it's our turn." Derrick tugged on his arm, pulling him toward an empty wagon. A man in a scarecrow costume was directing passengers where to sit. Dressed in ragged coveralls with a straw wig and tattered hat, he assisted a mother and child into the wagon. Caith stuffed the note into his pocket. Despite the painted face and triangular-shaped eyes, there was something familiar about the ride attendant.

"Dad." Restless, Derrick danced a few steps ahead.

The scarecrow waved them forward. "Move it, Caithelden. You're holding up the line."

"Merlin?"

Laughing, Veronica covered her mouth with her hands. "Oh, that's priceless! I wish I had my camera."

"Don't worry. Melanie took plenty of pictures after she got done stuffing me into this outfit. This is the thanks I get for having a friend who supplied the wagons."

Caith grinned. "So that would be your buddy the Tin Man?"

If there hadn't been children around, Caith was sure Merlin would have flipped him the finger. But there was no rancor in his reply, just the comfortable boasting of one brother to another. "You ain't in Kansas anymore, Caith. Get your butt in the wagon."

If Merlin was here, he couldn't possibly have dumped the glue. *Could he?*

Still grinning, Caith lifted the boys in, helped Veronica, then climbed in himself. Serving as makeshift seats, hay bales lined both sides of the wagon and the area behind the driver's station. Within minutes, the driver boarded, pausing to relay a somber warning that ghosts and ghouls haunted the grounds. He gave a snap to the reins, sending the wagon's horse down a dimly lit path, its harnesses jangling. Green glow sticks bobbed in the darkness as children turned eager faces toward the fields, hoping to catch a glimpse of a ghostly apparition.

Fog billowed from the ground and a garishly deformed creature lunged from the darkness. There were shrieks and screams as a series of flash pots erupted, piercing the fog with bursts of light. The illumination faded quickly and the creature was swallowed by shadow, trailing sinister laughter amplified through hidden speakers.

"That was so cool!" Derrick immediately turned to his cousins, and the three began mimicking how the creature had looked, making growling sounds and curling their hands into claws. Another blast of light came within minutes, sending the boys scrambling to see.

"You're shivering." Caith wrapped an arm around Veronica and pulled her close.

"I guess I should have worn a heavier coat."

"There's nothing that says two friends can't keep one another warm, is there?"

She tensed briefly, then relaxed against him. Permission enough, he shifted, positioning himself behind her rather than beside her. Bracing one arm across her chest at shoulder height, he held her snugly, a trifle too intimate for friendship. Rather than protest, she rested her head on his chest. Together, they watched the boys react with laughter and delighted yells as the hayride progressed.

"Aren's done a good job," Caith observed when the ride neared its end.

Veronica tilted her head to look at him. "Aren's perfect, didn't you know that?"

"A perfect pain in the ass."

She chuckled, settling more comfortably against his chest. "You're just jealous. Two brothers completely unalike. It's the same with you and Derry. He looks like you, but he's totally different in personality."

"You mean because he never shuts up?" Caith grinned, his question laced with affection.

Veronica smiled. "He's outgoing. You were always quiet, thoughtful. Merlin was the one who made friends, but you were the one who kept them."

For some reason, her words hit hard. *You were the one who kept them.* He hadn't kept Trask. He was responsible for getting Trask killed. Six more days would bring the seventeenth anniversary of his friend's death. Halloween. He usually passed it with a bottle of scotch after Derrick had gone to bed, the only night of the year he drank hard liquor. The only day he set out to get intentionally plastered.

He hugged Veronica closer. "I'm not the best at keeping friends. I almost lost you."

Her hand closed over his. She was silent a long time. "But you didn't," she said softly.

Chapter 11

Veronica tossed restlessly. The sweet scent of roses drifted from the dresser and wafted over her as she lay in bed. The jagged silhouette of the bouquet sprouted from her favorite cut-crystal vase, outlined in a faint glimmer of moonlight. The fourteenth rose, the one Caith had given her tonight, lay on the nightstand at her side. Tomorrow, she'd press the flower in a book, saving it as a treasured memento of their evening together as friends.

When the hayride had ended they'd taken the boys to the corn maze, then back to the story tent. By then, all three had been clamoring for barbeque and french fries, and Veronica had admitted she could eat something as well. Caith had found them a warm place inside one of the picnic tents, then returned later, his arms loaded with food and drinks.

He hadn't said anything more about what bothered him, but she'd known he was holding something back. Something about glue, and the scrap of paper Nick had given him.

When the evening ended, he had left Derry with Aren and drove her back to the lodge. Sweet and accommodating, he'd been a perfect gentleman. The same way he'd behaved all evening. As a result, she felt it only fair to tell him she and Merlin had decided to be friends. He'd merely nodded and kissed her good-night, a chaste peck on the cheek before retiring to his suite on the third floor.

Had she wanted him to kiss her? Had she wanted him to try?

Frustrated, she rolled onto her side. It was easy to recall the way his body moved with hers when they'd been together. She'd wanted him, still wanted him. She just didn't trust him to love her. He'd be leaving soon, a week, maybe two. Would he call from Boston? Would he ask her to visit?

The creak of a floorboard brought her thoughts to a shuddering halt. Someone was in the bedroom.

A spike of alarm rocketed from her head to her toes. Tensing, she lay still, barely daring to breathe. Eyes narrowed to tiny slits, she searched for any glimpse of an intruder in the darkness. From the corner of her eye, she spied a flash of gray shadow by the window, fleeting and quick. Lurching from the bed, she groped for the lamp, her heart hammering wildly.

Yellow light flooded the room. It took a moment for her eyes to adjust and her breathing to spiral into something controllable. Relief surged through her as she registered the cause of the disturbance. "Stupid cat. You scared the daylights out of me."

With a plaintive cry, her nocturnal visitor bounded from the windowsill and rubbed against her legs. Ghost-gray and short-haired, the animal had large green eyes. She recognized it as a friendly stray that often hung around the stables. She must have left the door to her apartment cracked when she went to bed, but how had it gotten into the lodge?

Feeling foolish for her earlier panic, Veronica bent and scratched the cat behind its ears. "How did you get in here?"

The answer hit her immediately. Someone was in the lodge. Someone who wasn't supposed to be there. After the last occurrence with the basement doors, Caith had made Lew install a heavy padlock. Even with that extra precaution, someone had found a way inside, and the cat had followed on their heels.

As if in confirmation of her suspicions, a woman's chill scream echoed shrilly from the lobby.

* * * *

The pattern was becoming all too familiar—sitting annoyed, helpless, and frightened while police officers trooped through the lodge. Merlin had arrived with Stuart and Galen with Aren on their heels. Kelly Rice would have a field day with the headlines: "Halloween Nightmare at Stone Willow Lodge."

It wasn't the shattered pumpkins that bothered Veronica, or the cow's blood splattered everywhere through the lobby. Even the couches, covered with manure, could be replaced. It was the thing hanging from the beamed ceiling—at first glance a woman dangling from a noose. Alma had found it on the way to the kitchen for a late-night snack, her blood-curdling scream waking everyone in the lodge.

The unknown intruder had dressed the dummy in clothes similar to those Veronica had worn to the hayride. They'd scrawled her name in cow's blood on a piece of white cardboard and roped it around the dummy's neck. At least the police thought it was cow's blood. According to Duke Cameron, a farmer had called earlier to report one of his heifers had been slaughtered and drained. In the end, it came down to a single ugly truth—some sick bastard had hung her effigy from the rafters of Stone Willow.

Someone wants to kill me.

Perched on the bottom of the stairs, a cup of weak tea in her hands, a blanket over her shoulders, she felt numb. Caith had wrapped her in the blanket and gotten the tea. What was it about Breckwood men always wanting to give her tea when she was upset?

The dummy and the ruined lobby were someone's idea of scare tactics, a trick that made her shiver. *Score another one for the bad guys.*

They'd done what they'd set out to do. A few of her guests had already left, terrified by the scene in the lobby. All would be gone by tomorrow, even the ghost-hunting Dean Bowerman. Stuart was closing the lodge temporarily. Most of her staff would receive a two-week paid vacation. Two weeks for BI and the Breckwoods to decide what to do with the lodge. A few essential personnel, like Lew and Ben Dunning, would remain. Lew tending to regular maintenance, Ben driving from town on a daily basis to care for the horses. Alma had already left, opting to stay in Coldcreek with her sister's family.

"This isn't a prank, and it isn't vandalism." Caith's angry voice cracked on the air, drawing her head around. Along with his brothers and father, he'd cornered Duke Cameron a few feet away. "It's a threat, Cameron, and you know it."

"*Sheriff* Cameron," Duke corrected.

Caith gave a vulgar snort. "A sheriff doesn't make the kind of rookie mistakes you have. You should have gotten off your lazy ass and done something when you found the dog."

"You're not a cop, and you have no authority here."

"The hell I don't." Caith shouldered forward, pressing his advantage of height. "I'm a Breckwood. I got my best friend killed proving it. That's got to count for something. We own the whole fucking town, right?" He drove his finger into Duke's shoulder. "You're incompetent, Duke, sitting around with your thumb up your ass, waiting for the answer to fall from the sky."

"Caith!" Stuart practically spat the name. "Back off. You're out of line."

Veronica couldn't hear Caith's muttered reply, but judging from Stuart's expression, she guessed it wasn't flattering.

With a dark look for his father, Caith joined her by the stairs. "Why don't you go home with Aren?" he suggested. "You can stay with Melanie tonight."

"No." She huddled deeper into the blanket, folding a handkerchief over her nose. The stench was becoming tolerable. In the beginning it had been unbearable, but after an hour with the doors and windows open to air the lobby, she'd almost grown used to it.

Caith exhaled, closing his eyes as if striving for patience. "Then go to your apartment. I don't want you sitting here, looking at that thing. It's going to be a while until they collect the evidence they need and cut it down."

Her eyes flicked to the grisly dummy. "I'm fine. It's my lodge. I need to be here."

"Veronica, no one expects you to be a stone." Caith sat beside her. "It's after one in the morning. I wish you'd try to get some sleep."

"Why?"

"Why?" Caith hooked his arm around her shoulders, pulling her against him with a sigh of exasperation. "I don't know. Maybe because I made a complete ass out of myself in front of Duke Cameron, the entire Coldcreek PD, my father and brothers, and I don't want you to see me do it again."

She chuckled. "Is that all?"

He was silent a moment. "Maybe I just care about you."

"That's not fair."

"What isn't?"

"I *am* tired. And saying things like that when I'm not thinking clearly could get you kissed."

He looked so surprised by her answer, she laughed. It was funny when she thought about it…sitting on the steps surrounded by manure and blood, police officers gathering pumpkin pulp for evidence, Caith's father so angry he might have throttled him given the chance. What did tomorrow or next week matter? It was foolish to pin her hopes on the future. There was only the moment, as absurd and tarnished as it was. If she died tomorrow she didn't want it to be with lingering distance between them. The awareness brought impulses she hadn't expected.

She wanted to kiss him. Not that chaste peck on the cheek between friends. She wanted to dig her hands into his hair and meld her mouth to his. To feel the heat of his tongue between her lips and strip the clothes from his body. He'd always been the leader. It felt good to be in control for a change. Especially with a crime scene photographer snapping shot after shot of her likeness dangling from the rafters.

Her gaze dropped to his lips. "Do you have to stay here?"

"Why?"

"Because I could probably sleep with you beside me. Upstairs." Her lips curled in a slow smile. "In your bed."

Caith groaned and dragged a hand over his face. As if torn, he shot a glance at his father and brothers, still talking with Duke. "I can't leave. I have a responsibility to stay here until this gets sorted out. BI hired me."

She shook her head, feeling foolish for making the overture. "I know I'm not very good at seduction, but maybe I didn't make that clear. I'm not interested in sleeping, Caith."

"You're merciless."

"I don't want to be alone."

He blinked in surprise. "Do you think the only way I'd keep you company is if you let me crawl into your bed?" He was serious. Not moody or angry, but sincere. He took her hand, turning those incredible blue eyes on her, his thumb tracking gently over her knuckles. "Tomorrow when you're thinking clearly, I won't use this against you. As much as I want us to be intimate, I don't want to lose your friendship. I spent twelve years without you, Ronnie. I don't want to risk that happening again."

Her sultry boldness faded. He was being Caith again. The Caith who'd sat up with her the night her grandmother died; the Caith who'd slugged Bill Parker in the nose for spreading false rumors about her after one date; the Caith who'd sent her yellow roses. She was tired, vulnerable, and feeling foolish for trying to seduce him.

"I..." She tried to find her voice. "I'll wait for you, and then maybe you'll stay with me." She lowered her eyes, ashamed by her earlier actions. "Stay. Nothing else. I don't want to be alone tonight."

He kissed her on the brow, pulling the blanket close about her shoulders. "I won't be long."

As he moved off to confer with Aren, a delicious sense of warmth engulfed her. The police were cutting down the dummy, but it didn't matter. Even with that ugly effigy hanging from the rafters, she felt safe.

Because of Caith.

* * * *

Veronica wasn't certain when she finally got to bed. She vaguely remembered falling asleep, huddled on the steps. When she awoke the next day, it was to fuzzy memories of Caith helping her up two flights of stairs to the Blackbird Suite. When she blinked the room into focus, she realized it wasn't a dream. She'd been asleep in his bed, huddled beneath thick quilts and warm blankets. Late morning sunlight streamed through an adjacent window, splashing a pattern of brassy gold squares on the floor.

"Caith?" She tossed back the covers, still dressed in the same clothes she'd hastily thrown on before the police had arrived last night—a baggy blue sweater and drawstring pants. With her feet snug and warm in thick socks, she padded to the bedroom door and peeked into the living area. Caith was sprawled on the couch, fully dressed, sound asleep.

He'd found a blanket somewhere, but it was half on the floor, tangled around one leg. Before she could withdraw silently, the door to the suite swung open and Merlin breezed in, carrying a tray laden with a coffee pot, three cups, and a creamer-sugar set.

"All right, that's enough slacking." He gave the door a forceful slam.

"Merlin!" Veronica stepped into the living area at precisely the same time Caith jolted awake. "Don't be rude."

"I bring coffee. I've even got cream, sugar, and those fancy little spoons you like, and I get accused of being rude?" Setting the tray on a low table by the couch, he cast a glance at his sleep-muddled brother. "What's the matter, Caithelden? Ten-thirty too early for you?"

Veronica tucked her hair behind her ear. Still standing in the doorway, she folded her arms over her chest. "What are you doing here?"

"I'm your morning wake-up call. I've got to leave, so it's time for you to take charge." He grinned, looking her over. "Have I mentioned how exquisite you look in shapeless sleepwear?"

"He's checking out your guests." Caith sat forward and rubbed grit from his eyes. "We arranged it last night. I'd stay with you, and Merlin would handle BI's part so you wouldn't have to be bothered." He poured a cup of coffee, drinking it black. After one swallow, he grimaced. "What the hell did you make this with, Merlin? Petrol?"

"So I like it strong." Merlin flopped into a chair across from him.

Still trying to adjust to the odd night and stranger morning, Veronica sat beside Caith on the sofa. There was something surreal about having Caith and Merlin working together in tandem, conversing without the usual verbal stings. She cleared her throat. "Has everyone left?"

"Even the guy who wanted to play Ghostbuster." Merlin reclined, hooking his left ankle over his right knee. With his elbows propped on the chair arms, he steepled a coffee cup between his fingers. "He wanted to pay extra to hang around, but Dad was adamant. No guests. I think

Bowerman was going to book a room in Coldcreek. As of now, Stone Willow is officially empty."

Caith slouched against the couch. He dragged a hand through his hair, adding to its early morning dishevel, and yawned. "How's the lobby?"

"We're not going to get any five-star awards, but Lew and his helpers have been working since sunup. Instead of smelling like cow shit, it smells like lemon-scented cow shit."

Veronica sighed and rubbed her eyes. "I wish I understood why this is happening."

"Somebody obviously wants the lodge closed," Caith said. "The question is why."

"And who," Merlin added.

They were silent a moment. Caith shifted, stretching his legs. "Whoever did this must have been at the hayride. That dummy was dressed like Ron. Whoever strung it up would've had to see her last night."

"That narrows it down to half the town." Merlin smirked and took a long swig of coffee. "How'd they get in this time? Pick a lock?"

Caith shook his head. "I checked last night. No sign of forced entry anywhere, windows or doors. Whoever's pulling these stunts either has an inside accomplice or a key. It's late to be changing locks, but it can't hurt. Lew should have done it after the incident with the dog."

Veronica looked away from his pointed stare. She knew he remained suspicious of Lew, but she believed the caretaker had nothing to do with BI's problems. "I'll call a locksmith."

"Have Lew do it." Caith stood and paced to the window. "I want you to spend the day with Melanie."

She blinked, certain she'd misunderstood. "Excuse me?"

"You heard me." He turned, his expression hard. "There's no reason for you to stay here and every reason to leave. I have to go into town, and I don't want you alone."

The heat of anger seeped into her skin. Clenching her hands, she stood stiffly. "I don't need protecting, Caithelden."

"I wasn't asking your permission."

Merlin chuckled. "Hey, can you two hold off until I make popcorn? This is better than reality TV."

Caith shot him a black glare. "I thought you were leaving?"

"And miss my childhood chums having a spat?"

"Merlin," Veronica snapped.

"All right." He raised his hands in surrender. "When you get this sorted out, I'll be waiting for the sequel." Still chuckling, he headed for the door.

Veronica never took her gaze off Caith. The moment Merlin was out of the room, she stalked forward, jabbing a finger against his chest. "You are not going to suffocate me or tail me around like some overprotective watchdog. I was dealing with the problems at this lodge long before you showed up."

"So successfully, too."

She was tempted to hit him. She settled for huffing out a breath and turning her back, folding her arms over her chest. "Go. I don't need your sarcasm."

Seconds passed. His hands settled on her shoulders. "What about my concern?"

The quiet sincerity in his voice tugged at her heart. She had no defense against his gentleness, only his anger.

"Please." The word was obviously hard for him. He wrapped his arms around her waist and dropped his chin to her shoulder. She allowed the embrace, but didn't relax her rigid posture.

"I don't want to spend the whole day worrying whether or not you're safe. You can help Melanie with the hayride and spend some time with Derrick." He hesitated. "I'd like for you to get to know him better."

Blindsided by the request, she fought the urge to gape.

A step toward commitment or was she reading too much into the suggestion? Had he, in a roundabout way, hinted he wanted her there in the future? She'd been convinced anything beyond friendship would only involve sex, not emotion. He liked the mechanics and heady gratification, but had mastered the art of disconnecting his heart. Or so she'd thought.

Not trusting her voice, she nodded.

Caith kissed her cheek. "Just don't go hay-riding with any scarecrows, okay?"

Chapter 12

The day turned out to be a pleasure. Unexpected balmy weather brought hordes of people to Aren's farm. Although the hayride didn't begin operation until nightfall, there were plenty of other activities. Veronica helped at the ticket booth until Balin, dressed in an elaborate Frankenstein costume, relieved her. Afterward, she spent the afternoon shepherding Derry, Noah, and Matt, allowing Melanie to oversee the festivities.

Aren was missing, helping Galen offset the fallout from last night's catastrophe. Kelly Rice had wasted no time in reporting the latest incident to plague Stone Willow. By noon, a new *On the Spot* column trumpeted all the ugly details. The insinuations were not as blatant as before, but the column hinted BI had orchestrated the episode in an effort to gain publicity for its failing retreat. Veronica spent ten minutes fuming over the article, then put it out of her mind.

Derry, Noah, and Matt kept her busy. When the twins vanished into the corn maze after lunch, she finally had a chance to sit down and draw a breath. Finding a comfortable spot on the grass with Derry, she watched the three witches who guarded the maze cackle over their cauldron.

"Are you sure you don't want to go with your cousins?" she asked.

"Nah, that's okay. I already did the maze a bunch of times." Derry sorted through the bag of marbles he routinely carried, spilling a few onto the grass. "If we're still here next week, will you go trick-or-treating with me and Dad?"

The question came out of the blue, catching Veronica by surprise. Before she could answer, he flopped onto his back, folding his arms behind his head. "Dad doesn't like Halloween."

"I know." She poked a fat blue marble with her finger. "Did he tell you why?"

Derry rolled his head on his arm to look at her. He wasn't wearing Trask's hat today, his hair a rumpled mass of black curls. "Because Trask died on Halloween. Dad said it was an accident. Something bad happened in the basement where they were playing."

"Playing." She said the word softly so Derry wouldn't hear. Caith hadn't told his son the truth, which was as she'd expected. "But he still takes you trick-or-treating?"

Derry nodded. "I know he doesn't like it. It's why he won't dress up like some of my friends' dads." He tilted his head to look at her. "I bet he'd dress up if you asked. He likes you, Ron."

Veronica's attention returned to the marble. "Did he tell you that?" She glanced up, needing to know.

"No, but I can tell." He grinned, much like Caith did. An extravagant, quicksilver smile that lit up his eyes. "Dad doesn't give girls flowers."

Veronica nodded knowingly. "But he does date a lot of girls?"

"No." Still grinning, Derry sat up. "His friend Jake—Jake's a cop—is always trying to fix Dad up on a date. Sometimes he goes to make Jake happy and I've gotta stay with a boring babysitter." He plucked at the grass on either side of his legs, pulling it from the ground as he talked. "Once, there was this really nasty lady with red hair and these long fingernails." He held out his hands to indicate nails no human woman could possibly have. "Jake and Connie—Connie's Jake's wife—brought her to the house to meet Dad, and she asked if I knew what 'keep quiet' meant. Dad got mad and kicked her out." He laughed at the memory.

Veronica laughed, too. She could picture Caith kicking someone from his home for slighting his son. "She was pretty stupid, huh?"

Derry nodded vigorously. "Not like you, Ron. I like you a lot. So does Dad. He'd never kick you out."

A sensation, equal parts pleasure and embarrassment, swept through her. Before she could say anything, Noah and Matt burst from the maze and ran to their lounging spot.

"I'm hungry," Matt declared, plopping down at Derry's side.

"Me, too," Noah chimed in.

Derry grinned and nodded his agreement.

"You just finished lunch," Veronica said with mock sternness.

"But not dessert," Noah protested. "There's pumpkin pie with Cool Whip, nut brownies, caramel apples, and—"

"Okay." Veronica held up a hand. "But you each get to pick only one."

Derry scooped up his marbles and stuffed them into the bag. "I want pumpkin pie."

The other boys began calling out their choices and pretty soon her small group was on its way to the food tents. As they walked, Derry slipped his hand into hers and tugged her along, the blissful sensation warming her heart.

* * * *

The locks at the lodge were changed by evening, the new keys limited to the Breckwood family, Veronica, and Lew. She spent the night at her apartment making an amaretto cheesecake for Sunday's get-together while Caith camped out in her small living room. Nothing eventful happened and by Sunday afternoon she was on her way to the Breckwood home with Caith for a family dinner.

From the corner of her eye, she watched him drum his thumbs against the steering wheel. "I wish you'd stop fidgeting. You're making me nervous."

"Huh?" He spared a distracted glance.

Veronica chuckled. "You look like you're going to your execution."

"Close enough."

The afternoon was going to be awkward. She felt bad for Caith, thrown into family socializing after a dozen years on his own. Derry, who'd stayed at Aren's farm the previous night, was coming with his aunt, uncle, and cousins. Judging by the cars parked in the driveway, the entire group was already there when they arrived. Even Galen and Balin, who each had driven separately, beat them. Caith had been gone so long, she wondered if he knew whether or not Galen and his wife had divorced. It would be awkward if he mentioned her. At least Galen had started to date again over the last year.

"You do know Galen and Bridget are divorced now, right?" she asked as they walked up the circular drive to the house.

"Aren told me. Can't say it surprises me."

"Caith."

He shrugged. "He's reserved, too focused on business."

"He's reserved with everyone. It's his way."

They stepped onto the porch, and she got the impression he was no longer listening. Stuffing his hands into his pockets, he stared at the front door as if undecided whether he should ring the bell or just go in. The decision was made when Derry burst outside giggling, Noah and Matt on his heels. Stuart charged behind them with a deep guttural roar.

Caith stumbled backward to excited cries of "Dad!" and "Uncle Caith!" Veronica barely had time to sort through what was happening before the boys were dancing around her, too.

"Ron, Grandpa's a monster." Noah tugged on her sleeve, shrieking with delight as Stuart made a false lurch to catch him.

Dropping his monster persona, Caith's father straightened with a grin. "Everyone else is in the back. Thought we'd keep it informal and do a cookout since it's so nice."

Veronica tried to relax, but it was difficult with Caith so tense. A cookout was just what they needed to put everyone at ease.

"Dad." Derry tugged on Caith's sleeve. "Grandpa said I can help him grill later. Come on. I'll show you where everything is."

After an initial bout of awkwardness, Caith seemed more relaxed as the hours progressed toward dinner. There was barbecued chicken, lean steaks, and fat hamburgers, all prepared in a mammoth outdoor bricked-in grill. A multitude of side dishes included hot potato salad, grilled vegetables, and plump sweet potatoes baked in foil.

After dessert, Balin disappeared in typical teen fashion, saying he had plans with his friends. Veronica sat with Morgana and Melanie on the glassed-in back porch, each with a cup of coffee. Outside, Caith tossed a small football with his son and two nephews while Stuart, Aren, and Galen fiddled around the grill. Merlin perched on the end of a stout redwood picnic table, looking chic and bored in designer khakis and an oyster-colored cardigan. There was little talk of BI or the troubles plaguing the lodge. It was a day for family and relaxing.

Because the weather remained mild, Morgana cracked a window. Within moments, the outside voices filtered indoors.

"Dad, catch!"

Veronica grinned as Caith made an elaborate show of catching the mini-sized football Derry lobbed to him. Bright orange with marshmallow white bands, it had nubby raised plastic where the stitching should be. Backing up slowly, he tucked it beneath one arm, giving Noah and Matt ample time to wrestle him to the ground. Within seconds, Derry joined them, and the three boys pinned him flat on his back. There was giggling and shrieking as Caith clawed free, catching first one boy and then another, spinning them upside down. When all three were clear, he allowed them to knock him down again.

Hearing the commotion, Aren glanced over his shoulder. "Look at that. Someone actually knows how to keep Caith in line."

"You're next." Caith tossed him the football.

Before Aren had time to blink, all three boys barreled down on him, giggling and laughing. Aren played along, jogging into the yard, the bright orange ball tucked under his arm. Caith tackled him from behind, taking him by surprise, and the boys hooted in delight. All three piled on the two men and soon all Veronica could see was a tangle of arms and legs.

"I love hearing that laughter." Morgana propped her chin in her hand, gazing wistfully out the window. "Do you realize this is the first time in twelve years I've had my entire family together?"

Veronica and Melanie exchanged an uneasy glance. "Now that Derry and Stuart have met in person, I'm sure Caith will be more open to visits," Veronica ventured. "It's going to be hard to keep Derry away from his grandfather."

"Caith indulges that boy terribly," Melanie inserted. "If Derrick wants to see Stuart——"

Morgana shook her head. "Anything to do with his father has always been Caith's sticking point. I used to plead with him to bring Derrick to Coldcreek, but he wouldn't hear of it. It's such a shame. Caith and his father were so close when Caith was a child, but Stuart took it badly when he changed his name. I don't think Caith realizes how hurtful that was to his father."

"But you know why he changed his name," Veronica insisted.

Before anything could be said, another shriek of childish laughter came from outside. The three boys had retreated to the edge of the patio while Caith and Aren closed on Merlin. The impeccably-dressed Breckwood brother suddenly found himself the recipient of the football.

"Don't even think about it," Merlin warned from his perch on the picnic table.

Realizing he was in trouble, he lurched into the yard, but wasn't fast enough to escape the inevitable. Caith caught him, tackling him low on the legs, and Aren piled on top of him. Merlin went down with a grunt.

"Get off!" he demanded. "Do you have any idea how much this sweater cost?"

Still holding him down, Caith exchanged a grin with Aren. "A couple of bucks?"

"Maybe even as much as that smelly aftershave you wear," Aren added.

"Off!" Merlin threw his weight into the effort, breaking free. Springing angrily to his feet, he looked down at his chest. Grass and dirt smeared the front of his sweater in grungy, vivid streaks.

Caith burst out laughing.

Grinning maniacally, Aren slung an arm over his shoulders. "I don't know, Caith, he looks mad. We might have a problem."

"Problem, my ass." Merlin lifted his head, the look in his eyes sending the other two backpedaling into the yard.

"Come on, Merlin." Caith's grin was wicked. "You could start a new fashion trend. Designer dirt for executives."

"You really want me to kick your ass, don't you?"

Aren hooted at the boast, looking delightedly between the two. Off to the side, Stuart and Galen stopped to watch the exchange. Caith raised a brow. "Think you can?"

Veronica caught something in his stance that went back to their childhood. The taunt was directed at Merlin, but the look in his eyes and the shift of his body sent a different message. A message that made them coconspirators in a silent plan.

"Oh." She covered her mouth with her hand, hiding a smile. "Aren's in trouble."

"What do you mean?" Melanie asked.

The silent communication that once flowed so effortlessly between brothers as children still worked as adults. With simultaneous battle cries, Merlin and Caith launched themselves on Aren. Completely taken by surprise, he went down like a stone. Popping from the tangle of tumbling arms and legs, the football rolled clear. Merlin scrambled free and scooped it up.

"Galen," he yelled. "Get Galen." And suddenly the football was flying through the air to be caught by a stupefied Galen.

Stuart wandered inside as his oldest son was bodily dragged into the fray. As the four tussled in the yard, Stuart raised his arm over his head and propped it against the glass to watch with a wistful grin.

"You should have stayed out there," Morgana said.

He shook his head. "Let them have fun. When's the last time you saw all of them together acting crazy? Galen's so mired in work he rarely smiles, and Merlin never has a hair out of place. It's good to see them acting foolish, behaving like brothers."

Eventually the rough-and-tumble dissolved into a game of pass-and-tackle with a regulation football Aren found in the shed. Caith teamed with Aren, and Merlin with Galen. Veronica was never sure who won but added her voice to Derry, Matt, and Noah's cheering section. The air got colder the closer it grew to dusk. After a time, the windows were closed, and the adults retreated inside. Derry and the twins continued to play in the yard, breaking out glow-sticks and rolling in piles of leaves.

Caith located a bottle of spring water in the refrigerator, drank most of it holding the door open, then carried the remainder into the family room. "Nice dinner, Mom." He gave her a kiss on the cheek, then sprawled in a plush easy chair.

"Did you tell your father?"

He shrugged, taking a sip from the bottle. Soon after the game had broken up, Galen left citing business, and Merlin followed. Aren and Melanie were off somewhere with Stuart, leaving Veronica with Morgana and Caith in the family room. "Maybe later."

Morgana sighed with a mother's longsuffering patience. "Caithelden, talk to your father. The two of you have danced circles around each other all day."

"Don't start." His gaze flashed to her face. "It's been a nice day, Mom. I didn't expect it to be, but it was. Can we leave it at that?"

Sensing a need to intervene, Veronica cleared her throat. "Morgana, did you get a new key to the lodge? Lew had the locks changed yesterday."

She nodded. "He dropped some at the house. I still can't believe anyone could do something as hideous as that mess in the lobby. And that horrid dummy!"

Caith hooked an ankle over his knee. "I know all about hideous," he said quietly.

Veronica shifted uncomfortably, never expecting he would insert Trask's death so casually into the conversation.

As if sensing what she was thinking, he shook his head. "I'm not talking about Trask. You don't spend the number of years I have as a cop and not see gruesome firsthand. At least whoever's behind this has limited it to vandalism and threats, nothing violent."

"So far." Morgana looked worried. "Veronica, I don't like you staying at the lodge after what happened. Maybe we should get you a place in town until this is sorted out."

If she didn't know Morgana better, Veronica would have thought Caith put his mother up to the suggestion. She sent him a sideways glance, and he arched a brow as if to say, "See? She thinks so, too."

"I'll be fine, Morgana. The locks have been changed, the basement's padlocked, and Caith's there. Besides, if the goal was to make BI close the lodge, that's already been accomplished."

Caith sat forward, lacing his hands between his knees. "The association with Warren Barrister bothers me. I picked up a book and tried to find some information online yesterday at the library, but the accounts of his life vary."

"That's usually the case with legends and myth." Morgana warmed to the subject as she did with anything involving shadowy half-truths and folklore. "You won't find this in most books, but Barrister was a Tolar. There was a great deal of them at that time."

Veronica exchanged a glance with Caith. So the Tolar connection was true. If a cult had existed in Coldcreek in its early days, could there still be stray followers of the religion even now?

"Wasn't that some kind of sect?" Caith asked.

Morgana curled her legs onto the sofa with surprisingly fluid grace for a woman in her sixties. "Yes. It's antiquated, but I believe there are still followers who practice it today. When Coldcreek was young, Tolars made up the majority of the population. Their belief system revolves around a prophesied leader, rising from a magical lake to lead the world to peace and prosperity."

"Stone Willow." Caith grimaced. "I can't believe any sane person would buy into that."

"Warren Barrister did. It was the reason he had all those secret passages built into his house. So he and other Tolars could come and go without being seen. He went mad eventually, waiting for something to happen that never would. That's why he killed his family. The children as they slept, his wife when she tried to escape to the lake."

"What a lunatic." Caith raked the bangs from his eyes. "I've seen the lake change. Once." He sent a self-conscious glance to Veronica. "But that can be explained by variations in atmospheric pressure and temperature drops."

"No, Caith." Morgana shook her head. "BI has commissioned countless studies of the lake, and no one has been able to explain its fire-like properties. Scientific teams from all over the country have studied it without success. Personally, I prefer it that way. The lake is an anomaly. There are few people who have ever seen it change, so count yourself lucky." She paused, a sly smile touching her lips. "There's another legend that has nothing to do with the Tolars. According to that one, if you see the lake dance with fire, you'll find your true love before the sun rises on a new day."

Veronica grew warm. *True love?* She wanted to scoff at the ridiculous notion. Maybe she'd found hers that magical night, but Caith had run off, tumbling another girl into bed a few weeks later. So much for true love and antiquated folklore.

He shifted, refusing to look at her.

"Dad!" Derry burst into the room with a shout, startling her with his abrupt entrance. Immediately, he zeroed in on Caith. "Uncle Aren and... and Noah and Matt and Aunt Melanie have to leave but-but—" He talked so fast, he tripped over the words, his face flushed, bits of grass snagged in his tangled black curls. "Grandpa says I can stay here." He leaned into

Caith's lap, planting his forearms on his father's knees. "Can I, Dad? Can I stay here tonight? There's no school tomorrow. It's one of those days teachers have off."

"An in-service day." Caith pulled a piece of grass from his hair. "We'll see."

"Puh-leeze?"

"I said we'll see."

Soon after, Aren gathered his family and left, calling it a night. Veronica expected Caith to do the same, but he surprised her by staying. Clearly pleased that he'd chosen to remain, Morgana talked at length about the lavish Halloween party scheduled a few days away, and how she expected them both to be there. In costume. Caith frowned, but didn't contradict her.

Across the room, Derrick plopped on the floor in front of the big screen TV. Instead of watching, he chatted nonstop with his grandfather over everything from how he was going to be a cop someday to the werewolf costume he planned to wear for Halloween, and how much he hated peas but loved cherry popsicles. Eventually, he tired, worn out from the day's excitement. Yawning, he climbed into the large chair with his father, curling against Caith's side. He was asleep in a matter of minutes. Without his constant chatter, the conversation lagged.

"He's pretty worn out," Veronica observed with a smile. She liked the way he curled so snugly against Caith, as if it were the most natural thing in the world.

"He had a full day." Caith slipped a finger beneath Derry's bangs, sweeping them from his forehead. "It's getting late. I better take him upstairs if he's spending the night."

It was something Veronica never expected to happen. Although Caith and Stuart had barely spoken to each other over the course of the day, she felt they'd gained common ground through Derry. She was proud of Caith for the effort he'd made, not only with Stuart but his brothers as well.

And, *ohhh*, she was attracted to him! That was the downside. Seeing him roughhouse on the grass with his nephews, son, and brothers, made him terribly endearing. He'd been relaxed, part of a family again. She loved that image and wanted to hold onto it forever.

Keeping an arm around Derry's shoulders, Caith stood, slipping his other arm beneath the boy's knees. Derry woke with a sleepy grunt as Caith lifted him. He shifted, wrapping his arms around Caith's neck, resting his head on his father's shoulder. Already accustomed to his highly-charged personality, Veronica found it amusing to see him so quiet and subdued.

Caith grinned. "Time for bed, partner. You can sleep here tonight, okay?"

"Thanks, Dad."

Veronica barely heard Derry's sleepy reply.

"Your old room will be fine," Morgana told her son as she followed Caith toward the stairs.

"I'll get extra blankets in case he needs them," Stuart said, trailing behind. Together the three of them left, fussing over Derry.

Veronica smiled.

With a little imagination, it was easy to envision them a family.

Chapter 13

The lodge felt strange without guests. Rooms were dark and vacant, the corridors draped with sinister shadows. Despite her initial reluctance to have Caith looking over her shoulder, Veronica was glad he was there. Even so, she felt guilty when he dragged blankets and a pillow into her living room, piling them on the sofa. Still fully dressed, she watched from the doorway of her bedroom.

"I'll be all right if you sleep in your suite tonight."

"No." Caith spoke over his shoulder, his back turned as he arranged blankets, folding them at the foot of the couch. "Two floors away won't cut it in the event of a problem. I'll stay here."

"You can't keep sleeping on the couch." She wished he would turn around and face her. The snug fit of his jeans was a little too distracting with him bent over the sofa. "Maybe if…you know…promised to behave, we could sleep in the same bed." She stood up straighter, clearing her throat when he glanced at her in surprise. "We're both adults, Caith. If you promised to stay on your side—"

"What about you?"

"Excuse me?"

He turned with a brash grin. "How do I know you won't pounce on me in the middle of the night? I've been told I'm not a bad looking guy."

She folded her arms over her chest. "Caithelden."

He gave a low whistle at the severity of her frown. "How many guys have you sent packing with that look?" Stepping closer, he brushed his hands over her arms, smiling less indulgently. "As much as I appreciate the offer, I don't think I could sleep in the same bed and not want to touch you."

Veronica lost the edge of sternness she'd managed only moments before. He was too close, the room too small, and she'd made a stupid mistake, blurting such an intimate suggestion. She averted her eyes. "Maybe we should call it a night."

"I don't want to do that either." Caith lifted his hand and hooked her hair behind her ear. He trailed his thumb over her cheek, watching her intently. When he spoke, his voice was lower, a husky whisper. "My kid's pretty stuck on you. He told me that today."

Veronica raised her head, her mouth dry. His eyes were winter and sea. "What about you?"

His lashes lowered as his gaze dropped to her lips. "I'm stuck on you, too."

Unconsciously, she leaned forward, a subtle invitation for his kiss. He bowed his head, angling his mouth over hers, sealing them together in a single heartbeat. The kiss was slow and deep, reaching into her soul. She hadn't known a kiss could be so possessive and tender at the same time. She was terrified he would continue, more terrified he would stop.

Caith pulled her into his arms, trapping her against him. "I can't stop wanting you," he murmured against her lips.

His fingers threaded into her hair. He kissed her with a hunger that left her senseless. Over and over again, until her heart shuddered and her knees grew weak. His breath was warm and ragged on her skin, as uneven as her own.

She quivered in his arms. "Take me to bed, Caith."

Bowing his forehead against hers, he cupped her neck with both hands, his thumbs tracking over her throat. "Are you sure that's what you want, Ronnie?" He kissed her brow, her cheek. "You have no idea what you do to me. I want you to want it, too."

"I do." Veronica nipped his earlobe. She gave a short startled cry when he scooped her into his arms.

His mouth never left hers as he carried her into the bedroom and kicked the door shut behind them.

* * * *

Sated and spent from their lovemaking, Caith lay in the dark, Veronica snuggled against his side. He hadn't been able to touch her enough, kiss her enough. There had never been a woman who stripped him of his senses so completely. In the matter of a single heartbeat, he knew he loved her. Beyond all reason, beyond all sanity.

"Ronnie." He bowed his face into her hair, unable to choke the words past his lips. "I—"

She seemed to understand what he wanted to say. "It doesn't matter." She kissed his cheek, his mouth. "You don't have to say it, Caith. I know this isn't forever."

He closed his eyes. *I love you.* The world wouldn't end if he said it. No one would snatch her away. No one would slide a knife between her ribs like they'd done to Trask.

His stomach twisted. The imagined scent of model glue nearly choked him.

"Veronica, I do care." It was as close as he could come. He wrapped his arm around her and hugged her closer, inhaling her scent. So clean, so pure. She cuddled against him, her warmth banishing the remembered nightmares.

He kissed her temple.

I love you.

But he couldn't—wouldn't— say it aloud.

* * * *

Veronica dragged herself awake at the insistence of Ash, the gray cat she'd adopted the night the lobby had been ransacked. A stray only a few short days ago, the animal had already adjusted to life at the lodge. Bounding onto the bed, the cat cried for a six a.m. feeding. With a sleepy grunt, Caith rolled onto his back, completely unaware when the light-footed feline strolled across his stomach. Suppressing a smile, Veronica nuzzled closer. It was still dark outside, blissfully snug and warm beneath the blankets. She wanted to stay where she was, cuddled against Caith, the heat of his body seeping into hers.

"Lie down, Ash," she whispered, gliding a hand over the cat's soft fur. It purred and rubbed against her, then waltzed across Caith again. She giggled against his shoulder. "All right. I'll feed you." When she slipped free of the covers, the feline sprang from the bed and darted for the kitchen.

Later, after attending to Ash and downing two cups of coffee, Veronica stepped into a hot shower. The water felt luxurious cascading over her bare skin. Its heated touch awakened memories of Caith, still asleep in the bedroom. Through the seductive hours of the night, she'd become familiar with every delicious inch of his body as they'd made love. He'd claimed her with tenderness and aggression, one moment impossibly gentle, the next driven by a need so fierce his passion consumed them both. As difficult as it was, she would accept the relationship at face value. She was in love with a man who couldn't love back. A man who had spent his entire life avoiding commitment.

Later, in her office, she checked her voice mail as Caith took his turn in the shower. Aren's voice greeted her, relaying a brief message that he'd be at the lodge around ten.

"I've got an overnight envelope for Caith," he informed her. "It came to BI from Boston. From someone named, um…" There was a pause as Aren checked the air bill. "Connie Clark."

Veronica felt a twinge of uneasiness. Girlfriend? Lover? Housemate? Her stomach clenched. He hadn't promised forever because he *couldn't* promise forever.

Stop it. Nervously she smoothed a hand over her navy slacks. Derry would have mentioned a woman if Caith was living with someone. She was just…just…

But she couldn't summon a solution. Just what?

"Ronnie?"

She reeled at his voice, looking up when he entered the office.

"What's wrong?" Caith crossed to the desk. "You look pale."

"N-Nothing." When he moved to touch her, she unconsciously flinched away. She loved him, but could she suffer hurt again? Could she watch him walk away into the arms of someone else? Her back stiffened. "Aren called. He should be here shortly. He said he has an overnight letter for you."

"From Connie?"

Veronica looked stunned. He wasn't even going to deny it.

"I didn't think she'd move that fast." Caith propped a hip on the edge of her desk. "I called on Friday, but…" He trailed off, noticing her expression for the first time. "Ron, what's wrong with you?"

Reaching for her desk calendar, she flipped the page, struggling to focus on anything other than the cold dread settling in her stomach. "How long have you known Connie?"

"I don't know." He shrugged. "Since before she and Jake got married. She was at the Fifty-Fourth before I was stationed there."

Veronica grew very still. "Married?"

"Yeah." Caith looked puzzled. "Jake's my ex-partner from the force, a good friend. Connie's his wife. She works in the records division at the Fifty-Fourth Precinct. I asked her to do some checking for me. Off the books. She's a first-rate snoop."

"Oh, no." Veronica propped her elbows on the desk and rubbed her temples. She felt like an idiot. "Jake and Connie are the ones who are always trying to fix you up with a date, right?"

"Yeah, they—" Caith stopped abruptly. "Hey, wait a minute. How did you know that?"

"Derry told me." As her jealousy drained, she realized how foolish she'd been. Suspicion melted into dry humor. "And about the redhead who had 'fingernails out to here.'" She held out her hand, mimicking Derry's exaggeration.

Caith frowned. "Derry talks too much."

"I like that he does." She favored him with a teasing smile. "It's amazing to think such an outgoing, talkative kid came from such a quiet, introspective father. I bet he doesn't bury his nose in books like you did."

"He does, and quit trying to change the subject." His frown was still in place, digging deeper. "Who did you think Connie was?"

"I—" Veronica clamped her mouth shut.

Aren's arrival couldn't have been timelier. His footsteps sounded in the hall as she frantically searched for an answer to Caith's question. Within seconds, BI's Chief Operations Officer rounded the corner.

"Aren." She smiled in relief. "You're early. There's coffee in the kitchen if you want some."

"No." He waved the offer aside. "I've been at the office since six and already downed a pot. Here." He slapped the overnight envelope against his brother's chest. "I would've sent someone else to play errand boy, but I needed a break." Huffing out a breath, he dropped in the nearest chair, running a hand through his sandy brown hair.

"Bad morning?" Caith pulled aside the perforated tab on the oversized envelope.

"The worst." Aren shook his head. "We've got a temporary plug in the top office at Boston Corporate, but can't come up with anyone to run the show."

His attention glued to the papers he pulled from the package, Caith plopped into a chair. "I don't know much about BI these days, but what's wrong with Merlin?"

"Nothing, except he's stuck on Baltimore. He could've had Boston ten months ago when I left. Instead we've been shuffling people around, settling on temporary fills. Dad's going to talk to him about it, but I'm not holding my breath." With a nod of his head, he indicated the papers in Caith's hands. "Who's Connie Clark?"

Caith flicked a glance over the top sheet. "Jake's wife."

"Your friend from the police force?" Aren looked confused. "I thought his last name was Jennings?"

"It is." Caith flipped to another sheet, frowning slightly. "Connie kept her maiden name when they got married. She thought it would be better since they both work at the same precinct. The Commissioner's office frowns on couples working together."

Veronica leaned forward. "What did she send you?"

He hesitated. "I'm not sure I want to tell you. You'll get angry."

Uncertain, Veronica exchanged a glance with Aren. "Why would I get angry?"

"Because I had Connie run a records check on Lew. She knows how to dig deeper than the normal databases."

"What?" She surged to her feet. Anger didn't begin to cover what she felt. Steel stiffened her spine as her mouth thinned into a furious line. "You had no right, Caith. He's part of my staff."

"I had every right." Shoving from the chair, he confronted her across the desk. "It's my job, Veronica. BI is paying me to get to the bottom of this, and if that means digging up dirt on your employees, then I'm damn well going to do it." Papers in hand, he pointed behind him to Aren. "Do you want to tell him your staff is off limits? The last time I looked, BI still paid your salary."

"Caith," Aren warned quietly.

Veronica felt her cheeks drain of color. He sounded like a Breckwood. An arrogant, wealthy Breckwood who knew his family was responsible for Coldcreek's prosperity. For her prosperity. She'd never heard him talk with such unflattering conceit.

"If that's the case, maybe I should charge you for last night, *Mr. Breckwood.*"

"Veronica." Caith's mouth thinned in irritation.

Furious, she shoved past him. How could the same man who'd made love to her with such passion turn around and treat her like a typed name on a pay ledger? He'd never been arrogant, and he'd never flaunted his family's wealth. After Trask's death, he'd even resented it.

But he used status and position now. He'd investigated Lew behind her back, even after she'd told him she trusted Lew implicitly. Even after Duke Cameron had cleared him.

Only later when she stormed into her apartment did Veronica realize she'd forgotten to point out the obvious. Connie Clark's search was bound to produce nothing on Lew except a big fat blank.

Chapter 14

"Well?" Aren nodded at the papers clutched in Caith's hand. "I hope that scene was worth something. What did you turn up on Lew?"

"Plenty." With grim satisfaction, Caith slumped in a chair. "Connie had to pull some strings to dig up what she did, all off the record." His gaze dropped to the sheaf of papers. "Lewis Frederick Earl Walden the third. He comes from old money. Banking, investments. Ten years ago his wife died. Up until that point, he was a practicing partner with a Hartford law firm." Caith sent Aren a speculative glance. "After he lost his wife, he started traveling, taking odd jobs for support. Seattle, Baton Rouge, Denver, Winston-Salem. He even did a stint on a film set eight years ago, helping the production crew."

Aren gave a low whistle. "So what makes a successful law partner pull up roots and become a handyman?"

"Grief?" Caith was silent as he considered. "A case that went sour? I'll do some digging. See if there were any high profile cases that imploded while he was with the firm."

Aren shook his head. "It sounds crazy. We're talking about Lew, a guy who barely strings three words together when speaking. A guy who looks and acts like a retro burnout from the sixties."

"Well, he was honest about one thing." Caith consulted the file again. "He does have a daughter in Pittsburgh. Galina Brady. Thirty-six, divorced, no kids. She's a VP for Roth-Deckman."

Aren looked up startled. "The media giant? This gets nuttier by the minute. Maybe Veronica shouldn't have been so quick to jump down your throat. What made you look at Lew in the first place?"

"Instinct." Caith tossed the papers on Veronica's desk. "Sometimes it's all you have to go on in my line of work. Lew's got the means to pull off these stunts, and I seriously doubt the passage from Hummingbird to the basement was a surprise. He's the caretaker, for crying out loud. He knows every square inch of this lodge, inside out." Pushing from the chair, he shook his head then began to pace. "Veronica's overreacting. And if that isn't enough…" His mouth twisted in a frown as a new concern reared its ugly head. "Dad's breathing down my neck, hoping I'll screw up."

Aren choked on startled laughter. "What?"

"He hasn't fired me, because he's hoping I'll blow it." It was a suspicion he'd carried around ever since the conference at BI. Originally, he'd thought his father hadn't fired him because of Derrick, but he'd since come to recognize the reason as something more personal. "He wants to rub my face in the fact I rejected BI. If I'm unsuccessful in cracking this case, it gives him the right to gloat. I chose this profession. He wants me to fail at it."

"That's asinine, Caith." Standing, Aren shook his head. "When are you going to stop looking for ulterior motives in everything Dad does? You've got a second chance. Not many people get the opportunity to fix their lives."

"There's nothing wrong with my life."

Aren sent him a pointed stare. "Like I said—you've got a second chance." Not waiting for an answer, he turned and left the room.

Muttering, Caith paced between the desk and the doorway. Aren had no business offering opinions, pointing out flaws. So his life wasn't perfect, but he made a decent living, kept his kid happy and sheltered, and was even occasionally at ease with his past. True, he didn't have an ideal relationship with his family, but Merlin had jumped ship, and his father…

With a disgusted groan, Caith dropped into the desk chair. Sliding both elbows onto the top, he leaned forward and rubbed his eyes. He couldn't fix his life now any more than he'd been able to seventeen years ago. Everything had gone wrong in that root cellar with Trask. Afterward, he'd counted on his family, his father in particular, to help him through the trauma.

But his father had lied.

Caith curled onto the bed, wrapping his arms around his stomach. It felt like someone had punched him in the gut. In sharp contrast to his mood, music and laughter floated up the steps and seeped beneath the closed door to his bedroom. He'd always enjoyed the lavish Halloween parties his parents had in the past, but not tonight. Tonight was the first anniversary of Trask's death.

Tonight, he wanted to be alone. In the concealing blackness with his grief.

Someone knocked on the door. "Caith?"

He curled into a tighter ball, hunching his shoulders. His mother had already been to see him. Stone-faced and tightlipped, he'd sent her away. Who was it now? Why wouldn't they let him be?

The door opened and a shaft of light spilled into the room. Within seconds, the beam was snuffed into obscurity as someone stepped inside and closed the door. "Caithelden?"

His father.

He recognized his dad's voice, his presence. Normally comforting, the intrusion made his skin crawl. He didn't deserve to be comforted. He didn't deserve affection or concern of any kind. It was his fault Trask was dead.

"You shouldn't stay up here alone." His father sat on the edge of the bed. "Merlin and your friends from school are downstairs." He paused, waiting as silence mushroomed between them. "You should see how pretty Veronica looks. She's dressed as a faerie princess."

"Go away." He managed to croak the words between clenched teeth. His stomach hurt so badly he thought he was going to puke.

"I'm not going to go away. Not when I know you're hurting." His father spoke softly, laying a comforting hand on his shoulder. "We'll get through this together, Caith. I know it seems unbearable now."

Caith scrunched his eyes shut. It wouldn't do to let his father see him cry. He was fourteen years old, well past the time when tears were acceptable. Even so, his shoulders shook as the betraying wetness leaked onto his cheeks. Images crowded into his head, fast and furious, punishing him with ugly accusations. It was his fault. Trask was dead, and it was all his fault.

The sob built in his chest. "Trask got in the way," he wailed. "It wasn't supposed to be him." Grief pummeled him. "It's not fair! We didn't do anything! We—we were just riding our bikes."

His father touched his cheek, must have felt the wetness there. "I know." Moving closer, he scooped Caith into his arms, cradling him against his chest. "Let it out, Caithelden. I promise I'll be here for you. No matter what happens, I'll always be here."

His father had lied.

Grimly, Caith shoved to his feet. How did Aren suggest he fix that?

* * * *

Caith waited until Lew left the caretaker's house, then picked the lock on the rear door and slipped inside. The home was small, a two bedroom ranch with a living-dining room combination and a boxed kitchen with a breakfast bar. The walls and furnishings tended to browns and russet, forsaking the vibrant jewel tones of the surrounding trees. With the shades drawn, the house felt confining.

Caith moved quickly and methodically, room to room, long accustomed to routine searches. Mail, letters, magazines, photographs, books, drawers, closets, clothing—all were examined. Some thoroughly, some briefly. He wasn't exactly sure what he looked for, but instinct kept him searching. A desk in the bedroom sported a framed photograph of Lew and a young woman with long, pale hair. The resemblance was clear, and Caith guessed the woman was Lew's daughter, Galina. Back issues of the *Coldcreek Herald* were stacked nearby, folded open to Kelly Rice's viperous articles about the lodge. As Caith leafed through, he saw each column circled in red.

Sitting at the desk, he tugged open the top drawer and rummaged through an assortment of old receipts, scratch paper, pencils, pay stubs, and paperclips. At the bottom of the pile he found a single sheet of paper folded neatly in half. Tilting it to the light, he realized it was a background check similar to the one he'd had Connie Clark pull on Lew.

The major difference was this profile had been run on Caithelden Fenwyck Lairen.

* * * *

Caith avoided Veronica and Lew for the remainder of the day. He left Lew's house exactly as he'd found it with the exception of the background profile, which he slipped into his pocket. Later, he visited with Derry and Morgana, taking care to leave before his father arrived in the evening. Worried that Veronica would be at the lodge by herself, he had his mother call and extend an invitation to dinner with the stipulation Veronica spend the night. Backed by Derry, Caith knew she wouldn't refuse.

Satisfied by his mother's assurance Veronica would be there shortly, Caith headed for the nearest hotel hoping to find Dean Bowerman. Like Lew, there was something about the self-professed ghost chaser that didn't ring true. Caith had done a thorough search of the Hummingbird Suite once the lodge closed, but other than the passageway to the basement which he'd discovered earlier, found nothing of note.

From the desk clerk at the Coldcreek Inn, he learned Bowerman was registered as a guest, but was currently out, timing that suited him fine. Caith distracted the young man by knocking a pen off the counter, then angled for a glimpse of the computer screen when the clerk bent to retrieve it. He apologized for his clumsiness, thanked the man, then left through the front door. Jogging to the back of the building, he entered by the rear entrance, located the nearest elevator, and rode it to the fourth floor. Bowerman's room number was 412.

"Room service." Caith knocked on the door. When there was no answer, he did a quick check to make sure no one was in the hallway. Even hotel keycard locks couldn't stand up to the small microcontroller he slipped from his pocket, a tool that read the code embedded in the lock and popped it within seconds. Available for purchase on the Internet, it was a device hotels and security firms had yet to find a safeguard against. He wasn't in the habit of breaking and entering, but knowing a trick or two definitely had its advantage.

Once inside, it didn't take him long to search the room. Bowerman had packed light. Even his clothing was sparse, a few pair of pants, some pullover sweaters, and flannel shirts. He found a digital camera with images of the lodge, lake, and boathouse stored on a memory card. There were even a few shots of the lobby, desecrated with blood and manure that Bowerman had managed to snap before police hustled everyone out. Three yellow legal tablets contained notes about the history of Warren Barrister and speculation about paranormal activity at the lodge. Tucked in the top drawer of the dresser, Caith found an ID badge with Bowerman's picture. The name on the tag read *Dean Porter, Paranormal Register.*

"Damn." The name clicked immediately. Kay Porter had told her brother about the apparition she'd seen. She'd also indicated he was an "expert" when it came to paranormal research. Considering he worked for a paper that regularly fed its audience sensationalistic garbage, Caith would have used the term loosely. A few facts and a lot of embellishment went a long way in selling supermarket tabloids. Irritated, he tossed the badge into the drawer. The last thing BI needed was another yellow journalist snooping around. Deciding to buy some insurance, he removed the memory card from the camera and pocketed it. Back at the front desk, he asked for paper and pen and scribbled Bowerman a note.

"Would you see that Mr. Bowerman gets this?" Caith slipped the note into an envelope, sealed it, and handed it to the desk clerk. "He'll know where to find me."

Three hours later, Caith headed to the Jade Club, arriving well before ten. He found a booth in the back facing the door where he could observe the bar, surrounding tables, and anyone coming or going. The waitress brought a beer, a steak sandwich, and an order of fries at his request, adding to the complimentary basket of pretzels already on the table. Passing over a bottle of ketchup, Caith chose instead to douse the fries with a liberal supply of yellow mustard. Eating with his fingers, he scanned the bar slowly.

Despite the somewhat trendy name, the Jade Club was nothing more than a neighborhood grill. The owners had dressed it up with a lot of brass and hunter green accents. The walls boasted sports memorabilia and candid black-and-white photos of various sporting events from the 1940s, '50s, and '60s. The bar curved in a smooth horseshoe rather than straight angles, and the booths and tables bore black lacquer finish.

Though it was late on a Monday night, the club was fairly busy, most of the tables full, a smattering of patrons at the bar. A hefty man with a ruddy face and crew-cut sat three tables away with a slim brunette. Caith didn't recognize the woman, but thought the man looked vaguely familiar.

Nick Fontaine stepped through the front door and their gazes met. Bursting into a wide grin, he crossed the room in a few quick strides and slid into the seat across from Caith.

"Damn! We didn't bump shoulders much in high school, but I sure as hell keep running into you now. Hey, uh…" Nick's lopsided grin faltered only briefly. "You don't mind if I hang out a while, do you?" Deciding the matter himself, he motioned to the waitress for a beer.

The hint of a smile touched Caith's lips. He'd already finished his dinner, was on his second beer, and it was still twenty minutes to ten. Nick Fontaine wasn't exactly his idea of company, but their rivalry was over twelve years old. It wouldn't hurt to pass the time with someone who had the inside track on Coldcreek, not to mention Kelly Rice.

"You weren't meeting anyone, were you?" Nick asked after the waitress deposited his beer and left.

Caith shook his head. "How about you?"

Nick took a swig from the long-necked bottle. "Dateless these days. I'm not ready to brave the fire. Divorce does that."

Caith leaned back in his seat. Across the way, the hefty man with the ruddy face pounded his fist on the table, talking sharp and rapid to the slim brunette. The woman cringed in her seat, hunching her shoulders and lowering her head.

Domestic abuse. Caith was sure of it. He'd seen enough as a cop to recognize the signs. As part of homicide, he'd also seen the end result when violence erupted in tragedy.

Nick followed his gaze. "Looks like McClure's winding up to a good drunk again. I pity poor Lucy when he gets there."

"McClure?" The name clicked somewhere in Caith's memory. "Lance McClure?"

"Yeah, you remember. Should anyway. He whooped your ass in the ninth grade. Course, he was three times your size. Whooped mine in eighth. These days he just beats on his wife, Lucy."

Caith frowned. Lance McClure had grabbed Veronica during lunch in the cafeteria, shoving his hand under her blouse. With Lance's friends watching and chortling like ogres, Caith had gone crazy, jumping on his back, wrestling him to the floor. Three teachers eventually pulled them apart and they were both suspended. A week later, Lance and his friends caught Caith alone behind the bowling alley. Lance hadn't needed much help in beating him senseless. The most his friends had done was yell encouragement and keep Caith from escaping. Without adrenalin and rage spurring him on, he'd been no match for the bigger boy.

Soured by the memory, Caith took a swallow of beer. He didn't want to think about McClure. "I'm sorry things didn't work out for you and Kelly."

Nick chuckled. "Sounds odd coming from you. Then again, you never were her type. Too brainy and quiet. You know why she went out with you, right?"

Caith kept a straight face. "You mean aside from the fact I'm wealthy and good-looking?"

Nick guffawed. "You ain't so bad, Breckwood."

"Lairen."

"Give it a rest. Nobody buys that shit, including you. I don't know what happened with you and your old man, but I bet you'd still turn cartwheels if he asked."

Caith cleared his throat. His beer was almost empty and the talk was making him dry. He thought about ordering another, but decided he needed his wits about him. A few feet away Lance McClure raised his voice, demanding to know if his wife thought he was an idiot. Tempted to answer for the whole room, Caith returned his attention to Nick.

"Why do you think Kelly has it in for BI?"

Nick shrugged. "Coldcreek ain't exactly heaven if you're not a friend of the Breckwoods." He popped a pretzel in his mouth and washed it down with a swig of beer.

"She wasn't always vindictive."

Nick scrunched his mouth to the side, considering. "She still talks to me even though our marriage went belly up years ago. She hasn't come right out and said it, but I'd bet money she's seeing someone. Or was. I know she took a bunch of weekend trips out of town. Once she even told me she'd met someone rich and powerful who was gonna change her life forever." Nick chuckled sourly. "I get the feeling that didn't work out like she planned."

"Any idea who?"

Nick hesitated. He dragged the silence out by finishing off his beer. Plopping the empty bottle on the table, he leaned forward and batted it back and forth between his hands. "Once when I stopped by her office, I saw a note in her appointment book. She was meeting someone with the initials GB." He cast Caith a wary look. "Your brother Galen goes out of town a lot, too. It might be coincidental, but his marriage was on the rocks long before it went sour. I figure when he didn't marry Kelly, she decided to put the screws to him. She couldn't out-and-out say what he'd done...what she'd done...so she started attacking him through BI and Stone Willow."

Caith let the insinuation wash over him. "You think my brother was having an affair with Kelly?"

Nick shrugged. "How many wealthy, powerful men do you know in Coldcreek with the initials GB?"

Lance McClure chose that moment to spew a loud stream of profanity at his wife. Distracted by the outburst, Caith watched McClure lurch drunkenly to his feet.

"Get up, you stupid whore," McClure snapped.

"Lance, please. Stop it."

Caith heard desperation in Lucy's quiet voice. When she made no move to stand, McClure wrenched her violently to her feet, manhandling her as he'd once manhandled Veronica. Her chair clattered to the floor, turning heads at nearby tables. The man had no concept how to treat women, then or now.

"Bastard," Caith muttered. He sent Nick a tight, darting glance. "Excuse me."

Before he could think it through, he slid from the booth and approached the quarreling couple. He'd dealt with drunks enough to know the situation required a calm, nonthreatening manner. Holding his hands away from his sides, palms open, he spoke in a placating tone. "Take it easy, buddy. What's the problem?"

Lance McClure narrowed his eyes. "Who the hell are you?" He gave a sharp, brutal tug to his wife's arm and she stumbled against him.

Caith caught a glimpse of her face. Her skin was bone-white, her eyes enormous and wet with tears. "Please, Lance," she whispered.

Conversation stopped in the bar as people turned to watch. A few of the men rose to their feet, ready to intervene. "Go home and sleep it off, Lance," the bartender yelled, disgusted.

"That's not bad advice," Caith said.

McClure squinted like an albino pig in the sun. "I know you." He swayed, licking his lips as the memory registered. "I kicked your runty ass good when you were a kid. You're a Breckwood. The brainy one." He belched and dragged the back of one massive hand across his mouth. "You know who that is, Luce?" He shook her shoulder until she staggered a step. "Ah, hell, maybe you don't. He bailed before you got to Coldcreek. I bet you wanna ball him anyway dont'cha, you little whore."

"Let her go, Lance." Caith took another step forward, his voice lower.

The drunk man tottered, dragging Lucy with him. "She's my wife. I'll do whatever the hell I want."

"Don't be stupid. No one has to get hurt." Another step, his hands still in front of him, his voice carrying the same smooth cadence it had from the beginning. "You need to take it easy. Let's sit down and talk about this."

"Screw you. I'm gonna have to kick your ass again." In one violent move, Lance shoved Lucy aside. Bellowing like a madman, he lurched forward, swinging at Caith.

Accustomed to dealing with violent offenders, Caith sidestepped with ease. He caught Lance by the arm, yanking it behind his back. His free hand clamped on Lance's neck like a vise. Thrusting him facedown across the table, he held him pinned in place. "Calm down. No one wants to hurt you."

"Fuckin' ass." McClure roared. "You're gonna pay for this, Breckwood. I swear I'll make you pay."

"I said calm down." Authority cracked in Caith's voice. "You either get it together or I'll have Cameron throw you in jail for attempted assault."

McClure grunted. He twisted sharply, his breath coming raggedly between clenched teeth. Caith increased the pressure on his arm and neck until he stilled. Eventually his breathing evened into a steady flow. Releasing him, Caith took a step backward.

"You best get home, Lance," Nick Fontaine said, appearing at Caith's side.

McClure looked ready to commit murder. He balled his hands into fists, silently looking between the two. With a black glare for his wife, he stalked from the bar.

Timidly, Lucy approached Caith. "Thank you."

"You shouldn't stay with a man like that."

Shamed, she lowered her eyes. "You don't understand."

"You're wrong, I do. I've seen too many situations like yours end in tragedy." He fished a business card from his wallet and passed it to her. "I'm staying at Stone Willow Lodge. If you need help, call me. I know people who can help you out of the situation you're in. There's no excuse for a man who treats his wife like property. You don't have to stay in an abusive relationship."

She smiled sadly, and Caith had the feeling the card would be forgotten the moment she got home. He'd seen the symptoms before. Terror, dominance, and dependency often went hand in hand.

"Thank you for caring." Pushing on tiptoe, Lucy kissed him on the cheek.

Nick gave a low whistle after she'd left. "What the hell kind of fancy move did you pull on Lance? I ain't never seen him handled like that." He laughed, enjoying the memory. "Ho-boy. It ain't every day you see Lance McClure shoved across a table. I'm guessing he's hot enough to piss blood. Probably yours."

Caith slipped his wallet into the back pocket of his jeans. "I only wish I could do more to keep him away from her." Frowning, he glanced at his watch. It was already a few minutes after ten. "I've gotta run, Nick. I'm late for an appointment. Stay out of trouble, huh?"

"Haven't you heard? I'm a saint." Nick sent him a salute as he headed for the door.

Voices and light dwindled behind Caith as he stepped into the darkness. The night air was cold, underscored with the promise of heavy frost. Caith moved from the front parking lot around the building to the rear. An overhead lamp illuminated a single door in a narrow cone of yellow light. Used solely by staff, the lot was unlined, its asphalt surface cracked and patched in numerous places. To the right of the doorway, a Dumpster overflowed with trash. The air smelled of barbequed steaks, fry oil, and sour garbage.

Caith glanced at his watch. Ten-oh-four. He stuffed his hands in his pockets, waiting as cold air scraped across his face. He heard a car pass out front, a dog yap in the distance. Dry leaves scuttled across the parking lot, clustering at the base of the Dumpster. Looking closer, he realized a square of white paper fluttered in the wind, anchored by a large stone.

Crouching, Caith retrieved the single sheet. In the mucous glow of yellow light, typewritten words became visible. The paper contained a single line: *Look closer to home.*

He barely had time to register the thought before heavy footfalls crunched behind him. Caith turned, half rising, unprepared for the sight of a baseball bat angling for his head. He raised his left arm on instinct as he shifted, taking the blow on his shoulder. The impact sent him reeling off balance in a sea of swimming darkness as the asphalt reared up to greet him. Something solid caught the edge of his cheek, splitting skin, igniting rockets in his head.

"I'm gonna make you pay, you fuckin' S-O-B."

Somewhere through the haze in his mind and the nausea waffling up from his gut, Caith recognized Lance McClure's voice. His vision cleared enough for a glimpse of McClure's fury-mottled face looming over him. Before he could roll clear, the bat descended a third time, catching him in the stomach. Caith was sure the world had upended. The food and drinks he'd consumed moments before threatened to spew from his gut. He drew his knees to his chest, shoving an elbow beneath him for leverage.

"Get the hell away from him."

A man's angry voice seemed to come from nowhere and everywhere. Something slammed into McClure, sending him teetering off balance. Recovering slightly, Caith hooked him by the ankle with a foot and spilled him to the ground. The bat clattered against the asphalt and rolled from his fingers.

"Keep your fucking hands off my brother," the newcomer commanded.

Caith blinked, pushing to his knees. Someone grabbed the bat. McClure struggled upward, spittle flying as he spewed vulgarities. The end of the bat popped him squarely in the face and he folded without a sound.

Breathing heavily, Caith looked at his benefactor. Shock coursed through him.

Merlin dropped the bat with a loud clatter. "One of you owes me a drink, and I don't think it's Cyclops here."

Chapter 15

Caith closed his eyes and tilted his head back against the sofa. He wasn't sure what hurt more, his shoulder, his stomach, or his pride. The ice pack Merlin had given him for the gash on his cheek helped mute the sting, but he'd be left with a nasty bruise. It wouldn't be the first time. Just the first in a long time. He was generally too cautious and observant to be taken by surprise.

"How's the arm?" Merlin dropped into an adjacent chair, carrying two open bottles of beer. He slid one across a glass-topped table to Caith. "Sorry I don't have anything stronger. I don't drink hard liquor."

"I always figured you for a wine and champagne man myself." Forcing his protesting body upright, Caith leaned forward with a groan. The label on the beer indicated it was pricey and imported. Dropping the ice pack in his lap, Caith retrieved the bottle, rolling his left shoulder experimentally. "Hurts like hell. I can't believe I let Lance McClure kick my ass again."

Merlin smiled smoothly. "At least you put him in his place first. Nick Fontaine said you threw him across a table."

Caith shifted and grimaced. "It was more like a pin. He was getting loud and mouthy with his wife. I just—"

"Stuck your nose where it doesn't belong." Merlin raised his bottle in a mock toast. "There's a lot of that going around lately." Their eyes met and held, and Merlin grinned.

Exhausted, Caith slumped into the sofa. Designed for looks, it wasn't exactly comfortable, but it felt like heaven after the drive to Merlin's home on the outskirts of town. Vaulted ceilings, an open staircase, and whitewashed hardwood floors reflected his brother's taste for contemporary styling. Sitting in the sunken living room, Caith found himself surrounded by shades of silver, crimson, and black.

"Merlin." Caith eyed the expensive art deco prints on the walls. It felt funny to be talking without sniping, to be conversing easily after so long.

He sent his brother a wary glance. "If I didn't say it before...thanks for helping me out tonight. If you hadn't stuck your nose where it didn't belong, I'd be a lot worse off than I am."

Merlin shrugged. "I like the Jade Club on Monday nights. They run a special on coconut shrimp. You're lucky it was so packed I had to park near the back. Otherwise I wouldn't have heard McClure shooting his mouth off about making someone pay." He took a long swallow of beer. "Besides, even if my mission in life is to piss you off, you're still my brother. No one takes a swing at you when I'm around. Especially not with a baseball bat."

Caith was surprised by the sincerity in his voice, just as he'd been surprised by Merlin's arrival behind the club. In truth, surprise didn't cover it. Shock, utter astonishment, even bewilderment fell short of what he'd felt when he'd spied Merlin standing over McClure, baseball bat in hand. Merlin, who fussed at getting a hair knocked out of place. Merlin who'd made it clear from that first day at Stone Willow, he cared little or nothing for Caith. There were too many years of silence between them, a host of buried and poisonous feelings. How could Merlin toss all of that aside in the matter of a heartbeat?

Because I'm his brother.

Caith frowned. "I keep screwing up, don't I?" The beer was sour in his stomach, the ice pack cold and wet on his legs. Right-handed and awkward, he tossed it on the table. "Aren told me I need to fix my life. I guess part of that includes you."

"Shit. Don't get sentimental, Caith. I'm not in the mood for a trip down memory lane."

"Neither am I, but it's unavoidable." Caith's expression was hard. "You've been at my throat since I came back. Over Veronica, over Trask's death. Then tonight you turn around and help me out of a jam."

With a snort of disbelief, Merlin slumped in his chair. He tipped the beer to his lips. "For as brainy as you are, you can be incredibly stupid, Caithelden."

"What does that mean?"

"It means, you stupid shit, it was never about Veronica and never about Trask's death. I can't believe after all this time, you still haven't figured it out." Irritated, he pushed from the chair. "I should find a fucking bat and finish you off myself."

Frustrated, Caith sat forward. He grimaced at the movement, cupping his right arm across his middle. "I don't know what you're talking about." He watched Merlin pace agitated rings around a grouping of scooped-back chairs. "You've been pissed at me since Trask died. You think it's my fault he got killed."

Merlin came to an abrupt halt, swiveling to face him. "Where did you get a crazy idea like that?"

"From you. You haven't spoken to me for twelve years."

"Why should I? You didn't need me when I was around. Why the hell would you need me when you were gone?"

Caith felt like someone had punched him in the gut. Everything he'd believed and held true for so long shifted out of focus. "I thought..." He swallowed, tried a different approach. "After Trask died, you were different. You kept pulling away. Year after year."

"Because you shut yourself off." Merlin leaned forward, gripping the back of a single chair. "Listen, Caith. I'm only going to say this once, because I'll feel like a damn idiot when I'm done. When we were kids, it was never about the four of us. It was about you and Trask. Veronica and I were there, but you and Trask—" He stopped suddenly, something dark and bitter compressing his mouth into a frown. "It was like he was your brother. Not me. Trask."

Blood thundered in Caith's ears. The knot in his left shoulder sent fire down his arm, and his mouth went dry. His stomach grew hollow as an unimaginable truth struck home. "Merlin." His voice was a hoarse whisper. "Are you saying...you were jealous of Trask?"

"Why would that surprise you? I'm shallow, conceited, self-centered. I'm the one everyone liked, but you're the one everyone wanted to *be* like. Chivalrous, smart, brave. Like one of those fricking knights Mom was always telling us about. Veronica fell in love with you the moment she saw you, and Dad was going to turn BI into a worldwide commodity with you on the team. When we were kids, everyone wanted your approval." He stared hard. "Even me."

Caith didn't know what to say. How could he possibly tell his brother he was none of the things Merlin imagined? He'd gotten Trask killed. He hadn't fought his way free and bravely thrown himself at the man with the knife. Instead he'd let himself be held, his arm pinned to a cold metal table while his captors joked about which finger to cut off. His father, Veronica, Merlin...they'd turned him into some kind of idea, a fabricated character.

"After Trask died, I thought things would be different." Merlin sank into a chair across from Caith. Shoulders slumped, he laced his hands between his knees. "I thought you'd start to rely on me. I thought I'd take Trask's place. Pretty low, huh?" He shot Caith a guarded glance.

"Merlin."

Merlin held up a hand. "You did confide in me for a while. I remember when you told me about the glue. I was proud you'd told me something no one else knew. Pretty sick way for brothers to behave. You were messed up in the head, and I was turning it into a competition with a dead kid. A kid who was my friend. The problem with you, Caith, is you're so fucking controlled you'd rather be miserable than admit you need help. So instead of getting closer, you kept shutting everyone out, trying to deal with things on your own. I got pissed, and then I stopped trying. When you left for college, I promised myself I wasn't going to call. I figured if you needed help, you'd pick up the phone, but you never did." He paused, smiling tightly. "You know what gets me the most? When we were kids, Aren was so much older than us, he was rarely around. Now look at the two of you. It's like you and Trask all over again."

Caith rubbed his temple. He couldn't think. The stillness in the room was suffocating. For twelve years, he'd harbored the misconception that Merlin blamed him for Trask's death. Stunned, he spread his hands. "Merlin, I'm sorry. I never realized." He faltered, too shaken to find the right words.

Merlin arched a brow. "Don't sweat it. I don't know why I was so stuck on being your best bud anyway. You got your ass kicked when you were a kid, and you got your ass kicked tonight. Some tough PI. You can't even take a drunk with a baseball bat."

"Maybe if he'd been a troll with a sword." Caith grinned faintly. "Why fight when you've got a wizard for backup?"

Merlin collected their empties and stood. "I'm glad that's out of the way. How about another round? We've got some catching up to do."

"Sure." Shifting stiffly, Caith dug in his pocket for his cell phone. "Just let me call the house. I want to make sure Veronica and Derry are okay."

By the time Merlin returned with two more beers, Caith had finished the call and was tentatively fingering the gash on his cheek.

"Your son's a good kid." Merlin passed him an open bottle and sprawled in the nearest chair. "Looks just like you. Talkative as hell, though. I took him, Matt, and Noah on a hayride and the kid never shut up. Is he like that all the time?"

Caith chuckled. "Afraid so." He set the beer aside, uneasy again. "Merlin, I need to ask you something. About what I told you…about the glue."

Merlin exhaled and dragged a hand over his face. "I knew you were going to get back to that. Okay, I admit it. I told Galen. I was pissed."

"Galen?" Caith thought back to his conversation with Nick and Nick's references to an affair between Kelly Rice and a man with the initials GB.

"I was pissed at you, and pissed at Galen and Aren for hiring you. So when Galen got back, I cornered him in his office and read him the riot act. If Aren had been there I would have done the same to him. I didn't mean to tell Galen about the glue. It sort of slipped out in the heat of the moment."

"How?"

Merlin shrugged. "I said something about you being unable to do a quality job when you freak and puke your guts over the tiniest whiff of model glue." He cleared his throat, looking shamefaced. "I didn't mean to tell him, Caith. I'm the one who called and ratted you out to Dad, too."

Caith barely heard, his thoughts racing. Galen had sent Aren to the Breckwood home to pick up BI documents, knowing he'd see Caith first. Had his brother figured Aren could talk him into going to the house? Once there, it was natural he'd visit his bedroom, almost guaranteeing he'd stumble over the glue in the nightstand. And the night of the hayride, Galen was the only one Caith hadn't seen. Was it possible he'd slipped through the shadows, dumping glue when Caith had been distracted with Nick?

He gnawed on his bottom lip. Why? To unsettle him? To distract him from what was happening at Stone Willow?

"There's no way Galen had anything to do with that glue in your bedroom, so if that's where you're headed, forget it." Merlin stretched, propping his feet on the glass-topped table. "The whole thing stinks if you ask me. We should have sold the lodge when we had the chance."

"Sold the lodge?" Caith looked at him blankly, momentarily forgetting Galen. "Are you telling me someone made BI an offer on Stone Willow?"

"Sure." He nodded to Caith's beer, sitting untouched on the table. "You're not drinking. Part of making peace with the past involves getting plastered together."

"Merlin." Caith leaned forward. "Who made the offer on the lodge? When did it happen?"

"I don't know. Before all the garbage started."

"A date," Caith snapped. "I need a date."

"I didn't pay much attention. No one was interested in selling, so we shelved the offer. Not long after that, the problems started."

"Why doesn't that surprise me?" Caith pinched the bridge of his nose. "I can't believe no one thought it important to tell me."

Merlin sprawled in the chair, flinging a leg over the arm. "Turn off the investigator, Caithelden. Whatever's going on in that analytical brain of yours can wait until tomorrow. You owe me. Tonight is about catching up on what we missed."

Caith hesitated. His mind was in overdrive, sorting details. Galen, Lew, Dean Bowerman. They were all connected somehow. He had the feeling it came down to the offer Merlin didn't want to discuss. As much as he wanted to pick at the puzzle and examine it from every angle, Merlin was right. He did owe his brother. Not only for tonight, but for the last twelve years and before.

"Okay." He picked up his beer. "Why don't we start with Veronica and how you feel about her?"

* * * *

Veronica returned to the lodge in the morning, stepping through the front door shortly after eight. Bare of furniture and rugs, the lobby felt vast, somehow intimidating. Ash greeted her, rubbing against her legs, insisting on breakfast. He left small wisps of gray hair clinging to her ankle-length, saddle-brown skirt as he trailed her down the hallway. Once inside, surrounded by familiar possessions, her uneasiness vanished. Later that afternoon, she was scheduled to meet with three furniture vendors to select new items for the lobby. The fate of Stone Willow remained undecided, but BI was moving ahead with refurbishing. Furniture, rugs, decorative accents, and potted plants would go a long way in making the empty space feel inviting, less eerie.

With Ash taken care of, she dug coffee out of the cupboards. As she turned on the faucet to fill the coffee pot, her mind wandered. She'd heard about Caith's run-in with Lance McClure. Most of the town already knew about it. News traveled fast in Coldcreek, especially when it concerned the Breckwoods.

She grimaced.

Lance was bad news. He was one of the few people who could make her skin crawl with a single leering glance. She supposed it went back to that incident in ninth grade when he and his friends had cornered her in the cafeteria. "Veronica?"

She jerked unexpectedly, dropping the coffee pot in the sink. "Caith. Where did you come from?"

As if realizing he'd startled her, Caith jabbed a thumb over his shoulder. "Your door was open."

"So you just waltzed in?" Her voice came out harsher than expected. Drawing a breath, she collected her scattered nerves. He looked disheveled, like he hadn't slept. There was a cut on his cheek, overlaid by an angry bruise more purple than black. She winced. "Look at what Lance did to your face."

"So you heard? It doesn't surprise me. I'm sure the whole town knows by now."

Veronica bit her lip. Turning back to the sink, she filled the coffee pot and set it on the burner. "I hope he looks worse."

Caith chuckled. "Sorry to disappoint you. He got the better of me."

Still gnawing on her lip, she looked at him worriedly. "Are you...are you feeling all right? You look tired, Caith."

"That's Merlin's fault." Moving closer, he leaned against the counter, facing her. "He bailed me out of the jam with McClure, then kept me up talking all night. We had twelve years of catching up to do."

Veronica grinned. Her wizard had turned into a white knight. Suddenly, her anger seemed childish considering Merlin and Caith had put twelve years of differences behind them. Her two childhood friends were acting like brothers again. "I'm happy to hear that." She couldn't mask the enthusiasm in her voice.

Caith reached forward, tentatively stroking her arm. "Does that mean I can kiss you?"

Her smile faltered. He was already under her skin. Before she could gather her wits to reply, he tugged her forward, gently pressing his mouth to hers. Her lips opened instinctively, inviting greater intimacy.

He kissed her slowly, thoroughly, his hand rising to cup her neck. She wanted to melt, to surrender to the heat and possessive warmth rolling from his body. The touch of his lips was deliberate, as if he sought to mark her as his own with every slow, seductive movement of his mouth.

When the kiss ended, she leaned against him, wrapping her arms around his neck. "I missed you." The truth brought a tight knot to her belly. If she missed him so dreadfully after a single day apart, how would she cope when he returned to Boston? When he finally told her *it's been nice, keep in touch, maybe we'll do lunch some day?*

Caith stroked a hand down her back, pressing his lips to her hair. "Derry said you read him a story last night."

She tightened her hold on his neck. Maybe if she never let go, he'd stay with her forever. Maybe, like the fairytales of her childhood, she'd find happily-ever-after. "He wanted to hear something you liked, so I went through the old books in your room. We started reading Robin Hood together." She raised her head to look at him. "He wants the three of us to have dinner tonight. Alone."

"He told me." He tipped her lips up to his and kissed her again. "My kid's playing matchmaker, Ron. You know that, don't you?"

She looked into his eyes, trying to decipher what she saw there, but he'd had too much practice at masking his emotions.

"What are you going to do about it?"

"Nothing." His mouth slanted over hers, sealing them together, and his kiss took her breath away.

* * * *

Veronica grew increasingly uneasy as she read the report on Lew. She thought she knew him, but the information Caith had unearthed related to a stranger. Worse, Lew had dug into Caith's background, running his own check for reasons she couldn't fathom.

"How could he obtain this?" Veronica asked, returning both profiles to Caith. They'd retreated to her living room where they sat side by side on the sofa, half empty cups of coffee and Caith's notes spread on a low rectangular table. Ash sprawled a few feet away in a bright patch of sunlight, blinking half-slit eyes, swiveling an occasional ear in their direction when some stray sound caught his attention.

Caith tossed the profiles on the table with the rest of the information. "Same as me. He has contacts, which isn't surprising given what he used to do for a living."

"I don't know what to say, Caith." He'd been right, and she'd treated him unfairly. "I shouldn't have been so defensive. You know your job better than I do. It's just that Lew..." She trailed off, unable to finish.

Caith squeezed her hand. "This doesn't make him guilty, Ron."

"But it looks bad." She brought her coffee cup to her lips, looking at the other papers on the table. "What about these?" She motioned to the two typewritten notes Caith had received from an unidentified source. "Who's leaving them, and what does this one mean? 'Look closer to home?'"

"I'm not sure. I've got some ideas, but nothing concrete. It could even be someone's idea of a joke. It's no secret who I am or what I'm doing in Coldcreek." He paused and switched tracks. "Merlin said someone offered to buy the lodge a while back."

Veronica nodded. "Another corporation. I think they wanted to use it for the same type of retreat we have, but limit it to their employees."

"Do you remember who it was?"

She thought a moment. "Galen took the offer. It was done verbally. He said the representative was testing the water to see if we'd be interested in a formal agreement. When BI declined, it didn't go much further. There was a secondary, higher offer, but that was declined, too. As I recall, your father made it clear he wasn't interested in selling at any price. Stone Willow's always been a Breckwood family project to him." Her brows drew together as she tried to remember details. "I think the name of the firm was Galicorp." She looked puzzled. "But I can't tell you anything about them or where they're based. I don't remember ever having anyone stay here, but if you need to know I could go back in the records."

"That would help. As for Lew and Bowerman, let's keep that information to ourselves for now."

Veronica grew uneasy. "I'm not sure I'll know how to act around Lew the next time I see him. If he's involved—"

"You'll act like you always do." Caith grinned crookedly. "Haughty and annoying."

Even though she knew he was teasing, Veronica frowned. She set her coffee aside. "Caithelden."

Still grinning, he hooked his arm around her shoulders and dipped her onto the couch beneath him. "Have I ever told you what an incredibly sexy way you have of saying my name?" He found the pulse point in her throat and pressed his lips to the chaotic dance.

It immediately escalated, thrumming up three notches. It was nine o'clock in the morning and she had insurance claims to file, furniture layouts to ponder. "Caithelden." She placed her hands on his shoulders, but didn't make a strong effort to push him away.

"There you go again," he murmured, moving his lips from her jaw to her ear. "All firm and disapproving. *Caithelden.*" He kissed her cheek, then found the corner of her mouth. "It makes me want to take you back in the bedroom." He grinned against her lips. "Or maybe just take you right here."

She laughed. "Stop it. I have work to do."

"So do I, but it can wait. I should probably warn you, I have every intention of making love to you right now." He kissed her softly, then trailed a finger to the hollow of her throat. "I can't keep my hands off you."

She didn't want him to. Not when he said things like that. Not when he kissed her so passionately, it left her head spinning, her body tingling in anticipation of his touch. Gently, she touched the bruise on his cheek, tracing the patch of discolored skin. "I should warn you, I have every intention of letting you."

* * * *

Later, twined together on the couch, both sated, their clothing scattered on the floor, Veronica's gaze strayed to the bruise below Caith's ribs. Tenderly, she traced her finger over the red-purple patch. "Is it sore?"

Caith shifted slightly, sliding his leg across her hips, trapping her beneath him. "Just stiff. My shoulder, too." He snared her fingers with his own. "I see Lance McClure is still the resident bully. What does he do these days aside from picking fights with his wife?"

"He has a welding shop. He took over the old rendering plant on the south side of town." Veronica turned as much as their positions allowed. Pushing on one elbow, she studied his face. "He isn't only mean, he's wacky, too. And in case you haven't figured it out, he hates the Breckwoods."

Caith smirked. "So between Lance and Kelly Rice, we have a regular fan club." He kissed her temple and disentangled himself. "As much as I don't want to, I should probably get dressed. You, too. I'm expecting a visitor."

Surprised, Veronica sat straighter. "Who?"

"A journalist." Caith grinned, the dazzling, heart-stopping smile she liked best. "I thought we should have a snoop on our side."

Chapter 16

Veronica was at the front desk looking over furniture layouts when Dean Bowerman barreled into the lobby. BI's design department had suggested a number of possible changes from the previous decor, still rustic and keeping with Stone Willow's remote location, but less somber than the heavy earth tones.

It was shortly after eleven in the morning, sunny and bright. Even the empty lobby felt inviting as the sun angled higher into the sky, streaming through towering windows, splattering the bare floors with patches of marigold light. Ash sprawled in the center of one sun-brightened square, soaking up heat, totally oblivious when Bowerman stormed up to the reception desk.

"Where's Breckwood?" he demanded.

Veronica kept her gaze unflustered and cool. "Which one?"

Before Bowerman could spit a reply, Caith appeared on the stairway. With a casual glance for his watch, he strolled down the steps. "You're late."

"You're lucky I'm here at all." Impatiently, Bowerman held out his hand, his expression flat. "I want the memory card you took from my camera."

Caith shrugged. He passed Bowerman a small object. "I wiped it clean."

Bowerman's face underwent a transformation that might have been comical under other circumstances. "You had no right."

"I had every right. You were here under false pretenses."

"Same as you."

"I was hired by the company that owns this lodge. But you..." Caith held out his hand and Veronica passed him a piece of paper. Looking over Bowerman's registration, he read from the sheet. "Claim to be a marketing manager with Farzfold Corporation. Isn't that where your sister works,

Mr. Porter? I wonder how the Farzfold board would feel about a tabloid reporter using their corporation for cover? Could cost your sister her job if they made the connection."

Unable to speak, Bowerman spluttered noisily.

Caith folded the registration and passed it back to Veronica. "I don't want to see BI or Stone Willow in the *Paranormal Register*," he said, "or any other paper for that matter. You're on private property. Being here under false pretenses makes you a trespasser. That alone gives BI the right to file a suit."

Bowerman squared his shoulders. "Are you threatening me?"

"You'd know if I was." Caith smiled tightly. "But I'd rather push all of this under the rug and have you on my side. I could use a good snoop."

"What does that mean?" Bowerman narrowed his eyes suspiciously.

"It means there's nothing paranormal going on here. It's a simple case of someone wanting what they can't have. That's a better story than the one you were angling for, and a lot more credible in news journalism."

Bowerman appeared to consider. He glanced between Veronica and Caith as if weighing the options. In her opinion, he had very little wiggle room.

It didn't take him long to realize the same. "I'm listening."

"Good." Caith sounded like he'd expected no less. "You help me out, check what I need looked into, and if I'm right—if the whole thing's a hoax—BI gives you an exclusive. But it doesn't end up in the *Paranormal Register*, agreed?"

"What if you're wrong? What if there really is something paranormal taking place?"

Caith flashed a tight grin. "Then you can call me a narrow-minded idiot in print, but BI and Stone Willow stay out of the *Register*. If I'm wrong, and there is something paranormal, you find yourself a credible science journal, and we'll talk possibilities. Fair enough?" Caith extended his hand.

Bowerman's grin was on the slippery side, but he gave a firm nod. "Deal."

"Perfect." Caith shook his hand. "This is what I want you to do...."

* * * *

Veronica watched Derry dig into his bowl of chocolate ice cream. He'd eaten most of his dinner, a hamburger and french fries, dousing the fries with an ample glob of yellow mustard instead of ketchup. Recognizing it as one of Caith's peculiar quirks, she found it comical to see Derry mimic the habit with no thought for its oddness. At five-thirty in the evening,

Bristlecone Tavern was only partially full, the perfect place for their dinner together. She'd already fallen in love with Derry, who made that deep affection so easy.

Not for the first time, she wondered what his mother had been like. Had she possessed the same outgoing, effervescent personality as her son? Derry certainly hadn't inherited his chatty openness from his father. What an odd pair Caith and his college sweetheart must have been.

Troubled by the thought, she glanced at her hands.

"What's wrong?" Caith sensed the shift in her mood.

"Nothing." From the corner of her eye, Veronica caught Derry watching her. She flashed a smile. "We should do this again sometime. Just the three of us."

"Yeah." Grinning, Derry dug into the ice cream. "It's fun."

Caith reached across the table, covering her hand with his. "I could get used to it. The three of us together."

Her heart thrummed a little faster, spurred by the underlying meaning in his words. Had she read too much into the simple statement? At her side, Derry grinned ear-to-ear, watching as Caith brought her fingers to his lips. "I'd like to show you Boston sometime. Maybe you'd like it there."

Her throat was tight. "Maybe I would." The waitress arrived with their check and he released her. Dry-mouthed, she watched as he searched his wallet for his credit card.

"Dad?"

"Yeah, partner?"

"I like Coldcreek better than home."

Caith pulled the card from his wallet. Surprised, he looked at Veronica, then at his son. "Well...that's good Derry, but I have a job at home. And you have friends. There's the house and—"

"But we could have all of that here," Derry objected. "And you could get a job with BI. Grandpa would give you one anytime you wanted."

"Oh, dear." Veronica couldn't halt her muttered dismay. Forcing a staged smile, she tried to overlook how still Caith had become. "You know, Derry, I think I'd like a taste of that ice cream." Picking up her spoon, she dipped it in the mound of melting chocolate. "Mmm." Her stomach felt abruptly tight and queasy, but she made a face that said the ice cream was pure heaven.

Derry laughed. "You didn't even get any of the chocolate sauce."

"Okay, where's that?" She dipped her spoon again, forcing him to focus on what she was doing.

"Excuse me." Caith collected the bill and stood. "I'm going to take care of this."

Veronica nodded, still talking to Derry. "I like the whipped cream best."

Derry watched his father leave. Veronica's heart went out to him as his eyes tracked Caith's every movement across the room. "I upset Dad, huh? I shouldn't have said that thing about Grandpa."

Veronica dragged her spoon through the sauce. "Your Dad's just a little touchy about your grandfather, Derry."

"I know." He sounded depressed. "Why can't they make up? I want to have a family like Matt and Noah with grandparents, and—and…" He looked at her awkwardly, then blurted the words in a rush. "I want to stay here. I want you, Dad, and me to be a family. I want you to be my mom, Ron."

Her spoon clattered to the table.

Looking sullen, Derry slouched in his seat. "Great. Now I said something else I shouldn't have. Dad's gonna be mad if I upset you."

"No!" She didn't know what to say. She wanted to laugh, cry, to marvel at the amazing thing that had just happened. "Derry…"A prickle of tears stung her eyes. Laughing, she hugged him close. "You're incredible, you know that? So incredible, I love you." She kissed the top of his head. Most eight-year-old boys would have fussed over the public spectacle, but Derry didn't have a mother and she imagined that made everything different.

The moodiness went out of his posture immediately. Beaming, he hugged her back.

"Hey. What's going on?" Caith slid into his seat.

Still smiling, Veronica brushed a finger beneath her eyelashes. She drew back, shaking her head. "Nothing. Did you pay the bill?"

"Yeah." Caith looked at his son who had his head lowered, a silly expression on his face. He picked up his spoon and dug into Derry's ice cream. "Well, if you two aren't going to eat this."

"Hey!" Derry sprang to life, suddenly animated.

Caith laughed.

Veronica watched as they finished the ice cream together. Caith stole only three bites, but made a game of each swipe. Derry glowed, the awkwardness of a moment ago already past. Wouldn't it be wonderful if they became a family someday? Her husband and her son. To say those words aloud and know they were true.

It would be like myth.

And magic.

* * * *

Caith stood in the doorway of the family room watching as Veronica and Derry told Morgana about their dinner at Bristlecone Tavern. A few minutes earlier his father had excused himself to take a call in his study. Deciding he needed more information about the offer from Galicorp, Caith roamed down the hall.

He felt edgy, crowded by memories. As a kid, he'd often gone to his father's study, perching on the edge of the wide window seat, swinging his legs as he talked with his dad. Not like Derry talked to him. Not endless ramblings about anything and everything, but only what mattered most. He'd talked about Veronica, Merlin, and Trask. About some accomplishment he'd been particularly proud of in school, or the latest test he'd aced. He'd routinely passed tests with ease and knew his father was proud of that. Once, when he was twelve, Caith had flunked a test just to see what it felt like. His teacher had phoned his parents upset, and his parents had grounded him for a week when they'd found out what he'd done. Even then his father had used words like Harvard and Yale. He'd wanted to put Caith in a private school, an accelerated school, but his mother wouldn't hear of it.

"Let him grow up with kids his own age," she'd said. "He's already younger than most of the kids in his class. It's why he's in the same grade as Merlin. Let him enjoy that. There's time enough for pressure later."

And because his father doted on his mother, Morgana had won. Still, Caith knew how much it pleased his father when he scored an A+ on a particularly hard test, so he always stopped by his dad's study to show him the results. His father would beam ear-to-ear, tell him how proud he was, and how they were going to accomplish great things together at BI one day.

And then Trask died and the world changed.

His father promised to be there in that horrible, harsh new world. Not just for a while until the bumps and pain passed, but forever.

"Shit." Caith dragged a hand over his face. Now wasn't the time to dredge up bitter memories. He needed to separate the past and his profession. Drawing a breath, he knocked on the door.

"Come in," his father called.

His dad had finished his phone conversation, and glanced up as Caith entered the room, surprise flickering through his eyes. Standing behind a massive mahogany desk, surrounded by towering bookshelves and soaring windows with diamond-paned glass, he looked every inch a wealthy and intimidating man.

The room was much as Caith remembered, furnished in deep shades of hunter green and rich crimson. A masculine room with leather chairs and gleaming woodwork, it contained row upon row of books stamped in gold leaf, a massive, antique globe that opened into a bar, and a couch that had once smelled sweetly of pipe tobacco. Had his father maintained his smoking habit, or given it up in favor of the health consciousness that generally comes with age? As a child, Caith had been reminded of Sherlock Holmes whenever he'd seen his father with his pipe.

The hint of a smile touched his lips, but quickly vanished. He hadn't understood the world's preoccupation with Sherlock Holmes until after Trask died. Until the analytical side of his mind made him hunt down detective fiction followed by casebook studies of actual crimes. Reference books, police procedurals, criminal investigations, even psychological examinations of convicted criminals became every day reading. His mother had worried when she saw his interest morphing into homicides, assault, and autopsies. He'd kept notebooks, writing down everything he'd learned, secreting them away for fear of upsetting his parents.

They'd never understood. At thirteen it had all looked so simple. He'd wanted to make the world a safer place.

He snorted quietly, stepping into the room. *What a stupid ass.*

"Got a minute?"

His father looked wary, but motioned him to a chair.

Caith chose to hover near the window, tracing his finger over the edge of the padded seat. The leather was soft and buttery, deep green like feral forests and dense woods. He cleared his throat uncomfortably. "Merlin told me there was a verbal offer to buy Stone Willow before all the problems at the lodge started."

"A coincidence." His father waved a hand in dismissal. "I asked Duke Cameron about it after the first incident, and he said it wasn't related."

"How does he know? Did he check into it?"

"He didn't seem to think it worth the effort." Easing into his chair, his dad inched closer to the desk. "It's a waste of time, Caith. I'd rather pay you for answers." He flipped open a ledger. "Assuming you can find any."

Caith tensed. Something dark and angry surged through him. With effort he tamped it down, spitting out words. "So, if I told you BI was showing a loss but not to worry, numbers would bounce back next quarter, you wouldn't look into it?"

His father eyed him mistrustfully. "What does that mean?"

"It means," Caith exploded, "that I wouldn't tell you how to run your company. Don't tell me how to do my freaking job."

"Enough!" Surging to his feet, his father stalked around the desk. "I knew hiring you was a mistake the moment I found out. I should have fired you when I had the chance."

Caith's gaze was stony. "Don't go soft on me now."

"Don't tempt me, Caithelden."

"Why not? You'd rather listen to Duke than anything I have to say. Shit, Dad. You've known him all his life. You know what he's like. He's shortsighted and lazy. He probably paid somebody to get where he is."

"Caith."

"All right." Caith held up both hands. He took a step backward, attempting to rein in his anger. "All I'm saying is you shouldn't rule out a connection between the offer and what's been happening. There's no reason we can't discuss this rationally."

"Agreed." His father paced to the globe and cracked it open, revealing a decanter with dark-colored liquid and a number of cut crystal glasses. "Fruit juice," he explained, indicating the arrangement. "I had the bar revamped with a built-in coolant system." Pouring a small glass, he turned to Caith who declined the offer with a shake of his head.

His father chuckled. "Can't say as I blame you. It's your mother's idea. She made me give up most of my vices when I had problems with my heart. Bourbon was the first to go."

Caith stared. "I…I didn't know you had problems." He felt abruptly uneasy.

His father rolled his shoulders, dismissing the reference. "Nothing serious. The doctor tells me I'm fit as a fiddle now. Probably all that clean living your mother makes me do." Walking to his desk, he tipped the chair back, reclining comfortably. "Don't hover, Caith. It bothers me."

Instinctively, Caith slid into the window seat, his perch from childhood. It felt natural, too familiar. Inwardly, he grimaced. To move now would only draw attention to his discomfort. "What do you know about the offer from Galicorp?"

His dad thought a moment. "It was substantial, more than generous given Stone Willow has never been extremely profitable."

"And that didn't strike you as odd?"

"It's not the first offer we've had, even if it was on the high side." His father sipped his fruit juice, considering. "Over the years we've had everything from historians and scientific groups, to private industry. Even a few Mom and Pop teams who wanted to turn the place into a quirky bed and breakfast and play off the Barrister legend. You know…ghost-related stuff. We get offers as a matter of routine. It's why Duke wrote Galicorp's inquiry off as inconsequential."

"But you said it was substantial."

His father nodded.

"Veronica told me Galicorp countered with a higher offer when you declined the original."

"That's right, but we declined that, too."

"Weren't you interested in the corporation? Curious who might be offering that much money for a mediocre retreat?"

His dad shook his head. "I left matters with Galen."

"Was he in favor of selling?"

"More than the rest of us. Galen's never been particularly fond of Stone Willow. He gave his son a name from mythology to make your mother happy, but he's as grounded as they come. The lake, Warren Barrister… He'd rather sell the place than deal with the curiosity it causes."

Caith considered that for a moment. "About Galicorp? You said Galen was in favor of selling. Was it because he wanted to unload the lodge, or did he have a personal interest?"

"Personal?" His father scowled. Sitting forward, he spread his elbows on the desk. "Listen, Caith. I didn't say he was in favor of selling. I said he favored it more than the rest of us. Galicorp is local, out of Pittsburgh. Galen liked that idea. Our profit margin would have been sizeable. As CEO, why wouldn't he advise us to sell?"

Standing, Caith stuffed his hands in his pockets and began to pace. Pittsburgh. Why did that bother him? "I understand Galen goes out of town a lot. Does he visit Pittsburgh?"

His father exhaled, growing frustrated. "I don't track his schedule. He's a grown man. He's my right arm. What the hell does it matter?"

Caith paused. The more he pieced it together, the more it felt wrong. What did Galen stand to gain if his family sold the lodge? He frowned. "Mind if I use the computer downstairs?"

"Help yourself." His father took a swallow of fruit juice and chuckled. "We've got state-of-the-art everything thanks to Balin. That kid's a real whiz when it comes to electronic gadgetry. Too bad he doesn't want to work for BI."

Caith was halfway to the door when he stopped and turned. "Huh?"

"You know how it is with kids today." His dad spread his hands, explaining. "Straight business is boring. He's already got his heart set on some school out west that teaches all of that blue-screen and CGI stuff. I don't understand any of it. The kid wants to make movies in Hollywood."

Caith hedged, digesting the information. Should he be concerned his nephew had more than a passing acquaintance with effects technology? Balin was part of the drama club, and the drama club had access to Aren's phosphorescent body paint. Would Galen have the same access through Balin?

When he remained silent too long, his father frowned. "What's wrong?"

"Nothing." Straightening, Caith drew a breath. "Do you mind if Derry and Veronica spend the night? I'll probably be hours on the computer."

"They're both welcome." His father hesitated, then cleared his throat awkwardly. He shuffled some papers on his desk. "So are you."

The muttered words made Caith wonder if he'd heard them.

"Thanks," he mumbled in return, unsure if his gratitude was for the use of the computer or a welcome twelve years overdue.

* * * *

Caith spent most of the night closeted in the downstairs den, trying to gather what information he could on Galicorp. He scoured several online databases including the Pittsburgh Chamber of Commerce, prominent business journals, newspapers, and community associations. He looked into business suits, civil suits, and clerk records. Checked deed registrations, fictitious name applications, and tax records. Later, he ransacked his father's personal office for everything he could find on Stone Willow, taking files, account ledgers, budget printouts, and copies of general correspondence to the computer room.

Around two in the morning, he checked on Derry to make sure he was sleeping soundly, then headed for the kitchen where he brewed a pot of strong black coffee. At three, he placed a phone call to an information broker he frequently used, dragging his disgruntled contact from bed. By three-thirty, he had expanded his search to include details on Lew Walden. At five-eighteen, he fell asleep hunched over the desk, a cold cup of coffee forgotten at his elbow, notes and papers scattered haphazardly on the desk and floor.

"Dad." Someone shook him, tugging on his arm. "Dad, wake up. I'm gonna be late for school."

Caith cracked an eye, forced the other open. The first thing he became aware of was a piece of paper stuck to his cheek where it rested on the desk. The second was Derrick's bright-eyed stare.

His son's face split with a sloppy smile. "See, Grandpa, I told you he'd wake up."

Caith groaned and forced himself upright. His body felt stiff, protesting with aches and pains below his ribs and around the shoulder where Lance McClure had battered him. He dragged a hand over his face, focusing on the eager expression of his son. "What time is it?"

"Seven forty-five." His dad hovered behind Derrick, his gaze sharp and critical. "Have you been here all night?"

Caith nodded. Even if he left now, he'd never have Derrick to school by eight o'clock. "Why didn't somebody wake me earlier?"

Derrick grinned. "Ron left early 'cause she's meeting Uncle Aren at BI, and Grandma decided to go with her."

"We thought you were up already," his father said. "In the shower." He glanced at his watch. "I have to be at BI at eight-thirty. I can drop Derry at school. He'll be a little late, but—"

"He's my responsibility." Still functioning in low gear, Caith shoved from the chair. He looked around at the papers scattered over the desk and on the floor. Bits and pieces of information he'd printed the previous night mingled with his own hastily scribbled notes of conjecture. Bending, he scooped a handful off the floor, stacking them in a messy, lopsided pile on the desk. Derrick's innocent statement nipped at his sleep-deprived mind. What the hell was Ron meeting Aren about? And with his mother?

"Too bad Balin didn't wake you when he was in here."

"Balin?" Caith sent his father a blank look.

"He keeps some books here. All that CGI stuff. He stopped to pick one up on the way to school. He's the one who told us you were asleep." He frowned as he noticed the files and records taken from his office. "I'd rather you asked for that information." A curt nod indicated a stack of ledgers and folders on the corner of the desk. "My private office is private."

Caith dragged a hand through his hair. He needed a shower, a change of clothes, and two pots of coffee to feel whole again. "I didn't want to wake you."

"Didn't want, or didn't feel like it?"

Irritated, Caith glanced to the side. "What does that mean?"

"It means you've always done what you wanted, the world be damned. Why should now be any different?"

Caith sighed. His body hurt, his mind was sluggish, and his mouth felt like sandpaper. Now wasn't the time to argue. Especially with Derrick standing three feet away, his eyes owlishly round as he looked between them.

"I'm not gonna do this in front of my kid," he said bluntly. "You want to argue, save it for when we're alone. I'll give you first shot." Pushing past his father, he caught Derrick's hand. "Come on. You're going to be late for school."

* * * *

Caith strolled into the lobby of the Coldcreek Inn, intent on finding Dean Porter. He'd managed to get Derrick to school by 8:10, which made him only fifteen minutes late for his meeting with Porter. He hadn't taken the time to shower or change, but a cup of coffee and a donut from the local bakery had made him feel marginally human. He'd eaten the donut in the Explorer with the coffee wedged into a cup-caddy between the seats. Unfortunately, he'd spilled half of it taking a sharp turn, sloshing it over his jeans. Even now he could smell stale coffee and wet denim as he entered the lobby.

A display of bright orange pumpkins, cornstalks, and hay bales greeted him inside the door. Fanciful spider webs dangled from the ceiling, and the desk clerk was dressed in full vampire regalia, complete with fangs.

Today was Halloween, the seventeenth anniversary of Trask's death. Seventeen years of thinking he should have done something differently, should have intervened. Seventeen years of wondering what it might have been like to grow up together, to attend the same college. Would Trask be married? Would he have kids? Bitterly, he shoved the thoughts aside and strolled toward the motel's tiny onsite restaurant.

Porter was seated at a table near the front, eating a fruit cup. Judging by an empty plate nearby, he'd already finished breakfast. "Nice of you to show up," he said sarcastically as Caith grabbed a chair and spun it around, straddling it backward. "I've got better things to do than wait on you."

Caith was in no mood and cut bluntly to the point. "I got tied up. What did you find out?"

Porter set his fork aside, leaving most of the fruit untouched. He motioned the waitress for more coffee. "You were right about Kelly Rice having an ongoing love affair with power and prestige. As soon as she learned who I worked for, she couldn't wait to rub my nose in the fact she was moving up the journalistic ladder and I was stuck at a tabloid."

Caith frowned. "Moving up where?"

The waitress arrived, refilling Dean's cup. Caith shook his head to indicate he didn't care for any and she moved away.

"She wouldn't say, but hinted she had an 'in' with Roth-Deckman, and was waiting for her connection to pay off. She bought the ploy I was looking for dirt on Stone Willow. Once she thought I was in her corner, the rest was easy."

Caith's brows drew together. He'd focused on the first half of Porter's explanation. "The media giant," he muttered, referring to Roth-Deckman.

"That's the one. At last tally, its holdings included a major TV network, a movie-production company, two book publishers, and a portfolio of high-circulation newspapers. Pretty much a journalistic dream. I know writers who'd sell their souls to get their foot in the door, let alone secure a cushy position like the one she hinted she has waiting."

Caith rubbed his temple. "GB. It makes sense now."

Porter sipped his coffee. "What does?"

"Never mind." Caith stood. "Doesn't look like you're going to get your paranormal story when this is done, but I've got something better for you. Hang around, and I'll get more than your foot in the door with Roth-Deckman."

* * * *

Veronica struggled to suppress a giggle as she eyed the Halloween costume. She'd been a fool to let Merlin, Aren, and Morgana talk her into this. "Aren, you've lost your mind. You are never going to get Caith to wear that."

Morgana fingered the trailing end of the black cape. "I don't know. I think it's dashing. A highwayman." Her eyes danced as she looked at Veronica. "It could be very romantic, my dear."

Veronica bit her lip. Caith in black pants, boots, a sleeveless black tunic belted over a white poet's shirt, and a swirling black cape. It was the stuff of fantasy. Aren had even tracked down authentic-looking extras— an eighteenth century straight sword, black gauntlets, a plumed hat, and a black scarf to double as a face mask. Just the thought of Caith in knee-high boots with the cape swirling behind him made her unsure if she wanted to swoon or laugh. She settled for dropping into the nearest chair with a heavy thud. "Caith hates Halloween."

Morgana waved a hand, shooing aside the statement. "This is for Derry. And when trick-or-treating is over, there's our yearly costume party. We've been tiptoeing around Caith since he got here, but he's coming, and he's coming in costume. If I have to box his ears and drag him, he's going to make this a family Halloween. For once in his life, he's not going to shut himself off in a room and sulk about Trask."

"With a bottle of Grand Marnier for company," Aren muttered.

Morgana continued as though she hadn't heard. "Don't you see how perfect it is, Veronica? He loved adventure when he was a child, and this costume even has a sword."

Caith with a sword. Caith in boots and a cape. She couldn't stand it any longer. Veronica clapped both hands to her mouth, giggling. "You're going to tell me I have to go as a troll, aren't you?"

Aren laughed out loud. "Wouldn't think of it. But just so you know, Merlin helped me pick these costumes. When Caith starts swearing a blue streak, I'm bowing out the back door and turning him loose on Merlin. As for you, milady..."Aren wiggled his eyebrows. He disappeared into an adjoining room, leaving the door yawning behind him. Within seconds he was back, a garment bag slung over his arm.

"For her ladyship." Aren performed a showy bow. He hooked the bag onto the same portable rack that held Caith's costume.

Veronica exchanged a glance with Morgana.

"Well," the older woman coaxed. "Don't sit there looking befuddled. Open it!"

Veronica drew the zipper down, feeling her breath catch as the gown slipped free. With Aren's assistance, she pulled the dress from the bag, hooking it onto the rack and stepping back to admire its lines. Soft and feminine, it flowed to the floor in shimmering folds of rose-colored satin. The waist was tightly cinched to offset a plunging Queen-Anne neckline. Puffed shoulders ended in short, snug fitting sleeves. Above-the-elbow white gloves added a touch of bewitching elegance. For adornment, a jeweled pendant was suspended on a silk choker, and twin hair combs were fitted with small faux pearls. An accompanying floor-length black cape was lined with the same rose-petal satin as the gown. To Veronica, the entire outfit resembled something out of a fairytale.

"Well?" Aren asked, when she continued to stare speechlessly at the gown.

Veronica fingered a glove. It had tiny pearl buttons running from elbow to wrist. "It's beautiful."

At her side, Morgana smiled. "You and Caith will make a perfectly romantic couple in these costumes." She patted Veronica's arm. "Derry isn't the only one who'd like to see the two of you together. I'm still young enough for more grandchildren."

Veronica flushed. Was she that obvious? Mortified, she glanced at Aren. "What about you and Melanie? What are you wearing?"

"She's going as a 1920s flapper, and I'm"—Aren grabbed a pen off his desk and stuck it in the corner of his mouth, talking around it like a cigar—"a mob boss, ya see? One a da Chicago boys, packin' heat." He mimicked holding a tommy gun. "Rat-a-tat-tat."

Veronica laughed. "Your tough guy persona needs work. Maybe you should—"

Before she could finish, the door banged open, cracking loudly against the wall. Caith barreled into the room, Aren's frazzled secretary trailing on his heels. "Sir, Sir! You can't just... Mr. Lairen, please! Your brother is in a meeting." She looked imploringly at Aren. "I'm sorry, Mr. Breckwood, but your brother—"

Discarding the pen, Aren held up his hand. "It's all right, Patricia. I'll take care of it." He waited until she left the room, closing the double entry doors behind her before he focused on Caith. "Well? Now that you've secured the floor, what's this about?"

"We've got a problem." Caith scowled and paced to the window. Digging his hands into his pockets, he stared out the glass. "Where's Merlin?"

Looking perplexed by the question, Aren glanced at his watch. "He should be here soon. He usually gets in around nine-thirty. What kind of a problem? What are you talking about?"

Caith kept his eyes turned out the window. "I need you to call a meeting. Get Dad, get Merlin, but keep Galen out of it."

Aren blinked. "Why not Galen?"

"Just do it." Caith glanced over his shoulder. He noticed the costumes for the first time. "What are those?"

"Something for later." Veronica wheeled the portable rack to the side, hoping to make it less conspicuous. Caith's body language indicated he was keyed up, functioning in high gear, his mind latching onto and dismissing information with breakneck speed. He wouldn't waste time with anything frivolous. Hopefully, Aren realized that, too.

"At the house," Caith said, returning his attention to Aren. "Set it at the house so Galen doesn't wonder what's going on."

Aren frowned, but moved to the phone and punched in an extension. "Dad," he said into the receiver after a slight pause. "Caith wants a family meeting. Without Galen."

* * * *

Two hours later, Caith observed the members of his family gathered in the living room of the Breckwood home. His father roamed restlessly, hands in his pockets, his face set in a perpetual scowl. His mother and Veronica sat together on the couch while Merlin sprawled in a high-backed wing chair. Aren blew out a breath and slumped into a seat, sending an impatient glance his way.

"You've got the floor, Caithelden. Why are we here?"

In the two hours since leaving BI, Caith had managed to shower, shave, and scrounge up new clothes. Operating on less than three hours sleep, the changes helped him feel halfway human. He was exhausted, but wired. As his gaze swept the group, he noted the expressions of the people he'd summoned. His mother and Veronica appeared curious, Aren wary, and Merlin bored. His father would be the problem. Plainly annoyed, he paced back and forth behind the sofa like a caged bear.

"I want to talk about Galicorp," Caith announced.

His father exhaled noisily. "We've already been through this. And why the hell isn't my CEO here?"

"Give me a minute." Caith held up a hand to stave off his anger. He tried to keep his voice level and controlled. "You said before Stone Willow is mostly a Breckwood investment. BI's ownership is marginal. You don't need your CEO to discuss that."

"But I need my son. The last time I looked, *he* hadn't changed his name."

Caith felt the blow like a punch to the gut.

"Stuart!" His mother swiveled on the sofa, sending her husband a withering glare. "Can we try and get through this without snarling, please? Will you at least listen to what Caith has to say?"

His expression black, his father said nothing.

Recovering, Caith plowed ahead. "I talked to Nick Fontaine the other day and he told me Kelly Rice was seeing someone rich and powerful. Someone she claimed was going to change her life forever." Caith paused, allowing silence to settle over the room. "Someone with the initials GB."

Alarmed, Aren sat forward. "Caith, you don't think Galen—"

"I did at first, but that's before I knew about Galicorp." Warming to the subject, Caith rushed to explain. "You had an offer from Galicorp. A substantial offer. One that didn't make sense given the lodge isn't overly profitable. When BI declined that, a higher offer was brought to the table. When it became clear you didn't want to sell, problems started at the lodge."

His father stopped pacing long enough to shoot him a glare. "I told you Duke Cameron said it was unrelated. We're wasting our time with this."

"Duke Cameron never looked into Galicorp, or he'd have realized the connection," Caith snapped. "It's a paper company. A tax shelter.

Registered on the books, but as functional as that lamp." He jerked his thumb, indicating a table light. "It has one principal owner. Galina Brady."

"GB." Merlin looked interested. "Who the hell is she?"

"She's Lew Walden's daughter," Aren said, thunderstruck.

"She's also a VP with Roth-Deckman," Caith continued. "I knew there was something about Galicorp being in Pittsburgh that bothered me, but I didn't make the connection to Lew's daughter until today. Kelly Rice wasn't having an affair. She was meeting with someone who could advance her career. Someone 'rich and powerful who'd change her life forever.' Galina Brady wants Stone Willow, and Kelly is doing her part to make sure she gets it."

"By printing unflattering articles in the *Herald*?" His mother looked skeptical.

"Yes. And helping stage paranormal events at the lodge. Whoever was walking around the lake in phosphorescent body paint was flesh and blood, not an apparition. I'd lay money it was Kelly."

"But she'd need someone on the inside," Veronica protested. "She couldn't possibly have gotten into the lodge without help, and she couldn't have pulled off that stunt in the lobby. What about the dog and the food poisoning? Kelly couldn't have done those things."

"Not alone," Caith agreed. "But she could have done it with Lew's help. And Galina Brady, through Roth-Deckman, would be able to supply them with high-tech special effects equipment. The hand in the fireplace, the woman sobbing, even the face Alma saw at the kitchen window. Lew would have the knowledge to make it work. He spent a year with a film crew in LA."

Merlin's brows drew together. "Lew?"

"There's a lot you don't know about him." Caith took a moment to fill them in on Lew's background and also the background of Dean Porter. Afterward, he told them about his morning meeting with the journalist. "So Kelly helps Galina get the lodge, and Galina gives Kelly a high-profile position with Roth-Deckman."

"But why would she want Stone Willow?" Veronica persisted. "Why would anyone put all that effort and money into a run-of-the-mill lodge?"

"It isn't run-of-the-mill. It's a landmark of Tolar activity." Caith dragged a hand through his hair. "I have my own theories involving the Tolars, but they're pretty farfetched. I'd rather not go into them right now. I think with the information we have, we should be able to get Kelly or Lew to supply the rest. We just have to trick them into it."

"Tricks." His father snorted at the suggestion. "So, basically you've got nothing to back up this elaborate claim of yours." His voice cut through the room like the crack of a whip. "Information on a tax-shelter and a lot of theory. You were always good at make-believe, Caith. Maybe now you can tell me why you've excluded Galen from this session of earth-shattering deductions."

Caith's face grew hot. It took every effort he had not to snap beneath his father's mockery. "I'm not certain he isn't involved."

"That does it!" His father stalked across the room, confronting him face to face. "It's one thing to waste my time listening to conjecture about people I don't know, or don't know well, but when you imply my son is involved, you've gone too far. You've given no concrete evidence—"

"Someone from the family is involved," Caith interrupted hotly. "Galen's the only one who makes sense. He's the only one who knew about the glu—" The word died in his throat. That would sound foolish. His father would make fun of the weakness and turn it into something mocking and demeaning. *You want to blame Galen because you blow your guts over model glue?*

"Knew about what?" His dad demanded.

Caith turned away. "Nothing."

"What a waste of time." His father strode from the room. A moment later, the door to his study slammed shut with a resounding bang.

"Caith." His mother moved swiftly to his side. She gave him a compassionate look and trailed her fingers down his arm in a feeble attempt to soothe. "He didn't mean it."

"He meant every word." He grew tired of pretending the rift could heal. He'd done everything he could to keep peace since he'd arrived. He had given his father every opportunity to see Derrick, and for Derrick's sake, he'd buried his resentment. But he was beat and irritable. He'd be damned if he'd let his father make him look like a fool.

Stalking from the room, he stormed down the hall and into the study uninvited. His father was seated behind his desk, the fingers of one hand drumming restlessly against the top. At Caith's abrupt entrance, his expression soured. "Get out."

"Not this time." Caith walked to the desk, stopping only when his thighs collided with the ornate edge. "You want a piece of me, you do it in private. Don't destroy my credibility on a job your firm hired me to complete."

"Hired without my consent. You're not part of BI, and you made it damn clear when you changed your name, you're not a Breckwood. Why am I even talking to you? I can go online and find a dozen down-on-their-luck PIs."

Caith stiffened. "I might not have your money, but I'm financially secure. And I didn't get there working for BI."

"Of course not!" His father snarled the words in disgust. "Why would you do that? Why would you want to do anything to advance your career? Do you realize how far you could have gone? Galen, Aren, Merlin—they all excel at what they do, but not one of them can match you academically." He sobered abruptly. "When you were a kid, I used to imagine how great it would be when you were part of the team. Then I realized I was shortchanging you. BI would have been a steppingstone, Caith. You could've been a national player, a world player."

"Those were your dreams. Not mine."

His father slumped in his chair. "Because of Trask."

"I don't know if it was because of Trask." God, his head hurt. This was too much thinking, too much talking. Spurred by anger, he'd expected a quick confrontation, not this laborious, painful dredging up of the past. "Even if Trask had lived, I don't think I would've fit with BI. I can't see myself in an office, or jetting around the world, tackling corporate concerns. I like what I do, and I liked being a cop."

"Liked it so much you took your son out of my life. Took my name from him."

"Damn it!" Caith slammed his fist on the desktop. His head was splitting open, fire shooting into his neck and eyes. "I did that to protect him. I kept your name until he was born. After that it was about Derrick, not about you or me. I'd already been through hell. I wasn't going to take the chance it could happen to my kid. Call me paranoid. I gave him a different name so no one would connect him to the Breckwood fortune."

"And that's supposed to make me feel better?"

"I don't give a flying fuck how you feel." The pain in his head made his anger boil over. "You've treated me like shit since I was eighteen. So I don't work for BI, and I changed my name. I'm still your son. You're the one who disowned me."

"Bullshit."

Disbelieving, Caith stared. "So you're saying all those years I struggled through college, you would have picked up the tab? That I didn't have to work double shifts to make ends meet, or work to get scholarships?"

Looking uncomfortable, his father glanced aside. "I wanted you to ask. That's all I wanted. To hear you admit you needed me. You're so stick-in-the-mud stubborn, you had to do everything on your own."

Caith sucked down a breath, grinding his teeth. The air rattled dangerously in his lungs. *To hear you admit you needed me.* The headache was blinding, pounding with the force of a thousand drums. Light streamed through the windows, hurting his eyes, making him wish for darkness and sleep. Blessed mind-numbing sleep where he could block out emotion and memories, tumbling headfirst into dull oblivion.

"You backed out of the deal," he said with rigid control. He balled his hands into fists, fighting the memory. "You lied."

His father looked confused, annoyed. "What are you talking about?"

"When Trask died." The clunk of his heart came faster. Opening the wound, digging into the past, left him unbalanced. It made him feel like a thirteen-year-old again. "You said you'd always be there. Always. You fucking promised me."

Hearing the change in his voice, his father stilled. "I don't know what you're talking about."

"That first Halloween. You knew how I was feeling. You came to my room and told me you'd help me get through it. Was that just a platitude? A cheer-up slap on the back, get-on-with-your-life-Caith? You said you'd always be there, but the first time we didn't agree, you laid down an ultimatum. About college. About my career."

His father looked away, a glimmer of remorse flickering through his eyes. "I was angry. It's not the same thing."

"You're wrong!" Furious, Caith leaned across the desk. "I chose a career I felt strongly about, and you didn't support me. You think nothing of Balin going outside BI to make a living. You even joked about it. But when I did the same thing, I got blackballed for it."

"Balin isn't my son."

"Well, I guess I'm not either." There was such angry bitterness in Caith's words, it made his voice crack. "You can't fire me. I fucking quit."

Chapter 17

Veronica shuddered at the sound of squealing tires. The high-pitched whine went through her like fingers on a chalkboard. A door opened and closed somewhere down the hall followed by the tramp of fading footfalls. She didn't need a crystal ball to know what had happened. The ugly storm brewing between Caith and his father had finally erupted.

"Oh, dear," Morgana whispered at her side.

Across the room, Aren swore softly and rubbed his temple. Merlin shook his head as if he'd expected the fallout all along. "That went well," he grumbled. "If I were a betting man, I'd lay money Caith just quit. Stubborn as he is, he'll head back to Boston as soon as Derry's out of school."

Veronica felt sick. It was happening again—Caith walking out of her life. She'd let him go once without a struggle, but he wasn't going to abandon her a second time. Not when she'd begun to entertain hopes they might have a future together.

"Excuse me." She walked briskly from the room, deciding it was useless to go after Caith. He'd only throw up walls, denying there was anything to talk about. Instead, she focused on Stuart. Judging from the sound of footfalls, he'd already left his study. She followed the path to its logical conclusion, sprinting down a back stairway and out onto the lawn.

Stuart stood just off the sprawling veranda, hands stuffed in his pockets, staring moodily across the rear grounds. Stepping to his side, she nodded toward a wooded thicket. "I remember when you made us a play fort in those trees."

He jolted, roused from his thoughts. "Veronica. What are you doing here?"

She moved closer, standing shoulder-to-shoulder with him as her gaze swept the gardens and woods. "There." Extending her arm, she pointed to a leaf-shaded path that wound into a cluster of sturdy oaks. "You made it because Caith asked you to. You could have hired someone, but you built it yourself. And when it was done, you stayed and played ogres and trolls." She smiled faintly. "You were a great troll, Stuart."

"Apparently, I still am."

"That's your opinion."

"It's his, too."

"Then change it." She touched his hand, curling her fingers around his. "It isn't too late to start over with Caith. He needs to know you accept him for the choices he's made. Is it so terribly hard to be proud of him?"

"You have no idea how I feel about him." Gruffly, he tugged his hand free. "This isn't your concern."

"I don't want him to leave."

He narrowed his eyes. "You're in love with him."

"Yes." If she made a fool of herself and Caith left tomorrow, she'd still declare it to the sky. "I've been in love with him since we were children. I've just been too cowardly to admit it. I don't want to lose him. And I don't want him to lose what he should have with you. You're his father."

"I thought I was." He paced a few feet away, kicking distractedly at a bed of dry leaves. "I understand why he took another name, but it doesn't soften the sting. Maybe if we'd been on speaking terms. Maybe if he'd told me all those years ago what he was thinking, I wouldn't have reacted so badly when he changed career plans at the last minute. Seems like a damn stupid sticking point."

"You're both stubborn, but you want the same thing. He needs to hear you say it." She paused, wetting her lips. "He's never made peace with what happened to Trask. Don't you realize how hard it's been for him to come back? To bring Derry?"

Stuart closed his eyes. "He's a good father. Better than I've been." He drew a slow breath, squaring his shoulders. "You're right. We've avoided each other far too long. I'm not making any promises, but I'll talk to him." He turned, the shadow of a smile hovering on his lips. "I don't want to be a troll all of my life."

Veronica closed the distance and planted a kiss on his cheek. "No chance of that. You're a prince."

* * * *

Caith threw two pair of jeans into his suitcase not bothering to look where they landed. He moved to the dresser, grabbed a handful of T-shirts, and tossed them over his shoulder. Half hit the suitcase, the other half the floor. Irritated, he kicked them aside on his way to the closet.

"Not a productive way of packing," his father observed neutrally from the doorway.

Caith rounded on him in anger. "What the hell are you doing here?"

Clearing his throat, Stuart stepped into the bedroom. "The outer door was open. I figured you'd be preparing to leave."

"You figured right." Ignoring him, Caith returned to what he was doing. He'd been operating on a hair-trigger since barreling out of the house. Lack of sleep kept him cranky, while anger made him defensive.

How would Derrick react to leaving Coldcreek? He had his heart set on trick-or-treating that night. Even if Caith took him to the weekend Halloween festivities in Boston, he'd miss sharing the experience with his cousins. And then there was the strong attachment he'd formed with Caith's father. Would Derrick forgive him for severing that?

Worse, he'd be leaving Veronica. If he asked her to give up everything and follow him to Boston, would she do it? Or would she insist on a commitment he still shied from giving? Could she love him despite scars that left him emotionally unstable?

"I need to talk to you," his father said.

"Too bad. I'm busy." Caith snatched an armload of shirts from the closet and carried the hangers to the bed. From the corner of his eye, he noted an oversized binder tucked under his father's arm. Popping a shirt from its hanger, he folded it into a semi-passable square and dropped it in the suitcase. "I told you I quit."

"'Fucking quit' is how you worded it." His father propped a hip against the dresser, holding the binder low against his stomach. "The last thing I want you to do is leave."

"Could've fooled me."

"Listen, Caithelden." Temper flared briefly in his father's eyes. "Maybe I haven't been exactly cordial, but you've been damn disagreeable yourself. I had reasons for riding you like I did this morning."

"Let me guess. You wanted me to look like an incompetent fool?" Wadding up a shirt, he shot it into the suitcase. Slamming the lid, he lobbed a glare across the room then stalked around the foot of the bed. "You wanted me to fail."

"That's not true."

"You wanted me to fail so you could prove to yourself I'm nothing without BI."

"BI has nothing to do with this. I jumped down your throat because I want you to stay."

"What?"

"Hard to believe, isn't it?" His father laughed humorlessly. "I've been trying to make you angry since you got here. I wanted your focus on me instead of the case."

A prickle of suspicion made Caith narrow his eyes. "Why?"

"Because if you resolve the problems at Stone Willow, you'll go back to Boston. I don't want that to happen, even if it means losing the lodge." Uncomfortably, he looked away. "I want you to stay in Coldcreek."

Caith stared, unable to believe what he was hearing. "Because of Derry?"

"Yes. But mostly because of you." Standing straighter, his father drew a breath and met his gaze. "I won't lie. I've made mistakes, Caith. I can't change that or the past. I only want you to understand why I've behaved the way I have."

Caith snorted. "I understand you slammed a door in my face."

"And you threw my name away like a thing of no value. What would you do if Derry grew up and changed his name? How would it make you feel if your son wanted no part of you?"

"I never said that." Caith brushed off the accusation, unwilling to admit his stubbornness had played a role in their rift. "It's not the same."

"It is. And you seem to forget you weren't the only one affected by what happened to you. When we'd found out you'd been kidnapped… those three days…" His father faltered over the memory, his voice unsteady. "Your mother and I thought the world had ended. You've no idea what it was like. We—"

He broke off abruptly, the words catching in his throat. Shaking his head, he tried another track. "When the police told us a boy had been killed, we were terrified it was you. When we learned it was Trask, I felt relieved." He closed his eyes briefly as if pained by the thought. "He didn't deserve to die, Caith, especially not the way he did. But no matter how hard I've tried over the years, no matter how many times I've told myself I should feel differently, I can't help being grateful it wasn't you."

Caith's mouth was dry. "He died trying to save me."

"I know that. And I know you thought of him as a brother, but you can't keep feeling guilty because you survived and he didn't. I thank God every day you were the one who lived." His gaze dipped to the binder. Absently, he smoothed a hand over the spine. "After what happened to Trask, I would have locked you in a cage to keep you safe. I took comfort in knowing you'd eventually settle into BI. It would have been a safe place for you. Policies, meetings, corporate fanfare. I'd be able to watch over you." He shook his head ruefully. "But what do you do? Out of college and into the police academy with barely a breath in between. From rookie, to robbery, to homicide. Did you have to choose homicide, Caith?"

"How did you know that?"

His father grinned faintly. "You'd be surprised what I know. Just because we haven't spoken for twelve years doesn't mean I haven't followed your career."

Caith shook his head. "It doesn't matter. It's not that easy." Words couldn't erase the sting of betrayal. Striding across the bedroom, he dragged a hand through his hair. "You went back on your word. You lied to me. You said you'd always be there. Do you know what that meant to me?"

"I'm sorry. I do now. And I should have realized what you were going through." His father offered the binder. When Caith made no move to take it, he set it on the bed, his expression hollow. "Your mother doesn't know I have that. Despite what you think, Caithelden, I am proud of you and what you've done for a living. Whether you believe it or not, I want you to stay."

Caith said nothing. His father waited the agonizing span of three heartbeats, then turned and walked from the room. In the resulting silence, the mausoleum-like shroud of the lodge settled heavily on Caith's shoulders. His gaze strayed to the binder as he noted the oversized pages and soft leather covering. A scrap book.

What was his father doing with a scrap book?

Moving to the bed, he sat on the edge and examined the binder. The first page held the clipping of an article that had run in a local Boston paper when he graduated from the police academy. A class photo accompanied the article. Someone had taken a red pen and drawn a ring around his head, setting him off from the others in the third row. He turned the page and saw a copy of the photo he kept on his mantel, a posed shot in full uniform. There was a candid shot beside it, snapped at the commencement reception. He was in the middle of a small group of uniformed graduates, all laughing. Still another with Aren, arms slung around one another's shoulders, each holding a beer. There had been a photographer at the reception that night. Had his father taken the time to track him down and obtain copies of individual photographs?

Turning the page, he discovered a collection of brief passages snipped from the paper whenever his name was mentioned in a passing article or police report. Highlighted sections in each article drew his eye.

Officer Caith Lairen of the 82nd Precinct was the first officer on the scene....

The robbery suspect was apprehended by Officers Caith Lairen and Paul Geiger, both of the 82nd Precinct. Lairen said the suspect's car careened out of control when he tried to make a wide turn at the corner of Claymore and 33rd....

Shots were fired in an early-morning robbery attempt when two men entered the Quick Stop Market on Dorchester Street shortly after seven a.m. Off-duty police officer, Caith Lairen helped foil the attempt....

Each page he turned brought more snippets. Some articles were lengthy, rounded out by accompanying photos, others nothing more than a few brief lines of newsprint.

Detective Caith Lairen of the Fifty-Fourth Precinct Homicide Division refused to give particulars on the grisly slaying, stating only a suspect had been taken into custody....

A high-speed chase shortly after two a.m. left Detective Caith Lairen with minor bruises and a broken collar bone when his car rolled down an embankment. Lairen and other officers were chasing a suspect wanted for questioning in the shooting death of a liquor store clerk.

And still farther into the book: *The Farrington Corporate Scandal was effectively brought to a close today when Private Investigator Caith Lairen, hired by the Farrington Review Board, submitted evidence incriminating three key executives.*

There was more. References to expert testimony he'd given in court, an ad for services clipped from an online listing, an article on charitable work that mentioned his name for contributing time and finances, even a business card for his investigation firm. A separate section detailed awards he'd won in the course of his career. Citations for bravery, merit awards, an extensive article written when he'd rescued two children taken hostage during a domestic dispute that had turned violent.

Scattered among the carefully preserved clippings were candid photographs, likely pilfered from his mother, Melanie, or Aren. There were pictures of him in college, his hair resting on his shoulders, pictures with Derrick shortly after his son was born, even a picture as recent as last summer when he'd spent an afternoon on the waterfront with his mother and Derrick. There were others as well, business photographs taken at city and municipal events he'd attended on behalf of the police department, and later as an investigator for hire.

Twelve years of his life in articles and photographs. His father had cared enough, been interested enough, to follow his career long distance. He'd obviously hired a clipping service to track down every scrap of available information on his son, even going so far as to pay others to attend events Caith frequented.

Swearing softly, Caith closed the book. In twelve years, he'd never once asked his mother or Aren how his father fared. He hadn't known about the complications with his heart, or other health problems that had come and gone. He'd been wrong to think the man had shut him out of his life.

His father did care. He was proud of him.

He simply wasn't able to say it.

* * * *

Veronica held her breath as Stuart returned to the house. All around them preparations were taking place for the Halloween party that evening. Vendors came and went. Florists, decorators, caterers, musicians. Aren and Merlin had returned to BI, but Morgana thrived on the commotion. Breezing from room to room, she directed the placement of this item, the removal of that. When Stuart walked into the main hall, Veronica sent him a silent, questioning glance. Wordlessly, he shook his head and retreated to his study, unwilling to discuss what had happened.

Her stomach clenched as a mixture of fear and dread skittered through her. The expression in her eyes must have betrayed her unease because Morgana took her by the arm and drew her aside. Across the hall, the caterer and florist were busily consulting with the head of Morgana's household staff. Three workers wearing black shirts that proclaimed *Ghosts & Ghouls, Inc.* wheeled a life-sized coffin through the front door. Having attended a number of Morgana's Halloween parties, Veronica knew trays would be fitted inside the open lid, bearing all manner of delectable treats.

"I know my son," Morgana said, cutting through the noise and activity. "He's stubborn, but he's not stupid. He isn't going anywhere, Veronica. He may not be willing to admit it, but he's in love with you."

"No." She tried to draw away. "Don't say that."

"It's the truth."

She shook her head. "Caith's terrified of love."

"He's terrified of loss."

Veronica clamped her mouth shut. Morgana was right. Even if Caith wouldn't admit it, she knew it was the defining emotion that had driven him all of his life. The reason he'd chosen a career designed to keep others safe, the reason he'd given his son another name, the reason he still couldn't bring himself to visit Trask's grave.

She wet her lips. "I have to see him."

"Give him time first," Morgana suggested. "Stuart said he was up all night working on the case. He's barely slept and probably isn't thinking clearly." She smiled encouragingly, hooking her arm through Veronica's. "You can stay and help me decide where the band should go. And the goblins. Did I mention we're having roving goblins?"

Veronica managed a small smile. The *Ghosts & Ghouls* people were pushing a series of crates through the door. Tall ones, large ones, squat ones.

"Mrs. Breckwood," a sandy-haired worker called. "Where would you like us to put the trolls?"

* * * *

Veronica waited until one-thirty before leaving. She swung by Aren's house to pick up the costumes for later that evening, hoping Caith would give her the chance to use them. Afterward, she headed for the lodge, her stomach in knots. Caith's Explorer was parked in its usual spot, shaded by a group of intertwined trees. Dry, shriveled leaves clung to the roof rack and more lay snagged against the wipers. He'd obviously been at the lodge for some time, a realization that helped quiet her nerves.

Tiptoeing into his suite, she found him asleep on the bed. The closet door was open, his suitcase shoved inside. A handful of sweaters were stacked on the dresser, but it didn't look like he planned on going anywhere. He'd kicked off his shoes but was otherwise fully dressed, wearing the same gray khakis and long-sleeved black shirt he'd had on earlier that morning.

Veronica sat on the edge of the bed, hating to wake him. It was after two o'clock, almost time for him to pick up Derry from school. Maybe she should leave a note and do that for him. Before she could debate the matter further, Caith shifted and stirred.

"Hey." She brushed a hand across his brow, sweeping stray bangs from his forehead. His eyes opened, blue as river water in the late day sun. Part of her wanted to know if he'd intended on leaving without seeing her. Another, more rational part, told her there had been enough dissent for one day. "I was worried you left."

"Not without you." His voice was hoarse, uneven. She blinked, surprised when he caught her wrist and drew her down beside him. "I'm sorry I stormed out. I never would have left without…I mean, since I've come back…" Frustration flitted through his eyes. "What I'm trying to say…"

She placed her fingers against his lips. "You shouldn't have to struggle to say it, Caith."

Clenching his jaw, he looked away. She felt a betraying ripple of muscle where their arms touched.

"Did Merlin ever tell you…" He swallowed, meeting her gaze warily. "You know?"

"Merlin is clueless about love. I never wanted him to say it and mean it. Not like I want you to."

He kissed her. To cover the lapse, she realized. Because he couldn't say it. Because in his mind, love and loss went hand-in-hand. She wrapped her arms around his neck, saddened it was all he could give.

At the very least, he had stayed.

* * * *

Veronica finished dressing, then stood back to survey her reflection in an oval, floor-length mirror. The Halloween gown was exquisite, nipped and tucked in all the right places, flowing softly over her hips and thighs. She'd pinned her hair with the pearl-encrusted combs, leaving the long column of her neck exposed.

All she needed was her highwayman.

Somehow, she and Derry had managed to coerce Caith into wearing the costume. It had taken persistent wheedling, but he'd eventually conceded, throwing up his hands in defeat. He might have refused either of them individually, but together she and Derry made a formidable team. Afterward, they'd shared a high-five and a root beer, giggling over their victory. When it came time for Derry to get dressed, he asked Veronica to help him with the werewolf costume.

She'd fussed over him, adjusting the hair-covered suit while Caith reclined on the sofa belting out snatches of Warren Zevon's "Werewolves of London." Singing purposefully off key, punctuating the lyrics with piercing howls, it didn't take long for his over-the-top performance to send her and Derry into another fit of laughter.

Eventually, they'd all recovered enough for her and Caith to affix pointed ears and tufts of facial hair to Derry's costume. When they were through, Caith had given his son a lesson on the finer points of howling and growling. It made her think that maybe, just maybe, the man notorious for hating Halloween would finally enjoy the holiday.

Wishful thinking, she realized as she stood in the bedroom adding the finishing touches to her costume. Retrieving a gold bracelet from the dresser, she slipped it over her wrist atop her satin glove. Seventeen years had passed without Trask.

Her gaze dipped to the floor as a sudden wave of melancholy washed over her. As much as Caith missed him, she missed him, too.

"I know you like Caith." Trask grinned at her, his eyes bright blue beneath the brim of his ball cap. He chewed on an ever-present wad of gum, then blew a huge bubble. It popped, and he immediately sucked the pink glob into his mouth. "Becky Kessler likes him, too. I think she's gonna ask him to the Sadie Hawkins Dance."

Veronica flung her hair over her shoulder. "I don't care what Becky Kessler does." Her gaze dropped to the pebbled bank beneath her feet. Walking along the edge of the creek always made her feel good, especially when she was with Trask. He was more understanding than Merlin, and his nearness didn't make her heart pitter-patter or her palms grow sweaty like they did when Caith was around. "Becky only likes Caith because he's rich. Besides, she's gossipy. Caith likes girls who are smart."

Trask picked up a stone then discarded it for another. "Like you?" He forked his arm to the side and the smooth pebble skipped across the water three times before plopping below the surface.

Veronica picked up her own pebble. "He's just a friend." She shot the stone across the creek, sending it skipping five times to the opposite shore.

Trask blew a huge bubble. "Bet you'd kiss Caith."

It was a challenge. She stuck her hands in the back pockets of her jeans and tried to decide if she should be honest. She'd heard some of the older girls at school talking about kissing, and for weeks now had wondered what it was like. Sometimes she'd lay in bed at night and dream of kissing Caith. Once she'd hugged her pillow close, pretending it was him, but she'd felt foolish and embarrassed. "Maybe."

He grinned broadly. "So you do like him?"

"Maybe."

Trask found another stone. He was silent, weighing it in his hands. "Hey, Ron?"

"Yeah?"

"If you do kiss him, can we still be friends?"

"What a stupid thing to say." She elbowed him in the ribs. "It'll always be the four of us."

"I guess so." He sent the stone across the creek and this time it made it to the other side. "Hey, did'cha see that? It went farther than yours."

"Did not."

"Did too."

And soon they were both picking up pebbles trying to outdo one another, boasting and bragging, enjoying a camaraderie Veronica had thought would last forever.

The thoughts flitted away as something moved behind her. The man she'd wanted to kiss all of her life wrapped a silk-clad arm around her waist and dragged her firmly against him. She watched in the mirror as he lowered his lips to her ear, tugging aside the black scarf that covered the bottom half of his face. "What's this? A genteel lady strayed from her coach?"

His voice was low, rich in timbre, bordering on dangerous. He'd donned the full costume with cape and hat, even gloves. The combination of so much black with his raven hair set off the electric blue of his eyes. "I can't let you go without payment, milady."

Veronica's breath caught as his teeth nipped her ear. He trailed his fingers down her side in a light caress, igniting goose bumps under her gloves. The sleeve of his costume was milk white, but the wide-cuffed leather gauntlet was black as India ink. It made a startling contrast against the soft rose hue of her gown, the starkness strangely intoxicating.

"And what do you demand, good sir?"

He blew in her ear, a gentle breath that sent a shiver racing to her toes. "A touch."

She closed her eyes, melting against him as his black-gloved fingers skimmed over her hip. "Only a touch?"

He slipped a finger beneath her chin, drawing her lips to his. "And a kiss."

She consented, nipping at his lips, smiling, teasing. It didn't take long for her playful squirming and soft moans of pleasure to push him toward aggression. With a throaty groan, he pressed her against the dresser.

Her eyes widened in shock. "Caith what are you doing?"

He covered her mouth before she could protest further, kissing her with such possessive hunger it left her whimpering.

"Remember all those tales about highwaymen ravishing innocent women?" He tossed his hat aside with a backward flourish and grinned wickedly. Her eyebrows shot up in alarm. Before she could so much as squeak out his name, he gripped her by the hips and lifted her onto the dresser.

"Cai—" His kiss silenced her protest. With his hand cradling the back of her head, he moved his mouth over hers, molding their lips in a slow, sensual rhythm. When the kiss ended, Veronica inhaled unevenly. "We have to go. Derry's waiting."

"I know." His breath was ragged. "That doesn't make it easier. I'm going to dream about making love to you all night." He bowed his head against her neck in a visible effort to collect himself. "That damn dress isn't helping. If anyone so much as looks at you...."

Her lips curved. She touched his cheek, drawing his head up. "And if someone does, would that make you jealous, Caithelden?"

Humor sparkled in his eyes. Stepping backward, he drew the sword belted at his hips. "Jealous, milady?" His voice rang with a lofty, staged accent. "I'd skewer the rake."

She giggled and scooted out of the way. "In that case I'd better defend myself. You were always lousy with a sword."

"Hey!"

Veronica made it to the door just as Derry appeared on the other side. He grinned at his father in the highwayman's outfit, then shyly told Veronica she looked pretty. A few minutes later Caith piled them into the Explorer.

"Wait a minute. I forgot something," he said.

"Dad," Derry whined, fidgeting in the back seat.

"I'll be right back," he promised.

Veronica fussed with Derry's costume, adjusting his ears, making sure he had his trick-or-treat bag while Caith ran back into the lodge. A few moments later he returned, an oversized binder tucked under his arm.

"What's that?" she asked as he slid it between them.

"Nothing important." He flipped up the visor and started the ignition. "Why don't you call Aren on my cell and tell him to meet us in town since we're running late?"

Veronica nodded, knowing Derry was eager. It would be another half hour before it grew dark, but Coldcreek's children would already be out in number, going house to house. Twenty minutes later, they met Aren, Melanie, Matt, and Noah in BI's parking lot.

"What a fun-looking group," Veronica commented when they drew together.

Noah was dressed like a pirate, and Matt as Spiderman. Impeccably dapper, Aren sported a wide-shouldered, black pin-striped suit, offset by a red tie and spectator shoes. A white hat banded in charcoal crowned his long hair, which he'd slicked down to exaggerate the length.

"The same goes for the three of you." With a flirty smile, Melanie sauntered over to Caith. She might have stepped from the roaring twenties, decked out in a beaded flapper's dress, short black wig, and sequined cap. "My, my, Caithelden, I didn't know you had it in you. What a hot-looking highwayman."

Aren rolled his eyes. "She always did have a thing for underdogs."

Melanie laughed. Returning to her husband's side, she wrapped her arms around his neck and planted a kiss on his lips. "You know I only have eyes for you, hot stuff."

"Eww, Mom, do you have to do that?" Noah protested.

"Yeah," Matt chimed in. "We want to go trick-or-treating."

Derry added his voice to the chorus, prompting all three children to prance restlessly.

"All right, all right." Aren held up a hand. "Let's get this show on the road. Who wants candy?"

The boys let loose a wallop of cheers. Soaring on adrenaline, they raced ahead, forcing the adults to follow them into town. Veronica strolled leisurely at Caith's side, delighted by Derry's obvious excitement. It wasn't long before the sun dipped below the trees, replaced by a full moon. Bloated and orange, it hugged the horizon like a lidless eye. A goblin moon, Morgana would have called it, whispering of winged creatures who roamed the sky and wraiths that slipped silently from nesting shadows.

Within the hour, the children had filled their bags with candy. Up and down the street, jack-o-lanterns flickered in windows and on doorsteps. Children raced among the sidewalks, waving glow-sticks while their parents trailed at a slower pace with flashlights. Higher in the hills, organ music drifted from outside speakers at the Breckwood mansion, sounding like the prelude to an Edgar Allen Poe movie.

"Are we going to the party now?" Derry asked his father. His trick-or-treat bag was already overflowing, but knowing Caith's mother, it would likely double once he was inside. "I wanna see the decorations, and I wanna have some candy."

"Only a few pieces," Caith warned. "You'll be in bed in another hour. Tomorrow's a school day."

"Dad…" Derry drew out the name in exasperation.

Caith glanced down at his son. "Derry…" he mimicked with the same inflection.

Derry laughed. He hooked his hand into his father's oversized glove as the group walked back to the car. Caith was doing an amazing job of keeping the spirit light, despite the heavier thoughts Veronica knew had to weigh on his mind. Hopefully, he'd manage the same ease at the party.

The house was teeming with people when they arrived. Costumed guests mingled in rooms transformed to mirror Halloween showcases. One resembled a night-time forest with leafless trees and moon-silvered, mist-covered grounds. Strategic lighting and portable fog machines created the effect. In another room, a miniature rendition of Stonehenge surrounded a band dressed as Druidic priests. Unlike the organ music pumped from outside speakers, this was upbeat and contemporary with a wide dance floor for those who wished to indulge. Ghosts, vampires, scarecrows, and an assortment of other creatures gyrated to the heavy bass beat pumped from hidden amplifiers.

Goblins and winged creatures threaded among the crowd, butlering silver platters with flutes of wine and hot hors d'oeuvres. Gossamer spider webs draped most every corner, and life-sized trolls greeted visitors in the foyer. Every time a door opened, it triggered a cackle or shriek. Dressed with black china and blood-red goblets, tables of food were scattered in every room. The lighting was low and muted, sometimes replaced by electric candles with flickering orange flames.

Caith kept a hand latched tightly on Derry's shoulder, preventing him from straying. "It's really crowded," he muttered.

Veronica wondered if he knew the guests came from neighboring towns in addition to Coldcreek, a few even flying in from out of state. The Breckwood Halloween party was an event not to be missed in the corporate world.

"It's early yet," Aren told him with a grin. "An hour from now and you won't be able to move without bumping elbows." He nodded toward the stairway. "Let's get the kids upstairs and out of their costumes. Melanie said she'd take them home once they've had a chance to wind down."

Caith nodded.

The children were not so easily put off, however, and kept up a steady stream of protests until allowed to race room to room, ogling the extravagant decorations and even more extravagantly costumed guests. Eventually, they collected their own bags of special Halloween treats from Morgana and Stuart, and reluctantly traipsed upstairs to change.

Veronica waited while Caith saw Derry safely tucked away in a bedroom with his cousins. She traded snatches of conversation with a few friends before rejoining him as he came down the steps. "How is he?"

"Begging to stay up all night and skip school tomorrow."

She chuckled. "Like that's going to happen."

"Excuse me." A woman dressed as a belly dancer bumped into them as she turned the corner. "Sorry, I didn't see you." Her face was completely masked, her eyes covered by brightly colored veils, spangled with flecks of gold. By contrast, her costume was composed of a skimpy strapless bra and low-riding harem pants. Veronica wondered how she managed to keep the bra in place.

"Veronica! Uncle Caith!" Within seconds, Balin appeared at the woman's side, dressed in the heavy brown robes of a Franciscan friar. Grinning, he slipped his arm around her waist. "Can you believe it?" He leaned forward to be heard over a particularly loud guitar riff rolling from the room with the band. "Grandma and Grandpa just make it better every year. Dad's around here somewhere." He waved a hand behind him. "We're gonna get something to eat."

Veronica nodded, preparing to introduce herself to Balin's date but the two left before she could utter a word. Unfazed, she smiled up at Caith. "Looks like Balin's having a good time. You might, too, if you'd relax."

"How? I've seen at least four guys leer at you since we walked through the door."

"Only four?" She enjoyed his jealousy. "I'm disappointed. I should have worn something skimpier like Balin's date. Besides…who's going to make a pass at me when I have a dashing highwayman as protector?"

Earlier, he'd shed his hat, cloak, and face scarf, hooking the gauntlets through his wide belt. The sword was gone, too. Yet dressed in a black leather tunic with a white poet's shirt, she could easily believe he'd ridden from the myths of their childhood.

He raised a brow. "Who's going to protect you from me?"

She had no will of her own when he looked at her like that. How could a man turn on charisma and sex appeal with the cavalier flip of a switch? Too bad Aren hadn't thought to add a paper fan to her outfit. She could use one right about now. "I think we should refocus on the party."

"I'd rather be back at the lodge with you." Linking an arm around her waist, he tugged her possessively against his side. The brush of his lips sent warm shivers racing down her spine. "In bed."

She placed a palm on his chest, enforcing distance. As seductive as he was, she wasn't going to compromise herself at a party. "Maybe we should dance."

He tightened his grip on her waist. "Or go upstairs to my old bedroom."

"Caithelden."

He chuckled. "Or dance."

The band had moved into a slow, sensuous song by the time they reached the room. False stars and a sickle moon hung suspended from a ceiling draped in black. The floor was shrouded in man-made fog, furthering the illusion of night on a desolate moor. Recessed lights cast an eerie blue glow on monolithic slabs of rock meant to resemble Stonehenge.

Veronica knew she was in trouble the moment Caith slid his hand onto the small of her back. The touch of his fingers was electric; heat raged through her veins. She linked her arms around his neck, gazing into his eyes. He moved with ease, guiding their bodies in a seductive rhythm. Nothing else mattered. Sound filtered into the background, distant and forgotten. She felt only the flow of their bodies twined together, heard only the thump of her heart. When he bent his head to kiss her, the world stilled, then shattered.

Shaken, she rested her head on his chest. "Caith, I'm in love with you." She cringed, horrified she'd spoken the words aloud.

Not now. Not on Halloween. Not on the anniversary of Trask's death.

How could she have been so stupid? She hadn't meant to tell him. Never to tell him. It was the magic of the night—their costumes, the music, the romance of the moment. She hadn't meant to say anything, only to feel it and hold it close to her heart. To know without a doubt he was everything she'd always wanted.

"Caith, I'm sorry."

"Veronica." He tensed and drew back.

"Hey, mind if I cut in?"

She blinked, startled to find Merlin at her side. Not the Merlin she was used to seeing, but Merlin dressed in the flowing silver robes of a wizard. He wore a wide-brimmed pointed hat and a sash embroidered with planetary symbols around his waist. A thin beard dangled over his stomach, bleached the same shocking white as the dye he'd used on his hair.

His hazel eyes darted to Caith. "How about it, rogue? Share your spoils?"

Looking unsettled, Caith released her hand. "I'll be in the other room."

"Hey." Merlin cast Veronica a puzzled look as Caith threaded quickly through the crowd. "What's the matter with him? He looks like he got hold of some bad food or something."

Veronica's stomach twisted in a knot. "Or something."

"Whatever it is, he'll get over it. He's edgy because it's Halloween." Merlin swept her into a dance. "He was always too intense, even as a kid."

"I suppose." She managed a weak smile. As the music swelled, she sent a worried glance to the doorway, certain she'd made the worst mistake of her life.

Chapter 18

Caith headed to a room he knew was private and off-limits to party goers. His father's study. On the way there he passed Galen, looking imposing and regal as a Mongol warlord, but didn't stop to talk. His brother was deep in conversation with their mother and a small group of people Caith didn't recognize. His mother easily outshone the others, dressed in a flowing white gown with silvery overlay. Gossamer wings, a wig of flowing blond hair, and a crowning circlet of wildflowers made her look the part of the Faerie Queen.

Myth. Magic. Happily ever after.

She'd taught him to believe in such things, to dream of what-ifs and might-have-beens. When he was a child, he'd enjoyed her love of fantasy and make-believe, but life had taught him harder lessons. Crueler lessons. People he cared about could be snatched away, all because of who he was.

A rich man's son.

Caith slammed the door to the study. Veronica was in love with him. More importantly, she wasn't afraid to admit it. She deserved someone who could say it in return. Someone whose throat didn't close up at the thought of uttering the words, who was able to separate love from fear.

Dropping into a chair, he bowed his face into his hands. He wasn't sure how long he sat, sounds of the party filtering through the walls. Music, laughter, voices. None of it felt real. Halloween had always been a day he associated with death. The one day of the year he wanted to lock himself in a room with a bottle.

He heard the opening click of the door and glanced up in time to see his father enter. For a moment it was like being fourteen again, when his dad had come to him during that first Halloween party.

"I thought I was the only one who hid out in here."

Caith raised a brow. "You're hiding? I thought you liked these parties."

"Your mother likes them." His father crossed to the antique globe that doubled as a bar and poured a glass of fruit juice. Dressed in the full regalia of a Union general of the Civil War, he looked like a veteran commander. "I'd rather sit out back with a carved pumpkin and watch the stars. Peace. Quiet. Just a candle in the jack-o-lantern, instead of all this hoopla." He waved a hand to indicate the extravagance taking place on the other side of the door.

Caith frowned. "I don't understand you. I'm beginning to think I never did." Beyond the walls of the study, the music stopped abruptly. He'd left Veronica on the dance floor with Merlin and should probably wander back. But how did he face what she'd told him: *I love you*? How could he answer in return?

Silencing the thought, he paced to the other side of the room and refocused on his father. "That scrap book—"

"Did you bring it back?"

"It's in my truck."

His father nodded. "It's my way of not letting go, Caithelden. Of hanging onto you, even when you shut me out."

Disgusted, Caith shook his head. He didn't need this. It was Halloween. Veronica was in love with him and his dad was talking like he wanted to be a father again. He pinched the bridge of his nose, feeling the onset of a headache. Through the walls, he could still hear voices, but the laughter had stopped. Coupled with the lack of music, the absence was disturbing. Now that Caith concentrated, the voices sounded off-kilter, jumbled and confused. Tensing, he stared at the door.

"Something's wrong."

His father scowled. "What?"

"Something's happened." Spurred by alarm, Caith reached for the door. It swung open before he could touch it, spilling a handful of people into the room–all three of his brothers followed closely by Veronica and Balin. Veronica looked shaken, her face a white mask. Balin hovered a foot behind, his skin a sickly shade of gray-green.

"What's wrong?" Caith drew Veronica aside. "Ronnie, are you all right? Are the boys all right?"

"Your mother and Melanie are with Matt and Noah." There was a tremor in her voice, barely disguised. "Caith, something terrible has happened."

"Derry." He pounced on the omission. "What about Derry?"

Aren gripped his shoulder. "Maybe you should sit down."

Panic rocketed through Caith. Sheer, stark, gut-twisting panic. In the space of a single heartbeat, he knew. Every fear, every unreasonable terror he'd harbored for seventeen years, crashed over him with bone-shattering force. Rounding violently on Aren, he gripped him by the lapels. "Where the hell is my son?"

"Caith, take it easy."

"He doesn't know. None of them do!" Balin's sudden wail broke over the room like a pent up storm.

"What did you say?" Through the blood pounding in his head, Caith registered his nephew's stricken face. Balin looked ready to collapse, his skin now bleached like the underbelly of a dead fish. Galen moved beside the boy, wrapping a protective arm around his shoulders.

"Caith, he didn't mean for this to happen. It was a mistake."

"What mistake? Where's Derry?"

"It was my fault. All of it. The lodge, the glue, everything." Balin was blubbering now, sobbing in earnest as he choked on tears. "No one was supposed to get hurt. I swear it."

"I don't give a shit about the lodge. Where's my kid?"

Balin appeared not to have heard. Shoulders slumping, he folded against the wall. "It was Galina...she wanted the lodge, and Kelly wanted that stupid job. I thought...I thought Kelly loved me. It-it's why I did all those things she asked." Choking back tears, he looked beseechingly from his father to Aren and Merlin. "She said we'd be together after Galina got the lodge. It seemed so simple, scaring people. Lance McClure helped, and Kelly dressed up as the woman at the lake."

Caith didn't care. None of it mattered. "Derry," he spat. "Where's Derry?"

But Balin appeared to be in a zone where events unfolded in a precise order, where clearing his conscience took precedence over everything else. Hitching in a breath, he looked directly at Caith. "Lance killed the dog, and he's the one who trashed the lobby and messed with the food stores. Galina paid him and that's all he cared about. I did the tech stuff... the hand in the fireplace, the woman on the third floor, even the sobs and the face at the window. I had copies made from Dad's keys so we could get in. And I'm the one who put the glue in the drawer at the house and dumped it at the hayride." His eyes darted to the side, guiltily sweeping the room as he fidgeted from foot to foot. Licking his lips, he ran a hand through his hair and plowed ahead. "I overheard Uncle Merlin tell Dad about how it does weird things to you. I told Kelly and she thought it would be a good way to mess with your head...that if you were bothered enough by what happened to you as a kid, you'd back off and leave things alone. Stone Willow would go belly up. Galina would make another offer and get the lodge. Kelly would get her job with Roth-Deckman. I never meant for anyone to get hurt. I wanted to be with Kelly. I didn't know she was using me. You gotta believe me, Uncle Caith."

Caith lunged forward only to be physically restrained by Aren. "You damn well better tell me where my kid is, or I'm gonna take you apart."

Acting as a buffer, Merlin stepped between them. "Balin, tell him the rest." Apparently, his nephew had already spilled his guts to everyone else before entering the room.

Balin sniffled, dragging a sleeve under his nose. "The other day when I stopped to pick up a book in the computer room, you were asleep at the desk. I saw what you'd been doing. All those notes on Galicorp and Galina. I figured you were getting close to working it out so I told Kelly. She and Galina…they said we had to come up with something really big. Something to make you forget about the lodge for good. Make you go back to Boston." Balin bit back a sob. He mopped the sleeve across his face, wiping up tears. "Kelly was my date tonight, the one you saw me with earlier. She told me she just wanted to talk to Derry. I didn't know she was gonna take him."

"You bastard." Furious, Caith broke free. He knocked Balin against the wall, rage and fear shattering the last of his control. He couldn't think, couldn't breathe. Someone locked an arm around his neck and tried to drag him backward. He thrust his forearm across his nephew's windpipe pinning him in place, a move he normally reserved for suspects and criminals. "You tell me where my kid is. Tell me before I rip out your throat!"

"Caith!"Aren was yelling at him, Veronica pleading, Galen and Merlin fighting to break his hold on Balin.

It all happened in a blur. A dizzying tangle of sickening impossibilities that left his head reeling, his gut roiling with acid. Someone had taken his son.

"Caithelden, let him go!" His father's powerful voice cracked over him at the same time Aren and Merlin snapped his hold on Balin. Merlin shoved him roughly backward. Red-faced, he jabbed a finger under Caith's nose.

"Calm down, damn you. You're not helping Derry this way."

Caith paced in an agitated circle, stepped forward, and was immediately shoved back by Merlin. Sirens wailed in the distance, growing louder.

Someone had obviously thought to call the police before bringing him the story.

"Where?" he snapped with a hostile glare for Balin. "Where did that witch take my kid?"

Unable to stand any longer, Balin sank into a chair. "I don't know. I brought him downstairs to talk with her. She sent me to get her a drink and, when I got back, they were gone. I never would have let anything happen to him, Uncle Caith, I swear. Never! I-I just thought she was gonna talk to him, tell him about what happened to you and your friend Trask. I figured she might try to scare him a little so he'd ask you to go back to Boston. I swear I don't know where she took him. She didn't even have a car. I picked her up before the party."

"She's going to deny she did anything," Aren said with a careful glance for Caith. "We don't have a witness who actually saw her take Derry from the house. With all these people, she might be able to convince the police Derry wandered off on his own, or that someone else took him."

"Let me get my hands on her," Caith snarled. "I guarantee she'll tell the truth." He sent Balin a scathing glare. "She probably didn't count on her teenage lover spilling his guts about the lodge. I know one thing." Outside the sirens fell abruptly silent, signaling the police had arrived. "I'm not leaving Derry's fate to Duke Cameron."

"Don't do anything stupid," his father snapped.

Halfway to the door, Caith glanced over his shoulder. His father's voice was controlled but his face had grayed, nearly the color of Balin's. "What does that mean?"

"Exactly what it sounds like. Do you think I don't know what you're feeling? Do you think I don't know what it's like to have my son ripped away? If you go off half-crazed—"

"Stay out of this," Caith stabbed a finger in his direction. "You made your choices, and I'm making mine."

"Wait!" Veronica's voice trailed him into the hallway. He'd only taken two steps before she caught up with him, grabbing him by the arm and forcing him to stop.

"Where are you going?" There was panic in her voice, fear that he'd never heard before. Looking into her eyes, he realized she loved Derrick, too. Not just with fondness, but a crushing, consuming tenderness that brought tears to her eyes.

"I'm going with you," she insisted.

"No."

"Caith, I love him, too."

"I know that." He touched her cheek, catching a tear that spilled over her lashes. "I need you to stay here, talk to the police. If Derry gets free, he'll come back. Or there might be a phone call. I can't concentrate on him if I'm worried about you. Ask around, see what you can find out. Maybe someone saw something."

"Caith."

"Veronica, I have to go."

She nodded, fighting for composure. "Be careful."

She gave him a quick kiss, and he sprinted down the back hall, avoiding the crowds who lingered in the party areas. A hush had fallen over the house, voices whispered rather than raised in laughter. Cold air hit Caith the moment he stepped outside, the temperature having dropped considerably since the hours of trick-or-treat. Slipping the gauntlets over his hands, he ducked the police with ease, heading for his Explorer. Two cruisers were parked in the driveway, the bounce of their emergency lights sending red and blue flashes through the darkness.

"Caith, wait up."

Merlin and Aren jogged up behind him as he reached the Explorer.

"What do you think you're doing?" he demanded.

Merlin raised a hand, dangling his keys in the air. "The same thing you are. We'll cover more area with all three of us looking. Aren can head east, I'll go west, you go north. When we're done, we'll meet on the south side and regroup. Assuming one of us hasn't already found Derry." He paused. "Galen would've come, too, Caith, but he needs to be with Balin."

"Yeah." There was bitterness in his voice, but he crushed the ugly emotion. It had been a long time since someone other than Aren stood beside him.

He looked steadily at Merlin. His brother had cast off his wizard robes and hat, but the false beard and the unnatural white dye in his hair remained.

Halloween. Damn, why did it have to be Halloween?

He swallowed a lump of fear. Just because Trask died on Halloween didn't mean Derrick would come to harm.

Exhaling, he dragged a hand through his hair. "Thanks. Both of you. I'll go by the *Herald* first."

Aren nodded. Popping the door on the Explorer, he pushed Caith toward the seat. "Get in and start looking. We're not going to let anything happen to Derry."

As Aren and Merlin darted away, Caith turned the ignition. With three of them looking there was a chance Derrick would be found. If nothing else, he had the strength of his brothers behind him, something he hadn't felt in years.

He pulled the vehicle out of the driveway and headed into town, trying to think rationally. Once he might have believed nightmares of this sort only happened to someone else, but experience had taught him differently. From the moment Derrick was born, he'd done everything imaginable to shelter his son from would-be predators. But none of it mattered now. Derrick was in the hands of a kidnaper.

Caith tightened his grip on the steering wheel until the pressure was painful. Worry over his son threatened to drive him insane. What he needed was a clear head. Sucking down a lungful of air, he pulled the Explorer onto the shoulder of the road and tried to rid his mind of distractions.

Don't hurt him!

Trask's voice echoed loudly in his memory, resurrecting another Halloween, another kidnapping seventeen years before. Angrily, he shoved it aside. Derrick was not going to end up like Trask. Derrick was not going to die. Not at the hands of some washed up prom queen and her VP boss.

Agitated, he drummed his thumbs on the wheel. Kelly didn't want to hurt Derrick. Hell, she didn't even have a car. Balin had brought her to the party. She wouldn't have run with Derrick on foot, so she must have had someone waiting. Someone with a car who could whisk her and Derrick to a secure haven at a moment's notice. She didn't know Balin had spilled his guts or the police would be looking for her. She had counted on his silence. Derrick was simply a diversion to shift Caith's attention from the lodge and send him back to Boston. By tomorrow, Derrick would probably be released, the scare alone sufficient to send them packing.

So, who would Kelly Rice employ as a driver?

She'd taken care to conceal her appearance with veils, ensuring even Derrick wouldn't be able to identify her later. Galina Brady would never involve herself in something better handled by subordinates, which left only one person.

Lance McClure.

"Fuck." Caith slammed his foot on the gas pedal. The truck lurched forward, exploding into the night. Veronica had told him Lance had a welding shop on the south side of town where the old rendering plant used to be. On a wild gamble, he swung the wheel around and headed south.

Slowing a block from the shop, he pulled off the road and parked beneath a willow tree. The area was dark, void of streetlights. Sprinting from the vehicle, he moved quickly through the shadows, approaching from the rear. When he was a child, deer and other wild animals struck by cars had been taken to the building for disposal. Sometimes even farm animals were carted by truck to the plant when their time expired.

He could still remember the smell. A strong odor that sweltered to an unbearable stench in the high heat of summer. Located at the farthest end of town, the building was isolated, several blocks from the nearest homes or businesses. Eventually, the townspeople complained enough that the plant was abandoned. Portions of the building remained boarded up and closed, but a hand-lettered sign with flaking paint hung over the side door: *McClure's Welding.*

Caith darted past, intending to go through the rear when something caught his eye. Squatting on the ground, he bent to pick up the tiny object, a bright white marble dropped by the door.

Derrick.

His heart beat faster, accelerating in a mad rush. Pressing his shoulder against the door, he tried the handle, but it wouldn't budge. Refocusing, he located a window ten feet to the rear that pried easily, allowing him to slip inside.

He found himself in an office, closeted by darkness. Images took shape gradually revealing the bare essentials of one-man operation—a metal desk, two drawer filing cabinet, and a rickety chair. A thin strip of light bled beneath a door, defining the exit. In the cramped room, his breathing was harsh, his heartbeat overly loud. It reminded him of another room, another time.

He swallowed hard, fighting to kill the images. Rather than fade, they crashed over him, propelled by a gut-twisting surge of panic.

Caith squirmed uncomfortably on the cold floor, his back pressed to a moldy block wall. He sent a darting glance to the man seated at a table near the door. For two days he'd watched Farrow assemble small plastic car models, piece by piece. The basement was cramped and dirty, smelling of wet rags and mildew. Light came from two bare bulbs dangling overhead and a small window butted against the ceiling.

Coupled with his own white-knuckle fear and the filthy surroundings, the smell of glue made his stomach churn dangerously. He'd already vomited once, retching up the cold soup and warm sandwich they'd fed him the previous night.

Richter had sworn a blue streak, cuffed him across the face, then made Farrow clean up the mess. The other man grumbled and threatened to beat him, but he'd eventually retreated to his station by the basement door. The blond man, Force, came to the room after that. Caith knew he was the one in contact with his parents and the police. Whenever he came to the room, the other two stopped what they were doing to listen.

"Soon," Force always promised. "We'll have the money soon."

Caith knew the names they used weren't real names, but he'd seen all three of their faces and that worried him. When his parents paid the ransom, would the kidnappers let him and Trask live?

Worried, he huddled into the thin blanket they'd given him for sleeping. Trask leaned against his shoulder, the two of them pressed closely together as much for comfort as warmth.

"It's my fault," Caith whispered. "Because of my dad and his money."

Trask turned his head. His eyes were wide, sunken into his face with harsh rings of shadow. "Will he pay?"

"Course he will."

"Will they let me go, too? I'm not worth anything."

Caith's stomach clenched. "Don't say that." The words came in a fierce hiss. "Don't even think it. It's my fault you're here. I won't go without you."

A feeble smile flickered over Trask's lips. "Like before...when we cut our thumbs?" His voice was thin. "Blood brothers?"

"Brothers," Caith affirmed. He didn't need blood mingled between them. Didn't need make-believe or words. What he felt in his heart was enough. He was responsible, and Trask was his friend. More than a friend.

"Hey. Quit whispering over there."

Farrow's sharp command made Caith cringe. Richter had hit him, but Farrow was the one who terrified him. Farrow with his models and glue and threats of violence.

"What are you boys talking about?"

"Nothin'." Caith squawked the word so quickly, air caught in his throat. At the sound of Farrow's chair scraping against the floor, he scrunched his eyes closed.

Don't come over...don't come over...pleasedon'tcomeover.

"Hey, Farrow," Richter hailed from across the room. "I'd leave the little punk go, 'less you wanna clean up another mess. He looks ready to piss himself."

Farrow gave a snuffling snort. "He'll do more than that if his parents don't ante up that ransom. Know what I think?"

Caith felt someone loom over him. A sinking sensation swept through him when he realized it had to be Farrow. His stomach twisted inside out, bubbling acid into his throat. He was cold. So cold he was shaking, yet sweat dribbled down the back of his neck.

"I think we need to convince his lordship's parents we ain't fucking around." Caith opened his eyes in time to see Farrow send Richter a broad wink. "I think they need physical convincing, hey?"

Richter chuckled. He was big and raw-boned, and when he laughed, he made a goat-like sound. "What do you have in mind?" He sidled into view from a chair below the window. His lips stretched in a macabre smile as he pulled a knife from a sheath at his belt. "Finger or an eye?"

Caith blanched at the sight of the stout knife with its thick blade. It was the kind the farmer down the road used to butcher deer. With a whimper, he scrunched against the wall.

Farrow folded his arms across his chest. "Those blue eyes are too pretty to cut out. I say we send them a finger. How about it, boy?"

The room reeled. Caith's stomach pushed into his throat. Farrow reached forward and yanked Caith to his feet, shaking him so violently his teeth clacked together. His head rolled backward and flopped to the side. They were going to cut off his finger, send it to his parents. Trask yelled, pleading with them to stop, but he had no voice of his own. Every nerve in his body had turned to stone. He couldn't speak, couldn't breathe, couldn't react.

They're going to cut off my finger.

Farrow flung him across the room and he crumbled to the floor.

"Don't!" Trask screamed. "Don't hurt him!"

Somehow he scrambled to his hands and knees, the uneven texture of the cold floor biting into his palms. A shadow loomed over him. He was going to be sick, spew his guts, and this time Farrow would surely beat him for it.

They're going to cut off my finger.

Farrow grabbed his collar and hauled him to his feet. His knees buckled. He managed a strangled gasp, half whimper, half protest, before being propelled toward the table. Farrow shoved him into a chair. The stench of model glue engulfed him in a suffocating cloud and he started to gag.

"Don't hurt him!" Trask screamed again.

Farrow pinned his arm to the table.

"Let him go!"

From the corner of his eye, Caith saw Richter approach with the knife. It was really happening. They were going to cut off his finger, maim him, and send the part to his parents as proof of his abduction. Tears blurred his eyes. Would he faint? How badly would it hurt? He prayed he wouldn't disgrace himself. He'd hurl in Farrow's lap to spite him if he could, but didn't want to wet his pants.

Tears trickled down his cheeks.

Richter was almost to the table. "Which finger?" He flashed the knife for effect. "Eeny. Meeny. Miny. Mo."

"Don't!" Suddenly Trask was there, hurling himself at Richter. Trask, a pitiful sack of stick-thin bones going against a man three times his size.

"No!" Caith found his voice.

Trask made a grab for the knife and Richter pivoted unexpectedly. The blade tore through Trask's stomach, burrowing deep, blundering out his side. It happened fast. So fast that when Trask crumbled in a boneless heap to the floor, Caith could only stare in horror.

Farrow released him, lurching backward. "You stupid shit!" he yelled at Trask. "It was a game. We weren't really gonna hurt him! We were having fun."

Caith pushed out of the chair, dropping to his knees at Trask's side. There was a new smell in the dingy basement. More powerful than the mold clinging to the damp walls and the glue splattered in bird-like droppings on the table. A hideous smell he would never forget.

The smell of blood.

"Help him!" He clamped his hands over the wound, felt something hot and slippery against his palm. Something that told him Trask was dying. "Help him!" He looked desperately at the men standing dumbfounded to the side, but neither moved, neither spoke.

"C-Caith." Trask grabbed his wrist. "Caith, I'm scared. I-I don't wanna die."

"You're not going to." But he knew with dread certainty Trask's life ebbed with each passing second. Hot tears flooded his eyes and spilled down his cheeks. He blinked, trying to focus. "Why'd you do it? Why didn't you just let them cut off my finger? Trask. Please don't go away, Trask!"

His friend's eyes flickered and closed.

"Please." It was no more than a whimper. The hand on his wrist went slack and tumbled free, thudding against the floor.

"He's gone, kid," Richter said behind him.

The world upended.

Blood, glue, shame, and every horrible fear he'd kept locked inside for two days exploded. Whirling, Caith threw himself at Richter. Something tortured and inhuman ripped from his throat, a savage animal wail he didn't recognize as his own.

"He was my friend. He shouldn't have even been here, you sick bastard! It's me you wanted." He flailed blindly with his fists, striking anything within range, consumed by hatred, ravaged by grief.

Trask was dead.

Only when Richter knocked him senseless did the agony stop.

Breathing raggedly, Caith dropped his forehead against the door. His son was on the other side, a prisoner like he'd been a prisoner. Like Trask had been a prisoner.

Derry, please don't go away.

He heard muffled voices through the barrier. A man and a woman, the deeper baritone farther removed. Caith cracked the door in time to see Kelly Rice, her face still covered by veils, walk briskly outside. Seconds later, an engine roared to life. Headlights cut through the room, then faded into the distance.

She must have left in McClure's car. Easing from the office, Caith crept into the main bay, noting it was crisscrossed by a series of catwalks overhead. When the rendering plant was in operation, carcasses must have been hoisted by crank, then lowered into vats for reducing, the entire procedure observed by workers stationed on the open bridges above. The glow from a single fluorescent tube cloaked the bay in weak half-light.

A banged-up car in the corner looked like it was being refitted with a roll cage, likely for use on a dirt track. Bicycle parts, pieces of farm equipment, and smaller projects in various stages of completion were scattered over worktables and on the floor. Cutting torches, oxygen and acetylene cylinders, pressure gauges, regulators, and an assortment of welding tools lined the walls.

Caith's eyes were drawn to the bottom of a narrow flight of metal steps. A single blue marble winked in the semi-dark. Derrick had left a trail.

He followed the path with his eyes, tracking to the catwalk suspended twenty-five feet above the floor. His heart caught in his throat when he saw Derrick being pushed along the elevated bridge by a man in a black ski mask. Uncontrollable rage rocketed through Caith. He bolted for the steps.

"McClure!"

The man on the metal bridge halted.

"Dad!" Derrick tried to break free, but McClure caught him by the collar, jerking him to a rough halt. With his free hand, he ripped the ski mask from his face and tossed it over the rail.

"You weren't supposed to know about this, Breckwood."

"Get your hands off my kid." Caith raced to the top of the stairs and stepped onto the catwalk. The shop yawned below in a web of dizzying shadow. A single rail created an ineffectual waist-high barrier on each side of the elevated walk. Ignoring the reeling height, Caith focused on McClure.

"Everyone knows. About Kelly and Galicorp, and how Galina paid you to cause problems at the lodge. Give it up, McClure. The cops will be here soon."

The last part was a lie. Duke Cameron didn't know and hadn't made the connection. Not even Balin knew where Derrick was, but the bluff was all he had.

Caith's gaze flickered to his son. Derrick's face was bone-white, fear in his eyes. But there was trust, too, the unmistakable trust of a child for his father.

"Let Derrick go." He took a step forward.

Sneering, McClure tightened his hold on Derrick's collar and gave a sharp tug. "Stay where you are or I'll toss him over the side."

Caith staggered to a halt. He was close enough to see beads of sweat glistening on McClure's forehead. A sour whiff of alcohol told him the bigger man had been drinking and probably wasn't thinking rationally. "Let him go. You're not going to gain anything."

"Screw that, he's my ticket out of here. Keep you and the cops off my back." McClure held Derrick in front of him like a shield. "Anyone tries to take me down, I'll break his fucking neck."

"You son of a bitch." Caith ground his teeth, forcing himself to stay rooted in place. "You hurt my kid, and I'll—"

"What? You think you can take me? You're an asswipe, Breckwood." He gave a short guttural laugh. "Too bad your boy looks like you. Makes me wanna beat the shit outta him for the hell of it."

"Dad," Derrick whimpered.

McClure snickered and started walking backward, dragging Derrick with him. A landing loomed behind him, connecting to a second set of steps that descended into the bay below. Caith spied a cutting torch and industrial lighter hooked to a post at the corner of the landing. A long curling hose connected the torch with two small tanks butted against the framework of the platform. If he could get close enough, he could use the tanks as a weapon. One hit and even someone as big as McClure would go down.

"Turning tail and running?" he challenged, inching forward to close the distance between them. "Afraid I'll kick your ass like I did at the Jade Club? If you hadn't had that bat in the parking lot, I would have taken you down there, too."

His jeering had the intended effect. McClure immediately came to a halt, his face puffing with anger. "Like you could."

Caith grinned tightly, moving even closer. "Try me."

The goading challenge was all McClure needed. Flinging Derrick onto the platform, he spun around and caught Caith squarely in the chest with the flat of his work boot. Caith reeled backward, stumbling off balance. Air exploded from his lungs as the metal side rail caught him in the small of the back, knocking the wind from him. He nearly plummeted headfirst over the barrier, but hooked his arm at the last minute, preventing a nosedive to the concrete below.

"Derrick, run!" By the time Caith regained his footing, McClure had snatched the cutting torch and striker from the post. From the corner of his eye, Caith saw Derrick pause at the top of the landing, clearly torn by fear and concern for his father. "Derry, run. Get the hell out of here."

Propelled at last, Derrick raced down the steps. Caith backed along the catwalk, retreating as McClure advanced. With a single click of the lighter, he sent a rod of flame shooting from the end of the cutting torch.

"You shoulda stayed in Boston."

Caith sent a glance below. He stood in the center of the catwalk, open space gaping on either side. As long as he kept McClure focused, Derrick stood a chance of escape. He tried to spy his son in the shadowy darkness below, but the light was too limited. Had he made it to the door?

Wetting his lips, he gripped the rail on either side. Beneath the leather gauntlets of his costume, the metal was slick without traction. "You're only digging a deeper grave, McClure."

"Think I give a fuck?" McClure swiped the torch at his face, making Caith wrench backward. "Galina's got lots of money. More than you. More than your whole good-for-nothin' family. She'll buy my way clear of anything. Know why?"

Another swipe of the torch. The heat hit Caith directly in the face, searing his skin as he flinched to the side.

"She's gonna resurrect the Tolars." McClure kept the torch in front of him. "It's why she wants the lodge and the lake. It's part of some cult she got involved with, thanks to her old man. He told her about the history of the lodge, and now she thinks she's a fucking Tolar Queen. Like I give a shit about some stupid mumbo-jumbo. All I care about is money." His lips split in a wolfish grin. "That and kickin' your rich, snotty ass."

Caith was prepared this time. When McClure lunged, he pivoted as far as the narrow catwalk would allow. McClure blundered into the opening, and he locked hands with the bigger man, straining to hold the lethal flare at bay.

"You're no match for me, whelp." McClure bared his teeth, pressing an advantage of height and weight. The hiss of the high-intensity flame was blinding at such tight quarters. Inch by inch, he forced the burning metal shaft closer to Caith's face.

Releasing him, Caith drove his fist squarely into McClure's nose. The bigger man staggered, dropping the torch to paw at his face. He lurched clumsily, inadvertently kicking the flaming rod. It clattered over the side, caught when the hose snapped into place like a bungee cord. Dangling five feet below the catwalk, the nozzle spit a steady stream of fire, cutting a halo of light through the shadows.

"You mother fuckin' S-O-B." With a roar, McClure plowed into Caith, snaring him around the waist and slamming him against the retention rail.

The impact ignited fireworks in Caith's head and sent pain boomeranging up his spine. Gasping, he drove his fist into McClure's midsection using his shoulder for leverage. McClure staggered and Caith caught him a second time, delivering a solid uppercut. The rage he'd felt earlier bubbled up like hot lava. "You tried to hurt my kid, you sick bastard."

McClure slumped against the rail. With a dazed expression, he raised his head. The blood from his nose dribbled over his mouth and chin. To Caith he looked ghoulish, a Halloween monster. Only monsters kidnapped children.

"Derrick shouldn't even be here." *Like Trask.* It was his fault all over again. Neither of them should have been there. "I'm going to make sure you get locked away." Somewhere in his head, past and present merged. "Like Richter, Farrow, and Force." With a savage curse, Caith kicked him in the ribs.

McClure grunted, but recovered quickly, grabbing Caith's boot at the last second. With a violent wrench of his hands, the thug rotated his ankle, twisting like a corkscrew. Pain ricocheted up Caith's leg. He crumpled with a groan, striking his head on the rail. Something wet and sticky streamed into his eye. Before he could recover, McClure straddled him, throttling him by the throat.

"You ain't lockin' me nowhere, Breckwood." McClure pinched his windpipe, cutting off his air. "And when I'm done with you, I'm goin' after your prissy kid."

No!

The scream was soundless, heard only in his head, but it echoed seventeen years of pain. The same unspeakable horror he'd felt when he'd watched Trask fall beneath Richter's knife. *Not again. Not Derry.* Panic, frustration, and fear mushroomed into rage so black and lethal, the loss of air no longer mattered.

Caith stopped fighting the pressure on his neck. He drove his fist into McClure's broken nose. Blood gushed over his glove as McClure loosened his grip. Sensing freedom, Caith wormed free. He hooked his leg around McClure's neck, and in a move reserved for self-defense classes, somersaulted the bigger man backward.

Unable to stop his momentum, McClure rolled to the edge of the catwalk. Weight carried him beneath the retaining rail as he scrambled frantically for a hold. At the last second, he locked onto Caith's leg, but gravity sent his greater weight plunging toward the earth. Dragging Caith with him, he tumbled from the catwalk.

Instinctively, Caith clutched the metal lip, halting his fall. McClure clung to his leg just below the knee, both of them dangling precariously in midair. When McClure cursed and tried to clamber upward, using his body like a ladder, Caith knew he was in trouble.

Heat washed over him and sweat dripped into his eyes. Suspended by the hose, the acetylene torch swayed near his leg, cooking him as it hissed flame. Growing lightheaded, he ground his teeth and tried to dislodge McClure. As the bigger man's fingers hooked into his belt, Caith released one hand from the rail and pivoted violently to the side. The jarring movement sent McClure careening face first into the flame-spewing torch.

With a gurgling scream, he released Caith, frantically pawing at his face. The stench of burning flesh filled the air, but Caith barely had time to register the horrific odor. McClure plummeted twenty-odd feet, his body landing with a sickening thud on the concrete below.

Swinging away from the torch, Caith tried for a better hold on the rail. His head rang and his ankle throbbed painfully. Grimacing, he wedged an elbow on the steel lip and tried to hoist himself up. His hand slipped and he fell back, losing what little advantage he'd gained.

Derry. Veronica.

The thought of his son and the woman he loved spurred him to try again. Straining for a better grasp, he tightened his grip. But the glove was slick, the metal too smooth. Risking a single-handed hold, he snagged one glove in his teeth, tugged it free, and spit it from his mouth. It fell to the ground like a flightless bird. Exhausted, he groped for the rail.

And encountered flesh.

Solid, wonderfully strong, impossibly anchoring. A firm hand locked onto his forearm, holding him in place when fatigue would have let him fall.

"Did you think I'd let you down, Caithelden?"

Caith tilted his head back and looked up into the eyes of his father. "Dad." His smile felt foreign, the warmth that accompanied the name, odder still. "Pull me up. I need to find Derry."

"Derry's safe." Reaching over the side, his father snagged his belt and hoisted him onto the catwalk. Somewhere in the distance a siren started, gradually increasing in volume. Caith got no further than dragging himself to a sitting position before Derrick barreled from the landing.

"Dad!" He flung himself into Caith's arms.

Relieved, Caith hugged him close. "It's all right, Derry. You're safe now." Soft curls brushed his cheek. A residual tremor of fear raced through Derrick's body. Gripping him by the shoulders, Caith pried him back. "Did he touch you? Did he hurt you?"

Derrick shook his head. Caith scanned his face, ran his hands over Derrick's shoulders and arms. He saw no visible damage, but emotional and psychological wounds were harder to heal. "Derry...this is all my fault. You shouldn't have been involved." He faltered for words, finding them tangled with secrets he'd locked away for too many years. His kid had a right to know. About Trask, about him, about why he'd been taken tonight. Cupping the back of his head, Caith pulled him close, hugging him fiercely. "If I'd lost you..." He couldn't finish the thought. The warmth of his body appeared to ease Derrick's fears, and his son's shivering gradually subsided.

His father laid a hand on Caith's shoulder. "I found him outside," he said quietly. He squatted, still wearing his Civil War costume. What a sight they must make—a highwayman, a Union general, and a terrified child. "I think he's more worked up over seeing you in that fight than what happened to him. He was petrified you were going to fall like McClure."

"You saw?"

"Most of it." The hand on his shoulder tightened. "You were both on the catwalk when we came inside, but I couldn't get to you in time."

"How'd you find me in the first place?"

His father shrugged, grinning crookedly. "It wasn't hard. I made myself think like you. I tried to imagine who Kelly would use as an accomplice, and that led me to Lance McClure and here. I've been following your career for so long, I know how your mind works. The moment I came inside and saw you on the catwalk, I called Duke Cameron on my cell. Not bad for an old man, huh? I would have helped you in the first place, but you left the house in such a damn hurry."

"I had to." The words caught again.

"I know." Reaching around him, his dad ruffled Derrick's hair. "I was worried, too. And not only about my grandson."

Derrick stirred in Caith's arms and raised his head. There were tears in his eyes, shining on the surface, blue and liquid as seawater. "Dad…that man. He said things. He was gonna hurt me."

"But he didn't." Carefully, Caith cupped his chin, and then smoothed a hand over his silky curls. "I know what you're feeling, Derry. It's okay to be afraid as long as you don't let it control you."

Derrick sniffled, nestling closer. "I don't wanna talk about it."

"I know you don't." He paused, making a decision. He didn't want his kid growing up with the same fear he'd kept bottled inside for so many years. A terror so constricting, it kept him from telling the woman he loved he wanted to spend the rest of his life with her. If his kid could put tonight behind him, he could do no less with his own past.

He's spent his entire life fearful his name and connection to the Breckwood fortune would put his son in danger, but his family was the one thing he never should have kept from Derrick. His family was his strength, not his weakness. There would always be unscrupulous people looking to profit from the misery of others, but he couldn't safeguard Derrick from everything. He couldn't expect his kid to live in a bubble, nor could he live in one himself. It was time to face the world for what it was, to let go of the chokehold Trask's death had held over him for far too long.

"Derry, Trask didn't die accidentally. We were kidnapped when we weren't much older than you." He swallowed hard and blundered ahead. "Trask died saving my life. When you're ready, I'll tell you about it. Maybe afterward, you'll tell me about tonight."

Puzzled, Derrick raised his head. "But you told me you were playing in a basement. That he got hurt."

"I know, but that's not what happened. It's my fault for not telling you the truth."

"Mine, too." Caith's father stood and offered his hand. "It's time we both faced the past, Caithelden. I have some explaining to do to Derry as well."

Caith looked from his father's hand to his son's shining eyes. Somehow, he didn't think either had anything to do with past events as much as future promises. It made him realize he still had one to give.

To Veronica.

Chapter 19

Idiot!

Veronica paced back and forth on the enclosed rear porch of the Breckwood home, trying to decide if she wanted to lynch Caith or kiss him. It was typical of the Caith she remembered to run off and do something stupidly heroic. What she couldn't conceive was why he hadn't called the police when he'd arrived at the welding shop.

Maybe he'd been distracted, thinking of his son and the past. Or maybe he was just so damn cocky and self-assured, used to solving things on his own, he didn't believe in police assistance.

A certifiable idiot!

Fuming silently, she passed an electric cauldron in the corner for the sixth time. Simulated orange flames danced across the top, sending ripples of light over the ceiling and floor. Earlier, the home had been cleared of guests, the ghoulish and fantastical landscapes now seeming out of place with only family remaining.

She'd cried herself silly when Caith brought Derry back, fussing over him like he was her own child. She'd helped Caith get him settled in bed, leaving only when Derry asked about Trask.

That was a private moment for father and son, one Veronica wasn't sure Caith would see to conclusion. But Stuart told her Caith had promised Derry the truth. He also told her about the fight between Caith and Lance McClure. She'd seen proof of it when he'd returned to the house. Bruising on his neck, a cut above his eye, and a swollen ankle that left him hobbling.

She'd wanted him to see a doctor, but he'd shrugged it off as unnecessary.

A certifiable macho idiot!

He definitely deserved to be lynched, not kissed. She was exhausted, on the verge of tears. The entire night had been an ongoing series of traumatic events. Duke Cameron had reported back to inform them Kelly Rice was now in custody, and warrants had been issued for Galina Brady. Balin was remanded to his father's care until the extent of his involvement could be determined. Lucy McClure was notified of her husband's demise, gossip spreading faster than it could be manufactured.

Stuart called a friend who was a doctor, begged a favor, and asked him to visit Caith at the house. By then, Caith's ankle had swelled to the extent the boot had to be cut from his leg. Fortunately, the doctor determined the swelling was the result of a bad sprain and it was highly unlikely anything had been broken. He suggested x-rays in the morning to be on the safe side. In the meantime, the ankle was wrapped, packed with ice, and Caith was given orders to remain off it as much as possible.

He'd used the time to stay with his son. Derry fell asleep, waking once with nightmares when she'd checked in. After an initial bout of bad dreams, he'd slept soundly.

Deciding her certifiable-macho-idiot boyfriend needed rest of his own, Veronica headed upstairs. It was still fifty minutes before midnight. Halloween's final hour.

She found Caith as he was leaving Derry's bedroom. He closed the door slowly, holding the knob to muffle the sound.

"Asleep?" Veronica asked.

Caith nodded. He looked haggard. He'd shed his tunic along with his remaining boot. The white shirt gaped at his throat, exposing purpling bruises on his neck. She wondered if the sight had disturbed Derry as much as it did her. Her eyes tracked to his bandaged ankle.

"You shouldn't be standing. I thought you were supposed to stay off your feet."

"I needed to see you. A lot's happened tonight." Catching her wrist, he drew her into his arms. His lips moved against her hair in a tender kiss. "God, you smell good."

She wanted to be angry for the danger he'd placed himself in but couldn't summon the effort. He'd reacted as she would have to protect Derry. It made her realize how much she loved them both.

"I need to talk to you." Taking her hand, he led her down the hall to the guest room she'd been given for the night. The late hour and concern for Derry kept the family gathered downstairs, bringing a sense of security and warmth long absent from the Breckwood home.

Caith pulled her into the room and closed the door. She'd been here earlier, leaving a small hurricane lamp burning on the nightstand. It created a halo of yellow that accompanied the moonlight streaming through high, steepled windows. A Victorian four-poster bed with a lace coverlet was draped in filmy white bed curtains. Another time, Veronica might have thought the ambiance enchanting, but her mind was too occupied with Caith.

"You really should sit down." Nervously, she moved to tuck her hair behind her ear and realized it was still caught up in combs. Clearing her throat, she motioned to the bed, hoping to mask her uneasiness. "Doctor Grossi said if you don't keep off that ankle, you're going to make it worse."

He grinned. "I think you just want to get me in bed."

His brashness took her by surprise, oddly out of place after the events of the evening. Befuddled, she fell back on sternness. "Caithelden."

He slipped his hands onto her shoulders, using his thumbs to tip up her chin. Heat flowed from his body, warm and inviting, promising passion to come. His lips hovered just shy of her own, ghosting her skin.

"I make a better lover than a highwayman." Bending forward, he moved his mouth gently over hers, sending sun-soaked warmth shooting through her veins. When the kiss ended, he looked intently into her eyes. "But I'd be a better husband than a lover."

Veronica's heart thudded against her ribs. "What?"

He cupped her face. "I love you."

Awestruck, Veronica watched a grin spread across his lips. Bright and dazzling, it was the smile she loved best.

"I've loved you since we were kids, but I couldn't tell you. I didn't want anything to happen to you." The smile faltered along with his words. Something clouded his eyes. "I've been an idiot, Veronica. I wasted years we could have been together. I wouldn't blame you if you hated me."

"Hate you?" It was happening too fast. Her head reeled as she tried to make the moment last. He'd said it, really said it: *I love you.* Words she'd thought him incapable of uttering.

"You need to know the truth." Anxiety crackled through him. She felt it as strongly as she'd felt his pleasure a moment ago. Taking her hand, he drew her to a seat on the bed. His thumb tracked over her knuckles, but the gesture was more likely meant to calm him rather than her.

"When we were together that first time at the lake...I loved you so much it scared me. I thought something would happen to you. Like Trask. That being with me could get you killed." Releasing her, he lurched from the bed and prowled a short distance away. "I know it's stupid, Ron, but I couldn't make it go away. So I wrote you that letter." He hobbled back and stood staring down at her. "There never was anyone else. It was always you. Only you. I made the damn thing up."

She shook her head, disbelieving. "Why, Caith?" Confusion, betrayal, and hurt rushed together, resurrecting the pain she'd felt when she'd received the letter. She'd carried that scar for years. Even now, as much as she loved him, the wound was bitter. To know he'd inflicted it deliberately...

"Why didn't you talk to me? Tell me what you were feeling?"

"I couldn't. Don't you get it?" Anguish flared in his eyes. "You would have wanted to stay with me. I couldn't have that. I couldn't live with the possibility of something happening to you because of who I am."

"The heir to a fortune." She said it bitterly.

"Yes."

Veronica stood. "And now?"

Caith lowered his eyes. "Now I know I've been a complete ass. To you, my father, my family, even my kid. I'm my own person with or without the Breckwood name." He drew a breath, meeting her gaze squarely. "I told Derry about Trask tonight. I told him everything. I don't want my son growing up with the same fears I had. Ten years from now he could meet someone and make the same stupid mistake. It might be too late for us, but I'm going to work like hell to make sure that never happens to Derry."

Veronica's heart sank to her stomach. "Do you think it's too late for us?"

"You need to decide that." Caith moved forward. She saw fear in his eyes. Not the obsessive fear that had controlled his life, but fear he would lose her. Fear she would turn and walk away now that he was ready to make a commitment.

"I love you, Veronica. I couldn't say it before, but if you give me the chance, I promise to tell you for the rest of your life."

Hot tears flooded her eyes. When he took her hands, her whole body trembled. She tried to blink past the watery haze, but her vision only blurred further. Still holding her hands, he crouched awkwardly on one knee.

"Your ankle."

"My mother will skin me alive if I don't do this right. One knee. It's in all of the books."

"Caith."

"We've played at myth all of our lives." He looked into her eyes. The smile was back. Not as self-assured as before, but full of love nonetheless. "I don't want what-ifs or make-believes. I want you, Ronnie. I'm sorry I don't have a ring for you. I didn't plan on proposing tonight. After what's happened, I just know I don't want to spend another day without you." He drew a breath, tightening his grip on her hands. "Veronica Kent, will you marry me?"

Tears crested her eyes and flowed down her face. Her throat closed up but she managed a pitiful squeak.

Looking worried, Caith tilted his head. "Is that a yes?"

"Yes!" She flung herself into his arms, remembering his ankle too late. Off balance he reeled backward, taking them both to the floor. Veronica laughed. "I'm sorry. Your ankle."

Grinning, he rolled on top of her, tucking his knee between her legs. "I'd rather have the bed, but this will do." His mouth closed on hers, warm and giving, sealing his promise.

She wrapped her arms around his neck and kissed him back. Only then did she realize he'd proposed on Halloween. Perhaps somewhere in a realm where myth and magic combined, a blond-haired boy in a green baseball cap watched and smiled.

Trask would approve.

* * * *

Veronica gave Dean Porter a quick once-over as she passed him the key to his suite. It was amazing the difference a few months had made in the scrawny writer. He hadn't gained weight as much as confidence. His suit was immaculate and his thinning hair styled for distinction. Going from hack tabloid writer to respected journalist with a major newspaper had done miracles for his self-esteem. Wanting to keep Roth-Deckman out of the press, the CEO had been more than willing to listen when Caith suggested an introduction to Porter. While the tabloid writer flourished in his new position, Galina Brady had been stripped of hers. Both she and Kelly were disgraced but free on bail, pending trial.

"Third floor," Veronica told Porter, with a nod for the steps. "But we don't call it the Hummingbird Suite anymore."

Porter read the engraved name on the old-fashioned key tag with a shrug. "Camelot?"

Veronica smiled. "Fit for a king. Or in this case, a journalist."

The observation made him puff up with pride. Preening, he headed for the stairs.

Veronica sighed, satisfied to have the lodge full again. There was no longer a need for anti-stress sessions, or bans on cell phones and laptops. The lodge was open to the public, replacing its corporate theme with one of myth and romance. It had been Morgana's idea, changing the theme and the name.

Myth and Magic had replaced Stone Willow Lodge in mid-November. Veronica still had occasional single guests like Porter, but more often, couples came to celebrate anniversaries, honeymoons, and romantic holidays. The rustic decor had been replaced with soft pastels, romantic lace, and antique furnishings. Theme suites, meals, and events were built around famous couples from folklore—Arthur and Guinevere, Tristan and Isolde, Robin Hood and Marian. At first she feared the idea wouldn't take, but the lodge had received favorable write-ups in countless magazines and online sites, most courtesy of Roth-Deckman.

Veronica grinned. Sometimes there were benefits to having a private investigator for a husband. Abandoning the registration counter, she walked to the rear of the lobby, then stood staring out over Stone Willow Lake.

When Caith proposed, she'd never expected him to stay in Coldcreek. But a week later he'd made arrangements to sell the house in Boston. They'd bought a two-story Colonial not far from Aren's farm. The wedding had been small, family and a few friends. Jake and Connie from Boston and Nick Fontaine, with whom Caith had developed an amazing, if unusual, rapport.

Her parents flew in from Florida with Melanie acting as matron of honor and Aren standing as Caith's best man. The wedding was simple, an evening candlelight ceremony at the Breckwood mansion. Afterward, they'd taken an island honeymoon, enjoying sun-drenched afternoons surrounded by sparkling water and lazy nights of making love sheltered by palm trees. They returned in time for the opening of the new lodge and for Veronica to assume her place as manager.

Content, she folded her arms over her chest.

Beyond the windows, the ground was covered with snow, tumbling to the edges of the lake. Christmas was three weeks away, the first with her new husband and son. A time for rejoicing and love. As she watched the play of sunlight on water, she thought back to the first time she'd made love with Caith on the bank. They'd been children really, seventeen and eighteen, but the water had turned to fire, resurrecting buried myth.

Magic, Morgana had insisted when she'd told her mother-in-law about the experience a few short days ago. *The assurance of true love.*

Veronica still wasn't certain she believed in the legend of Stone Willow, but she believed in Caith. He'd changed. He was mellower since Derry's abduction, smiling more often and wanting to spend time with his family. It was as if in saving Derry, he'd finally made peace with Trask.

Derry was a little less open with strangers, but his natural exuberance and curiosity hadn't suffered from his experience. Veronica credited a good portion of his recovery to Caith's frank discussions about his own kidnapping. Their marriage brought additional stability and, within two days of the wedding, Derry began calling her "Mom," a name she found simultaneously thrilling and terrifying.

Balin suffered the most, working hard to convince his family he'd learned a valuable lesson and would never make such a dreadful mistake again. A light jail sentence was later suspended in favor of community service. Two nights a week he helped at a center for homeless children in a neighboring town. Veronica had no doubt Caith would eventually come around and ease up on his nephew. He'd even hinted as much to Merlin on the phone.

High-profile and fashionable, Merlin had decided it was time to leave Coldcreek. After several discussions with Stuart, he'd finally convinced his father to give him BI's Balitmore office, the golden carrot he'd coveted all along. Shortly after, Lew Walden left Stone Willow to stand by his daughter. While his wife's death had propelled him to wander, Galina's incarceration motivated him to consider law again.

Although he'd suspected her involvement, he'd convinced himself someone in the Breckwood family was at fault. Pegging Caith as a private investigator from the start, he'd run a background check, and then left anonymous notes hoping to steer Caith away from Galina. He'd prayed his suspicions about her weren't true, but in the end, she'd only dug herself deeper.

Because of the Tolars, Veronica marveled silently. It reaffirmed the staggering thought that even people in high-ranking positions could fall prey to cult propaganda. Lew had apologized profusely, as he was the one who'd first sparked Galina's interest in the Tolars. After starting work at Stone Willow, he'd learned the history of the property and shared the information with his daughter. According to him, Galina had long held a fascination with old world religions, but he'd never expected her to embrace the cult and lose perspective.

Veronica assured him she held no animosity toward him. It certainly wasn't his fault his grown daughter had taken it upon herself to spin a complicated web of deceit and criminal behavior.

"Enjoying the view?"

Caith appeared behind her and wrapped his arms around her waist. He dropped a kiss on her neck. "Our son wants to go to the movies tonight. Since it's Friday, I told him we'd go for dinner, too."

"Mmm. Sounds good." She leaned against him, hugging his arms close. He wore a long, black wool coat over a bone-colored turtleneck and faded jeans. The scent of wood-smoke and wet winter grasses clung to his clothing.

"You're cold," she noted. "Where have you been?"

"The cemetery."

Stunned, Veronica turned. Ruddy color was high on his face, brightening the arctic spark of his eyes. In all the years she'd known him, he'd never visited Trask's grave.

As if sensing her shock, Caith shrugged. "I owed Trask a visit. It was overdue."

He kept the words light, but she could tell by the look in his eyes, he didn't want her to make a fuss. He'd simply wanted her to know. After years of torturing himself, he could walk into the cemetery without guilt, without fear.

Veronica touched his cheek. "I'm glad."

Caith caught her hand and kissed her fingertips. "I've got something to show you." Grinning, he slipped a business card from his coat pocket, flashing it between two fingers. "Dad thought it was time I made it official. You should have seen him when these arrived. He was like a kid at Christmas, passing them out to anyone who came within five feet."

Veronica took the card, immediately recognizing the BI logo. She'd seen it displayed countless times on everything from letterhead and presentation folders to pens and corporate signs. Never, though, in conjunction with the name emblazoned in black script beneath it: *Caithelden Breckwood, Investigative Services.*

Breckwood. Not Lairen.

He'd made the name change legal before their marriage, giving his father an early Christmas present. Now after years of estrangement, he was on BI's payroll.

Something warm and tingly spread through her stomach. "It's beautiful. I don't know why the two of you didn't think of it before."

Caith chuckled. "Stubborn, I guess."

She was surprised to hear him admit it. "No argument there." Smiling, she slipped the card into her pocket and wrapped her arms around his neck. She knew he'd already hired Nick Fontaine as a field assistant. "But are you going to like corporate investigative work? It's not what you set out to do."

He kissed her forehead. "It made up sixty-five percent of my clientele in Boston. And Force, one of the guys who kidnapped me and Trask, was mid-management in BI. He just hired two thugs to help him pull off the kidnapping. Yeah, they were eventually caught and ended up with life sentences, but that doesn't mean I've forgotten where they came from. Besides, being on retainer for BI doesn't mean I won't take cases outside of the business. Only now my motivation is different." He trailed a thumb over her cheek. "I don't want to wage a private battle in Trask's memory any longer. I have a family to think about."

His touch sent a shiver racing down her spine.

Family.

It was a beautiful word. Resting her head on his shoulder, she leaned against him. "I'll love you whatever you do."

He chucked a knuckle beneath her chin. "You love me because I'm good looking and rich."

"I thought you were brainy and gifted."

"That, too. You just want to hear me say I'm madly in love with you."

"Well?" She drew back, arching a brow.

He traced his thumb down her jaw, and feathered it across her lip. When he spoke, his voice was husky and low, his eyes the deep blue of twilight seas. The humor melted from his gaze, replaced by something warm and giving. "I always will be."

Pulling her close, he covered her mouth with his, sweeping her into a dizzying kaleidoscope of emotion. His kiss filled her with the promise of eternity, sealing what she'd known since they were children.

All the myths in the world couldn't compete with the magic of true love. She didn't have to look outside to know Stone Willow Lake burned with fire.

Meet the Author

Mae Clair opened a Pandora's Box of characters when she was a child and never looked back. Her father, an artist who tinkered with writing, encouraged her to create make-believe worlds by spinning tales of far-off places on summer nights beneath the stars.

Mae loves creating character-driven fiction in settings that vary from contemporary to mythical. Wherever her pen takes her, she flavors her stories with mystery and romance. Married to her high school sweetheart, she lives in Pennsylvania and is passionate about cryptozoology, old photographs, a good Maine lobster tail and cats.

Discover more about Mae on her website and blog at www.MaeClair.net

Turn the page for a special excerpt of Mae Clair's

Weathering Rock

Drawn together across centuries, will their love be strong enough to defeat an ancient curse?

Colonel Caleb DeCardian was fighting America's Civil War on the side of the Union when a freak shower of ball lightning transported him to the present, along with rival and former friend, Seth Reilly. Adapting to the 21st century is hard enough for the colonel, but he also has to find Seth, who cursed him to life as a werewolf. The last thing on Caleb's mind is romance. Then fetching Arianna Hart nearly runs him down with her car. He can't deny his attraction to the outspoken schoolteacher, but knows he should forget her.

Arianna finds Caleb bewildering, yet intriguing: courtly manners, smoldering sensuality and eyes that glow silver at night? When she sees Civil War photographs featuring a Union officer who looks exactly like Caleb, she begins to understand the man she is falling in love with harbors multiple secrets--some of which threaten the possibility of their happiness.

Finding a decent guy who'll commit is hard enough. How can she expect Caleb to forsake his own century to be with her?

On sale now!

Chapter 1

The June moon rode a ragged ridge of bone-white clouds, filmy and pale as the translucent skin of an onion. Honeysuckle mingled with the aroma of sweet clover and drifted through the open window of Arianna Hart's Chrysler Sebring. It was a pleasant night, touched by fog and ripe with all the scents and sounds that heralded summer's arrival. In the distance, the rooftops of Weathering Rock jutted above the trees, silvered with the ice-white blood of the moon.

The old manor home predated the Civil War and had been a landmark for the town of Sagehill as far back as she could remember. Ball lightning and freak storms were said to roll through the surrounding fields like a tempest of Earth and sky, giving rise to superstition and legend. Even now, tendrils of fog twined among the trees. Arianna didn't care about the weather anomalies or myths. It was the past that fascinated her, a passion she'd carried into her career as a teacher of American history at the local middle school. Engrossed in her thoughts, absently humming along to Lady Gaga on the radio, she was unprepared when a man on horseback plunged from the trees.

"Shit!" With a shriek of horror, she slammed on the brakes sending the Sebring fishtailing across the road. The horse reared upright, trapping the rider in the beam of her headlights, his hair a blaze of bright silver. She watched in horror as he lost his battle to stay mounted and tumbled backward to the ground. The horse wasted no time in thundering off between the trees, and was swallowed by ribbons of fog.

"Oh, God!" Arianna popped the door, fumbling off her seatbelt and stumbling in her haste to reach the prone man. "I'm sorry, I'm so sorry. I didn't see you." She was babbling, her heart in her throat, nerves in the stratosphere. "Are you all right?"

Of course he wasn't all right! He wasn't even moving. He looked to be in his early thirties, dressed in jeans, a dark t-shirt and an archaic-looking frock coat. The garment was straight out of a history book.

"Sir?" Arianna knelt on the roadside. Now that she saw him up close, she realized his hair was blond, not silver, cut longer than fashionable. He had a lean but muscular physique and--she couldn't help noticing--was handsome as sin. If she was going to mow someone down, why not go for the gold? "Um--" She prodded his shoulder, jumping when he responded with a groan. Arianna sank back on her haunches. "Thank God!"

The man stirred and rolled his head on the asphalt, dragging one leg upright. He made an abortive attempt to wedge it beneath him, and raised a hand to his head. "What happened? I need to reach Meade."

"Who?" Arianna didn't like the way he was holding his head. "Uh, look...I'm not sure who you are, but I'm going to call an ambulance. My cellphone is in the car--"

"No." Wincing, he struggled to sit.

Arianna did what she could to assist, surprised when he completed the action by climbing to his feet and steadying himself against her. He was taller than she'd thought, six foot-one or two, every inch of him dazed and wobbly male. She could feel the press of his body to hers--sinew and muscle, the taut, well-formed lines of a denim-clad hip and thigh.

"I don't need an ambulance." His eyes were touched by an eerie silver sheen. Like an animal's at night when reflecting light. "I live at Weathering Rock.

"You might have a concussion."

"No hospital." He looked away and his face fell back into shadow. It made her wonder if she'd imagined that feral glow. When he spoke again, his speech carried a formal inflection. "May I impose upon you to drive me home? It appears I require assistance."

"What about your horse?"

"It knows the way." He pressed two fingers against his temple, his eyes narrowing to painful slits. "I didn't see you. Like Seth at Crinkeshaw."

His distraction worried Arianna. It made her reconsider calling an ambulance, but he seemed to read the thought in her eyes. "My... brother...is at home. He's a doctor."

"Your brother lives at Weathering Rock?"

"We both do. It's not far."

"I know the way." Forcing herself to speak calmly, Arianna guided him to the passenger's side of the Sebring. She didn't know if she was crazy or foolish for helping a stranger into her car. She said a silent prayer he was harmless and wouldn't turn out to be a deranged serial killer.

"I'm going to call a friend. He's a cop."

"No." He grabbed her wrist and held fast. "I won't hurt you."

She balked, disturbed he'd read her mind so easily. He needed to have his head examined if he thought she was going to take his word at face value. Wasn't she always getting something in her email, forwarded by a well-meaning friend that warned of men who preyed on unsuspecting women? There was nothing to stop him from stuffing her in the trunk and driving off.

Except if he'd wanted to harm her he would have done it by now. Not everyone was an ax murderer or a fugitive from *American's Most Wanted*.

She pulled her arm free. "What's your name?"

"Caleb." There was pain in his voice, the answer spoken through gritted teeth. "Caleb DeCardian." He opened the door of the Sebring and folded into the seat. With his face turned away, Arianna did a visual check, searching for blood. She couldn't see any, but suspected he'd hit his head when he'd fallen. He appeared dazed enough to be nursing a concussion.

Squelching her panic, she rounded the vehicle and climbed in the driver's side. She left the door hanging open, the dome light brightening the interior of the car while she fished in her purse for her cell. "I have insurance."

"It wasn't your fault. I rode out in front of you."

At least he was honest. What kind of an idiot went for a horseback ride when it was almost midnight? A handsome idiot.

No question about it. His platinum hair was wavy and thick, highlighted by streaks of white-gold. It dipped beneath his collar in the back and covered his ears. The style meshed well with his tailored black frock coat, a strange contrast against the faded denim of his jeans and the tightly defining fit of a navy t-shirt. The clothing molded his body well, accentuating long legs and a broad chest. He must be as eccentric as he was good-looking.

Locating her cell, Arianna punched out her home number and closed the car door. A half-hour earlier she'd left her friend's home for the night. She didn't want to worry Lauren over her whereabouts, but thought it wise to play safe. Dating a cop for a year had taught her the value of being cautious. When her answering machine kicked in, she pretended to have a conversation with her friend.

"Hi, Lauren?" Pause. "No, I didn't get home yet. Something came up. I'll call you in about twenty minutes, as soon as I get in the door. I'm stopping at Weathering Rock--you know that old house on Blackberry Lane?" A longer pause. "No, I'll explain later. Talk to you then." She felt foolish for pulling the charade, but wanted Caleb to think someone was waiting to hear from her.

"Are you all right?" she asked again as she started the ignition and eased the car onto the road.

He gave a noncommittal grunt. It made her think of lawsuits and catastrophic medical bills. Everyone was sue-happy these days. He'd admitted to riding out in front of her, but how quickly would that change once a fee-hungry lawyer sank greedy claws into him?

She could always call Lucas for help, even if she didn't want to involve the police directly. Her ex-boyfriend would know what to do, though asking for advice was guaranteed to trigger one of his *you-need-a-keeper* spiels. It was no wonder they'd split up. As Lauren liked to say--there were no King Arthurs left in the world, just Arthurs who expected to be treated like kings.

"Sagehill isn't far," she said, contemplating her liability, court dates and how complicated the whole situation might become.

"Weathering Rock is closer." In the half-gloom of fog and moonlight, Caleb's eyes flashed like crystal. "What's your name?"

She considered lying, but smothered the impulse. "Arianna Hart. My friends call me Ari."

"Annie," he said, still sounding confused.

She would have corrected him, but grew distracted when he stretched his legs in an attempt to get more comfortable. He was almost too tall for the tiny vehicle, his proximity charging the air with a goosebump-crackle of electricity. The taut pull of faded denim over his thighs was disconcerting, especially when her glance wandered higher, revealing how well his jeans defined all areas of his lower anatomy.

Abruptly warm, she turned her attention back to the road. She had a history of failed relationships, but that didn't mean she couldn't appreciate the male physique. Especially when a man was as well put together as Caleb DeCardian.

"Who's Meade?'

"What?"

"You said you had to reach Meade." She eased into a left turn. Overhead, the sky was a patchwork of clouds and stars. "Is that a person or a place?"

"Uh…" The word stuck on his tongue. "Nothing important." He tilted his head against the seat, his lashes sweeping closed as he dismissed the question. "Thank you, Annie."

"Ari," she corrected, falling silent. Weathering Rock was only moments away, but it felt like an eternity. Life would have been much easier if she'd spent the night at Lauren's like her friend had wanted. Instead, she'd insisted she could navigate the roads, the hour not too late for a drive she'd made countless times before.

Yet in all those times she'd never come upon a rider on horseback wearing a 19th century frock coat. Caleb. Even his name was archaic, his speech and diction distinctly formal. What did she expect from an odd encounter in the middle of the night?

Another curve in the road and Weathering Rock came into view, only the rooftop visible among layers of low-lying fog. Memory told her the house was set back from the road a good hundred yards by a rolling expanse of lawn. Squat pines and a fringe of ash flanked the driveway.

"Almost there," Arianna told her passenger as she turned the Sebring up the sloping drive. The lane rose at a steady incline, paving the way to a carefully preserved manor home with a broad wraparound porch, white pillars, and multiple chimneys. She stopped at the top of the drive in time to see a man sprint around the house. He raced for the car.

"Are you Doctor DeCardian?" She'd barely managed to open her door before he reached the vehicle.

"Yes!" He shot a glance through the windshield at her passenger, then wrenched open the door. "Caleb? What the hell happened? Ranger came pounding back without you. I thought Seth--" He stopped abruptly as if realizing he'd said too much. "Are you hurt?"

"Headache." Caleb swung his legs to the ground.

Arianna felt her stomach clench. "What can I do?"

"Get the front door," the other man--Winston, if she'd heard correctly--instructed.

With a nod, she hurried up the steps, nearly tripping on the narrow front stairs. Behind her, Winston kept one hand clasped around Caleb's arm as he steered him toward the house.

Panicked by the thought she might have caused him permanent harm, she wrapped a sweat-sticky palm around the doorknob and shoved inside. She should have called Lucas or the cops. She should have done something. But it was too late to be courting shoulda-coulda-wouldas.

She waited as Caleb hobbled past with his brother, then trailed behind them, following down a central hallway. An open arch led to a parlor with blush champagne walls and furnishings of wheat, navy and gold. Her heels clacked on the walnut floorboards, echoing shrilly, rattling her already frayed nerves.

"Sit here." Winston steered his brother to a medallion-backed sofa with clawed feet. It looked as comfortable as a slab of rock, but Caleb folded into it with an appreciative groan. He bowed his head and massaged his temple.

"I couldn't tell if he was bleeding," she blurted to Winston as he breezed past and ducked into an adjoining room. He came back within seconds, carrying a plastic pill vial, prompting Arianna to continue as if he'd never left. "I…I almost ran him down with my car."

"It wasn't your fault," Caleb said. "I should have been paying attention."

"Too worried about Meade or some other dumbass garbage," Winston muttered, uncapping the vial and tumbling several white tablets into his palm. He thrust two under Caleb's nose. "Here. I'll get water."

"I don't need it." Taking the pills, Caleb swallowed them dry. He sagged against the cushions and flicked Winston a sour glance. "Quit looking so damn irritable. I'm not bleeding, I took a spill from my infernal horse."

Infernal? Arianna cleared her throat. "I know I'm not a doctor, but couldn't he have a concussion?"

Winston DeCardian looked at her as if seeing her for the first time. As tall as his brother, he had dark wavy hair and shockingly blue eyes. "Of course he could, probably does too, the damn idiot. Caleb suffers from headaches and had one earlier tonight." He eyed his brother with a frown. "Which is all the more reason to not go riding after dark. You're lucky this woman was driving by, Caleb."

"You don't understand." Arianna stepped closer, certain he'd drawn the wrong conclusion. "I'm the reason his horse reared. I mean, my car… It wasn't his fault."

"It wasn't yours either," Caleb said again. He motioned toward his brother. "Winston, meet Arianna Hart. Arianna, my brother Winston."

"Wyn is fine." The doctor managed a halfway agreeable nod for Arianna. "Caleb is the only one who calls me Winston." He waved toward the windows, indicating the road beyond. "Whatever happened out there, I'm glad you stopped to help."

"I think Arianna should spend the night," Caleb said, tilting his head against the rear of the sofa and cupping a hand over his forehead.

"What?" She laughed, startled by the suggestion. Damn, if she hadn't been staring, focused on the way the light defined strands of white-gold and ash in his longish hair. It didn't help he sat with his legs braced apart, his jeans pulling taut, defining the muscular lines of his thighs. Unlike Lauren, she'd never been attracted to blond men. Lauren's ex-husband, Rick Rothrock, was the perpetual golden boy of Sagehill--young, handsome and successful.

Feeling her checks flush, she cleared her throat. "I live in Sagehill." She was thankful neither man had noticed her straying glance. "Twenty minutes and I'll be home."

Caleb lowered his hand long enough to meet her eyes. "The fog is growing worse and it's late."

"He's right." Absently, Wyn laced his fingers through his rumpled black curls. He looked like he'd only woken up, sloppy in comparison to his fair-haired brother. She guessed he'd dressed in a hurry when he heard Caleb's horse outside. The physical resemblance between the two was slight, and Arianna would have never pegged them as being related.

"I'll be fine driving home," she said.

"I'd rather you didn't." Caleb cast his brother a pointed glance, but his words were for Arianna. "It's not safe tonight."

"Excuse me?"

"The fog," Caleb clarified with an easy smile. "It's building."

Before she could protest, he stood and gathered her hand in his, the touch igniting sparks along the pads of her fingertips.

"I'd feel better if you stayed here. If you need to call your husband--"

"I'm not married." Normally she could tell when a man was fishing, trying to discover if she was involved with someone. She'd been on the singles' scene long enough to know the rules and spot the players, but Caleb bewildered her. Her eyes dropped to his left hand, noting the absence of a wedding ring.

"I live alone." She cringed as soon as she said it, realizing her blunder. Nothing like announcing she lived by herself and wouldn't be missed. Why not ring the dinner bell for anyone unscrupulous enough to ditch her body in a remote area where the remains wouldn't be found for months or years? "Uh, but I'm still friends with my ex-boyfriend. He's a detective with the Sagehill Police Department and we check in with each other regularly."

"I see." Caleb released her hand. "You can call him over there." He nodded to a table where Arianna noted a wireless handset among a clump of other items--car keys, pens, a pocketknife, unopened mail and a handful of loose change.

She shook her head, embarrassed to appear distrustful when he'd been nothing but understanding. Caleb had a way of looking at her that made her feel like an awkward teenager. He couldn't have been more than thirty-two or thirty-three, yet seemed older.

"I should go now." She didn't believe either man was a threat. They would have harmed her already had that been their intent, but she didn't want to spend the night with strangers. The only danger outside was a naturally occurring fog, something she'd encountered countless times before.

"I'll leave my insurance information in case there's a problem."

Caleb traded a glance with Wyn, something nonverbal passing between them. "The least I can do is escort you to your vehicle and ensure it wasn't damaged."

She couldn't argue with that. Rummaging a pen and paper from her purse, she jotted down her contact information and left it on the table by the phone. Afterward, both men walked with her outside, Caleb holding the door as she stepped onto the porch.